A Few Right Thinking Men

A Rowland Sinclair Mystery

Sulari Gentill

Poisoned Pen Press

First U.S. Edition 2016
Large Print Edition

10 9 8 7 6 5 4 3 2 1

Library of Congress Catalog Card Number: 2015957972

ISBN: 9781464206368   Large Print

Poisoned Pen Press
6962 E. First Ave., Ste. 103
Scottsdale, AZ 85251
www.poisonedpenpress.com
info@poisonedpenpress.com

Printed in the United States of America

*To all the right thinking men I have known,
and the libertines who keep them in line.*

Acknowledgments

It takes a village to raise a child…and to write a novel. Certainly there were many people who contributed to both this book and the maintenance of its author's sanity. It is a debt I wish to humbly acknowledge here.

My father, who did not once question my decision to spurn an ostensibly respectable career in order to write stories; who read all my manuscripts and approached my newfound passion with all the support and enthusiasm that he gave my schemes as a child. This, despite my past teenage proclivity to grandiose disasters…who can forget my ill-fated forays into the world of stuffed toy manufacture, T-shirt design, and, of course, film production?

My husband, Michael, an historian, an Old Guardsman in spirit if not in fact, whose historical knowledge, political insight, and natural disposition I shamelessly appropriated for the purposes of this book; who married a lawyer and then found himself financially tied to someone who just wanted to tell stories…and refused to do anything else. Thank you.

My boys, Edmund and Atticus, who at times impersonated laptops to gain a spot on my knee; who wanted Rowland Sinclair to be a werewolf; whose fearlessness and belief in all possibilities is both noisy and inspiring—though Rowland Sinclair is not a werewolf.

Leith, my childhood friend, with whom I plotted world domination when I was twelve; to whom I turned in those "who am I kidding" moments; who, most delightfully, retells passages from my novel, forgetting that they are not her personal memories of old friends. Thank you.

The intrepid J.C. Henry who bravely took my author photos with the brief that he must "improve on nature."

My sister, Devini, who read the manuscript and then sent me suggestions for casting the movie; who has some quite bizarre ideas about who should play Rowland Sinclair, but whose belief in me and this novel meant a great deal. My sister, Nilukshi, who on hearing of my latest mad obsession, enabled me with a gift of enough paper to sustain several long novels.

My dear friend, Wallace, who offered his

services if I needed to do anything "dodgy" to get published. I didn't have to resort to that in the end, but it could have been fun.

Jo-anne O'Brien, whose hand I held tightly as we jumped naively into the world of aspiring authors; with whom I shared paperback dreams over coffee and various types of cake. Thank you.

Rebecca Lachlann, fellow writer, who has, for as long as I've know her, been both generous and timely with her advice, her interest, and her friendship. Alastair Blanshard, who both willingly and unwittingly helped me research this novel. Michelle Wainwright, Sarah Kynaston, MaryAnn Marshall, and Stanley Sparkes—that most precious literary resource—friends who could read and were willing to do so.

Whoever it was behind the Australian Newspapers Digitisation Program—brilliant idea! The online access to the times in which Rowland Sinclair lived was invaluable. All but two of the newspaper extracts featured in these pages were taken from actual articles appearing in Australian newspapers in 1932 or thereabouts. The specific dates and the names of the publications in which they appeared have been altered to better align with the story—in some instances, even that was unnecessary.

Finally, I would like to acknowledge the rich

background to the era and its personalities that I gained from the writings of Andrew Moore, Keith Amos, David Hickie, and the memoirs of Eric Campbell himself. Thank you, gentlemen, for preserving this fascinating, if occasionally ludicrous, period of Australian history.

Well that's my village. Thank you all. S.G.

CRIME WAVE
BRUTAL MURDER

SYDNEY, Thursday

Late last night, police attended a shocking murder scene at one of Sydney's foremost suburbs.

The deceased gentleman, Mr. Rowland Sinclair, died in his own home, after or during a brutal attack by unknown assailants. Authorities were alerted by his housekeeper who discovered his bludgeoned body. The victim was from one of the State's pre-eminent families: the Sinclairs of Oaklea near Yass.

It is a sign of the times that the lawlessness that has taken hold of Sydney's streets has invaded the homes of even the most well-to-do. Violent crime, on the rise since the Great War, has been further exacerbated by the current political tensions, as well as the ever-mounting numbers of unemployed. Burglaries and robberies from the person, often with firearms and violence, are now daily events, with the meanest classes of thefts reported from all quarters. Last evening was no exception.

According to police sources, Mr. Sinclair's attackers were merciless. The investigation is continuing, though Superintendent MacKay was not available for comment.

Superintendent MacKay has come to prominence for his efforts to suppress the Razor Gangs waging their murderous warfare in Sydney's streets and terrorising honest citizens.

Colonel Eric Campbell, the Commander of the New Guard, attributes the current crime wave to Communist elements conspiring to destabilise the State. Last night, he again offered the assistance of his men to the State Police Force.

Colonel Michael Bruxner, of the newly formed United Country Party, and a friend of the Sinclair family, paid tribute to Mr. Sinclair before calling upon Premier Lang to urgently address the rampant crime facing the citizens of Sydney. "People can no longer feel safe in their homes," he said.

The Sydney Morning Herald,
December 11, 1931

Chapter One

Five days earlier

It wasn't right. He leaned to the left, squinting, but no change of perspective improved it. Swearing at the canvas was also unlikely to help, but he tried that anyway. A reasonable man would have walked away long ago.

It was ridiculous to be working in the evening, by the light of an electric bulb. He knew that. Of course, the colours would be wrong. It seemed some destructive urge compelled him to render it completely irredeemable, rather than to leave it simply unsatisfactory. Still, he continued, hoping that by some accident he would find the precise combination of pigment and stroke to resurrect the landscape. Under the broad bright sky of morning, the painting had shown such promise.

He stood back and cursed again. It was no use. He had finessed it beyond redemption. He could not even bring himself to sign the lifeless work. Not that the signature of Rowland Sinclair was of any great consequence in the world of art. Perhaps in time.

Rowland gazed out the window as he cleaned his brushes. The grounds of Woodlands House were immaculate and traditional. The distant front hedge was made just visible by a street lamp, which added its radiance to the muted light of the moon. Somewhere beyond that hedge stretched the fairways of the golf-links, and further in that direction, the great harbour of Sydney. It was hard to believe that so many struggled and despaired under the weight of the Great Depression; the leafy streets of Woollahra seemed beyond the reach of the economic crisis.

Rowland wiped his hands on his waistcoat. Not so many months ago, it had been a quality item of gentleman's attire. Now, it was stained with paint and smelled of turpentine. Rowland preferred it that way. He looked again at the painting with which he had battled all day and which, in the end, had defeated him.

"Hmmm, that's rather awful—embarrassing really." The voice was Edna's. She peered over his shoulder and spoke with all her customary bluntness.

He smiled. "Yes, I should have stopped when it was merely bad."

Edna laughed, and slid into the tall wingback armchair where she often posed for Rowland. She pulled off her hat and gloves, tossing them carelessly onto the side table as she shook out her dark copper tresses. "I sold *L'escalier* today."

"That's smashing," Rowland said, impressed. *L'escalier* was one of Edna's larger pieces—difficult to sell in the financial restraint of the times. "Who bought it?"

"Some academic friend of Papa's…I had to discount it a little."

Rowland saw the flicker in her eyes. "I wouldn't fret about that, Ed. Most of us aren't selling anything at all these days." He groaned as he looked back at his landscape. "Obviously, the buying public recognises true talent."

Edna dismissed the last. Rowland Sinclair was by no means untalented, but painters were susceptible to self-doubt. Edna created art in clay and bronze. Her mother had been a French artist of some acclaim in her own country. Before she died, she imbued in her daughter a determination, a belief in her own artistic destiny, and a certain European disregard for the social expectations of conservative Sydney, whose elite still clung to the Empire.

"I don't know why you spend so much time trying to paint trees," she said, as Rowland pushed his easel into a corner. "You're not very good at it... and you capture people so beautifully."

"Trees don't complain quite so much." Taking to the chair beside her, he took opened his notebook and began to sketch her face, glancing up occasionally with intense blue eyes that observed every contour and movement, each nuance of expression. She ignored it, accustomed to being the subject of his scribbling.

"Rowly, do you remember Archie Greenwood?"

"No."

"Yes, you do. He was at Ashton's when you first started there."

"If you say so." Rowland remained focussed on his notebook.

The Ashton Art School was where he had first encountered Edna. It had been the twenties, a time of thrilling optimism, a time when crashing markets had been unthinkable. Rowland had been barely twenty-three and not long returned from Oxford.

"You must remember Archie—he had that dreadful lisp, but talked all the time anyway. Considered himself the next Picasso."

Rowland looked at her blankly. In truth, he hadn't noticed much at Ashton's after Edna, and he had noticed her immediately—how could he not? She was enchanting. Her face was mesmerising, as open as a child's, yet full of passion and an unshakable sense of self. Her hair was that glorious fiery shade featured time and again in the works of the great masters. A spirited, laughing muse, she had captivated and mystified him. Still, their association had not started well.

"Come on, Rowly," Edna insisted. "Archie used to paint those appalling pictures of erotic fruit."

"Oh, him! He had an interesting way with bananas." Archie Greenwood and his lewd still lifes came back to him.

To his recollection, the Ashton school overflowed with odd characters; and yet, it was Rowland Sinclair whom Edna had seemed to find ridiculous, somehow trivial. She had often left him feeling so. Admittedly, he had not been typical of the students there.

"I saw Archie today."

"What's he doing?"

"Oh, Rowly." Edna wrapped her arms around a cushion and hugged it under her chin. "He was picking up cigarette butts from the platform. I think he may be sleeping at Happy Valley." She shuddered. The unemployed camp out at La

Perouse was a desperate, violent place—the refuge of those without any other choice.

Rowland stilled his pencil. "He wouldn't come with you?" He assumed Edna would have tried to bring Greenwood back to Woodlands House. The Woollahra mansion, the Sydney residence of the Sinclairs, had for some time hosted a succession of artists, writers, and poets. Some stayed a short time, others longer. Some came to live and work in an atmosphere of creativity; others because they had nowhere else. Edna had been there two years.

She stood, frowning as she thought of the broken man who had once dreamt of artistic triumph. "He would barely talk to me. He was so embarrassed."

"Greenwood knows how to find us?"

Edna nodded. "I gave him my card."

"Do you know how to find him?"

"No, I ran into him by chance."

"Not much we can do, Ed. He knows his own mind, and a man has his pride, if nothing else."

Edna leant against the back of the armchair, which Rowland's late father had imported from London. "Not just men. I wonder when things will get better."

Rowland glanced up. The life-sized portrait of Henry Sinclair glared down at them from the wall behind Edna, as if he disapproved of her being anywhere remotely near his chair, or his son. For that moment, Rowland's choices were silhouetted against his background. His father had presided over a rural fiefdom—vast pastoral holdings near Yass, in the west. His sons were born into a world of extraordinary privilege and conservative tradition. The Sinclair boys had been raised as gentlemen: New South Welshmen, but British, nonetheless.

And yet, Rowland had been drawn Edna's world. She had been raised among the city's intelligentsia, in salons rich in thought and debate. Through her father, a professor of philosophy at the University of Sydney, she had developed a sympathy for the ideas of the left and, with it, a suspicion of the almost incomprehensible wealth of those in the great houses of Woollahra.

Despite her initial misgivings, Edna had come to like Rowland Sinclair. He had surprised her with his willingness to absorb the ways of her world, her politics, her friends, and her causes. She knew that he was in love with her—on some level at least—but he had never asked that his feelings be reciprocated. Indeed, he called her "Ed," as if she were one of his mates. Edna liked that. To her, their relationship was clear; they were the best of friends—they would storm the world together with their art and their ideas.

She had introduced him into her circles—artists

and intellectuals who fraternised across the class lines that segregated polite society from the rest. In time, Rowland was accepted among them, forgiven for the absurd opulence of his background.

Rowland looked over as the housekeeper entered the room. Mary Brown had been in his family's employ since before he was born. She managed the day-to-day running of Woodlands House, supervising the domestic staff, including the gardener and the chauffeur. A solid woman of formidable disposition, Mary sighed audibly as she surveyed the drawing room. She pulled a cloth from her apron and pointedly rubbed the drops of paint from the lacquered sideboard. She sighed again.

Rowland winked at Edna. Mary Brown had an entire language of sighs.

At one time, when Mary had still been the downstairs maid, the Sinclairs had spent much of the year in Woodlands House. Then in 1914, Britain declared war on Germany, and Australia fell enthusiastically into step. Rowland's brothers joined up, eager to fight for the Empire's cause. He was not yet ten when he waved them off on the troop ships bound for Egypt. Wilfred had been twenty-four, Aubrey just nineteen, and the three of them had been friends, despite the years between them.

Aubrey was killed in action a year later. Mrs.

Sinclair deserted the whirl of Sydney society to mourn her son in the seclusion of their country property. She never returned. She had never been the same.

Wilfred eventually came back from the war, but he was changed. He, too, retreated to Oaklea, and Mary Brown became keeper of an empty house.

Sent to school in England soon after the war ended, Rowland remained there for over eight years. Through all that time, there were no Sinclairs in Woodlands House, though Mary Brown ensured it was ready for the family to walk back in at any time.

"Will you be dining in tonight, Master Rowly?" She addressed him as she had since he was a child.

"I think so, Mary." Rowland glanced at Edna. "But we should probably wait for Milton and Clyde. Ed, do you know where they are?"

"I think they went to the pub," she said. "Clyde's been struggling with his commission, and Milton…well he just likes to drink."

Rowland smiled. "It might be a while, Mary."

She nodded and left the room, her face set and unreadable. Mr. Sinclair would not have approved of his son's friends; of that, she was sure. He certainly would not have been happy that his home

had become a shelter for all manner of shiftless artists and Communists. To Mary Brown, the terms
were synonymous. Still, she had known Rowland
since he was a baby. He had been a quiet, sensitive
child, but she had thought him a good boy. She
hoped he would see the error of his ways. In any
case, it was not her place to say.

"What are you doing tomorrow, Rowly?"
Edna asked suddenly.

"Lunch with my uncle, at his club," he replied,
wondering what else she had in mind.

"Sounds frightful."

Rowland grinned. Edna objected to gentlemen's clubs on principle. "Uncle Rowland likes it.
It's not that bad."

His Uncle Rowland, his namesake, was his
father's younger brother. He had never married and
had spent much of his life travelling. An unrepentant and flamboyant hedonist, the elder Rowland
Sinclair worked diligently at indulging in all the
pleasures of life, with hardly a thought for anything
else. It was not that he was unkind or intentionally
indifferent. He just seemed to assume everyone had
the same resources as he.

"He's rather taken with you," Rowland said,
cringing a little as he remembered how outrageously
his uncle had flirted with Edna on the few occasions
they'd met. She could easily have been offended,

but the sculptress had taken it in her stride, telling the elderly rogue that if she ever did decide to take up with a Sinclair, it would indeed be an old one.

"He's a character," Edna's eyes twinkled. "You know, he doesn't seem to be the least bit bothered about us all." She could not imagine any of Rowland's other relatives being so at ease with the manner in which he had turned their grand home into a luxurious artists' commune.

"I think he's rather tickled that there's someone else disgracing the family name," Rowland replied.

"You'll be finished by three, won't you?" Edna ventured. "Even your uncle can't eat for more than three hours…" She had become resigned to the fact that Rowland occasionally had to return to the world to which he was born.

"I can be finished by three," he said. "What do you need me for?"

"There's a meeting tomorrow afternoon. At the Domain. We should go."

Rowland knew she meant a meeting of the Communist Party. He was not a Communist, neither was Edna, at least not officially. "Why?"

"Morris is speaking," she replied. "He's very nervous—I'm sure he'd appreciate it if we were there."

Rowland had now met many Communists, Morris among them. The returned serviceman was sincere in his conviction and committed to his ideology, but he was no orator. The crowds at the Domain had grown during the harsh Depression years. The exchanges between the rousing speakers and the equally fervent hecklers were often so entertaining, that those who could no longer afford shows flocked there for amusement, if not enlightenment. As far as Rowland could tell, the local Communist Party had nothing to fill its agenda except for the impassioned speeches by its members. To date, Morris had avoided the duty, but with the Depression dragging on, and more people turning out, every Party member was required to do his bit to rally the masses.

"Come on, Rowly," Edna pleaded, as she poured him a drink. "We can clap and cheer at the right times, and hopefully he won't have to stand up for very long."

"Yes, why not?" Rowland replied as he put down his pencil and took the glass of sherry.

"Good." Edna smiled, satisfied. "We'll meet you there at about quarter past."

"We? Who else have you drafted?"

"Just Milt and Clyde. Morris will be very grateful," she added earnestly.

"He needn't be." Rowland picked up his pencil once again.

Chapter Two

SYDNEY DAY-BY-DAY

(By A Special Correspondent)

SYDNEY, Sunday

The new Masonic Club building is in accord with the recent progress of the city. It rises to 150ft yet seems even taller. A view of North Head and the Pacific beyond may be obtained from the roof.

The building was made possible by activity in the real estate market. The former premises were disposed of at a surprising profit. The club purchased a block of land running from Castlereagh Street to Pitt Street between Market and Park Streets, and it soon sold the Pitt Street half at a price which gave it a site free with a large sum of money to go toward the cost of the building.

The present value of the property is about £180,000.

The Argus, December 7, 1931

The grand dining room of the Masonic Club, an establishment of reputation and elegance, was thoroughly removed from the bleak hardship of those walking the streets in search of work outside its thick cedar doors. The murmur of polite voices was deep, for the patrons were exclusively male. The club was a dominion of impeccably dressed and well-connected men. They dined with each other under elaborate chandeliers that hung from high ornate ceilings, trimmed with intricate cornices and plaster roses. Rowland had become a member at his brother's insistence, but he generally used the club only on his uncle's invitation.

The elder Rowland Sinclair was already seated at the table. He was a large man whose body and features spoke of years of indulgence. His hair was thick, swept back from his face. It had once been as dark as his nephew's—now it was white. His eyes had, with age, become a little weak, but they were still the distinct blue that marked all the Sinclair men.

"Rowly, my boy!" he said as he stood in

welcome, moving his substantial girth with some difficulty and catching the table.

"Hello, Uncle. Have you been waiting long?" Rowland lunged to save the nearly empty bottle of wine which wobbled precariously on the table's edge.

"Not that long—there may still be a drop left for you." He resumed his seat and, taking the bottle from Rowland, drained its remnants into a glass. Rowland sat down.

"So how are you, my boy? I haven't heard much of you for a while. I had hoped I could rely on you for at least the odd minor scandal…but there has been nothing! When I was your age I would not have allowed myself to become so respectable! It's tremendously uninteresting."

Rowland smiled in the face of the old man's barrage. "I'm well."

"And how is your painting going? I can't tell you how many people have commented on that lovely piece you gave me last summer….your brother, particularly."

"Wilfred was here?" Rowland was surprised. He had not seen his brother in months.

"Just a few weeks ago. Some sort of business… Now tell me about your work. I expect you will be submitting something to the Archibald Prize?"

"Not this year, Uncle. Maybe next."

They paused their conversation as the waiter took their orders.

"I don't blame you," the elder Sinclair went on, as he knifed a thick layer of pale butter onto his dinner roll. He lowered his voice. "The competition is rigged—the trustees seem think one has to reside in bloody Victoria to be able to paint!"

Rowland laughed. Much to the ire of the Sydney art community, Victorians had dominated the prize since its inception, but he was reasonably sure it was not a conspiracy of any sort.

The meal continued in effortless company. Rowland's uncle carried the conversation, but that was not unusual. Intermittently, his acquaintances would stop by to speak with him. Rowland observed that a certain indulgence was extended to age under the auspices of eccentricity. It was obvious, however, that he would not be afforded the same tolerance. Most responded warily to any introduction. Although Wilfred Sinclair was a gentleman of reputation, his youngest brother was known for avoiding the company of men of standing. The esteemed members of the Masonic Club declined any extended conversation with the younger Rowland. It seemed that Woodlands House and its current residents had not escaped the notice of Sydney society, and, regardless of what his uncle thought, Rowland was not quite respectable.

After a dignified passage of time, lunch was complete. Rowland glanced at his watch as his host smoked and recounted some tales of his most recent visit to London. It was nearly three o'clock. He could walk to the Domain from the club in about ten minutes. He finished the last of his wine in a single gulp.

"I must be off," he said, standing before his uncle could order yet another round of port.

"I'm glad to hear it, son. A young man like you should have better things to do than dine with old relatives. Go now. Do something interesting!"

"We shall do this again, soon." Rowland shook his uncle's hand.

"Of course, of course…"

Rowland retrieved his coat and hat. The Masonic Club was in the heart of the city, only a short walk from the parklands of the Domain. The day was dull and although it was December, the breeze was brisk.

There were many men walking in the same direction. Some, like Rowland, walked with a sense of destination. Others seemed bent with unseen burdens, tired men who were walking that way because they had nowhere else to go. Honest men, criminals, and those who resorted to theft and menace because they saw no other option. Later, once darkness had emptied the Domain, they would find refuge in the rock shelters of Mrs. Macquarie's Point.

Occasionally, he was stopped by beggars and men bearing pamphlets decrying some ill or promoting some cause. He always carried coins for the former and politely declined the latter.

Rowland placed a hand on his hat as he ducked through the congestion of motorcars and horse vans near the grand iron gates at the Domain's entrance. He made his way toward Speakers' Corner, where the Communists met on Sunday afternoons to exercise their right to free speech in the open air, and to rally support for their cause. When he reached the outer Domain, a large crowd was gathering, and he could already hear the rabble of fiery speeches. Eventually, he spotted Edna talking earnestly with a man whose arm was bandaged in a sling about his neck. Milton and Clyde stood beside them.

"Ed!" Rowland hailed them all with her name. Edna waved.

"What on earth are you wearing?" Milton asked as soon as Rowland was in earshot.

"He's been lunching with the ruling classes," Edna explained.

Rowland laughed. There was really no point denying it. The dress regulations of the Masonic Club, and the expectations of its members, were strict and particular. Still, it was not as if he was wearing tails. In fact, he was dressed pretty much as he always was, though he had taken special care to find a jacket and a shirt that were not streaked with paint.

"Just trying to keep pace with Milt," he replied.

Milton's attire was not expensive, but it was distinctive, much like Milton himself. He had a preference for unusual colours and extravagant cravats. He wore his hair well below his ears in the style of the old aesthetes. On a lesser individual it may have been peculiar, but on Milton it rarely raised mention. A childhood friend of Edna's, he had moved into Woodlands House the previous year, and he and Rowland had formed a close and unexpected friendship. Though his formal education was minimal, Milton was a product of various Literary and Mechanics' Institutes, organisations which promoted personal improvement and often provided the only libraries to which working men had access. Essentially self-educated, he called himself a poet; but though Milton was extremely well-read, Rowland was yet to see an original verse, sonnet, or even a couplet penned by his friend.

"What happened to you, Morris?" Rowland asked the man with the injured arm. Now he was closer he could see the ex-serviceman also sported a black eye.

"Bit of trouble in Redfern, mate," Morris replied as he rolled a cigarette with his uninjured hand. "Fell foul of a couple of bailiffs."

"Repossession," Edna added.

Rowland understood. The Australian Unemployed Workers' Union often organised resistance to help those about to lose their homes. Returned soldiers like Morris used what they had learned in the battlefields of Europe to barricade homes against the bailiffs. It was trench warfare in the suburbs, not quite as bloody, but often just as desperate.

"Are you all right?"

"I'll live."

"Are you ready?"

Morris sighed. "I'm up next," he said balefully as he glanced at the makeshift podium, a stepladder, from where a squat man addressed the masses in a faintly Irish accent.

The Irishman roused the crowd with volume and passion. Rowland sketched him mentally—hawkish nose, jutting chin, eyes almost hidden beneath a craggy brow, and a cigarette balanced precariously on his lower lip like an exclamation mark to his words. He danced as he spoke, like a boxer.

"Who's that?" Rowland hadn't seen this man before.

"Patrick Ryan," replied Morris.

"Struth, he's getting them worked up," Clyde

pulled at his braces as he looked out at the crowd. He was only a little older than Rowland and Milton, but the years had settled early on his face. Like Rowland, he saw pictures in the scene. They were painters; it was what they did.

Ryan was railing about the inequities of the Depression. The capitalist classes, he claimed, had created the disaster but it was the working man who'd lost his job, who'd lost his home. It was the working man who suffered.

Rowland listened. Despite coming from the class that Ryan was casting in villainy, he was not affronted. He was who he was; but he was not unsympathetic. Somehow in the years since he had returned to Sydney, since he had started moving in Edna's circles, he had fallen into a sort of gap between the social classes, observing them both from a distance.

Rowland's eyes moved around the crowd. It was mostly male. Troubled faces wearied by hardship nodding at the stirring rhetoric, and murmuring assent.

And then, a lone cry of dissent. "Get a job, you Red mongrel!"

Rowland's gaze shifted immediately toward the voice. The heckler was not far away—among a group of men whose crisp suits didn't show any signs of wear. There was a certain militaristic uniformity in their posture and stance, their arms folded rigidly across their double-breasted chests.

Ryan responded to the derision by escalating his own fervour. The response from the crowd increased, both for and against him. When Ryan called for revolution, the jostling began and within minutes a scuffle broke out near the group that had started the heckling. Several men were now attempting to drag Ryan from his podium and Morris ran forward to help his comrade. Despite the numbers they'd attracted, the Communists were grossly outnumbered, especially when reinforcements emerged to support the men who took exception to the words of rebellion.

Milton took exception to the imbalance. "Come on!" he motioned to Rowland and Clyde, a split second before he leapt into the fray after Morris. Rowland glanced quickly at Edna and did likewise.

The skirmish was now in earnest. Rowland and Clyde fell in behind Milton who was already in the thick of things. Rowland had boxed at Oxford, but Clyde, who had spent those same years on the wallaby, in search of work, really knew how to fight. He seemed to move very little but men staggered all around him. From within the mêlée, a defiant voice belted out the first bars of "The Internationale," and soon the Communist anthem rang out. To Rowland, it was a bit surreal.

He ducked a fist and tried to pull Milton back, but the poet would have none of it. Clyde called out to him, but too late, and Rowland caught a blow to the jaw. He recovered quickly and turned toward his assailant, finding himself face-to-face with a blond man disfigured by a jagged scar that ran from his ear to his chin. Rowland remembered the scar.

"What the...?" the man started, his eyes widening in shock. For a moment he seemed confused and then realisation dawned.

A hand grabbed Rowland's and jerked him away. It was Edna.

"Ed! Watch out!" Rowland pulled her into him as a plank swung wildly. It missed her and glanced off his shoulder. He cursed and looked for a way out through the incensed factions.

"Hey! Back off!" The scarred man who had punched him just a moment earlier intervened to block the blow of a pick-axe handle.

"Rowly, Ed!" Clyde beckoned for them frantically. They followed him and, after considerable weaving and dodging, and some belligerence, he managed to lead them out of the worst of it. Policemen were now a presence, separating the throng with force and batons.

"Where's Milton?" Edna looked back anxiously.

"Morris dragged him out a little while ago," Clyde assured her. "He's fine."

"That was getting nasty," Rowland murmured, rubbing his shoulder.

"Morris got out of speaking." Clyde replaced his hat over tousled sandy hair. "He'll be stoked."

"Come on, let's go." Edna adjusted her own hat, which had been knocked awry in the brawl. "Milt will turn up."

Even as she spoke, the poet emerged from the crowd, looking dishevelled but cheerful.

"That was a hoot!"

"For heaven's sake, Milt." Edna rolled her eyes.

"Though a quarrel in the streets is a thing to be hated, the energies displayed in it are fine; the commonest man shows grace in his quarrel," Milton proclaimed to the world at large, throwing his arms wide into the air in exhilaration.

"Keats," Rowland added. Milton's reputation, as a poet, came from his ability to quote the great bards, and his propensity to do so without attribution. Of course, Rowland Sinclair's traditional British education made such blatant appropriation a little difficult when he was around.

With many others, they spilled out of the Domain, leaving the violence behind. It was now early evening and the shadows had started to lengthen. Most businesses were closed, and as the trams were not running, they began the long walk back toward Woollahra.

Milton threw an arm about Rowland's shoulder. "What do you say, Rowly? Shall we go to the pub? If we hurry we may make it before closing time."

"What would we do with Ed?" Edna was unlikely to wait quietly in the ladies' bar while they drank.

Milton looked at Edna, "Damn."

"You and Clyde go," Rowland offered. "I'll take Ed home."

"No, she'll be right," said Clyde. "We'll come with you."

"We needed you to pay for the drinks, anyway," admitted Milton. "We're both a bit skint."

"You're shameless!" Edna slapped his arm. She was not, however, particularly concerned. Milton was a genuine friend; he just dealt with economic realities pragmatically. She would not have allowed him to simply use Rowland.

Braced by the cold wind, they arrived at Woodlands House. Milton and Clyde availed themselves of the contents of various decanters and bottles in the main drawing room, while Rowland picked up his notebook and sketched, from memory, the figures from the battle at the Domain. His drawings were quick and rough, but they captured the essence of their subjects in just a few strokes. He began with Patrick Ryan, and moved on to a study of Morris. And then he drew the blond man who had both struck, and defended him.

"Do you want a drink, Rowly?" Milton poured Scotch. Rowland glanced at the bottle the poet held aloft.

"No," he said thinking briefly of Wilfred. His brother had often accused him of drinking like a woman. Whisky was a man's drink, Wilfred insisted. Rowland hated the taste of whisky, but he'd drunk it with Wilfred, in the hope that they could be friends once again. In the end the spirit had made him sick and their relationship was still uneasy.

Clyde walked over to see what Rowland was doing, and rested his brawny arms on the back of the armchair. "Who's that?"

Edna looked over his shoulder. "That's the man who hit you," she exclaimed. "I think he recognised you—looked as though he'd seen a ghost."

"He probably thought he had."

"What do you mean?" Milton fell into an armchair with his drink, careful not to let any escape his glass. He slung his leg up over the arm and pulled a slim dog-eared book from out of his pocket.

"This is Henry Alcott." Rowland marked in the scar. "I've not seen him in years. He was Aubrey's best friend." Rowland looked up at the framed photograph which had adorned the mantelpiece since he was a child. The young man was in uniform, about to go to war. Even in sepia tones, his eyes were arresting. His hair was dark, and his mouth hinted at a smile despite the austere formality of the pose. It could easily have been a photograph of Rowland who, it appeared, had grown to be the image of his brother.

Edna took the picture down and ran her finger over the handsome face in the frame. She had never taken the time to scrutinise it before.

She knew that Rowland had lost a brother in the war. He had once mentioned that his mother had never recovered from Aubrey's death, but that was all. He spoke very little of the Sinclairs.

"Do you think he thought you were Aubrey?"

Rowland shrugged. "Maybe for a moment… but he knows Aubrey's dead—they were in the same regiment. I remember him at the memorial service."

Milton put down his book and took the photograph. He looked from it, to Rowland. "Still, it would have given him a shock." He passed the frame to Clyde.

"I rather think he worked it out in the end," Rowland said on reflection. "I really should look him up. I'm sure he tried to help us out."

"Good of him," Clyde agreed. "And handy. Those thugs weren't playing games."

Edna nodded. "They were New Guardsmen."

Rowland hadn't thought of that, but he wasn't surprised to hear it. The ranks of the New Guard had swelled of late, and they were no friends of the Communists.

"They've been breaking up all the meetings, lately," Milton said as he sipped his scotch. "There's rarely a Party meeting or a union rally that doesn't end in some sort of dustup."

As the popularity of the Communist Party had risen through the Depression, so, too, had patriotic organisations at the other extreme. The daily papers often carried the severe images of the Fascist leaders in ascendancy in Europe. In Italy there was Mussolini and, in Germany, Hitler was becoming ever more powerful. Mosley was pushing the Fascist cause in Britain. In New South Wales, Eric Campbell had come to prominence. Rowland was aware of the popularity of the New Guard, chiefly among the wealthy, but he was not particularly interested in politics. He had in any case always regarded Campbell and his followers as a bit of a joke.

Edna was less blasée, making her position clear with frequent anti-Fascist rants. Clyde, too, was concerned about the New Guard movement, but he had always been the most earnest among them. Only Milton shared Rowland's tendency to dismiss the New Guard as ridiculous.

"I'm surprised you weren't recognised by a Guardsman, Rowly," Clyde said replacing Aubrey's picture onto the mantelpiece. "I'll wager most of your neighbours are in the movement."

"Well, since the neighbours don't call by anymore, I wouldn't recognise them either."

"You," Clyde pointed at Rowland with his cigarette, "should take them seriously. They're dangerous."

Rowland laughed. "I'll tell Mary to be on the lookout for an imminent attack by the neighbours, then."

Chapter Three

Filth and Hate

In Communist's Home
Stones Thrown At Mother At Father's Order

SYDNEY, Monday

The police proceeded to Punchbowl yesterday and found a woman with a baby in her arms who alleged that her husband, a Communist, assaulted her and used filthy language toward her because she would not join the Communist Party.

The man declared that his wife's story was untrue, but sang "The Red Flag" in the presence of the police.

The Sydney Morning Herald,
December 8, 1931

Rowland sat at the mahogany bar of the Australian Club, scanning the paper as he waited. Behind him, the pick of Sydney's gentlemanly elite reclined in leather-studded armchairs, engaging in polite conversation as they drank and smoked. A large portrait of George V gazed imperiously, but benevolently, over his loyal colonial subjects. The adjacent wall held a gallery of smaller portraits, the Australian Club's presidents since 1838.

Elderly statesmen in the armchairs closest to the bar discussed the new Sydney Harbour Bridge and its unfinished roadway which grew ever closer from either side of the harbour, under the colossal structure of its arch.

"I tell you it's damned inconvenient. The noise from the locomotives will be intolerable—we wrote to the Authority and Game of course…but it seems Lang is determined to build this infernal bridge and destroy the serenity of the foreshore."

His companion sighed. "Nothing so civilised as gathering one's thoughts on the ferry crossing— be a thing of the past, I'm afraid, as the populace goes hurtling across that grey atrocity."

Rowland checked his watch, and returned to his paper. There was an account of the previous Sunday's violence in the Domain. Apparently a police officer had been injured when he fell under the wheels of a buggy trying to escape the fracas.

"Sinclair."

Rowland turned as Henry Alcott extended his hand. "Rowland Sinclair. Good Lord, I haven't seen you since I came back from the war. It seems you've grown up. You were still at Kings when..."

Rowland shook the man's hand. "How are you, Henry?"

Alcott smiled broadly, the wide scar on his jawline highlighting the stretch of his mouth. "I can't complain."

"What's your poison, then?"

"Scotch."

Rowland motioned to the barman, and Alcott took the stool beside him.

"I didn't get a chance to thank you for your assistance on Sunday..." Rowland started.

Alcott dismissed his thanks with a wave. "Glad to help, old man." He looked intently at Rowland. "How did you get caught up in that anyway?"

"Usual way—followed a mate."

Alcott said nothing for a moment, and then, "I say, Rowly, I'm sorry I haven't been in touch since Aubrey passed on. We were such chums, Aubrey and I...it was difficult."

Rowland sipped his beer. "It's all right, Henry, we didn't expect—"

"My Lord, you look like Aubrey!" Alcott

shook his head. "It's like having a drink with Aubrey again."

Rowland listened as Henry Alcott talked of Aubrey: tales of boyhood larks, schooldays, and the war in which they'd served together. Henry had been injured first, and so had not been with Aubrey when he died. Rowland could see this weighed heavily on Alcott's conscience. Intermittently, Alcott would interrupt himself and say, "My Lord, you could be Aubrey."

Rowland let him go. He'd been just a child when his brother had fallen and Alcott's memories gave him some he'd never had himself. The pair toasted Aubrey Sinclair many times that afternoon.

It was a couple of hours before Alcott asked about the Domain. "What were you doing at Speakers' Corner, Rowly? Did you know what kind of men speak there?"

Rowland felt a mild rise of annoyance. Alcott spoke to him as if he were a child. "A friend of mine was due to speak next."

Alcott's face darkened. "What? For the Communists?"

"Yes."

"You were there to listen to the Communists?"

"I was there to listen to a friend."

"Do you have many friends among the Communists, then?"

"Quite a few."

Alcott looked away for a second.

Rowland regretted this turn in the conversation. He did not wish to alienate Henry Alcott, who now seemed unable to return his eye.

Suddenly, the ex-serviceman smiled. "Look, Rowly, what say I introduce you to some chaps? Aubrey would want me to look out for you."

"What chaps?"

"Right-thinking men, Rowly. Loyalists who love this country. Men like Aubrey. We could have a few drinks…get you back into the right crowd."

Rowland chose his words carefully. He suspected these men Alcott mentioned would be of the same conservative ilk as his brother, Wilfred. He was being invited to attend hour upon hour of patriotic ranting. "Look, Henry, I don't think I'm your man. But I'm always available if you want to have a drink."

Unhappy, Alcott drained his glass. And then he laughed. "Aubrey always said you were a pain in the royal…" He laughed again and wagged a finger at Rowland. "I'm not letting this go. Aubrey would want me to straighten you out.….Introduce you to the right sort of people. Good Lord, you look like Aubrey." His voice caught a little.

Rowland drank with him for a while longer.

"Well, I'll keep in touch." Alcott stood,

offering Rowland his hand. "You give my regards to Wilfred, and to your mother." He smiled. "You'll come round, you know."

Rowland's brow rose, irritated by Alcott's presumption, but he didn't bother arguing with the man.

Chapter Four

CAUSES OF CRIME

SYDNEY, Wednesday

According to Reverend H.S. Craik, chairman of the Congregational Union, the present crime wave is not due only to leniency of punishment, or the educational system, or the lack of home education or moving pictures, but to the four combined, and underlying all are evil thoughts.

The Canberra Times, 10 December 1931

The elder Rowland Sinclair relaxed in his favourite chair, with his after-dinner pipe and a generous glass of brandy. He closed his eyes, savouring the combination of cherry tobacco and the warming liqueur. When he lifted his lids again it was to gaze, with a familiar satisfaction, at the nude hanging above the fireplace. The woman in the painting stared right back at him, unabashed, uncompromising. And yet there was vulnerability in the set of her lips, a hesitance underlying the strength. It was as if, for a moment, her face had been more naked than her body, and the painter had caught it. He was not a great connoisseur of art, but Rowland enjoyed the painting, and he always surrounded himself with those things he enjoyed.

The aging playboy settled his significant proportions into the well-padded seat. An American jazz orchestra blared from the wireless. Despite his age, he saw himself as a man of modern tastes. A strict rural upbringing and the dual millstones of tradition and obligation were, for him, a distant past. Rowland Sinclair pleased himself now. He sipped his brandy contentedly, stretching his feet toward the fire. To his mind this was a perfect way to see out the evening.

The knock was, at first, barely audible over the music, and then it became more insistent.

"Mrs. Donelly!" Rowland bellowed for his housekeeper. There was no response and the knocking became louder.

"Mrs. Donelly!" Still she did not reply. He put down his glass and dragged himself from the comfort of his chair, cursing the old housekeeper's creeping deafness. Wondering who would be calling so late, he shuffled into the foyer to answer the door. He sighed. Manners, it seemed, had become a thing of the past.

"Steady on!" he called as he fumbled with the bolt. The latch lifted and he stepped back hastily as the heavy door swung in wildly under sudden force.

Edna dragged a frock over her head as she dressed hurriedly. She had been asleep only moments before, but something serious was going on downstairs. From her bedroom window she could see police vehicles in the driveway, and the voices carried upstairs. She pulled on stockings and slipped her feet into shoes, wondering if Milton had managed to find some sort of trouble. Not that Milton was a criminal; he was just more reckless than the rest of them. She didn't bother with her hair, merely smoothing out the tresses with her hand as she left the room.

The entire household was up. Edna walked into the main drawing room and stood tentatively by the doorway. No one noticed her at first.

Two police officers sat stiffly on the brocade couch. The elder of the two was speaking quietly, a notebook open on his knee. His partner stared at the easel. Apparently Rowland had been up, working on his painting of the rally at the Domain, when the police arrived. He sat in the armchair in front of them. His elbows rested on his knees and his face was in his hands, his dark hair clenched in his fingers. Milton stood behind him; Clyde leant against the mantelpiece.

Edna hesitated, unsure. Rowland looked up suddenly, as if he sensed her standing there. His face was pale and hurt, and even from across the room, Edna could see the sadness that clouded his eyes.

He motioned her to come in and introduced her to Constables Peters and Delaney. They looked at her with faint disapproval.

"What's happened, Rowly?" she asked, frightened, sensing the answer would be tragedy.

"My Uncle Rowland's been murdered, Ed," he said calmly.

For a moment Edna's voice was lost. "How?"

"It seems he was attacked in his home, poor old…"

"As I explained, sir," said Constable Peters, "we have been unable to reach your brother, Mr. Wilfred Sinclair. We'll need you to identify the body, I'm afraid. But it could wait till morning if you prefer?"

Rowland shook his head and stood. "I'll come now." He glanced down at his paint-spattered waistcoat. He'd always cleaned up before he visited his uncle. As silly as it seemed, he did not think it right to do anything less now. "I'll just get a clean jacket."

Milton pressed his shoulder. "I'll come with you."

"Have Johnston bring the car round." Rowland turned to the policemen. "We will follow you, gentlemen."

"Mr. Sinclair's body has been transported to the morgue, sir," the constable replied. "We have left an officer at his house for tonight. His housekeeper," he consulted his notes, "a Mrs. Donelly, found the body. She was understandably distraught…quite incoherent. The detectives will want to examine the house again in the morning."

Rowland nodded. The constables waited in the foyer while he took the stairs two at a time, to change.

When he returned shortly thereafter, he looked less like Rowland and more like a Sinclair. He turned to Edna and Clyde and smiled tightly. "Better get this over with. We shouldn't be too long…."

Edna embraced him. "I'm so sorry, Rowly. This is just horrible."

"Thank you, Ed. He wasn't a bad old chap, you know."

He felt the grip of Clyde's strong hand on his back. "Do you need us to call anybody, mate?"

Rowland shook his head. "I'll do that when

I get back." He opened the door and followed the policemen out.

In the darkness of the driveway, Johnston, the chauffeur, opened the rear door of the Rolls-Royce saloon. The Sinclairs were in the minority who had kept their cars on the road. Even in Woollahra, many vehicles had been placed on blocks as people waited for better times. The Sinclair fortune was of a scale and kind that made no such measures necessary.

Milton followed Rowland into the backseat.

"Do you know where the Coroner's Court is, Johnston?" Rowland asked his driver.

"Yes, sir, I do." Johnston put the car into gear and swung it out of the sweeping driveway. For a while there was silence and then the chauffeur spoke again. "My condolences, sir…Terrible business this."

"Thank you, Johnston. You knew my uncle, didn't you?"

"Yes, sir. The other Mr. Rowland were a young man when I come to work for your late father… 'Course it were carriages then. Terrible business this."

Rowland nodded. It was a terrible business.

The morgue was located in the basement of the Coroner's Court building in The Rocks, near Circular Quay. An unimposing structure, it stood between the Sailors' Home and the Mariners' Church, and was neither austere nor foreboding, despite its unhappy function.

Peters and Delaney guided them to the rear of the building. As they descended the stairs to the morgue, the smell confronted them. Rowland paused, steadying himself against the banister. He gagged, trying to disguise it with a cough.

"You all right, Rowly?" The poet was less affected by the stench. It was hardly pleasant but, unlike Rowland, he had spent his life in far less salubrious haunts than the clean, polished world of Woollahra. Disagreeable odours did not penetrate the better suburbs, but they were a reality of lesser addresses.

"You'll get used to it in a moment, sir," said Peters, reassuringly.

"God, I hope not!" Rowland straightened and took the stairs slowly.

They entered the central mortuary. The acrid smell was more intense. There were seven tables in the room, with clean white sheets sombrely protecting the dignity of those who lay beneath.

"The coroner will conduct his postmortem on the body tomorrow," Peters pulled back the sheet on the table nearest them.

Rowland stared, then stepped closer, silently.

"Bloody hell," he said almost under his breath.

His painter's eye took in too much. His uncle's face was swollen, battered. Blood had congealed in his snowy hair and stained the smoking jacket which bore a Cambridge crest. It had seeped into the crevices of the wrinkles in his skin, deepening the purple bruising with etchings of red. Flat on the table, the body looked too small. Rowland Sinclair had been large in life. Milton put a hand on his shoulder.

Rowland felt sick. "Yes…that is…Rowland Sinclair."

Delaney pulled the sheet back over the body and the older Rowland Sinclair again became little more than a draped mound on a table.

"Thank you, sir." Peters motioned them to the door. "The detectives will want to talk to you in the morning."

Rowland nodded. He and Milton followed the constables up the stairs, where they left Peters and Delaney to their paperwork, and returned to the car. Johnston started the engine and Milton opened the drinks compartment built into the back of the front seat. He poured Rowland a drink from one of the crystal decanters.

Rowland choked on the first gulp. "I really hate whisky," he said, handing the glass back. Milton shrugged and not being a man inclined to waste, he drained the glass himself. Rowland found the port and drank that instead.

"Who would beat an old man to death?" he said, gazing into his empty tumbler.

"Is that what killed him?"

"I don't know." Rowland rubbed his forehead. "I guess the coroner will figure that out."

"I'm damned sorry, Rowly," Milton refilled his friend's glass. "I know you were close."

Rowland sat back in the seat. "He taught me to play poker, you know—I used to spend school holidays with him during the war…" He smiled faintly. "Until my father found out where he was taking me of an evening. It's hard to believe…" He didn't finish, retreating instead into a silent private grief.

Milton let him be.

Edna and Clyde were up waiting for them.

Rowland slumped into the armchair and loosened his tie. "Well, that's done."

"Was it awful?" Edna asked.

"Yes."

"What happens now?"

"The coroner has to do his bit." Milton distributed beverages yet again. He found that most situations could be helped with a stiff drink. Or several.

Rowland took the glass. "The police will want to speak to me tomorrow, Milt. I can't be drunk."

"You won't be drunk," the poet insisted. "Perhaps just a little hung over."

"Why would they want to speak with you?" Edna curled her legs up on the couch as she rolled her glass between her hands.

"Murder investigation." Rowland said the words slowly, getting used to the reality behind them. "I assume they'll need some sort of background on my uncle—though I don't know how much help I'd be. They'll probably learn a lot more from that housekeeper of his."

"Poor old thing," Edna murmured. "It would've been a terrible shock for her."

Milton raised his brow. "It didn't look as though the old boy went quietly...surely she would have heard something going on...."

"Mrs. Donelly is about a hundred and six." Rowland blanched as he thought of his uncle's final moments. "I don't think she hears too well."

Clyde examined the unfinished painting on Rowland's easel. "This is going well, Rowly," he said. "You've got the light on Ryan's face just right...it makes him look almost biblical."

Milton laughed. "He'll just love that! Who'd have thought...? Paddy Ryan leading the workers to the Promised Land...Not bad for a godless Communist!"

Rowland tried to smile. "I might get back to it tonight."

"You should get some sleep." Edna reached over and rubbed his hand. "There will be things to deal with tomorrow...and not just the police."

"Talking of which," Rowland said, putting down his drink, "I really should phone Wilfred. Let him know what's happened." He stood, and walked into the hallway to ring through to the exchange.

Milton replenished Rowland's glass, and they all listened while he spoke, first to the telephonist and then to his brother.

The conversation between Rowland and Wilfred Sinclair was strangely formal. Direct, but sad. Rowland recounted what the policemen had told him; then after some silences, during which Wilfred must have been pressing for more information, Rowland told his brother what he had seen at the morgue. Clyde and Edna were shocked by his description, and moved by the distress in his words. Then there was another series of silences interrupted only by Rowland saying: "Yes," or "All right."

When he came back into the drawing room, Rowland did not resume his seat, but headed straight to his easel. His eyes seemed a greyer shade of their normal blue, and they were distant. Edna recognised the look. He didn't want to talk anymore. She uncurled herself from the couch and said goodnight, squeezing his hand gently as she left. Milton and Clyde stayed a while, watching him work, and drinking in companionable silence. In time, they too retired, leaving Rowland alone with his brushes, his canvas and his thoughts.

Chapter Five

Housekeeper's Suit Against Grazier's Estate Action for £10,610

MELBOURNE, Thursday

Alleging an oral promise to be "provided for during her life", Maude Winifred of Mentone, spinster and housekeeper, brought an action against the trustee of the estate of John Francis Darby, of Studbrook, Birregurra, claiming £10,610...The late Mr. Darby, who was a grazier, left an estate valued at approximately £68,000.

The Argus, December 11, 1931

Edna took the tray from the downstairs maid and carried it into the drawing room. Rowland was still at his easel. It wasn't difficult to see that he had not slept. The suit he had worn to the morgue was now spattered with paint. His hair, too, was streaked where he had dragged his fingers through it as he worked. Edna smiled. Rowland had always been a little chaotic in the way he painted. She placed the tray on the sideboard and poured coffee into a fine china cup.

"Here, drink this," she ordered.

Rowland took the cup but left the saucer in her hand. He drained it in a single gulp and handed it back to her with a smile. The night at his easel had apparently lifted his spirits somewhat.

Edna looked past him, to the painting: Ryan's speech at the Domain. She was awestruck by Rowland's detailed recall. It was as if the figures had been posed before him while he painted. She saw the passion and conviction in Ryan's face as he spoke from his makeshift podium…the men in the crowd, some enthusiastic, some sceptical, and the New Guardsmen, hostile. Edna motioned Rowland out of the way and looked more carefully at the faces of the last, militant and determined, like soldiers.

"Oh my, Rowly, you're good," she said, almost to herself.

Rowland said nothing, but he was pleased. Edna was sparing with her praise.

"Do you want any of this?" he asked finally as he poured more coffee.

She grimaced. "Heavens, no." Edna drank only tea. This month anyway.

Rowland gulped his second cup. "Wilfred caught the train early this morning. He'll be in Sydney by afternoon—wants me to meet him at Uncle Rowland's house."

"Why there?"

Rowland shrugged. "I guess he's got to find papers and deeds, hide the odd skeleton...that sort of thing."

Edna stepped over a wet palette that Rowland had left on the floor. She had never met Wilfred. He preferred the country and came to Sydney infrequently. On those occasions that he did, Rowland would dine with him at the Masonic Club. She wondered if Wilfred had ever seen any of Rowland's work.

"You're finished then?" She looked again at the painting.

"Maybe." He pushed his hair back from his face. "Sometimes it's difficult to know when to stop...What do you think?"

Edna stood back, tilting her head to one side as she considered the picture as a whole. "I think you need to put in a couple more figures."

"Really?"

"Here, and here." She pointed to two spots on the canvas. "You have the Communists here and the New Guardsmen facing them in opposition. But there were others there too…ordinary people who were somewhere between the two. It won't be complete without the people in the middle."

Rowland stepped back and considered his work. The people in the middle. He thought of Alcott. Yes, she was right. "What would I do without you, Ed?"

"Nothing worth hanging, anyway."

He grinned as he picked up his brush and started dabbing at the mess of colour on his palette.

Milton sauntered in, fussing with the cuffs of a cream jacket he had paired with a red brocade waistcoat and cravat. He carried a pale buckskin fedora with a jaunty feather stuck into its band. Where and how Milton procured his idiosyncratic apparel was a mystery to his friends. The poet had his own contacts. Rowland assumed there was an insane, colour-blind tailor among them.

"Oh, you're still at it." Milton kept well clear of Rowland and the paint, lest his immaculate attire be spattered. He pointed vaguely toward the dining room. "Breakfast is served. Are we ready to partake, wot? Those cooks, how they pound, and strain and grind, and turn substance into accident, to fulfill all your greedy appetites."

"Chaucer," Rowland said, without taking his eyes from his canvas. "Tell Mary I'll eat later."

Milton nodded. "You coming, Ed? Clyde's working too. Don't make me eat alone."

Rowland worked through the morning. Absorbed, he didn't notice the time. Clyde came in at some stage to borrow some viridian blue and Rowland could hear Edna and Milton in the conservatory. It was where Edna sculpted the clay models she'd use to make castings for her bronzes. Despite the tragedy of the previous evening, the morning seemed almost normal.

It was afternoon when Rowland finally cleaned his brushes. His brother had arranged to meet him at four. Johnston, the chauffeur, was to meet the train at Central Station at two-thirty with the Rolls. Wilfred Sinclair had some business in the city he needed to attend to first, but Rowland knew he wouldn't be late. Wilfred was never late.

Rowland showered and changed, going through several shirts and waistcoats before he found one free of paint, and only then did he wander into the kitchen in search of food. Mary Brown shooed him out, sighing repeatedly, and banishing him to the dining room while she reheated the meal he'd earlier missed.

His stomach settled, he stuck his head into the sunroom where Clyde painted.

"What's your hurry?' Clyde began, tapping his pocket watch in case it had stopped. It read just half-past two and the elder Rowland Sinclair's house was not far.

"I thought I'd have a chat to Mrs. Donelly—the housekeeper—before Wil arrives," Rowland explained. "The poor old thing might have calmed down by now and have something to say."

"The police didn't get anything useful out of her."

"Yes, but she knows me…has for years. She might be able to remember something if I ask her."

"Would you like a mate?" Clyde asked, a little too eagerly.

"No. You finish your commission…the sooner you get that blasted harridan out of my house, the happier we'll all be."

Clyde sighed. A struggling artist could hardly turn down commissions, but the wealthy subject of his current work had few redeeming qualities. The portrait was taking Clyde much longer than usual because he was struggling to balance accuracy with his artistic desire to produce something pleasing to the eye. "It's hopeless," he said, despondent. "Its only value as a portrait is that it does actually look like her."

"You should've painted her from behind," Rowland grinned. "You could have said it was avant-garde—Lady McKenzie would have loved that."

"Get off!" Clyde snorted. "From the back, I would have had to paint her hump and bristles!"

Rowland laughed. He was glad he didn't have to take commissions. "If you make sure the frame is spectacular," he advised, "and match the colour of her dress in the painting to the curtains in her drawing room...she'll be more than happy."

"But look at it!" Clyde was in despair. "It's almost cruel to give it to her."

Rowland pondered the portrait. There was nothing wrong with it, except that it did depict Lady McKenzie in all her triple-chinned, buck-toothed squint-eyed glory. The woman had not one good feature that Clyde could highlight to distract the viewer from the bad ones. Indeed, having met the subject, Rowland thought that Clyde had, if anything, been kind. He remembered the hairy mole on Lady McKenzie's cheek as a good deal more prominent.

"I don't know, Clyde. She owns a mirror...it shouldn't be a great surprise."

Clyde grunted and turned back to the portrait.

Rowland understood. He knew Clyde to be a truly decent man, more considerate than most artists. Clyde felt a responsibility to find the beauty in even cantankerous, vain Lady McKenzie. But nothing presented itself, and Clyde couldn't escape the fact that a portrait did have to look at least vaguely like the sitter.

Clyde picked up his palette. "I've put together some stretchers for you. I'll stretch the canvases this evening."

"You don't have to do that," Rowland replied, knowing it was useless to argue. Clyde insisted on doing odd jobs about Woodlands, and no amount of assurances that it was unnecessary would dissuade him.

Clyde waved Rowland away as he went back to work.

Rowland left the house for the old stables that now served as a garage. The Rolls was of course out, but he never drove that himself anyway. To do so would probably have offended Johnston.

He climbed into his yellow Mercedes Benz, patting the bonnet affectionately as he did so. He had brought the supercharged tourer back with him from England. The car had once belonged to a Lord Lesley, with whom Rowland had played cards at Oxford. The Sinclairs meant very little to English society. There, they were looked down upon as colonial upstarts of dubious breeding. Lord Lesley had been no exception, and made no secret that playing poker with an Australian was akin to dining with savages. The evenings were regularly peppered with barbed witticisms about convicts and bushrangers.

Rowland had found it grating, but he was playing poker. He kept his face closed.

Perhaps it was because of this that the Englishman could not simply walk away as he started losing. By the time Lesley had bet his newly acquired motorcar on a single hand, a significant crowd had gathered to look on. The triumph of the colonial upstart was a public sensation. Rowland would probably have forgiven the wager to anyone else, particularly since the car in question was German. But it was too sweet a victory. He drove the Mercedes whenever opportunity allowed, even if the distance was short enough to stroll.

The engine roared into life. Rowland smiled, satisfied, as he savoured the familiar vibrations. He pulled slowly out of the stables and into the street, and in all of three minutes he turned into the driveway of what had been his uncle's home.

Though smaller than Woodlands House, the residence was similar in style and grandeur. Its gardens were formal, framed with box hedge and kept in park-like condition by a permanent gardener. The door was opened before Rowland could knock. The Mercedes had announced his arrival. It was not a quiet car, and had penetrated even Mrs. Donelly's deafness.

"Mr. Rowly!" She was obviously pleased to see him.

"Hello, Mrs. Donelly," Rowland replied in a strong, loud voice.

"Oh, Mr. Rowly, do come in, sir." She opened the door wide for him.

"I am so sorry about Mr. Sinclair—he was very good to me."

"As, I am sure, you were to him."

His uncle's house was as it had always been: richly decorated and crammed with trinkets and other objects from his many travels. The old man had always liked to call them his "*objets d'art*," but Rowland never quite saw them that way.

The stooped housekeeper ushered him into the dining hall, and insisted on bringing him tea.

"How are you, Mrs. Donelly?" he asked when she ceased fussing long enough for him to speak.

The housekeeper was almost startled by the question. Rowland shifted uncomfortably as her eyes become moist. He had not intended to distress her.

"I am so terribly upset, Mr. Rowly." She sat in the chair he pulled out for her. "Last night, I was sure I was going mad...."

"It must have been terrible to find him like

that," Rowland said, his mind flickering to his uncle's body on the morgue table.

Her tears came. "Poor Mr. Sinclair. They were cowardly, beat him so badly…he was not a well man, you know…He went to see Dr. Jones every other day these past weeks…"

"They?" Rowland interrupted her. "Did you see who did this, Mrs. Donelly?"

The housekeeper clutched the silver cross that hung from her neck. "I saw something, Mr. Rowly," she whispered.

"What?"

"It was not of this world, sir."

"All right," said Rowland carefully, trying to keep the scepticism out of his voice. "What was it exactly, Mrs. Donelly?"

She was now gripping her cross with both hands. She kissed it before she spoke again. "Ghosts, Mr. Rowly. Dark spirits."

Rowland was not sure how to respond. His uncle had never mentioned that Mrs. Donelly was mad, and he had never before noticed it either. "What did these apparitions look like?" he said eventually.

"Like ghosts, sir, but they were dark…grey…" She shuddered and kissed her cross again. "I saw them leave and then I found poor Mr. Sinclair."

"Did you tell the police this, Mrs. Donelly?" Rowland asked gently.

"Yes, I did."

"And what did they say?"

"They brought me a cup of tea." Rowland smiled slightly.

The housekeeper's face was distraught. "Mr. Rowly, what am I going to do, sir? I've been doing for Mr. Sinclair for so long…I don't have any other home. My nephew's out of work…he can't take me in—the poor boy can barely feed himself…"

Rowland was a little surprised. He hadn't considered what the death of his uncle meant for the staff he employed, particularly those who lived in.

"Don't worry, Mrs. Donelly," he said tentatively. "You can stay on here for as long as you want. We won't be selling the house." Wilfred usually made such decisions, but Rowland resolved to talk to him. If worst came to worst, surely his uncle's staff could be retained at Woodlands House. The Sinclairs had always been good employers.

He finished his tea and wandered back into the foyer where his uncle had died. The police had obviously finished with the scene, for the black and white chequerboard tiles had been scrubbed clean. Rowland felt a sudden surge of anger. Till now, he had crowded his mind with his work and with things more mundane, but as he stood where his uncle had died, he was staggered by a deep sense of loss and outrage.

Rowland had been close to his father's younger brother. The elder Rowland Sinclair had always been a man of grand pleasures and passions. He had travelled the world and enjoyed a life of luxurious adventure. He'd been unrelenting in his pursuit of the interesting and had taken a mischievous pride in corrupting his nephew. In Rowland, he had finally found a kindred Sinclair. Rowland, for his part, had loved the incorrigible old man.

He was still standing in the foyer when Wilfred came in. Now head of the Sinclair dynasty, Wilfred wore the mantle well. In his early forties, he reflected the establishment in his carriage and demeanour. His fair hair was receding, but only slightly. He was stockier than Rowland and his face more stern, but his eyes, which regarded the world over the tops of bifocals, were the same vivid blue.

"Rowly." He shook his brother's hand.

"Hello, Wil."

"I see you're still driving that Fritz monstrosity."

"She's a good car." Rowland's voice tightened, knowing what was coming.

"The Germans killed our brother." Wilfred's response was cold. Rowland sighed. This was not a new quarrel, and Wilfred was not alone in seeing the Mercedes as a betrayal of Aubrey. Rowland saw it differently.

"Let's not get into it, Wil."

For a moment Wilfred Sinclair looked like he might continue, but instead he said, "Shall we go into the sitting room?"

Wilfred turned without waiting for a response, and headed straight to the sideboard where he poured drinks. He handed Rowland a whisky and sat in the armchair closest to the fireplace. Rowland leant against the mantelpiece, holding the whisky, which he had no intention of drinking.

"I trust Kate and Ernest are well." Rowland spoke into the awkward silence.

"Yes, yes, they're both fine," Wilfred replied. "Ernest is riding unassisted now…He's only just turned four!"

Rowland smiled. It seemed to him that his brother only softened when he talked of his son.

"I spoke with the police commissioner," Wilfred said as a matter-of-fact. "Apparently the coroner believes that Uncle Rowland died of a heart attack brought on by the assault. Of course, he hasn't filed his report yet, but that is what it will say."

"Oh. Do they have any idea who…?"

"They're working on the idea it was someone to whom Uncle Rowland owed money."

"You told them that was ridiculous?"

"I directed them to our accountants. They'll explain how unlikely that notion is." Wilfred sipped his whisky and glanced up at the painting of the nude above the mantelpiece, his expression somewhere between appreciation and disapproval. "Anyway," he went on, "they should be releasing his body in a couple of days, so I'll wait to accompany it back to Oaklea. And you should make plans to come home for the funeral."

"Of course," said Rowland, irritated that his brother thought that he needed an instruction to do so.

"In the meantime, I'll be meeting with the old man's solicitor to make sure his affairs are properly settled."

"Shall I have Mary make up a room for you?"

"I'll stay here."

Rowland's relief was obvious. Wilfred glanced at him and shook his head, "I take it that Woodlands House is still full of your guests?"

"Not quite full," Rowland replied, "but I'm not lonely."

Wilfred's face darkened. He drained his glass. "I've made reservations at the Masonic Club," he announced, standing. "Finish your drink, Rowly, and let's go…you always did sip your drinks like some kind of debutante!"

Chapter Six

ART OR INDECENCY?

The Nude in Pictures—
Inspector "A Trifle Prudish"

ADELAIDE, Friday

Whether the nude in art is indecent was raised in the Adelaide Police Court on Friday, when Drew Brown, of Rundle Street East, was summoned for exhibiting indecent pictures in a shop window in contravention of the Indecent Advertisements Act.

The Advertiser, December 12, 1931

They returned first to Woodlands House, so Rowland could dress for dinner. The house was quiet. Wilfred wandered into the main drawing room while his brother ran upstairs.

When Rowland returned, Wilfred was in an armchair smoking, and glaring at the easels and canvases that now crowded what had once been called the most elegant parlour in Sydney.

"Ready to go?" Rowland asked hopefully.

At that inconvenient moment, Edna came home, escorted by a dapper man in a double-breasted white suit. Rowland recognised him as Bertram Middleton, another journalist writing the great Australian novel, and one of the sculptress' many gentlemen callers. Rowland swallowed. Edna was enchanting in the pale green dress that she reserved for the theatre or for gallery showings. The couple came in, deep in conversation and unaware that they were not alone. Rowland felt a familiar rise of ire when Edna placed her hand on Middleton's arm, but he remained unreadable.

"Oh, Rowly, you're back!" she said, finally noticing him.

"Hello Ed...Middleton." Rowland smiled at her and nodded at her companion.

"You look formal, Rowly!" She beamed at him in a way that told him that she'd been drinking a little. "Are you going out?"

"Yes." He stepped aside so that she could see into the drawing room. Wilfred stood hastily.

"Ed, this is my brother, Wilfred," Rowland

said awkwardly. "Wil, Miss Edna Higgins…oh… and Mr. Bertram Middleton."

Edna stepped toward Wilfred, while Middleton stayed by the door looking distinctly uncomfortable. She extended a gloved hand and bestowed him with her most beguiling smile.

"Mr. Sinclair, what a pleasure to make your acquaintance."

Wilfred shook her hand slowly, staring. "The pleasure is mine, Miss Higgins…Though I do have a feeling we have met before."

Edna giggled. "Possibly." She looked around her. "I have been living in your house for two years…but I do think I would remember."

"Indeed," replied Wilfred, without taking his eyes from her face. "And Mr. Middleton, do you live here too?"

Edna laughed. "Bertie? Oh no…we're all too noisy for him." She leant conspiratorially toward Wilfred. "He's trying to write a novel…he's very serious about it."

Middleton looked mortified and Rowland tried to feel sorry for him, but couldn't quite manage it. "Didn't you say we had reservations, Wil?" he said, looking pointedly at his wristwatch.

"Yes, of course." Wilfred put his glass down on the sideboard and moved to the door.

Wilfred said nothing as Johnston drove them

into the city. Rowland couldn't help smiling, certain Wilfred would make the connection eventually. He didn't look forward to the conversation that would inevitably follow, but he could see the amusing side of it.

Realisation came to Wilfred as he was in the process of ordering from the menu. Rowland could see the sudden suspicion in his face. As soon as the waiter had gone, Wilfred spoke. "Miss Higgins…I was wondering why she seemed so familiar…She looks a little like the woman in the painting in Rowland's house. The, er, nude above the mantelpiece."

"Well that's a good thing, I suppose—it is a painting of her."

"Oh, my God!" Wilfred pushed his glasses back up to the bridge of his nose. "Are you sure?"

"I should be," Rowland said as the waiter returned with the jug of iced water. "I painted it."

"You did what?"

Rowland waited until the waiter left before he said again. "I painted it."

Wilfred's expression lingered somewhere between envy and disgust.

"For the love of God, Wil, people have been painting and sculpting nudes for thousands of years—it's not exactly a dangerous, new art form!"

Wilfred started to reply, but then stopped. He took a sip of water. "Rowly, you've been back for over three years now, don't you think it's about time you stopped this nonsense and settled down?"

"Not dead yet, Wil," said Rowland curtly. "When I'm dead you can bury me on the property, but until then I'm staying here."

"It's not about where you are, Rowly," Wilfred reasoned. "It's about the way you behave, the kind of people with whom you associate. Look at what you're doing to our father's house!"

"I'm living in it," Rowland snapped, "which is more than any other Sinclair has done for years."

Wilfred paused, and then tried a different tack. "Lucy Bennett has just returned from her tour of Europe. She's grown into a very handsome young woman. Perhaps we could have her to luncheon when you're home?"

Rowland nearly laughed. "Just what I need, some society belle who's travelled through the great dress shops of Europe. Lovely."

"Don't you think you should at least meet her before you decide that?" Wilfred demanded, trying valiantly to keep his temper.

"No. I've met hundreds of Lucy Bennetts… they're all the same."

"Yes, well a decent girl might not provide the entertainment of your Miss Higgins…"

"Careful," warned Rowland, his back tensing.

Wilfred stared at his brother, at first in disbelief

and then in horror. "Bloody oath, Rowly, you're not…Miss Higgins and all your other freeloading friends are only after one thing!"

"And what exactly would be Lucy Bennett's interest in me?"

"Lucy is a jolly decent girl from a good family," Wilfred replied. "Rowly, you must be careful. You are a wealthy man. Women like Edna Higgins have ways of ensnaring men like us…"

Rowly groaned. "For God's sake, Wil! I'd be entirely happy for her to 'ensnare' me, but you needn't worry—Ed can do much better than a Sinclair."

There was an uncomfortable silence. Rowland wondered if Wilfred had been struck dumb by the mere notion that the Sinclair name was not enough to attract a woman. He hoped that the conversation would move on.

They ate their soup in relative silence. Over the main course, Wilfred mentioned the painting he had seen on the easel in Woodlands House.

"Is that one of yours, too?"

"Don't tell me you liked it?"

"I've never pretended to know a great deal about art, Rowly." Wilfred was non-committal. "I must say the subject intrigued me.…Were they real people?"

"Yes." Rowland told him about the meeting in

the Domain and the ensuing violence, carefully, for he was surprised that Wilfred was interested, and he was sure that some sort of censure would follow.

He was not disappointed.

Wilfred drank deeply from his glass. "What the devil is wrong with you, Rowly?" he said in frustration. "Don't you realise how dangerous the Communists are! What's the point of me—" He stopped suddenly.

"Point of you what?"

Wilfred said nothing for a moment. "What's the point of me fighting for this country if my brother is going to undermine it? What's the point of Aubrey dying if you're going to join up with the enemies of our way of life?"

"That's a bit dramatic, Wil. Have you joined the New Guard then?"

"Don't be a fool." Wilfred slammed his fork on the table. "Campbell's Boo Guard is a band of radical no-hopers. I daresay their hearts may initially have been in the right place, but they simply don't have the calibre of men required to do anything but aggravate the situation!"

"Oh, they were certainly inflaming things at the Domain last Sunday."

"That's beside the point, Rowly." Wilfred glared at his brother over his spectacles. "What are you doing consorting with the Red Army? Aside from being wrong, it's bloody unseemly."

Rowland sighed. "A few men in the Domain are hardly the Red Army, Wil. When did you get so paranoid?"

Wilfred wiped his lips with his napkin. Rowland braced for a lecture.

"I want you to get your unemployed, Communist friends out of my house."

Rowland's voice became steely. "It's my house as much as it is yours, Wil, and as you said, they are my friends. They stay as long as they choose to."

And so the Sinclair brothers returned to silence as they finished their meal, and parted in anger.

"I'll send Johnston around for you in the morning," Rowland said as Wilfred got out of the Rolls at their uncle's house. "I can use my car."

Wilfred nodded abruptly and walked into the house. As Johnston drove off, Rowland watched Wilfred through the rear window. He had not intended for their meal to end this way.

When Rowland walked once again into Woodlands House, Bertram Middleton was still there. A jazz recording was playing on the gramophone and the aspiring novelist was teaching Edna and Milton the steps of some new dance, while Clyde tapped the final nails into a newly stretched canvas. Rowland slumped into the armchair and removed his tie without interrupting them. He took his notebook from its usual place on the side table and doodled absentmindedly as he listened to the laughter and good-humoured banter. He was, at that moment, completely happy with the way he chose to live his life.

Once she had tired of the dance lesson, Edna suggested cards, and they played poker until Middleton gave up all hope of having Edna to himself and went home.

"I thought he'd never go," Edna said as the door closed behind him.

"Of course he didn't want to go," Rowland replied. "You shouldn't lead the poor chap on, Ed."

"Whatever makes you think I'm leading him on?" Edna huffed.

"Going to marry him, are you?" Milton asked raising a chuckle from Clyde.

"I might." She tossed her head.

Milton rolled his eyes. Edna was just about stubborn enough to do so, simply to prove a point.

"Oh, yeah? And what are you going to tell Alby Jones, Sam Harrington, Fred Turner, and that other bloke with the funny voice?" asked Clyde, listing just some of the artists and musicians who came calling to vie for her attention.

"I wouldn't worry about that last one." Milton

restacked the deck. "He's more interested in seducing Rowly."

Edna smiled. "I'm not going to marry Bertie, not unless his novel proves a lot more interesting than he is."

Rowland dealt the next hand. "What's the book about?"

"Some tragic ponderous epic about unrequited love, and justice for the downtrodden...I don't know too much. Frankly, I don't like to get him started on it," she picked up her cards. "I'm heartily sick of talking about Bertie. How did things go with your brother?"

"You made quite an impression on him."

"I'll bet," said Milton as he studied his hand,

"Did you speak to the housekeeper?" asked Clyde, remembering why Rowland had left the house early that afternoon.

Rowland nodded and recounted his conversation with Mrs. Donelly.

Edna's mouth dropped open. "She thinks your uncle was murdered by ghosts?"

Rowland nodded. "Dark ghosts, apparently."

"Do you think she's off her rocker?" asked Clyde.

"I don't know. The police obviously do."

"She's not a Theosophist?" suggested Milton thoughtfully. The spiritual movement, which had reached its height over the last decade, still had many local adherents.

"I doubt it." Rowland shook his head.

Milton stroked his chin. "Hmmm, mysterious, wot."

Edna groaned. Milton was an avid reader of the works of Sir Arthur Conan Doyle. "Grow up Milt!" she scolded. "Rowly's uncle was murdered. This is not the time to play Sherlock Holmes."

Rowland, however, was not offended. He, too, had been intrigued by the housekeeper's claim. Despite his initial reaction to her story, he was not inclined to believe she was mad. "He's right, Ed," he said in Milton's defence. "It is odd; I wonder what the old girl actually saw?"

"Nothing wrong with using our own brains, my dear Edna," Milton added smugly. "The amateur reasoner could well have a part to play in the resolution of these sad events."

Now Rowland laughed. "I just meant that I should talk to the police again about what Mrs. Donelly saw. I'm not suggesting that we buy pipes and move to Baker Street!"

Regardless, Milton regaled them with the anecdotes of the fictional detective as they played poker into the first hours of the next morning.

◇◇◇

The night had been hot and Rowland rose early, despite having played cards until the small hours. It was fortuitous. He had just drained his cup of coffee when Mary Brown informed him the police were at the door. He asked her to show them in, and met them in the drawing room.

There were again two: Peters, who had come to tell him of his uncle's death, and an older man not in uniform, but a charcoal suit.

"Mr. Sinclair," he said as Rowland shook his hand. "Inspector Bicuit, like biscuit without the 's'. You've met Constable Peters."

"Inspector Bicuit…Constable." Rowland gestured toward the chairs. "I take it you have come about my uncle."

"We have," Bicuit agreed, slipping himself into a wingback.

"Have you discovered who murdered him?" Rowland asked eagerly.

"Are you aware, Mr. Sinclair," Bicuit went on ignoring his question, "how long the housekeeper, Mrs. Donelly, was in your uncle's employ?"

"Since before I was born," Rowland responded. "About thirty years I'd say…she'd be able to tell you more exactly herself, I expect."

"Do you know, sir," the inspector asked, "of any family or male associates that Mrs. Donelly may have?"

"Not really." Rowland wondered where Bicuit's line of questioning was heading. "There is a nephew, I think, but I haven't met him."

"Are you able to tell me, Mr. Sinclair, if any valuables were taken the night your uncle died?"

Rowland shrugged. "No, Mrs. Donelly is probably the only one who would know for sure exactly what bits and pieces Uncle Rowland had. Has she noticed anything missing?"

"Mrs. Donelly claims that nothing was taken," Bicuit replied tersely.

"So it wasn't a robbery then?"

"Perhaps."

"I spoke with Mrs. Donelly yesterday," Rowland volunteered. "She is certain that she saw what she described as 'dark ghosts' when she found my uncle. Perhaps there was something she mistook for spirits….I know how it sounds, but I doubt Mrs. Donelly is insane."

"I also doubt that, sir." Bicuit exchanged a glance with Peters.

"Mr. Sinclair," the inspector continued, "your uncle's body was found by the entrance door, as if he had just answered it." Bicuit looked around at the genteel opulence of Woodlands House. "Was it Rowland Sinclair's custom to answer his own door?"

"Not in my experience."

"Who would normally have done so?"

"Mrs. Donelly, I expect. I'm not really sure what arrangements my uncle had with his domestic staff."

"Why do you suppose that, on this occasion, your uncle answered his own door?" Bicuit leaned toward Rowland.

"I don't know," Rowland said slowly. "She's a bit deaf…perhaps she didn't hear the knocking." He suddenly realised where the inspector's questions were leading. "I say, you don't think Mrs. Donelly had anything to do with it? That's preposterous!"

"Perhaps not quite as preposterous as the notion of dark ghosts," the inspector replied.

"What would she possibly have to gain?"

"Well, that rather depends upon what, if anything, was taken from your uncle's house. At the moment, we only have Mrs. Donelly's word that nothing was taken."

"Why would an old woman suddenly turn to crime? Murder?"

"You may not have noticed, sir," said Bicuit coolly, "but we are in the midst of a Depression. These times have seen many otherwise honest people driven to crime." He looked around the drawing room, his eyes settling on a large silver urn on the sideboard. "Perhaps that has escaped your attention."

Rowland glowered at him. The silence was brittle, icy.

"Your uncle was a wealthy man," Bicuit spoke first. "Are you aware, sir, who stands to inherit his estate?"

"My brother and me, I expect…possibly my nephew…his solicitor could tell you."

"In fact, his solicitor has already told us," replied Bicuit almost triumphantly. "You are the primary beneficiary of Mr. Sinclair's will."

"Your point, Inspector?"

"As I said, Mr. Sinclair, your uncle was a wealthy man…."

"I don't mean to sound crass, Inspector," Rowland said evenly, "but I am already a wealthy man."

"Where were you the night your uncle was killed, Mr. Sinclair?"

"Right here," said Rowland.

"Can anyone verify that, sir?"

At that moment Edna entered the drawing room bearing a tray laden with tea. Rowland smiled to himself. Subtlety was not Edna's talent, and she was by nature inquisitive. The men stood as she put down the tray and poured tea.

"Gentlemen, this is Miss Higgins. Ed, you remember Constable Peters, and this is Inspector Bicuit."

"Like Biscuit without the 's'," intoned the inspector, staring keenly at Edna.

"Charmed, gentlemen," said Edna demurely passing them cups of tea. She held out a plate of shortbread. "A biscuit, Inspector Bicuit?" she asked.

The inspector declined, but Peters took one, clearly enjoying her thinly disguised impudence.

"I couldn't help but overhear, Inspector," said Edna, "you asked whether anyone could verify Rowly's whereabouts on the night he lost his uncle so tragically. Well, we were all here."

"And who exactly constitutes 'we'?" Bicuit asked, unable to take his eyes from Edna.

Rowland recognised the look—a mixture of realisation, scandal, and a little guilt. He'd seen the same expression on Wilfred. Apparently the inspector had noted the painting above his uncle's mantelpiece.

"Those who live here, of course." Edna sat so that the men, too, could resume their seats. "Admittedly, I was asleep, but Clyde and Milt were with Rowly in the drawing room."

"She means Clyde Watson Jones and Milton Isaacs," said Rowland.

"And Messrs Watson Jones and Isaacs are your houseguests?" Bicuit asked warily.

"As is Miss Higgins."

"I see."

"Clyde and Milt are still asleep, but they are here if you need to speak with them," Edna chirped.

"That won't be necessary," replied Bicuit. "If you would just ask them to come into police headquarters to give their statements?"

"Certainly, Inspector." Rowland rose to show them out.

But Bicuit stayed in his seat. "Mr. Sinclair... I'm afraid this is a somewhat delicate question, but it must be asked. Are you aware if your uncle had any romantic liaison or attachment?"

"He was seventy-two." Rowland replied, aghast. But even as he said it, he lost confidence in his own outrage. His uncle had been an inveterate flirt. Perhaps the old man...

"We did find a pair of, er..." he stopped, looking at Edna.

"Please go on," said Rowland.

Bicuit cleared his throat. "We discovered a pair of fishnet stockings in his house. We haven't yet asked Mrs. Donelly, but I think it safe to assume they are not hers."

Rowland smiled faintly, as an absurd image of the ancient housekeeper wearing fishnets flashed upon his inner eye. He shrugged. "I'm afraid I can't help you, Inspector."

Finally, Bicuit rose to leave. Constable Peters had used the extra time to finish his tea and did likewise. They stopped by the easel where the Domain painting still sat, and studied it for a moment. "You and your uncle have some interesting artwork, Mr. Sinclair," the inspector said as he walked out.

Rowland closed the door behind them. "What was all that about?" he asked Edna as he returned to the drawing room.

"What do you mean?" she said with a look of wide-eyed innocence.

"The tea and charm thing," he persisted. "Surely you could have just eavesdropped at the door."

"I had to come in," she replied sipping her tea. "That man…Biscuit without the 's'…he was about to accuse you of murdering your uncle!"

"He only asked me where I'd been, Ed," he said, amused. "I'm sure it's only routine."

"I don't trust him…He kept looking at me strangely."

"I rather think he recognised you from the painting I gave Uncle Rowland."

"Oh," she said, understanding now. She laughed and then suddenly became serious. "Perhaps you should put that painting away, Rowly."

Rowland was surprised. He was not the first or last artist Edna had sat for. It was not like her to be coy. "Why?"

"I was so fat back then…it's embarrassing."

Rowland smiled. Edna had lost some weight over the last year, but it was hardly an extraordinary amount. In any case, he did not think her more or less beautiful as a consequence.

"You know yourself, Ed," he said. "The eye likes curves. A gentleman's eye in particular. I'll take it down if you really want me to, but it would be a jolly shame. It's probably my best piece."

She sighed. "All right, leave it then. I'm just not sure I like all these strange men knowing how extremely plump I was."

Rowly wasn't quite sure how to respond. "I doubt they noticed your weight, Ed."

Chapter Seven

After the Polo

Town and Country
FRIENDS ENTERTAINED

YASS, Saturday

One of the most dazzling receptions in the Polo Week gaieties was given last week at Oaklea by Mr. and Mrs. W. H. Sinclair. The guests, who numbered almost 400, included many country visitors, and there was a delightfully friendly and informal atmosphere about the gathering, making it a happy start to the pageantry of the Polo Ball.

The Argus, December 14, 1931

Rowland latched the wooden case containing his paints, and wrapped his brushes into their roll. The maids had just completed the rest of his packing, under Mary Brown's watchful eye, but he would trust the tools of his trade to no one but himself. Through the window, he could see his trunks already being loaded into the Rolls-Royce for the trip to Central Railway Station. Wilfred would send a car to meet his train at Yass and take him back to Oaklea, where his uncle Rowland was to be buried the next day. Wilfred had left Sydney with the coffin the day before. As it was so close to Christmas, Rowland would stay in Yass for a few weeks, returning in the New Year.

He was searching for his notebook when Edna and Milton came in.

Edna looked him up and down, clearly dissatisfied. "What are you wearing?" she demanded. "You're going to the country…"

"What do you mean?" he said looking down at the dark suit for a paint stain he may have missed when he selected it.

"I just thought you'd look a bit more…rural." Edna handed him the notebook she'd just picked up from the couch.

"She wants a big hat and some kind of rope, Rowly." Milton grinned as he adjusted his own cravat to sit perfectly within the collar of his shirt.

Rowland laughed. "Obviously someone needs

to take you to the country, Ed," he said. "You'll find old Banjo Paterson's taken a bit of licence."

"I'd like to see you droving," she said mischievously, "mustering cattle through the bush...."

Rowland shook his head. "I hate to upset your conviction that I'm Clancy of the Overflow, but Oaklea is a sheep property, and the last time I rode was in a polo match."

"Oh." Edna did seem genuinely disappointed. "So what do you do out there? Didn't your family make their fortune growing sheep?"

"They're pastoralists, yes, but the last couple of generations have had the good sense to put the actual running into the hands of men who know what they're doing." Rowland was as always amused by Edna's romantic notion of his background. "Wil handles the business side, but the managers take care of everything else."

"Don't you do anything?" asked Edna.

He smiled. "I'm the youngest son, Ed...My role is to keep bad company and squander the family fortune."

"As long as you have some sort of purpose." Milton picked up Rowland's case of paints. He was surprised by its weight. "Will you need all this? How long do you plan to be gone?"

"Not long, I hope," Rowland replied, "but if

I don't have something to do, my brother will feel the need to drag me around with him."

Clyde wandered into the drawing room holding before him a large canvas, the painted side facing his chest. He put it down and beamed at Rowland. "Lady McKenzie is finished, at last. I'm taking her to be framed with the most lavish gold leaf frame known to man!"

"So let's see her."

Clyde swivelled the canvas round. For a moment there was silence as they gazed at the dreaded portrait. Rowland broke it first.

"Clyde, old boy, you're brilliant!" He applauded.

Clyde had depicted Lady McKenzie accurately, but she was no longer the focus. The foreground was now dominated by a poodle, with large, beseeching eyes which, by distraction, softened its owner's severe and unwelcome features.

"My friend, you have painted Medusa without turning us all to stone," waxed Milton.

The classical allusion was lost on Clyde, but he gathered it was a statement of approval nonetheless. "I don't know why I didn't think of it earlier." He grinned. "She loves that mutt."

"She'll be really happy with it, Clyde." Edna stood back to observe. "It's such a handsome dog!"

"It's a vicious, smelly beast, actually," Clyde replied, "but it is a lot prettier than the good lady."

"I'd better get going," Rowland checked his watch. "You know where to reach me. Try not to upset Mary, and don't burn down my house."

They walked him to the Rolls and between them managed to squeeze his remaining cases and easels into the limited space left in the trunk.

Rowland passed his time on the train comfortably. He occupied himself as he always did, sketching. He made drawings of the people who stood on the platform as he waited for the train to pull out; the elegant ladies and suited gentlemen about to enter the first-class carriages, the people who headed for second class and even the furtive shabby men who loitered in the shadows, waiting for an opportunity to jump into an open freight car. After the train left the station, he had to draw from memory. The private compartment in which he travelled meant he was deprived of unsuspecting models.

At midday, he took lunch in the dining car. The cut glass of the chandelier tinkled above his table with the rock of the carriage. Eating alone, he observed his fellow diners, making occasional scribbles in his notebook. The two men who sat at the table closest to him were discussing the divisive state premier. The conversation was not unfamiliar. Premier Jack Lang incited heated passions one way or the other. Here, in the first-class dining car, opinions on the socialist leader were unlikely to be positive.

A young woman, fashionably dressed in a fitted cream ensemble that seemed a size too small, sat smoking by the open window. She spoke with an older woman, who Rowland assumed was her mother. Despite their hushed tones, Rowland gleaned that she was to be married in a month and that her dress was being shipped from Paris. It was a remarkably long and involved conversation about a single dress. He captured the bride-to-be with barely more than five lines, marks as controlled and sharp as her face. He stopped when she noticed his gaze. She blushed and smiled coquettishly. Her mother's glance was more severe. Rowland unfolded his newspaper, making a note to be more subtle in future.

The train pulled into Yass Junction by the middle of the afternoon. It was hot, but dry. The wind was warm from the north. Already, Rowland missed the cooling coastal breezes.

The car waiting for him was another Rolls-Royce Phantom, though a more recent model than the one at Woodlands House. The chauffeur—he must have been new—introduced himself as Alfred Meakin before loading the trunk. Rowland removed his jacket and climbed into the backseat. It would still be a twenty-minute drive to Oaklea.

The township of Yass itself was busy and, for a country centre, its main street was crowded. Yass thrived as a natural break-point in the long journey between Sydney and Melbourne. Despite the times, visiting travellers contributed significantly to its economy and the activity of its business district. There were also other travellers, of vastly different circumstance. The tired men on the wallaby track, who moved from town to town in search of work, and were marked by the ragged swags that weighed down their backs. They, too, came to Yass.

The countryside here was already parched. The summer, though barely begun, had been intense and dry. The pastures had long turned gold and the road was dust under the wheels of the motorcar.

The low stone walls marking the home paddock of Oaklea seemed to hold the dryness of the landscape at bay. The lawns were irrigated and lush. The long driveway was lined by large oak trees underplanted with purple-bloomed agapanthus. It circled in front of the main house, around a segmented rose bed which lent its heavy perfume to the afternoon air.

Despite the heat, Rowland slipped his jacket back on. Wilfred was particular about such things and there was no need to start out on a bad footing.

Several other cars were parked outside the house. Rowland expected they were people who had come to pay their respects at the funeral—the usual births, deaths, and marriages company of distant relatives that appear only on such occasions. Fortunately, so close to Christmas, they were unlikely to stay long.

He stepped out of the car as soon as it stopped on the gravel.

Oaklea loomed before him. It had changed since his last visit, well over a year ago. The original homestead had been a Victorian building, with rubblestone walls and Romanesque features. Over the past three years, however, it had been expanded and remodelled under the direction of his sister-in-law. The verandah had been widened and softened with wisteria, the blooms now hanging in their pendulous purple clusters. Several bay windows had been added to the ground floor, as well as a projecting porch at the entrance. Another wing had been constructed and the roofline now included gables. Even the garden sported large arboured walkways and meandering dry rock walls he had not seen before. The extensive modifications interested more than disturbed him, but he wondered what his mother thought of them. She didn't like change.

Rowland straightened his tie and ran up the steps to the front door. He braced himself. Homecomings were difficult.

Mrs. Kendall, who had been the housekeeper at Oaklea since before the war, was holding the door open for him. Her husband was head gardener and her sons both worked for Wilfred on the property. Mrs. Kendall was a substantial woman with perfect rose-hued skin, and a face that was warmth and welcome itself.

"Mr. Rowland!" she exclaimed. "Come in, come in…"

As he entered the house, he saw the interior had also been renovated. It was much lighter now. Many of the original dark and ornate features were gone, replaced with modern touches.

"Mr. Sinclair is with funeral guests in the main drawing room," Mrs. Kendall said conspiratorially. "Why don't you go into the library and I shall quietly tell him you're here? You won't want to be talking with visitors immediately after you've arrived, not after such a long trip."

Rowland smiled. Mrs. Kendall looked on him as a twelve-year-old. In her maternal heart, he remained the shy boy who'd been her charge. If he'd not grown so tall, she'd probably still be licking her hand to smooth down his hair. He embraced her whilst Wilfred was not around to disapprove of such familiarity. She was probably the only person at Oaklea who still missed him.

When he finally entered it, he noticed that the

library, too, had been modernised with oak panelling and a sandstone fireplace. Wilfred, it seemed,
had added to his father's already substantial collection of books. Rowland leant on the back of a
leather armchair, letting his eyes scan the shelves
for familiar titles.

"Rowly," Wilfred walked in and shook his
hand. "It's good to see you back here. What do you
think of Kate's changes?"

"She's been busy."

"Yes, it keeps her occupied." Wilfred clearly
believed the occupation of his wife to be a good
thing. "Kate will be down in a moment—she just
went to fetch Mother from her room."

"There's no need for that." Rowland glanced
uneasily toward the doorway. "I could just go up…
How is Mother?"

"Good days, bad days," said Wilfred grimly.
Their mother had never quite recovered from the
deaths of her son and her husband.

Elisabeth Sinclair came into the room just
ahead of her daughter-in-law. Now in her mid-
sixties, she was still a handsome woman. Her hair
was the snowy white that spoke of auburn origin,
and she wore it stylishly back from her face. Always
dressed immaculately and tastefully, she moved
with a considered grace. Her face, however, was
hesitant, her eyes tragic and bewildered. Until she

saw Rowland. She rushed to him, as he stepped quietly toward her, and reached up to clasp his face between her hands. "Aubrey." Her voice trembled. "My dear, dear Aubrey."

Rowland returned her smile sadly. His mother had started mistaking him for Aubrey when he first came home from Oxford. In the last couple of years she had acknowledged him as no one else. It was as if she eased her grief by convincing herself that he was his dead brother. Rowland occasionally wondered what she thought had become of her youngest son, but he had given up trying to disillusion her.

"Mother, this is Rowly," Wilfred corrected her calmly.

"Rowly? Don't be silly, Wilfred. Do you not recognise your own brother?" Despite her words, her eyes welled with tears at the mere suggestion that it was not her beloved Aubrey returned.

Rowland glanced at Wilfred, a sign to say no more. "How are you, Mother?" he said. "You look well."

He spoke gently with her for a while. He wasn't sure if his visits helped or hurt her—she seemed more and more fragile each time he came home.

Eventually, Wilfred suggested their mother take her afternoon rest. "No, Wilfred." She stamped her foot like a small child. "I want to stay with Aubrey."

"I'll be here for a couple of weeks," Rowland said as Mrs. Kendall took his mother's arm. "You go and rest; I'll come up to see you later." Elisabeth Sinclair smiled, sunshine again. "Yes, I believe I am a little tired." She stopped briefly at the doorway. "Aubrey, darling, did Wilfred tell you? Rowland has died…it's so sad."

There was an awkward silence after she left.

"I'm sorry, Rowly."

"You don't need to be, Wil," Rowland replied. He turned to his sister-in-law and kissed her briefly on the cheek. "How are you, Kate? And where's my nephew?"

Kate Sinclair smiled shyly. She was a pretty young woman, a couple of years younger than Rowland. Naturally slim, the slight swell of her belly was already obvious, though Wilfred had not yet mentioned that they were expecting a second child. She had married Wilfred when she was barely twenty. To Rowland, she still seemed nervous in her role as the mistress of Oaklea.

"How lovely to see you, Rowly," she said. "It's been too long…Ernest has gone out with Gerard to select a suitable horse. Gerard will start breaking it for him, so it's ready when he's old enough to swing a polo mallet."

Rowland nodded. The selection of one's first polo pony was something of a Sinclair tradition. By the time young Ernest was of an age to start playing, the animal would be both experienced and quiet.

Wilfred considered his brother critically. "There's a match next Saturday. Do you want to play?"

"Polo?"

"You still look reasonably fit—the city doesn't appear to have softened your body at least."

"Yes, why don't you play?" Kate piped in.

Rowland grimaced. "No, thanks. I'm afraid that riding around in the midst of several men wildly swinging mallets never seemed very sensible to me."

"But you used to play," Kate persisted.

"I wasn't ever very good—just ask Wil." Rowland tapped his temple. "Too scared of head injuries."

"You always were a bit skittish for polo," Wilfred agreed, remembering the few matches that Rowland had played. "Stop alarming Kate—next thing she'll be telling me that it's too dangerous for Ernest."

"Well, we couldn't have that." Rowland nodded toward the drawing room. "Who's here?"

"The Hamiltons, the Castlemaines, and the Oldmans," Kate replied. All three families were cousins of sorts to the Sinclairs. "And Canon Radford, of course."

The small chapel on Oaklea had been built by the first Mrs. Sinclair, and it was here the service was conducted, before Rowland Sinclair was laid to rest in the family plot behind it.

Elisabeth Sinclair didn't attend either the service or the burial. Rowland suspected the decision was Wilfred's, not her own. His brother did not want the world to know how unsteady their mother's mental state had become and, with her insistence that he was Aubrey, it would be obvious. Rowland suspected her frailty was no secret, but he did not blame Wilfred for trying to protect her dignity.

Wilfred and Rowland shouldered their uncle's coffin with the men who had been the old man's closest friends. The lacquered oak casket was heavy. Rowland wondered, fleetingly, if the weight would finish off any of the aged pallbearers who shuffled and wheezed beside them.

But the elderly men did not falter, and Rowland Sinclair was placed into the ground without incident. A large crowd attended to see him to his final rest, most of whom Rowland recognised only vaguely. They all returned to Oaklea afterwards, where the funeral guests took refreshments in the cool of the Sinclair ballroom.

It was not until after all the guests had finally departed that Wilfred spoke again to Rowland about their uncle. "What do you want to do with the house, Rowly? He left it to you, you know."

"The inspector mentioned it." Rowland shrugged. "I don't really care, Wil. Do whatever you think best…Just make sure Mrs. Donelly and the others are taken care of."

"Inspector Biscuit thinks Mrs. Donelly was involved."

"It's Bicuit," Rowland smiled. "No 's'. He told me his theory…frankly it's idiotic."

"They have to investigate everything, I suppose." Wilfred absently fingered the Returned Soldiers' badge on his lapel.

"Did Bicuit tell you about the stockings?"

"Yes." Wilfred exhaled with vexed disapproval. "I don't want to speak ill of the dead, Rowly, but it would be just like the old bugger to have some harlot on the side."

Rowland grinned. "Could be worse, Wil—maybe they were his."

Wilfred glared at him, unamused. "With respect to the house," he said, "there's no need to do anything yet…It might be handy to have another house in the city once Ernest starts school…particularly since you've…"

"You're right," interrupted Rowland before his brother could relight the fiery topic which had led to them parting in anger just days before. "Another house in the city would be useful."

At that moment, a little boy slipped quietly into Wilfred's lap. He did not say anything, but stared at Rowland from the safety of his father's knee with bright blue Sinclair eyes.

Wilfred ruffled the boy's hair. "Are you going to talk to your Uncle Rowly?"

Ernest shook his head. Rowland smiled. The boy had not yet said a word to him, but he wasn't surprised—he had no talent for small children. To him, they were strange inexplicable creatures.

"Let him be, Wil," Rowland said as his brother tried coaxing some conversation from the boy. "I'm going to sit with Mother for a while." Rowland stood and removed his jacket, retrieving his notebook and pencil from the inside pocket. He liked to have something to do while his mother chatted to him, or rather to Aubrey, about things that happened years ago as if they had occurred only yesterday.

Chapter Eight

Trotsky's Plans

Australian Visit Mooted!

MELBOURNE, Monday

A Melbourne journalist has received a letter from a friend in Paris stating that Leon Trotsky is endeavouring to secure permission to visit Australia in order to study conditions here and write a book.

From other quarters, however, it is reported that Trotsky's desire to visit Australia is part of his effort to reconcile with Stalin.

The Canberra Times, December 16, 1931

Rowland sat on the verandah with the latest edition of *Smith's Weekly*. The paper gave a particularly patriotic and conservative perspective on events.

Favoured by returned soldiers and old men, it was not Rowland's usual fare.

The front page carried an alarmist account of supposed Communist plots aimed at setting the countryside ablaze. According to the journalist, the hot dry summer was just what the Bolshevik insurgents required to bring rural Australia to its knees. Rowland regarded the article with amusement, though not surprise. For some time, the popular press had been inflaming the public's fears of a Communist uprising by painting bleak and bloody pictures of a Socialist future. Socialism, even Communism, was regarded far more kindly among the artistic and intellectual communities of Sydney. In any case, Rowland was fairly sure that the man the press vilified as Australia's Trotsky was rarely sober enough to lead any sort of offensive.

Wilfred approached, and regarded his chuckling brother with clear disapprobation. Rowland stopped smiling, and put down the paper. Wilfred took *Smith's Weekly* very seriously.

"Thought we might go out and look at Ernest's new pony," Wilfred said curtly. Dressed for a day on the property, he wore a tweed waistcoat and jacket over his crisp white shirt; his wool trousers pushed into knee-high gumboots. It was early, but already the day was hot.

"Yes, of course." Rowland stood. He grabbed

his notebook from the wickerwork chair on which he had tossed it earlier.

"Don't you want your jacket?"

"For God's sake, Wil, it's over a hundred degrees!"

"If you wish to be mistaken for one of the shearers…"

Rowland groaned. He'd never seen a shearer dressed as he was, and he didn't really care, but it was clear that Wilfred did. He dragged on his jacket irritably.

"I'm not wearing gumboots," he muttered. "It hasn't rained in six weeks—you look like you're going for a walk in the marshes at bloody Balmoral."

Wilfred ignored him, flicking his eyes over the paper Rowland had discarded. "They'll find we're ready for them."

"Who?" Rowland slipped his notebook into the inside pocket of his jacket.

"The Communists, who else? They'll find we're not so complacent here as in the city!"

Rowland thought about responding, but only briefly. It was in moments like these that the years between them seemed greatest. He sighed. "Let's go look at this horse then."

They strode out over the lawns at the rear of the house, past tennis courts flanked by rose beds in full bloom.

Rowland took in the colour. "Flowers look good, Wil."

Wilfred had been passionate about the rose gardens since his return from the war. He oversaw their planting and spent hours designing extensions to the beds. He had even managed to breed a new cultivar. Rowland usually avoided reference to the blooms as Wilfred took any such mention as an invitation to expound on the finer points of pruning or grafting. This time was no exception.

"Kendall's brought on a Chinese lad to help McNair with the beds," he said. "It's made all the difference."

Rowland glanced at McNair who was shuffling about with a hoe. Another veteran of the Great War, McNair had returned without his right arm and with a permanent limp. It was amazing he managed to do anything at all, but his job at Oaklea was secure. Over the years, Wilfred had simply hired extra men to compensate.

They stopped to discuss aphids with McNair who had a great deal to say on the subject. It amused Rowland to watch the gardener in conversation with his brother. McNair spoke in consecutive strings of profanity, making no attempt to modify his speech for Wilfred's sake. Wilfred, for his part, did not seem to notice and responded with his customary, genteel civility. Although Rowland found McNair quite difficult to follow, he gathered that the veteran wished to rout the "bloody flowers" to make room for vegetables. Wilfred listened patiently, and then suggested that McNair put the vegetables in the kitchen garden, where they were traditionally planted. In any case, he would certainly not tolerate his driveway and tennis court being lined with tomatoes and pumpkins. McNair seemed to find his employer's attitude somewhat frustrating and stalked off with words which may have been translated as "Be it on your own bloody head!"

They watched him go in silence, though Rowland could not keep from smiling. McNair had always been thus.

"He's a good man," was all Wilfred would ever say.

It was over an hour after they'd originally left the house that they reached the exercise yard beside the stables. Regardless of his brother's protestations, Rowland had again removed his jacket, and carried it slung over his shoulder.

Ernest was hanging over the rails as Gerard, the groom, handled a young colt in the yard. It was a sizable bay animal, well-proportioned and with an intelligent head.

Ernest jumped down from the rail and ran to

his father. "So, what do you think, Rowly?" Wilfred tipped his head toward the horse.

"He's rather big." Rowland folded his jacket over the fence.

"Ernest will grow. Won't you Ernie?" Wilfred tousled the boy's hair.

"He'd better…It's a good looking horse, Wil. Where'd you get him?"

"Crookwell—Philip Ashton—they did jolly well last year."

"So I read." The Ashton brothers' triumphant polo tour of England had been enthusiastically reported. Rowland had known them most of his life, and had gone to school with Philip, the youngest of the four. On matters of polo they had no peer, and Rowland could not remember Philip ever expressing an interest in anything but.

Wilfred caught his eye and seemed to know his mind. "Philip hasn't changed," he said, "but he does know his horses."

"What did you call your horse, Ernie?" Rowland asked.

"Fred." Ernest gazed up at him.

"Good name…I had to ride a horse called Bubbles."

Wilfred laughed. "I'd forgotten about that. Why did…?"

"Mother named him." Rowland shook his head. "Fred is a much better name, Ernie."

Gerard walked Fred over to them, and Rowland stroked the horse's sleek neck while Wilfred discussed its progress with the groom. Fred was a steady animal despite being a colt. In time, he would be an ideal first polo pony.

Wilfred climbed into the yard still deep in conversation with Gerard.

Rowland took out his notebook and drew quickly; the lean, weathered face of the groom, sharp eyes, tight mouth and strong hands; Wilfred, straight-backed, confident, his jacket still buttoned in spite of the draining heat.

"What are you doing?"

Rowland looked down and was met by Ernest's solemn eyes. He squatted so the boy could look over his shoulder.

"That looks like Daddy," Ernest said, pointing to the sketch.

"I'm glad you think so."

"Could you draw my horse?"

"Perhaps." He sketched the colt on a clean page, and when it was completed to his nephew's satisfaction, he tore it out and handed it to the boy. Ernest accepted the drawing silently and held it tightly in both hands.

"What's that Ernie?" Wilfred rejoined them.

Ernest showed him. Wilfred tickled the back of his son's neck. "Do you go anywhere without that flaming notebook, Rowly?"

"Swimming maybe," Rowland replied as he closed it. "It helps me see."

"What's wrong with your eyes?"

"Nothing." Rowland tried to explain. "I just see things more clearly once I've drawn them."

Wilfred rolled his eyes and then glanced at his pocket watch. "We had better get back—see what Mrs. Kendall's organised for lunch." He swung Ernest up onto his shoulders. Rowland grabbed his jacket from the fence and farewelled Gerard with a wave.

Walking back across the paddocks to the house, they were on the lawns when Kate beckoned them over to the conservatory. "It's so terribly hot, I thought we might eat out here," she said as Wilfred lifted Ernest off his shoulders.

"Off you go, Ernie. Mrs. Kendall will have lunch for you in the kitchen."

The child nodded in his grave, quiet manner, and ran into the hallway still clutching the page torn from his uncle's notebook.

"Mother won't be joining us today." Wilfred turned to Rowland. "Mrs. Kendall will take her a tray—she's a little tired."

Rowland looked suspiciously at the round

table. Set for four, it was draped with starched white linen and centred with a massive arrangement of roses and spinning gum.

"You boys go and wash up for lunch," Kate said brightly, as she fussed nervously with an elaborately folded napkin.

"Are we expecting someone?" Rowland asked.

"Just an old friend from school," Kate looked away. "She's just returned from abroad."

Rowland glared at Wilfred and walked into the house.

"You'll want to put this back on," said Wilfred, tossing him the jacket that he had discarded over the back of a chair.

When Rowland returned to the conservatory, Lucy Bennett was sipping lemonade from a tall glass and chatting with Kate. She was a pretty girl, fashionable, but in a very wholesome way. Her hair was blond, almost white, beneath a pink hat that matched her shoes and dress. She spoke with studied tone and inflection and played with the pearls about her neck as she talked.

Rowland closed his eyes briefly and sighed.

"Rowly, here you are!" Kate moved quickly to his side and touching his arm, ushered him toward her guest. "You remember my dear friend, Lucy Bennett."

"Of course," Rowland replied. "Miss Bennett."

"How nice to see you again, Mr. Sinclair." Lucy looked up at him from beneath the brim of her hat and smiled.

"Lucy's just returned from a tour abroad." Kate initiated the conversation like the perfect hostess she was.

"Yes, Wil did mention that." Rowland glanced at his brother.

"Lucy was just telling us about Paris when you walked in."

Lucy continued her tale of Paris, a jocular account, gushing in its enthusiasm for France's fashions and peppered with clever witticisms about the peculiarity of its citizens. Rowland played the polite guest, listening quietly and feigning interest. It was a familiar charade.

By the time the first course arrived, Kate had noticed that the conversation was clearly one-sided. She seized the opportunity when Lucy mentioned some apparently riotous misunderstanding at the Louvre while viewing the *Mona Lisa*, and interjected. "Did you know that Rowly paints, Lucy?'

Wilfred snorted, and Rowland almost choked on his bread.

"Don't be like that, Wil." Kate patted her husband's hand. "Ernie showed me the picture Rowly drew of Fred; he's really quite good."

"How interesting, Mr. Sinclair," Lucy effused.

"My Aunt Mildred Bennett took up painting when her eyes grew too weak for embroidery. Her pictures had quite the impressionist feel to them."

Rowland held down his urge to laugh.

"Fred is Ernest's pony, isn't he?" Lucy carried on. "Do you only do horses, Mr. Sinclair?"

Rowland cleared his throat. "No, I—"

"Rowly draws just about everything, he's always sketching," Kate answered for him.

"Why don't you show Lucy your notebook, Rowly?" Wilfred forked the last of his fruit cocktail into his mouth.

Rowland glanced darkly at him. "I'm sure Miss Bennett would not be interested…"

"Why, Mr. Sinclair, I'd be fascinated!"

They all looked at him expectantly. Reluctantly, Rowland reached inside his jacket and retrieved the slightly battered, leather-bound notebook. Kate mistook his hesitance for modesty and smiled encouragingly. "You mustn't be shy, Rowly."

He handed the notebook to Lucy Bennett, and she thumbed through its pages eagerly. "Why this is very accomplished, Mr. Sinclair."

"Thank you, Miss Bennett," Rowland replied, hoping she'd give back the notebook and return to her trivial tour of Europe.

"I've always thought it lovely to have a hobby at which one can achieve some level of proficiency,"

Lucy twittered. "Look Kate, here's a picture of your Wilfred." She laughed, though Rowland couldn't see why the drawing was so hilarious. Her laugh was high and tinkling. It reminded Rowland of breaking glass. He thought briefly of Edna, who often laughed so hard that she often forgot to breathe and ended gasping in the nearest chair.

Kate caught the softening in his expression and smiled with satisfaction.

"And who is this?" Lucy asked studying a sketch. "He looks terribly dangerous—Daddy says the city is full of criminals these days and the streets are just teeming with the unemployed. Something should really be done—it's not safe."

Rowland glanced at the page. It was Clyde.

Lucy then found a series of drawings of Edna. She flicked through them slowly at first.

"I know!" Kate said suddenly, "Rowly, you must paint Lucy." Rowland looked up, his face blank.

Lucy blushed, laughed inexplicably again and fluttered her lashes so hard that Rowland thought her afflicted with a tic. "Oh, I couldn't trouble you, Mr. Sinclair."

"Nonsense," boomed Wilfred. "Rowly needs something to do instead of following me about all day!"

Lucy turned another page of Rowland's

notebook, then snapped it shut. Her face was flushed a much deeper shade of pink than her hat. "No, I really couldn't," she said. "I just couldn't." She pushed the notebook back across the table toward Rowland.

Kate looked at her friend, dismayed. Wilfred appeared distinctly disgruntled. Rowland's lips hinted a smile, but he tried to seem politely disappointed. He slipped his notebook back into his pocket. He knew Lucy had found the pencil studies he had done of Edna for the nude he'd given his uncle. He was relieved. There was nothing interesting about Lucy Bennett; nothing worth capturing on canvas. As far as he knew, she didn't even own a poodle.

After that, the meal was somewhat subdued. Lucy seemed unable to look at him, which only aggravated his conviction that she was ridiculous. Poor Kate became increasingly distressed as her meticulously planned luncheon floundered.

Three awkward courses later, Lucy Bennett made her farewells, despite Kate pressing her to stay longer in a last attempt to salvage the day from disaster. At his brother's pointed suggestion, Rowland walked the young lady to the motor waiting for her in the driveway. Since what she'd seen in his notebook had mortified her into silence, he felt forced, finally, to make some conversation.

"It's been a pleasure to see you again, Miss Bennett," he lied, though admittedly, it had not been entirely unentertaining.

"Goodbye, Mr. Sinclair. I hope you understand why I cannot sit for you."

"Of course," he replied with painstaking civility.

Lucy Bennett smiled coyly as she climbed into the backseat. "Perhaps then I shall see you again, Mr. Sinclair."

Wilfred was in the drawing room when Rowland got back to the house.

"Don't ever do that again, Wil," Rowland warned as Wilfred handed him a glass of whisky.

"Lucy's an old chum of Kate's. Perfectly natural we should have her to lunch."

Rowland put down his glass. He removed his jacket, loosened his tie and dropped into the armchair.

Kate walked into the room with her son. Ernest left his mother's side and climbed into Rowland's lap. "Will you draw me another picture of Fred?"

"Please, Uncle Rowly," his mother corrected.

Rowland sat up. "If you'd like…or I could show you how you can draw Fred."

Ernest looked at him as he considered the proposal. "No, I'd rather you did it."

Rowland smiled. "He's a Sinclair already, then," he said, taking out his notebook once again. He found a clean page and drew Fred from memory. Ernest watched every stroke carefully. Rowland glanced at him, and added a small boy astride the horse. He tore the page out and Ernest ran to show it to his mother.

"You know, you really are very talented, Rowly." Kate looked closely at the sketch. "Why don't we have any of your work here? We really should. Would you paint something for us?"

Rowland suspected his sister-in-law was trying to make up for Lucy Bennett's lack of enthusiasm. "Of course."

"Perhaps you could paint the billabong," Kate continued. "It's the prettiest part of Oaklea. Of course the arboretum is best in the autumn, but even now it's lovely."

"I've been told I don't paint trees very well." He looked at her intently. "But why don't I paint you, Kate? You could sit for me...you're a lot prettier than Lucy anyway."

Kate coloured. "Me...Really...? I don't know...What do you think, Wil?"

Wilfred looked dubiously at Rowland. "I agree—you're much prettier than Lucy."

Kate gazed so adoringly at her husband that Rowland began to feel quite uncomfortable.

"Excuse me for just a minute," she said picking up her son. "I'll just put Ernie down for a nap." She hurried out of the drawing room, still blushing.

Rowland watched her go, amused. "You need to compliment that girl more often, Wil. That one surprised her so much she had to leave the room."

Wilfred's eyes narrowed accusingly. "What are you playing at Rowly? I've seen what you call a painting!"

Rowland faltered, surprised, but only for a moment, and then he laughed. "For the love of God, Wil, she's your wife! She can keep her clothes on."

Chapter Nine

WHAT SHALL WE DO WITH COMMUNISTS?

CANBERRA, Wednesday

...Of course we all believe in free speech—with certain limitations. A man may be free to advocate the adoption of any system, whether Communistic or anti-Communistic. But this freedom should not extend to advocacy of revolution. Let the Russian people enjoy their own methods—if they can. That is their affair. But when they send emissaries into other countries to sow the seeds of revolt, the people so attacked are surely justified in defending their own liberties. They are not exceeding their rights when they deport foreign disruptionists or declare an organisation which teaches revolution an unlawful association. They are merely acting in self-defence.

The aim of Communism is to break up and destroy the "capitalist" state. With this object, religion is attacked and derided, children are taught subversive doctrine, strikes are encouraged and industry is held up, basher gangs are organised or assisted, the police are assaulted, and trouble is fomented in every way.

The Canberra Times, December 17, 1931

Rowland was trying to coax his sister-in-law to relax. "Just be comfortable, Kate. I'll work out the rest."

Kate Sinclair shifted, but returned to her stiff, tense pose. Rowland stepped away from his easel and sat in the armchair opposite her.

"I'll tell you what," he said, opening his notebook. "I'll do some quick sketches first. It'll let me work out the best angles and you can get used to me looking at you…all right?"

Kate gave a tiny nod, trying hard to move her head as little as possible.

"You don't have to sit still for this part…" He tried to distract her from his scrutiny. "Tell me, what's this meeting of Wil's all about?"

Having established there'd be no nudity, Wilfred had become quite a proponent of the portrait.

It was he who had suggested that they start right away, that same evening. He'd been quite insistent about it, as he had a meeting and could not entertain his brother.

"I don't need to be entertained," Rowland had protested. "Don't you need me to be at this meeting, too?"

Wilfred usually took the rare opportunities of Rowland's visits to drag him through various items of family business, to sign documents, meet with solicitors, and the like. This time, however, he was adamant that Rowland was not required, a shift which piqued the younger man's interest.

Wilfred's meeting was to be conducted at Oaklea in the library. He directed Rowland to use one of the sunrooms at the back of the house for the sitting, ostensibly to avoid the artistic process being disturbed by visitors. Rowland was reluctant to start work without natural light, but Wilfred was determined he should spend the evening that way. Eventually, Rowland conceded, allowing himself to be banished, with Kate, to a room as far from the library as possible. He was certain there was more to the arrangement than Wilfred would admit. All of which intrigued him even more.

"I don't really know," Kate replied. "Something to do with politics, I expect."

"So why was Wil so determined that I stay out of sight? You'd think he was ashamed of me."

Kate missed his attempt at humour and was at pains to assure him otherwise. "Oh, no, Rowly, I'm sure he's not. He's always this way about his meetings. Even the servants aren't allowed near the library while his guests are here."

"Who is he meeting with?" Rowland scribbled quickly now that she had relaxed. Ernest, who had been playing on the floor by his mother's feet, came to stand by him and watch.

"I don't know." Kate beckoned her son to come over to her. He climbed into her lap. "Wil doesn't talk to me about them at all."

"What makes you think it's politics then? Wil isn't standing for office is he?"

"Oh, no." Kate stroked Ernest's dark curls as he climbed into her lap and lay drowsily in her arms. "He's far too busy for that. It's just that he's always so agitated after these meetings. Wil's very concerned about the Communists, you know."

Rowland sketched Kate with Ernest asleep in her embrace. He liked the gentle composition, the natural tenderness in her face. Already he knew that this was how he would paint her. "So, what is Wilfred planning to do about them? The Communists, I mean." He spoke with a smile, not really expecting an answer. Raging against the Communists had become something of a populist pastime among the armchair armies.

"I'm not sure exactly," Kate said quietly. "But I know he's doing something. Wilfred wouldn't let us be unprotected…Your brother's an amazing man, Rowly. I know he seems stern at times, but that's just because he's making sure we're all safe."

Rowland started pencilling a closer study of her face. He liked the expression in her eyes when she spoke of her husband. He hadn't really expected to find Kate such an interesting model. He was also becoming more and more curious about this meeting of Wilfred's.

"You know, he worries terribly about you," Kate continued, a little hesitantly.

"Really, why?"

"He says you don't understand the way these people work. He believes you're too trusting." Her voice was almost a whisper now. "These people are clever—wicked, but clever."

"Oh, Kate…" Rowland wasn't sure what to tell her. She seemed genuinely frightened for him.

"Rowly, you must listen to Wil," she said earnestly. "He knows about these things."

"Uh huh…" Rowland concentrated on shading his nephew's sleeping face. There was no point trying to persuade Kate that her husband might be overreacting. She was obviously convinced that

Wilfred Sinclair was all that stood between them and the Red Army.

"How often does Wil have these meetings?"

"It's hard to say, more often lately…Rowly,"—Kate changed the subject—"what do you think of the changes?"

"Changes?"

"To the house. Wil says I must do whatever I want, but it's difficult to know what's right. I don't want to upset anyone."

"Kate, you're Mrs. Wilfred Sinclair." He felt a little sorry for her. Kate's family hailed from Glen Innes in the north—he was only now starting to understand that she must be feeling somewhat alone on the property. "This is your house. Paint it pink if you want. For the record, I think your remodelling looks smashing."

"Sometimes I suspect your mother…"

"My mother is living in 1913." Rowland was firm. "Try not to let her upset you."

"Oh, she doesn't. She's very kind, really," Kate said quickly.

Rowland knew his mother was polite and softly spoken; but she was formidable, even now. She did not always remember that there had been a changing of the guard, that she was no longer the mistress of Oaklea. "In a couple of years, Ernie will be at school and you can spend more time in the city," he offered as consolation, despite her assurances that his mother was kind.

Mrs. Kendall stepped into the room, whispering so as not to wake the boy. "Shall I take Master Ernest up to bed now, Mrs. Sinclair?"

"Yes, I think so," Kate kissed Ernest's head. "I might come up with you…" She glanced apologetically at Rowland, "He likes me to sing to him if he wakes up."

"You go ahead," he replied. "I've got everything I need for tonight…I'm going read for a bit and turn in myself."

Mrs. Kendall took Ernest from Kate's arms. "It seems only yesterday I was carrying Mr. Rowland up to bed."

"What are you reading?" Kate turned as they walked out of the door.

Rowland held up the dog-eared copy of Lawrence's *Kangaroo*. "I've been trying to finish it for about a year," he admitted.

"Is it dull?"

"No…just a little farfetched."

Rowland waited until he heard their footsteps fade on the staircase. He slipped his notebook into the pocket of his trousers. The night had not cooled the stifling heat, and once again his jacket lay discarded on the back of an armchair. He left it there and padded quietly down the long hallway toward the library.

He saw that the door to the library was shut and two men stood outside. Rowland was baffled. Why would Wilfred feel the need to post guards in his own house? Now he was determined to find out who was cloistered inside the room.

He retraced his steps, then climbed out of the large open window onto the verandah. The library was on the south side of the house where there was no verandah. Rowland did remember, however, that there was an old oak tree right outside the window. His father had always thought it too close to the house, but his mother had refused to allow its removal as its shade kept the library cool. Dark, but cool.

Rowland cut across the lawn toward the tree, slipping unnoticed past the limousines and saloons parked in the driveway with their waiting chauffeurs chatting amongst themselves. The oak's branches were pendulous away from the house, but on the other side, had grown up against the wall. The trunk was only a few feet from the library window, which had been opened to catch any breeze. He could see why his father had wanted to remove the oak—it was an absurd place to plant a tree that would grow so large.

Rowland looked up and decided on his path

through the branches. He had often climbed this tree as a child, but both he and it had grown since then. He hoisted himself up slowly and silently. He could already hear the murmur of voices just a few feet above his head. The canopy was dense— he would be able to get right up to the window without detection.

He smiled, feeling ridiculous. Somehow he had regressed to his eight-year-old self, stalking his older brothers in the hope he'd be included in whatever they were doing.

Rowland shimmied along a branch as close as he dared to the window. It creaked somewhat, but he was pretty sure it would hold his weight. He stopped just a couple of feet from the opening where he could see and hear what was going on inside.

The library was crowded with at least a dozen men. A dozen dark suits in a haze of cigarette and pipe smoke. Rowland didn't recognise anyone except his brother, but that was not surprising. He and Wilfred had moved in different circles for several years now. A tall, slim man with a military moustache was formally chairing the meeting. His manner was measured and purposive, with an obvious air of authority. Rowland heard one of the other men call him Roger. Wilfred sat to his right. It seemed Kate was correct that the meeting was about politics. The conversation concerned the impending Federal election. Rowland was a little disappointed.

Carefully, he pulled out his notebook and with the pencil he kept sheathed in its spine, he began to draw the faces of those gathered in the library.

For some minutes, he was engrossed—concentrating in the dim light and because he was hanging in a tree—but then he caught something that made his pencil stop. The speaker was a heavy-faced man in a tweed jacket that stretched to button over his portly torso. Rowland had already captured his face in full round lines.

"We have received further confidential intelligence from the Victorian organisation that the time is nearly at hand for the Communists to initiate their final effort. As reported earlier, they mean to act on one of two plans—a general strike or a *coup d'd'état.*"

Rowland listened in sceptical amazement as possible paths of revolution were detailed, as well the measures taken to meet such an uprising, including the procurement of arms. The man in the taut tweed then went on to describe the "cleaning up processes" where "right-thinking citizens" such as themselves would expel local subversives from towns across the state, whether the constabulary helped or not. It became clear to Rowland that preemptive frontier-style justice was to become the order of the day—the country was going mad and somehow he hadn't noticed.

Finally the speaker concluded his disturbing report with an allusion to an internal betrayal. "The membership has been warned to take no further notice of Millar who, as we know, has defected to the New Guard. That blaggard Campbell may find his new country organiser is far less effective than he hoped."

The last statement was greeted with a murmur of assent and the odd "Hear! Hear!"

"A lot of damage has already been done." Wilfred leaned forward. "Campbell has been recruiting from our ranks for months and there is a groundswell in his favour among the younger men."

"Surely that's just in the city," protested a grey-haired man who puffed on a pipe with the rhythm of an industrial machine. "Campbell's megalomania will not wash here."

"I have spoken to our people in the Graziers' Association," said the man they called Roger. "Campbell's funds will begin to dry up shortly, and he will soon find he has no friends to bankroll his narcissistic bid for power."

"Reid's staff has called a meeting to discuss amalgamation," Wilfred replied. "Obviously Campbell feels that there are enough among us who will fall in behind his reckless campaign, and Reid seems to agree."

"The big worry is Charles Hardy. He has far more appeal out here than Campbell." Roger was clearly frustrated. "Hardy will be able to bring men to the New Guard through the Riverina Group, and he has been campaigning vigorously."

At this, the portly man who had spoken of the *coup d'état,* exploded into a tirade about Eric Campbell and his New Guard.

Rowland was intrigued. What exactly was this organisation considering amalgamation, albeit reluctantly, with the New Guard?

"Obviously, Hinton, you will speak against the motion," Wilfred said when the man's outburst finally subsided.

"Most certainly!"

"Well then, the future of the Old Guard will be decided in Cootamundra, my friends." Wilfred looked grim. "In the meantime we must not lose sight that the real enemy is Lang and the Communist hordes into whose hands he plays!"

The Old Guard? Rowland looked up sharply, too sharply. What on earth was the Old Guard, he wondered as he struggled to regain his balance. He tried to right himself, but the branch he grabbed for was weak and brittle. It snapped and he fell.

Rowland heard the alarmed voices as he hit the

ground, but he did not stop to look up. There were shouts and then a gunshot from the window. The bullet grazed him. He clutched his side gasping as he pressed himself into the shadows of the house.

He could hear Wilfred's voice, "Put that damn thing away, you fool! You'll have the entire district here!"

Rowland moved quickly. He slipped back onto the verandah as the chauffeurs ran toward the sound of the shot. Lights were switched on in the house. He climbed back in through the window, trying to catch his panicked breath. Cursing, he removed his hand from his side. There was no time to examine it properly. He hoped it wasn't too bad, but saw it had already bled a telltale red patch on his shirt. There was movement in the hall—if he didn't emerge soon it would look suspicious. He slipped on his jacket and buttoned it. Wiping his hands on the rags he kept in his paint box, he poured himself a drink and after taking a large gagging gulp, he walked out with the glass in his hand.

Rowland could hear engines starting in the driveway. Wilfred was outside the library door, which was now ajar. He was speaking to Mrs. Kendall. "Just tell Kate and mother there's nothing to worry about. One of the boys mistook a possum for a burglar...no need to worry," he repeated. "I'll be up in a moment."

"What the hell is going on, Wil?" Rowland asked. "Did you shoot someone?"

"Just a mistake." Wilfred scowled. "One of the chaps overreacted."

"Solicitors and accountants carry revolvers these days, do they?" Rowland knew it would be odd if he did not appear at least a little interested.

"Where were you?" Wilfred asked.

"Where you bloody put me." Rowland did not hesitate. "I was having a drink when I heard the shot."

Wilfred looked at his brother's glass. "Since when do you drink whisky?"

Rowland smiled. "As you keep pouring it for me, I thought I'd better give it a chance."

Wilfred assessed his brother. Rowland was pale and his hair was damp with perspiration. "You don't look so too well." The comment was sharp with accusation.

Rowland put his glass on the hall table. "Precisely why I don't drink whisky," he said as calmly as he could. The warm sticky patch under his jacket was spreading. He felt a little light-headed, but he waited a moment until Mrs. Kendall had left. "So what happened, Wil?"

Wilfred's eyes narrowed. "It might have been a burglar, but there's no need to alarm Kate."

"So you didn't see him?"

"No, it was just a noise really."

"Bit risky to shoot at a noise."

"Riskier not to."

"Well, if nobody's dead…" Rowland started brightly.

Wilfred continued staring at him.

"Unbutton your jacket, Rowly."

"Not words I thought I'd ever hear from you." Rowland battled to maintain his smile.

Wilfred had had enough. He reached forward and tore open Rowland's jacket. They both gazed mutely at the red, which now soaked half of Rowland's shirt, as a jacket button rattled to rest on polished floorboards.

Wilfred only just caught his brother as he stumbled.

Chapter Ten

THE DRUG HABIT

Growth Among Soldiers

ADELAIDE, Wednesday

Attention is drawn to the annual report of the Inspector of Inebriate Establishments (Dr. W.E. Jones) to the growth of the drug habit. He said some returned soldiers had exhibited this failing. He could not help an uncomfortable feeling that the medical profession was responsible for many cases of the drug habit through the indiscreet provision of prescriptions.

The Advertiser, December 17, 1931

Rowland sat on the scrubbed oak of the kitchen table with a towel pressed against his side, and waited. Wilfred had made some calls, then disappeared upstairs briefly to reassure Kate and their mother. He'd put Rowland in the empty kitchen and directed him not to move. He hadn't said much else, too furious even to speak to his brother. Mrs. Kendall and the servants had retired to their own quarters under Wilfred's direction. When Wilfred returned to the kitchen, he was accompanied by a bearded man with a leather bag.

Rowland recalled him from the meeting in the library.

"As I said, Maguire," Wilfred closed the kitchen door, "this is my idiot brother. Just make sure he doesn't bleed to death."

Maguire's expression was almost as hostile as Wilfred's. He spoke only to instruct Rowland to remove his shirt and the towel he'd been holding against the wound. While the bullet hadn't actually lodged, it had gouged a four-inch lesion as it passed. It wasn't dangerously deep, but it did require stitching.

"A little to the right and this could have been ugly." Maguire sounded almost disappointed. "I could give him some morphine before I start."

"Absolutely not." Wilfred was resolute.

Rowland didn't argue. Having served with men who were destroyed, not by the enemy's guns, but by their addiction to the morphine they'd been given for their injuries, Wilfred was adamant it be used only in the most extreme circumstances. Clearly, he also felt any pain was, in this case, deserved.

Maguire didn't pursue the matter either, muttering only, "Hold still," before he started to clean and sew the wound.

Rowland gripped the table and hoped the man was actually a doctor. As Maguire silently stitched and dressed the lesion, Wilfred looked on without the slightest flicker of compassion.

Eventually Maguire replaced his instruments into the leather bag, and turned to Wilfred. "I should inform Roger about this."

Wilfred shook his head and shot Rowland another look of disgust. "There's no need. I'll take care of Rowly—he will not present a problem."

"I don't know, Sinclair. This is too important…"

Wilfred put a kettle on the Aga cooker. "I think I still know how to make a cup of tea. Sit down Maguire." He motioned Rowland to the door. "For pity's sake, Rowly, go and get dressed. You'd think you were raised by savages!"

For a moment the brothers glared at each other, then Rowland limped painfully out of the kitchen, leaving Wilfred to negotiate with Maguire.

Back in his room, he found a clean shirt and tie, tossing the bloody shirt into the back of the cupboard. He made a mental note to see his tailor; between paint and bullets he was running out of clothes. Rowland gingerly tested his side. Perhaps morphine would not have been such a bad idea. He wondered what kind of lunatic organisation met in secret and shot at shadows…though admittedly he had not been a shadow.

He would much rather have slept at this point. He was tired and in pain, but he was also fed up with Wilfred trying to send him away like a child. They'd shot him, for God's sake—he wasn't going to just sit quietly in his room. Resolved and now quite ready for the inevitable confrontation, he had turned the handle to head back to the kitchen, when Wilfred pushed his door open and stepped inside. "Suppose you tell me what the hell you were doing, Rowly!" Wilfred's voice was flat but livid.

"I was trying to figure out what it is you're doing." Rowland used the bed post to steady himself. "What is this Old Guard, Wil? What's all the cloak and dagger about?"

Wilfred stepped toward him. "That is not your concern…I want the truth. Were you spying for your Bolshevik friends?"

"For pity's sake, Wil! I know you think there's a Communist lurking behind every tree, but on this occasion it was only me!"

Wilfred's face reddened. "This is not a game, you idiot. It's about time you grew up."

"Look, Wil, I'm sorry. It was stupid to be hiding in a tree...but what are you mixed up in? Who were those men?"

Wilfred turned away from him, his fist clenched. "Honestly, Rowly, if you weren't my brother...You are to mention nothing of this to anyone...Do you understand?"

"Believe me, I'd rather no one knew my brother was involved with the New Guard!"

"I am not involved with the damn New Guard! The men you saw tonight..." Wilfred stopped and studied Rowland, deciding how far he could trust brotherhood. "Our intent, the Old Guard's intent, is to counter the coming revolution, to protect law and order, and to defend our way of life against the Communist threat. Campbell was originally among us, but we saw his militant approach was almost as dangerous as Lang's coddling of those bloody Red traitors. Campbell was invited to resign—an invitation he accepted."

"But now his New Guard wants to amalgamate back with your Old Guard?" Rowland said, confused.

"Campbell is seeking validation." Wilfred turned away, pacing. "We will hear him out, but he will not get what he wants. As I said, the revolution

Campbell is advocating simply plays straight into the hands of the Communists."

"So why all the secrecy, Wil?"

"We are on the verge of civil war, Rowly. One never shows one's hand to the enemy."

Rowland laughed, wincing as he did so. "Civil war? You can't be serious."

Wilfred stepped toward him again, his eyes incensed. Rowland instinctively stepped backwards.

"Yes, civil war! Perhaps it's time you behaved like a man and decided on which side you will fight." Wilfred leant forward and poked Rowland in the chest, ignoring his wound. "If I find out you are indiscreet with anything you've learned here, I will let them bloody well shoot you!"

"They already shot me." Rowland refused to be drawn into his brother's madness.

The comment seemed to startle Wilfred. "Well, next time, you may not be so lucky."

Rowland moved his hand to the wound. Lucky? It hurt like blazes. "Who in their right mind shoots out of a window into the darkness? It might have been anyone out there. Doesn't that strike you as even a little bit crazy, Wil?"

Wilfred's face hardened again. "It wasn't anyone. It was you. You'd better bloody well hope that Maguire trusts me enough to keep his mouth shut!"

Chapter Eleven

COMMUNISM

New Regulations Against
Seditious Literature First Step In Policy

CANBERRA, Saturday

The first step taken by the newly-elected Lyons Government against the threat of Communism is likely to be the tightening of regulations covering the importation of literature and propaganda.

The Canberra Times, December 20, 1931

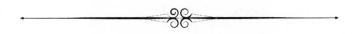

Rowland leant against the wall, observing the celebrations in the ballroom at Oaklea. The newly formed United Australia Party was now in control of the Federal Parliament under the leadership of J.A. Lyons. Wilfred and Kate were hosting an election party—an elegant and formal affair, befitting the glorious restoration of the nation to the conservative forces. Elisabeth Sinclair had made a brief appearance at the start of the evening, but had long since retired.

The ballroom glittered with the rural establishment. Rowland wondered idly if this change in Federal government would do anything to lessen the rampant paranoia of a Communist revolution.

He sipped his champagne enjoying a brief respite from the rigours of eligibility. Kate seemed determined to introduce him to every unmarried graduate of finishing school west of the Divide. He had done his best to be gracious and conceal his lack of enthusiasm. The effort had left him a little weary.

Wilfred, he'd noticed, had spent the evening moving between tight furtive circles, in a series of earnest conversations with stalwarts of the Right. He had barely spoken to Rowland since the meeting in the library.

Rowland saw Lucy Bennett moving in his direction, and slipped away. Regrettably, Miss Bennett had recovered from her shock at the scandalous sketches in his notebook. Back in the sunroom which had become his studio for painting Kate, he removed his dinner jacket and resumed work on her portrait. The new hostility between him and

Wilfred had seen him seek refuge in front of the canvas, and the work had progressed quickly as a result. He stretched gingerly. Maguire had removed the stitches that morning, but he was still a little tender.

He lost himself in painting. For a while he forgot where he was, consumed by pigment and stroke.

It was morning when Wilfred walked in. "My God, Rowly, have you been here all night? You're getting a bit fanatical…"

Rowland laughed. Wilfred, who was raising a secret army, was calling him a fanatic. "Everyone's gone then?"

"You're not hiding are you, Rowly?"

"Your wife's rallied every spinster in the State to Oaklea. What else could I do?"

Wilfred smiled. "Kate does get a bit carried away…But there are worse things than settling down—you've been sowing your wild oats for years now."

"Wish that were true, Wil," Rowland mumbled as he cleaned his brushes. "Haven't we already had this conversation?"

"Probably," Wilfred admitted. He looked toward the canvas, which was faced away from him. "Are you finished?"

"Pretty much."

"May I look?"

Rowland stepped back so his brother could come behind the easel. Wilfred gazed at the painting for some time.

Rowland became a little nervous in the extended silence. "Well, what do you think?" he asked, tentatively.

For a further moment, Wilfred said nothing. Then, when he spoke his voice was thick, plainly emotional. "I didn't know you were painting Ernest as well."

Rowland was surprised, but gladly so. He'd never really hoped to reach Wilfred. "You have a beautiful family, Wil."

Wilfred nodded.

Rowland returned to cleaning his brushes while his brother continued to stare at the painting.

"I have a meeting," Wilfred said eventually. "I'll be back tomorrow."

"Cootamundra?" Rowland remembered the discussion in the library about amalgamating the Old and the New Guards.

Wilfred nodded, warily.

Rowland didn't know quite what to say next.

Wilfred spoke first. "Rowly, I don't like leaving Oaklea at this time…God knows what might happen…"

"It's only one night, Wil."

"It could start at any time…we right thinking men need to be ready." Wilfred reached into his jacket and extracted a revolver.

"Oh, for God's sake!" Rowland recoiled from the gun.

"Rowly, I'm leaving my family in your care… The threat is real and it is imminent! The Communists are armed—and we must be too."

Rowland shook his head. "Wilfred, the Communists are not about to do anything."

Wilfred pointed at his brother. "That is exactly why they are so dangerous! They lull the complacent into thinking they're harmless—poets, painters, clerks, labourers, even accountants and lawyers—they infiltrate every level of society, all arms of government." Wilfred grabbed Rowland's hand and pressed the revolver into it. "Rowly, it's time you stood up and took some responsibility. This country needs men like us to stand against the Red tide!"

Rowland met his brother's eyes. Wilfred was absolute and sincere in his conviction that revolution was at their doorstep. "Wil…this is insane…I'm not shooting anyone!"

"Bloody hell, Rowly! You're a Sinclair. How about you give something back to this family for once?"

"So you want me to sit on the verandah, with a gun, in case Trotsky drops by!"

"Just bloody well take the gun and be watchful. As you said, it's only one night!" Wilfred stalked out of the room leaving his brother staring after him with a revolver in his hand.

Rowland knew how to use a gun. Paramilitary training had been part of the curriculum for boys who had gone to school in the shadow of war. Even so, he had no intention of shooting anyone in the streets of Yass. He wondered uneasily how widespread this lunacy was. He really had to get back to Sydney.

He placed the firearm in his paint box, burying it beneath tubes of paint and colour-stained rags. He closed the lid and secured the latch, and decided to forget about it.

Refusing to concede a single thing to Wilfred's call for vigilance, he showered, changed, and slept for a couple of hours. By the early afternoon, he was ready to accompany his mother for a walk in the gardens. Despite the dense shade of the oaks and claret ashes, it was oppressively warm. In the absence of Wilfred, Rowland walked in the relative comfort of unjacketed shirtsleeves.

Elisabeth Sinclair chatted happily, to Aubrey, chastising him gently for coming home so infrequently. Occasionally she referred to "the baby," but that was the closest she came to remembering her youngest son.

As Rowland listened to his mother, his conscience was pricked with vague feelings of guilt. It seemed that his entire family was mad—his mother conspicuously and his brother secretly. Kate was lucid, but she believed unquestioningly in her husband's paranoid ramblings. Rowland wondered if he might have abated their slip into insanity if he had not absconded to Sydney. He thought of his nephew—the aptly named Ernest—and resolved to visit more often, if only to give the boy some link to reality.

At about three o'clock, Rowland took tea with his mother and Kate on the verandah. It was the elevation that allowed him to see over the hedges and make out the car parked outside the entrance to Oaklea. A black Oldsmobile. He wondered if it had broken down; it had been there for the entire hour they had been enjoying their tea and cake. Wilfred's misgivings came back to him but he put them firmly aside. This was silly. "I'm just going to walk down and see if that car needs help," he told Kate as he stood.

"McNair can go. I'll call him…"

"No, it won't take a minute. I know a bit about engines."

He grabbed his hat and set off down the

driveway. It was a good quarter mile to the gate. As he approached, he could see there were two men in the Oldsmobile looking at him. As he raised his arm in a greeting, the engine gunned and the car pulled away. Rowland watched it disappear, wondering whether it was odd or whether he was just succumbing to Wilfred's suspicions.

Chapter Twelve

Rowland's eyes went again to the sitting room window. The impulse to check repeatedly for the black Oldsmobile was making it difficult to read. The road remained clear, and he smiled at his own folly—Wilfred was infecting him with his paranoia.

His restlessness diverted to brooding over the brutality of his uncle's murder. He had long ago dismissed Inspector Bicuit's suspicion of Mrs. Donelly. Still, Rowland could not imagine who would want to hurt the harmless old man. His uncle had been, as far as he could see, inoffensive. He was not aligned particularly with anything, politically, religiously, or even socially. The elder Rowland Sinclair had many friends, but had never bothered with enemies. He'd had no real passions beyond food and entertainment, though Rowland did now wonder about the mysterious fishnet stockings. There was no conceivable way that the assault could have been precipitated by debts…no Sinclair was short of funds.

Rowland played with idea of Mrs. Donelly's "dark ghosts," drawing shadowy figures repeatedly into his notebook in the hope that something would trigger…but he came no closer to any earthly explanation for what she might have seen.

Toward the end of the day, two men came to the gate, hats in hand, asking for work. It was not unusual. With so many unemployed, these hopeful, hopeless appeals were a daily occurrence. There were no vacancies at Oaklea, but Mrs. Kendall always fed them in the servants' quarters before sending them on their way; it was a long walk to the next property and the men were invariably hungry.

Not long after they'd gone, Wilfred returned from Cootamundra, buoyed, and Rowland guessed that the proposal to amalgamate with the New Guard had failed. He was relieved. He had no wish to find himself at war with his brother; but he could see himself standing against the belligerent excesses of Eric Campbell's men. He was glad that doing so would not pit him against Wilfred. With any luck he could remain outside whatever it was that his brother's group was planning—as long as they didn't start shooting again.

Days at Oaklea fell into an indulgent pace and pattern—a series of dinner parties, graceful entertainments and refined company. Evenings with the wireless, often spent listening to the rousing broadcasts of the Sane Democracy League. Tennis parties at the courts behind the homestead. For most of the time, Rowland felt only half awake.

Kate was both delighted and embarrassed by Rowland's painting. It was only when she saw the completed work that she realised how closely her brother-in-law looked at the world, how much he saw and understood. It disconcerted her, but the finished portrait was arresting. Rowland had painted Kate as a mother, but he had not lost her in that role. He had found a girlish dreaminess in her eyes, a gentle strength in the way she held her son. Wilfred had it framed and hung proudly in the main drawing room. Rowland was unexpectedly gratified. He had not known that his brother's approval meant anything to him.

There were no more meetings at Oaklea, although Wilfred often left the property on the pretext of business. Rowland had decided to avoid the topic of revolutions and insurgents, and simply hope that the head of the Sinclair family would come to his senses.

Christmas was a private affair at Oaklea but Boxing Day was different. On this day Oaklea was festooned with bunting and marquees for the annual Sinclair garden party in the aid of the

Australian Red Cross. The garden parties had been held at Oaklea since the war, and were usually very successful fundraisers. Rowland's mother played the hostess with surprising ease; though it was Kate, as the new Mrs. Sinclair, who had organised the day.

Rowland surveyed the celebrations with a kind of distant interest as he listened to Lucy Bennett enthuse about the extraordinary philanthropy of his family. Rowland had, for the past couple of years, allowed Clyde to guide his own charitable works, relying on his friend to point out those who did not otherwise enter his world. In the days before Clyde had moved into Woodlands House, he had himself eaten often at the soup kitchens which fed hundreds of desperate, hungry people around the city. He had not forgotten those days and so, at his suggestion, Rowland Sinclair had become a benefactor. It was a stark contrast to the champagne that accompanied charity at Oaklea. It was not that Rowland found the excess uncomfortable; it was just that now he noticed it.

Even before the year turned, the summer became more intense. The northerlies blew in strong gusts bringing the fire season in earnest. Grass fires had to be dealt with quickly. If they were permitted to grow, it would be too late do anything but allow the blazes to burn themselves, and whatever lay in their paths, out.

There were many men who lived and worked on Oaklea but, at the first signs of fire, all hands manned pumps and beat flames. Rowland fell in wherever needed, and took orders from the farm-workers, who knew better than he how to control a blaze and protect the property. Wilfred approved. While he didn't feel it was appropriate or necessary that he, as head of the family, participate in such a direct manner, he thought Rowland's involvement a good thing. If nothing else, he hoped that his brother was finally showing an interest in the property to which the Sinclairs owed so much.

Having spent so little time on the property in recent years, Rowland was much less identifiable than Wilfred. The smoke, grime, and panic in fighting the fires, helped him keep a sort of anonymity. There was no time for chatter under the circumstances, so the telltale British plum of his speech was barely heard. In any case, Edna had so often ribbed what she called his pretentious accent, that he had learned to adjust it to the company he kept. He did it subconsciously, and quite well now. Indeed, Wilfred often complained about the common manner in which he used the King's English.

The grassfires cracked the languid pace of life at Oaklea, giving Rowland some purpose now that Kate's portrait was hung. The small blazes were more a nuisance than a potential disaster, though the season was a dangerous one. Much further west, bushfires were gathering force and forming massive fronts. Here, they were mere skirmishes by comparison, but even so, they couldn't be allowed to get out of control.

At times, Rowland wondered if Wilfred's involvement with the mysterious Old Guard was his brother's attempt to break the luxuriant and frivolous monotony of the landed gentry. If so, he could understand it.

On New Year's Day 1932, Wilfred called Rowland into the library shutting the door behind them. Rowland took a seat. By Wilfred's manner, it was a matter of some gravity. The older Sinclair poured two glasses of whisky, placed one in front of Rowland, then sat and lit a cigarette. "Rowly, I want to talk to you about our responsibility to this land."

Rowland groaned. "I'm not coming back to Oaklea, Wil."

Wilfred sighed. "I don't care where you live— just listen. I would not have thought to bring you into this, but since it seems you have stumbled into things, I can only hope you have enough common sense and love of country, to work with, rather than in opposition to, us."

Rowland toyed with his glass wordlessly. Obviously, Wilfred was about to make a speech.

"Rowly, we have undeniably been raised in a privileged world, exposed to the best education, society, and morality that the British Empire can offer. With that, comes an obligation to guide and lead men who are not so well-equipped to grasp the intricacies of politics and good government."

Rowland relaxed a little. This was going to be another of Wilfred's "ruling class" speeches, which always finished with him demanding that his brother find a more fitting occupation.

"The world is on a precipice," Wilfred continued. "The Communists have Russia and they seek to extend their power much further. Europe is in flux. Both Germany and Italy have sought to stand against the influence of the Bolsheviks with men who know that Communism must not be treated gently."

This, Rowland could not let lie. "I've met men who have not been treated gently by Germany." Artists and writers had already started fleeing the increasingly Fascist regimes of Europe, where dissent was dealt with brutally.

Wilfred ignored him. "There are patriots, organisations of men, ready to defend His Majesty's peace against the enemy—prepared to lead this country out of the destruction and terror to which Russia has succumbed."

Rowland let him carry on, hoping Wilfred would get to the point soon.

"Rowly, I must admit that given your tendency to associate with lesser elements, I would not have normally thought to ask you this." Wilfred stubbed out his cigarette. "I am hoping that your behaviour is simply a manifestation of your age…"

"For heaven's sake Wil, I'm nearly twenty-seven, not ten!"

"The other evening, you saw a meeting of the Old Guard. We are a membership of right-thinking men from all over the state. Our men are loyal to both King and Country and are committed to turning the Red Army from our shores."

Rowland exhaled impatiently.

"The organisation values secrecy. Only Maguire knows it was you who spied upon us."

Rowland's brows rose as he waited for Wilfred to meander to some sort of end.

"Rowly, I want you to join us. You could bring us valuable intelligence through your less savoury contacts. It will assure me that I can rely on your discretion and, frankly, you owe it to your family and your country!"

Rowland was taken by surprise. This wasn't quite what he expected. "Wilfred…No."

The ensuing argument was heated, and bitter. Rowland was not a Communist, of course, but he did not share his brother's hatred of them. Wilfred was motivated to give his son the same world he had himself inherited, and determined that all the Sinclairs should enlist in the defending the status quo.

"You don't need to worry about my discretion, Wil," Rowland snarled. "I'm not about to tell anyone that my brother is raising some clandestine, tweed-jacketed army because he thinks Stalin is heading south! Who the hell would believe me, anyway? I can barely believe it myself. You're crazy, you know."

"How like you to leave it to other men to defend the life you take for granted." Wilfred was contemptuous.

Rowland had worn this criticism before. In a country that revered its returned soldiers, he was a man unproven in war. He responded sharply and defensively. "Wil, I was fourteen when the war ended, if you recall?"

"You're not fourteen now, and this war is on our doorstep. If the Communists rise up…"

Rowland stood. "No." He opened the door and walked out, quickly, because at that moment he wished very much to hit Wilfred.

He would have left for Sydney immediately—he

certainly wanted to—but his mother stood in his way. She heard him throwing his things into a bag—he was angry and so not quiet about it. Elisabeth Sinclair came out of her room, and when he tried to say goodbye, she clung to him frantically, her eyes terrified. "Aubrey, Aubrey, you mustn't go," she whispered and wept. "They'll shoot you…they have guns…they'll shoot you…" She shook uncontrollably. Her legs gave way but still she gripped the lapels of his jacket as if they were her last grasp on life. Kate came to help him, but Elisabeth would not let go of her son. She began to wail. "Dear God, they'll shoot you, Aubrey…stay here with me…it's safe here, darling…"

Wilfred emerged from his study. "Kate, call Maguire—tell him we need him."

Rowland was struggling to keep his composure and console his mother. She would not release him, frantic to save her Aubrey. Eventually, he carried her back to her bed.

Maguire arrived. He treated Elisabeth Sinclair with a sedative and, finally, she loosened her grip on Rowland. She was confined to bed rest and her warring sons were warned to upset her as little as possible. Accordingly, it was decided: his mother wanted Aubrey to stay, so Rowland could not leave.

Chapter Thirteen

ATTENDANCE FIGURES

MELBOURNE, Friday

Attendance at the Motor Show on Saturday was 12,411, which is 400 more than attended the show's first Saturday last year.

Around the Exhibits
Mr. Hoette is also displaying the Mecedes-Benz motorcars in two models— the new two-litre type and the six-litre sports model. For the smaller engine, remarkable and rapid acceleration are claimed, and the supercharged sports model possesses unusual speed and road-holding qualities.

The Argus, January 9, 1932

Rowland was sketching on the verandah, trying

once more to manage a likeness of his mother. For some reason, he had never been able to do so. This time, he blamed the chirp of countless cicadas whose background scream was almost physically uncomfortable. Even so, he was reluctant to go inside. His mother had become difficult, constantly demanding to see Aubrey, as if she were afraid he would vanish at any moment. Rowland sighed. She was probably right in a way, though he was beginning to get the desperate feeling he would never escape Oaklea. He and Wilfred had started butting heads regularly now. It was, on reflection, how his visits home had usually ended. Wilfred had taken Ernest riding and Kate had gone with them.

His mother was resting and he was free to brood in peace. Well, a sort of peace if he ignored the cicadas.

A cloud of dust billowed in the distance. Rowland squinted and saw that the cloud contained a vehicle which was turning into the long driveway. As it got closer, the roar of the engine struck him as familiar.

He rose and walked down the entrance stairs. For a moment he stood motionless as the Mercedes hurtled toward the house with Milton at the wheel and Clyde and Edna waving madly. Milton skidded the car to a stop sending gravel in all directions and over Rowland. Before he could shout at

Milton, Edna had jumped out and wrapped her arms around his neck. "Rowly! Surprise!"

"What on earth? What are you all doing here?" Rowland asked. "I can't believe you let Milt drive my car. Who said he could drive my car?"

Edna laughed. "Don't be ridiculous, Rowly… He was quite good, after a bit of practice."

Clyde and Milton jumped out of the tourer to shake his hand. Rowland was unreasonably happy to see them. It was like standing on solid ground again after months at sea. "What are you all doing here, really?" he asked again.

When Rowland had phoned Woodlands House with the news he was staying longer than expected, Edna decided he had not sounded himself.

"Lady McKenzie paid Clyde for the portrait," Milton replied. "So we decided to have a holiday in the country…unfortunately we spent most of Clyde's fee feeding this flaming monster." He patted the bonnet. "She's a guzzler, isn't she?"

"You've got to treat a lady well, Milt—they like to be fed." Rowland smiled. Lady McKenzie's commission was Clyde's only income in months. They were all like that—his friends—both generous and utterly irresponsible with what little they had.

"Mary Brown is bloody scary when you're not around," confided Clyde. "And we have some news for you."

"Well, you don't need to tell me in the drive-way," Rowland motioned back at the house. "Grab your bags and come in."

"No, Rowly, we won't." Edna was firm. "Your mother's not well…We've taken rooms at the Royal in town."

"Yes, mate." Milton slapped his friend's shoulder. "We just thought we'd bring you the car… figured you'd be missing her by now."

Rowland was happy to see his car; that was true. If things hadn't already been so tense between him and Wilfred, he might have insisted his friends stay at Oaklea. As it was, perhaps this was better. "Just give me a minute," he said as he opened the French doors into the main drawing room. "I'll drive you back to the Royal."

They followed him in and sat primly in the immaculate formality of the drawing room, while they waited.

He walked quietly into the house and found Mrs. Kendall. He told the housekeeper that he would be going into Yass.

"If my mother awakes, assure her that I'll be back later," he said a little guiltily.

"Don't you worry about Mrs. Sinclair, Mr. Rowland." The housekeeper dismissed his concern. "She won't be getting herself so upset if you're not here to see it." She patted his hand. "You go and have a nice time. I'll bake you some shortbread tomorrow."

When Rowland returned to the drawing room, his friends were stopped in front of Kate's portrait.

Edna stood closer than the men. The painting was mesmerising; it pulled her into it—into the depth of the bond between the sitter and her child. The light came in from the window to bathe the boy in an almost ethereal glow, and yet it was the woman who was the true subject of the piece. Rowland, she decided, was developing a very distinctive style.

"Who is she?" Milton asked.

"Kate. She's my sister-in-law, and that's Ernest, my nephew."

"She's not a bad model," Clyde murmured appreciatively.

"You'll have to paint me like that one day, Rowly," said Edna softly.

Milton grinned. "It's illegal to kidnap children, Ed."

Rowland laughed but Edna snapped back at Milton in a less than charming manner, which would have shocked the real Kate if she'd been there to hear it.

They left the house and Rowland slipped behind the wheel of his beloved Mercedes. He listened to the roar of the engine as though it were some kind of symphony, refamiliarising himself with the sound of the pistons and the workings in the already warmed machine.

Edna squeezed next to him and Clyde and Milton jumped into the backseat. Milton handed him back the driving gloves he had borrowed from their place in the glovebox, and Rowland swung the car around the driveway and accelerated toward the ornate gates of Oaklea. He had engaged the supercharger by the time they turned onto the road into town.

They pulled up outside the Royal Hotel oblivious to the curious, somewhat disapproving stares of the local citizenry. Rowland spoke to the proprietor and arranged for refreshments to be sent up.

They took their tea on the wide balcony which skirted the building, or rather, Rowland and Edna had tea while their companions sampled the establishment's other beverages.

"So what do you have to tell me?" Rowland asked.

"We have news about who killed your uncle," Milton replied, smugly.

"Really? Why didn't Inspector Bicuit telephone me? Did he come by Woodlands?"

"Bicuit? Forget that fool," Milton replied. "This piece of deduction was the product of a mind far more evolved than poor Bicuit's."

Clyde laughed. "It was hardly deduction, Milt." He turned to Rowland, "Paddy just told us."

"Told you what?" Rowland demanded.

"Paddy—you remember—the speaker at the Domain that day…?" Milton started.

Rowland nodded.

"He was beaten up last week; they broke into his house and did him over."

"Who?"

Milton drummed his fingers against the side of his glass. "Dark ghosts…" He paused for further effect while Clyde rolled his eyes.

"Just get on with it, Milt," said Edna, irritated.

"Paddy says it was four men dressed in black Ku Klux Klan outfits—you know?—robes and hoods. Dark ones."

"You're joking," Rowland sat up. "Paddy wasn't drunk, was he?"

"He's usually drunk," Milton admitted, "but not that night."

"Was he badly hurt?"

"He took a fair hiding."

"But they didn't kill him?"

"No, but then your uncle died of a heart attack, not from the assault itself."

Rowland nodded.

"Anyway, Rowly," Milton went on, "that's not all, see. Clyde and I had a good chat with Paddy."

At this point Clyde shook his head and Rowland gathered that the chat had been in furtherance of Milton's Holmesian fantasies.

The poet detective continued, "While their garb made them impossible to identify individually, Paddy is sure his 'dark ghosts' were New Guardsmen!"

"What?" Rowland was sceptical. "How on earth does he reach that conclusion?"

"It's happened before," said Edna. "Almost all the men these 'dark ghosts' have been targeting have been speakers for the Communist Party or from one of the unions."

"Paddy said there was a lot of bad language, which I won't repeat in front of Ed…generally it was not exactly complimentary of Communists," Clyde added.

"Yes, but Uncle Rowland was no Communist."

"Are you sure?" asked Edna. "Perhaps he had a side he kept hidden from you?"

"That's insane…" Rowland started, but then it occurred to him that he had been saying that a lot of late. Perhaps he was expecting too much. Perhaps madness was actually the normal state of affairs. Certainly, Wilfred had surprised him. That his Uncle Rowland was a Communist was unlikely, but not quite as farfetched as what his own brother was doing.

Deciding to ignore Wilfred's insistence on secrecy, Rowland began to tell his friends of the meeting at Oaklea and subsequent events.

"You hid in a tree?" Edna was quite aghast at the indignity.

"Did I mention they shot me?" Rowland repeated.

"And this Old Guard is different from the New Guard?" Clyde's weathered face furrowed with effort of following the subtle distinctions between establishment militias.

"So it seems." Rowland tried to explain. "Campbell was once a member of the Old Guard, but at some point he got peeved and started his own little club."

"Surely they're just a bunch of old codgers playing secret armies…They'd be pretty harmless, right?" Milton put his feet up on the side table.

"I don't know, Milt—they seem fairly organised and I'm guessing many of them are returned soldiers. They're convinced there's going to be civil war any day now."

"Civil war? Who would…?" Milton clapped his hand on his forehead in realisation. "Bloody Catholics! I knew the Tykes were planning something…all that bloody Hail Marying!" Milton folded his arms in indignation.

Clyde, who was a Catholic of sorts, clipped the side of Milton's head as he got up to refill his glass.

"They're talking about the Communists, you idiot!" retorted Edna, a little worried that Milton might only be half-joking.

Milton laughed. "There aren't enough Communists to stage a dance, let alone a revolution, but there's plenty of Catholics."

"That's what I'd thought," agreed Rowland, "but I think they're counting all the unions, the unemployed, and anyone who's ever tipped his hat to Premier Lang."

Milton stood rubbing his chin. "Well, let's just gather the facts, shall we, my friends? And, with the application of superior reasoning, determine the culprit in this foul deed."

Clyde groaned.

"My God, you're annoying." Edna poured another cup of tea.

"Do you think the New Guard may have targeted your uncle because of friction with your brother and the Old Guard?" Clyde ignored the poet and directed the question at Rowland.

"I suppose so…maybe…but it…" Rowland shrugged. "This whole thing's bizarre."

"So what are we going to do?" Edna moved to sit next to him on the wicker settee.

"I guess I'll go see Bicuit when we get back to

Sydney," Rowland replied. "Tell him about Paddy's assault and the others. It's a theory at least."

"When are we heading back?" Clyde looked at Rowland sheepishly. "My commission will only cover us here for another two nights."

"Don't worry about that," Rowland didn't blink. "I'm not entirely sure when I can get away—my mother's a bit fragile at the moment—but we should be out of here in a few days."

"You take your time, Rowly." Edna placed her hand on his arm. "We don't have anywhere we need to be."

"Yeah, mate," Clyde assured him, "we can keep ourselves occupied for as long as you need."

Rowland drained his cup and smiled. He felt relaxed for the first time in weeks. "That might not be so easy," he said. "There isn't a lot to do in Yass. But I'm really glad you came."

Milton reached over and ruffled his hair. "I knew it. He's lost without us."

Rowland pushed him away. "Actually, I missed my car."

They talked of other things for a while—the new ground being trod by the avant-garde movement, Cubism, Picasso, Lindsay, and of course the latest gossip. Clyde spoke in enthusiastic detail of the Harbour Bridge, which had in its various stages of completion been part of the Sydney skyline for some years now. He raved about the suspension cables, the great arches, and the flex of the structure. Clearly he was besotted with the industrial magnificence of it.

"For pity's sake, Clyde, it's a bridge!" Edna was less impressed.

Finally Rowland stood. "I'd better go," he said reluctantly. "Telephone me at Oaklea if you need anything…but I'll see you tomorrow anyway." Before he left he spoke to the proprietor of the hotel, and settled the accounts ahead of time. The old hotelier was a little uneasy. He did not recognise Rowland personally, but he understood he was the youngest of the Sinclair boys—perfectly well-presented despite the rumours he was somewhat wild. It was his friends who were questionable—Sydneysiders and flappers, no doubt. The woman particularly; she was altogether too familiar with her companions. They were not the kind of people he usually welcomed into his establishment. Still, times were difficult and even some of his respectable customers had stopped paying their accounts. And no sane businessman of Yass would risk offending the Sinclairs.

Rowland drove back to Oaklea without haste, relishing the ride. It was nearly dark when he pulled into the driveway. Ernest hurtled down the front steps, his eyes grew large as he saw Rowland's yellow car. They sat together in the front seat for a time while Rowland helped the boy explore the supercharged tourer.

The Sinclairs generally had Rolls-Royces, in black. To Ernest, the flamboyant yellow Mercedes with its pointed radiator, and external exhausts was completely exciting. Rowland explained proudly that the car could get to sixty miles an hour in twenty seconds, among other things. Ernest did not really understand what his uncle was talking about, but to his four-year-old mind the car looked fast…and that was good.

"Uncle Rowly, who are you?" Ernest knelt on the driver's seat and gripped the steering wheel.

"I'm your daddy's brother," Rowland replied, a little unsure of the question's intent.

"Grandma calls you Audrey."

Rowland smiled. "Aubrey. She gets confused sometimes."

Ernest looked hard at him. "I saw your picture at the chapel on the pointy stone."

Rowland knew what he meant. There was a memorial at the Sinclair chapel. "That's not me, Ernie, that's your Uncle Aubrey."

"It looks like you. What happened to him?"

"He was a soldier. He died."

"Daddy was a soldier."

"Yes. They went to war together."

"Were you a soldier?"

"No."

"Why not? Wouldn't Grandma let you go?"

"Something like that. I was too young."

"Daddy gets sad when we go to the pointy stone."

Rowland was quiet for a moment. "He probably misses your Uncle Aubrey."

"Daddy's cross with you, isn't he?"

Again Rowland smiled. Young Ernest seemed to have his finger right on the pulse of everything.

"Yes, but we're brothers. Brothers get cross with each other sometimes. It doesn't really matter."

Ernest nodded sagely. "You've got to do as you're told," he advised. "Then Daddy won't get cross."

"I'll try to remember that, Ernie."

Ernest returned to steering. When Kate came outside, Rowland was sketching the Mercedes into a page of his notebook, with his nephew watching intently.

"Oh, Rowly, you're back." Kate took in the car a little anxiously. "Your mother has been asking for you. She wants you to play the piano for her."

Rowland sighed. "I can't play the piano, Kate." He tore out the page for Ernest, and climbed out of his car without mentioning that Aubrey had been a brilliant musician.

Chapter Fourteen

MACHINE GUNS

Alleged Disappearance From Stores

CANBERRA, Monday

In the Senate yesterday, the assistant Minister (Senator Dooley) was asked by Senator Duncan whether an investigation of the stock of ordinance stores in Sydney had revealed that a number of machine guns had disappeared mysteriously.

Senator Dooley said that he was not acquainted with the facts, but if the question were placed on the notice paper he would endeavour to obtain information.

The Canberra Times, January 12, 1932

***

Rowland looked up and waved to Edna who leaned

out over the hotel balcony and blew him a kiss. Two matrons walking past turned their heads in together and tutted disapprovingly of the exchange. Rowland tipped his hat politely.

He waited in the Mercedes for his friends to join him for the trip back to Oaklea. Kate was excited at the prospect of meeting his friends from the city. He hadn't seen the need to mention it to Wilfred, who had gone to Galong for yet another meeting.

Milton vaulted into the backseat. Clyde used the door and Edna climbed into the front, pausing to check her reflection in the side mirrors and pull her hat down over her ears. Milton leant over and yanked it off her head as she shouted at him to give it back.

Rowland looked back over his shoulder and saw Milton was sporting a black eye. "What have you been doing?" he asked.

"A minor altercation," Milton replied, waving off the question.

"Milt found himself in disagreement with some of the local lads," Clyde cut in. "One of them decided to make a point on his face."

Milton sniffed indignantly. "Don't mean to slag off your hometown, Rowly, but the place is full of misinformed rednecks!"

"What on earth were you brawling about?"

"Milt decided to educate the locals on the principles of Communism," Clyde replied, recalling the moment with a grin.

"Whatever for?"

"Because the good people of Yass have no idea what they're talking about." Milton adjusted his cravat. "It irritated me. They seem to think the Communists are responsible for everything, including the drought!"

"So you decided to give a lecture?"

"Yes."

Edna laughed. "You should have been there, Rowly. It was really funny—until they hit him... and then Clyde had to rescue him."

Rowland smiled. "Well, try to keep your head down from now on," he warned. "People out here don't seem to be all that rational when it comes to Communists."

As they drove out to Oaklea, Milton and Clyde saw fit to sing drinking songs at the top of their lungs. Between the engine's roar and their hearty voices, they arrived at the property in a manner that announced itself. Ernest ran down the steps and Kate came out to greet them.

Edna was again taken by the homestead. "My goodness, Rowly, it's so huge!"

Rowland looked round. "I suppose it is." He'd never really thought about it. Rowland made the appropriate introductions, hoping his friends would not frighten his sister-in-law unduly. Hers was a polite and quiet world, in which the modern-living flappers were spoken of only with a note of scandal.

Kate was, of course, gracious, if a little nervous. Edna decided to make a friend of her, and soon the two were chatting without any distance. The party became relaxed. Clyde refused to let Ernest be banished to the kitchen to eat, and pulled the boy onto his knee for the meal. Rowland was not surprised. Clyde was from a large family. He had left his parents' home as soon as he was able, not because he didn't love them, but because there were too many mouths to feed. Without him, there was a little more for his younger brothers and sisters. It was not an uncommon story; many boys had been forced into early independence in the supposedly "roaring twenties." For a lot of people, the hardship began long before the markets crashed.

Edna was at her charming best. She talked to Kate about the Red Cross, listened to tales about young Ernest and showed more than polite interest in the remodelling of Oaklea. Even her vowels became more rounded and her manners more genteel. She ate petitely and said "Goodness me!" quite often. The men who lived with her found it all rather amusing, but said nothing, as it seemed to make their hostess more comfortable.

It was while they were taking tea in the parlour that Elisabeth Sinclair made her entrance.

Kate glanced anxiously at Rowland.

"Aubrey, where have you been? I told you not to go out there." Elisabeth's voice shook slightly.

Rowland didn't flinch. He kissed his mother's cheek and settled her in an armchair, before he introduced his friends. He didn't bother to introduce himself.

Elisabeth seemed delighted to meet new people and enquired of each how they knew Aubrey.

Rowland had never mentioned the peculiarities of his mother's memory outside the family. Clyde and Milton took it in their stride, appearing not to notice. Edna was flustered, calling him both "Aubrey" and "Rowly," and then deciding not to refer to him at all, to avoid the problem. While the older Mrs. Sinclair was cordial and seemed quite cheered by the company of "Aubrey's friends," Kate fluttered about nervously with a teapot.

It was late in the afternoon when Edna asked after the sheep. So far, she hadn't seen a single animal on the grounds.

"They're in the paddocks, Ed," Rowland replied. "We don't keep them at the house."

"Goodness no!" said Kate. "Wil would be inconsolable if they came near his roses!"

"I'll drive you out to see some before I take you back, if you like." Rowland checked his watch. "Though they've not long been shorn; they'll look somewhat pathetic."

Keen to experience the real countryside, and to escape the discomfiture of the parlour, Edna stood enthusiastically.

"You're not going are you, Aubrey?" Elisabeth was panicked again.

Rowland squeezed her hand gently. "I'm not going far, Mother. You should have a rest now. I'll be back before supper."

◇◇◇

"How long has your mother...?" Edna began as soon as they were in the car.

Milton frowned. "Ed, shut up."

"It's fine," Rowland said quietly. "It's been a few years now—since I came back from abroad."

"Rowly, I'm so sorry," Edna said, distressed for him. "It must be awful."

"More awkward than awful." He turned over the engine. "My mother's always been a bit emotionally fragile. Aubrey's death was more than she could take and then, when my father died..."

Edna rested her head on his shoulder as he drove. "Still, I'm sorry."

Rowland didn't respond. As he said, it was awkward.

He drove them out along the road that branched from the driveway to the house. The borders of the homestead paddock defined by the stark change from green to scorched yellow. Still, the paddocks were not short of feed. To Edna's delight, Rowland found a mob of sheep that had lambed late. Clyde climbed through the fence and chased after a ewe, catching it quickly and expertly so that Edna could hold her lamb.

"I worked on a property, roustabouting, for a while," Clyde tried to catch his breath, releasing the bleating sheep while Rowland handed her leggy offspring to Edna. He jiggled the top wire of the fence. "This is a bit loose, Rowly. I could restrain it for you…"

Rowland laughed. "Sixty-two men work on Oaklea, Clyde. I'm sure someone will get round to it."

Edna held the lamb, burying her face in the springy, oily softness of its short fleece, pondering how she could reproduce the texture in clay. She had been contemplating a rural series since they started their drive out here. Unlike Rowland, Edna never made sketches. Her sculptures drew on feelings and sensation rather than visually accurate form. She let the lamb go and, as it sprang back to its mother, she closed her eyes and memorised the sense of its energy.

The gentlemen she lived with waited patiently until she'd committed all she needed to memory and opened her eyes once again.

"What's that, Rowly?" Edna pointed to a massive building, surrounded by yards, in the middle of the paddock surrounded.

"That's the shearing shed. The wool clip's been in for about a month so there's nothing in there now."

"Can we look inside?"

"Yes, if you wish, but it's not that interesting." Rowland led the way to the great shed and stopped to allow Edna to enter first. The smell of lanolin was heavy in the heat. The wooden boards and beams had been impregnated and darkened by the natural oil after years of exposure to fleece.

Rowland pointed out the pens and shearing stands and showed Edna where the wool classers would do their work. Clyde was fascinated by the motor housed in a large side room.

"That's the lister." Rowland watched as his friend tugged at the belts and pulleys. "It mostly runs the stands, though Wil's had a line run out to the battery house so he can listen to the wireless of an evening."

"You could power Sydney with this," Clyde said in awed admiration.

"Wil does have a tendency to over-engineer," Rowland agreed. He returned to Edna. "The bales are put into the wool room so they can be moved easily onto the stage when the trucks pull up." He pointed to the large sliding doors, beyond which was the stage.

"Do you put all the wool in crates?" Edna asked.

"Crates? No, they're baled."

"Oh, what are these then?" Edna jumped up beside two large wooden crates.

"I don't know, machinery maybe. Wil was talking about getting another engine so he could run more stands; this would be the most sensible place to deliver things like that, I guess."

"They're pianos." Milton read the stamp on the closest crate. "Beale's pianos."

"Really?" Rowland approached and saw that Milton was right. "That's odd."

"Why?" asked Edna. Two pianos seemed a bit excessive, but having seen the grandeur of the estate, it was not extraordinary that they would find space for more than one.

"Well, because there are already two pianos at

Oaklea," Rowland replied. "And since Aubrey died, nobody really plays." He looked at the crates. The events and revelations of the past days had made him suspicious. He looked around for something with which to force open the lid. In the end, he found a box of tools stowed near one of the shearing stands. He rummaged through and brought out a large flat-headed screwdriver.

"What are you doing?" Clyde climbed onto the stage behind him.

"I'm going to open it." He began to pry at the edges of the crate.

"Why?"

"Don't know. Just wondering why Wil wants a piano in every room." With a little effort, and the occasional swallowed profanity, he managed to lever off the lid.

He pulled aside the straw packing. "Bloody oath." He gazed at the contents in disbelief. Milton and Clyde peered over his shoulder and Edna stood on tiptoe. The crate was packed to the top with guns.

Milton exhaled a whistle. "Could have a hell of a sing-a-long with these."

Chapter Fifteen

Pull Lang's Nose

Senator Hardy Talks Big

YASS, Monday

"It would give me great pleasure to go to Macquarie Street and pull Lang out by the nose," said Senator Hardy, addressing a meeting of farmers.

He added that trades-unionism and city capitalism was not going to help the country man in the least.

The Canberra Times, January 12, 1932

Rowland tapped the nails back in with the handle of the screwdriver.

Clyde looked at him. "Clearly, your brother's

serious about this secret army thing. Is he planning to march on Parliament?"

Rowland shook his head. "No…they're just stockpiling to halt the advance of the Red Army. Wil must think Stalin has his eye on Yass."

Milton sniggered, but even he was unnerved.

"Shouldn't we do something?" Edna asked tentatively, aware that his brother's involvement put Rowland in a very unpalatable position.

"I'll talk to Wil." Rowland glanced at Milton. "Don't get into any more fights," he advised. "They're probably all carrying guns."

"Wonderful." Clyde shook his head. "The countryside is teeming with Fascist lunatics, all armed to the teeth."

"People out here have always had guns"— Rowland spoke more casually than he felt—"mostly, they shoot rabbits."

Milton's brow arched. "So they've been practising."

They walked to the car, in a mood that was decidedly subdued, and Rowland drove them straight back to the Royal. He shook Milton's hand as they parted. "Remember, try not to be noticed until we can get out of here."

"Don't worry." Milton winked. "I'll be good."

Rowland smiled. "Just try being quiet."

The Sinclair brothers spent the following morning at the offices of Kent, Beswick and Associates. There were papers to sign to settle their uncle's substantial estate. Rowland was content to allow Wilfred to make the decisions, despite his growing doubts as to his brother's judgment in other respects. Indeed, even as the learned gentlemen talked and advised, Rowland's mind drifted back to the rifles packed in the piano crates. It was difficult to fathom what Wilfred could be thinking. He wondered if the Old Guard was dangerous. For some reason he found that hard to believe, regardless of the arsenal in the shearing shed.

Having signed whatever was put in front of him, Rowland followed his brother out into the main street. They were to attend a lecture of some sort, sponsored by the local Graziers' Association. Rowland trailed unenthusiastically behind as Wilfred walked briskly toward the Soldiers' Memorial Hall, wondering all the time what had made him agree to spend the next hour stuck in a disquisition about the marvels of the wool clip. Still, he hoped, it might give him the opportunity to speak to his brother about the guns, though he had no idea what he could possibly say to make Wilfred see sense. Nothing he'd said, thus far, had had any impact whatsoever. Short of setting the shearing shed on fire, there was nothing Rowland could think of to get rid of the weapons himself. He pondered if it was illegal to have so many guns—he wasn't sure.

The main street had become densely crowded in the time they had been at the solicitors'—there were hundreds of men gathering near the Hall's entrance. Rowland began to pay attention. Surely sheep and fodder couldn't be this exciting.

Wilfred led the way through the press of bodies, many in the crowd stepping back to allow them to pass.

They stopped outside the two-storey hall building. No expense had been spared in the construction of the memorial, raised in honour of the district's fallen and returned soldiers. It was a large building, but not so large it would hold the crowd already gathered in the street outside it. Rowland could now see the men on the freestone balcony above the columned entrance. He assumed they were waiting to speak. There was an unmistakable air of anticipation.

A soloist, a baritone, opened the proceedings with "God Save the King." Rowland scanned the gathering—an excessive, but respectable, congregation of the middle and upper classes. Many kept their jackets on despite the oppressive heat in the January sun. They sang the anthem with something akin to religious fervour, as they clutched their hats over their hearts.

The Mayor of the Yass Shire stepped forward to introduce the speakers, the first being a local of sorts, Harold McWilliamson. He spoke of the plight of rural New South Wales labouring under the weight of its Socialist government, the insanity of the Lang Plan and the economic disaster it would wreak. By the time he sat down again, the crowd was ringing vocal in support of McWilliamson's indictment of the Premier. Rowland watched, keenly observant, eye and mind recording faces and figures, movement and manner. He reached inside his jacket for his notebook. Wilfred's eye caught him and a warning jerk of his head stayed Rowland's hand.

The mayor introduced the second speaker, Senator-elect Charles Hardy Jr. of Wagga Wagga. Rowland was immediately alert to the name: it had been mentioned in the library, when the Old Guard met at Oaklea. It seemed Wilfred was still trying to recruit him.

Charles Hardy was a handsome man in his early thirties, whose strong smiling face appealed to men and women alike. His suit and hair were well cut, and his eyes, piercing. He stepped forward with the relish of a natural orator and he began. The crowd, already warmed to his message, became a chorus of concurrence as he launched his attack on Communism.

Suddenly, unexpectedly, a dissident emerged. The challenger pushed in from the back. He wore no tie and pinned prominently to his lapel was a large Soviet badge, clearly visible in its red and yellow. Rowland was both surprised and intrigued. So, this was one of the mysterious Communists that his brother believed were lurking around every corner.

The crowd surged against the radical, but then Hardy called for calm. He engaged the man in debate. What ensued was an extraordinary exchange between the leader of the Riverina Movement and a man who expressed all of the classically attributed sentiments of a Socialist intent on a workers' revolution. Still, Hardy persisted with his impassioned rhetoric, appealing to the man's sense of patriotism and country. In the end, the Communist tore off his badge, threw it to the ground and stomped upon it, in a public declaration of political conversion. Hardy welcomed him to the congregation of right thinking men and the hall broke into applause, as one more soul was brought back to the path of loyalist righteousness.

Rowland was dumbfounded. He leant over to Wilfred.

"Who is that? Is he a local?" He motioned toward the man who was a Communist no more.

Wilfred rolled his eyes. "You'll find he's attached to the O'Brien Publicity Company," he replied under his breath.

"What?"

"Let's just say he's been to a number of Hardy's rallies—that badge of his has been trodden on a few times now."

Rowland laughed out loud, but sobered quickly under Wilfred's glare. It appeared that though Wilfred did not applaud the pantomime, he had no intention of decrying it either.

With the erstwhile Communist now firmly in his support, Charles Hardy addressed the street again. He proclaimed himself an unashamed Fascist. "There are perilous signs, my friends, that the constitutional government of New South Wales is on the cusp of collapse, leaving us in a state of national emergency." Hardy paused dramatically, waiting till the silence was absolute and every ear strained for his next words. "The Premier's financial misrule, with hundreds of thousands of unemployed primed for an upheaval of social disorder, makes chaos a likelihood, far more than a possibility!"

The crowd responded on cue with shouts of horror and agreement. "If this calamity occurs, my friends, the Riverina Province Council will be ready to undertake immediate self-government!"

"What's the Riverina Province Council?" Rowland asked Wilfred.

"The need for a provisional government is a sad reality, Rowly." Wilfred didn't take his eyes away from Hardy. "Charles Hardy is not the only man to see it. It's simply a matter of time before Lang's administration collapses."

"You're all mad," Rowland muttered. Wilfred chose not to reply.

Hardy continued, berating the "worst elements of the community" who, clothed as workers, were trying to set up a Soviet state on the pattern of Russia. He explained that in such dire circumstances the Movement had to be prepared, indeed was prepared, to defend the country and install the Province Council to govern the Riverina. It appeared clear to Rowland that Hardy was styling himself as some kind of dictator of the region. The crowd was with the senator. There were shouts for immediate action. Hardy was living up to his title as the "Cromwell of the Riverina."

Hardy leaned over the balcony and pointed at a man who had just called of action. "By all that is good and holy, you are right!" He slammed his fist on the stone balustrade. "It is time those godless Red terrorists knew the wrath of right thinking men! It is time they knew they are not wanted here, that we will not tolerate them among our wives and daughters."

The roar that ripped down the street was deafening.

"Let every Communist traitor be on notice," Hardy declared. "You have till midday to leave the patriotic district of Yass!"

The crowd cheered. Someone began a chorus of "For He's a Jolly Good Fellow" and soon five-hundred-odd men sang it with one voice. Hardy looked down from the balcony, a messiah before his people.

Rowland thought the ultimatum presumptuous, considering Hardy was not from Yass, but it was just rhetoric. Even so, it would be wise if his friends headed back to Sydney soon…very soon.

"Come on." Wilfred grabbed Rowland's arm and jostled him through the throng toward the building. He ushered his brother inside, past the vestibule where Aubrey Sinclair's name was inscribed in marble, and up the staircase to the second floor. Hardy was still on the balcony. Wilfred spoke to someone from the Graziers' Association, who stepped out to fetch the leader of the Riverina Movement. It was several minutes before Hardy tore himself away from his crowd to come inside.

"Sinclair! Good to see you." He took Wilfred's hand between both of his.

"Charles," said Wilfred warmly, "I see your election to the national parliament hasn't stemmed the flow of men to the Movement. To the contrary." He glanced out of the window at the men now lining up outside to join Hardy's cause.

"New South Wales is still in the hands of Lang." Hardy looked down proudly at the new recruits. "Precarious times need stout-hearted men."

The clock in the post office tower struck twelve, the chimes barely audible over the still-cheering crowd.

Just as Wilfred introduced Rowland, Harold McWilliamson approached with two other members of the Graziers' Association, and joined the conversation. As usual, Rowland attempted to remain politely neutral.

Presently, Wilfred pulled Hardy aside leaving Rowland in the company of the graziers, who were still railing about the scourge of Jack Lang. They occasionally looked to Rowland for a grunt of agreement, but otherwise he was not called to participate to any great extent. His attention was in any case drawn to Wilfred and Hardy. The pair spoke earnestly, but he could not catch what they were saying. He could see the increasing tension in Wilfred's neck. The discussion was becoming strained, and then Wilfred's voice raised enough for Rowland to overhear "Campbell." Hardy responded calmly, but he seemed resolute. Wilfred was clearly annoyed.

Quite suddenly, Wil turned on his heels, leaving Hardy standing there, and motioned to Rowland to follow him down the stairs.

"What was all that about?"

"The Riverina Movement is full of good men, many of them ours," Wilfred responded curtly. "But Hardy is making alliances with Campbell, and Campbell is as dangerous as the bloody Communists."

"Oh." It occurred to Rowland that perhaps these good men were confused as to which secret Fascist army they belonged, but he decided against voicing this.

As they walked out, Rowland noticed that the crowd had, in large part, dispersed or moved on. "Looks like everyone went home to check their sheds for Communists."

From behind them came a laugh. The brothers turned. It was McWilliamson. "They didn't need to go that far, son. Apparently some Red blew in from the city." He glanced at his pocket watch. "It's twenty past twelve."

Rowland stared at him, horrified. Surely he

could not be serious. Surely Hardy could not have been serious.

"The boys went to get him from the Royal about a quarter of an hour ago." McWilliamson smiled, his moustache bristling as he inhaled the patriotic atmosphere of the street with gusto.

Rowland began to run but Wilfred grabbed his arm and pulled him back.

"Let me go, Wil!" He wondered if Wilfred's conversation with Hardy had been orchestrated to keep him occupied, while a mob went after Milton.

Wilfred pushed him back toward the Hall. "Rowly, you are not getting involved in this. Your friend made himself a target."

Rowland swore, furious and dismayed. He tried to break away from his brother, but some of the graziers stepped in to bar his way and hold him still. Wilfred remained calm. "There's nothing you can do, Rowly. You saw how many men were here before."

"Where the hell are the police?" Rowland demanded. "What happened to the King's laws you're so keen on defending?"

"What do you expect two constables to do against five hundred angry citizens?" Wilfred returned. "You're staying out of this, Rowly."

"They'll kill him!"

"No, they won't—he'll just get what he deserves."

McWilliamson laughed again. "Doubt the Red mongrel's seen service. The feathers may quite suit him."

Rowland felt sick, panicked. He tried another tack. "Wil, I'm your brother. Don't do this to me."

Wilfred regarded him intently. He checked his pocket watch. "Let him go," he instructed. To Rowland he said, "Get the other two and go back to Sydney now—I'll have your things sent on."

"And Milt…?"

"When the mob's finished with him, I'll have him taken back to Sydney, quietly."

Rowland wondered why Wilfred thought he'd be satisfied with that. Perhaps his brother really did think him a coward. He shook his arms free of the graziers and ran toward the Royal.

The establishment was barricaded shut. Rowland hammered and demanded entry. Who the hell tarred and feathered people? It was the thirties, for God's sake. Where would one even get hold of boiling tar?

The hotelier poked his head out of an upper window and recognised Rowland. He signalled him to come to the back. Rowland did so quickly. Yass appeared to have become a frontier town in the space of a single morning.

He entered through the kitchen. The hotel-keeper, obviously nervous, muttered something about having done all he could. Rowland nodded, glad the man had showed the good sense to close the hotel. Edna was in the office, seated. She wore no hat, and her hair was dishevelled. She was silently sobbing. Clyde sat beside her, holding a wet towel to his face, his white shirt spattered with blood.

Edna looked up as Rowland entered and threw herself into his arms. "Oh God, Rowly, they've taken Milt!"

Rowland held her, but he spoke to Clyde. "I know. Are you all right? Do you know where they took him?"

Clyde took the towel away from his face. One eye was blackened and his nose was swollen and bloody. He shook his head. "There was a heap of them…on some kind of Communist hunt." He stood up. "They said something about tarring and feathering him." Clyde's temper flared. "Apparently that's not illegal, not out here!"

"They're going to kill him," wept Edna.

The hotelier, who had been in the room behind Rowland all this time, spoke up. "I wouldn't worry about it too much, Miss," he said. "The boys talk about tarring and feathering, but nobody ever remembers to bring the tar or the feathers. And it's not as easy as that anyway, is it?

Tar cools so quickly…it's not as if you can carry a bucket of hot tar around with you to pour over a man…"

Rowland was alarmed by the man's detailed knowledge of vigilante reprisals. Edna just became more distraught.

"Look!" Rowland struggled to think calmly. "Where would they have taken him?"

The proprietor rubbed the grizzled stubble on his chin. "To the shire boundary, most likely, but I reckon they'll stay near the river—that way they can throw him in."

"Where exactly?" asked Rowland, his mouth grim. It was obvious now that this had happened before, and the innkeeper was beginning to try his patience.

The proprietor of the Yass Royal caught his tone, and gave him vague directions to the place he thought would be the most suitable site for a Communist eviction.

"Right." Rowland headed for the door. "Clyde, are you all right to go?"

Clyde tossed the towel onto the desk. "I'm fine. Let's go get Milt."

"Ed, you should probably stay here…" Rowland began. It was a futile attempt. The sculptress would have none of it.

"You're not leaving me here, Rowly. These

people are mad—what if they come back?" She glanced at the proprietor and whispered. "Do you seriously trust him to protect me?"

Rowland gave in—Edna had a point. "Okay, you two wait at the back door and I'll bring the car around. There's still a fair mob out the front." He turned to the hotelier. "I assume you've alerted the police?"

The man reddened and looked at his shoes. Clearly he hadn't. Rowland tried to keep his temper. "Once we leave, I presume you will immediately make the authorities aware of the situation."

"Yes, of course, Mr. Sinclair."

Rowland ran out the rear door and back to where he had parked. Despite the antagonism in the centre, the Mercedes was exactly as and where he had left her. A wry relief. This was the country after all—kidnapping was one thing, but property, even a German motorcar, was respected.

Clyde and Edna emerged from the hotel as he pulled up directly outside the back door and, after they piled in, Edna told Rowland more fully what had happened. They had stayed inside—taking care as Rowland had asked—when twenty or so men stormed the hotel and dragged Milton away. Clyde had gone to his aid, but no one else had helped them. "Do you think they'll hurt him?"

"No," he said, more confidently than he felt.

"Not on purpose, anyway. Hopefully they're not organised enough to have tar and feathers on hand."

"What is wrong with these people?" Edna was both terrified and disgusted.

Rowland kept his eyes on the road. "He'll be all right, Ed."

"Rowly," Clyde leant toward him, "Milt can't swim."

Rowland did not reply, just gritted his teeth and engaged the supercharger again.

As they approached the shire boundary, the wide expanse of the Murrumbidgee River came into view. Rowland cursed—there were hundreds of men by the bank. Periodic cheers indicated that someone was giving a speech. Rowland drove the car as close as he could. Again he tried to talk Edna into remaining behind, and again she refused, adamant that she was safer with him and Clyde. In the end they got out and, keeping Edna between them, pushed their way into the centre of the crowd.

"What the hell are we going to do?" Clyde was at a loss.

Rowland shook his head. He had no idea. Milton was being restrained by four men, while another stood upon a tree stump and rallied the crowd against the Communist traitor in their midst. Nearby burned a campfire over which was hung what Rowland assumed was cauldron of tar.

For his part, Milton looked more contemptuous than anything else.

"Righto." Rowland glanced at Edna, wishing he had insisted that she stay behind. He could not see this becoming anything but ugly.

The trio moved toward the fire, huddled close, shielding Edna as much as possible. The crowd was focussed on Milton. One man waved a set of shears. "Let's cut the dingo's hair," he yelled. Of course, the crowd roared.

Rowland saw his chance. He bent down and, seizing one of the longer branches protruding from the flames, he used it to topple the cauldron onto its side. As the sticky black liquid spilled onto the coals and the dirt, someone tackled Rowland. Edna screamed and Clyde joined the fray. The crowd pressed in dangerously.

"Good on you, Rowly," Milton was defiant.

When Rowland was released from the dirt, he and Clyde were beside Milton, and the mob leaders were arguing about how to deal with both the loss of the tar and the additional Communists. Edna was ignored. This was a business for men.

The same baritone from the town rally began to sing "God Save the King." As before, the mob removed their hats and joined him. At the precise point when the anthem called for the monarch's long reign, Milton's captors lifted him bodily and hurled him into the water. Clyde struggled to get to his friend's aid. Rowland, who knew the river, was less frantic. Milton stood up in the waist deep water, covered in mud and swearing furiously just as the chorus became loud enough to drown him out.

The blood of the mob was high but Milton was not going quietly. He began to sing "The Red Flag," off-key, but as stridently as the others were singing their anthem.

Men waded in and dragged him back to shore. The outraged crowd was not going to be satisfied with a mere dunking, and Rowland had thwarted their intention to tar and feather Milton. Suggestions were shouted.

"Give them all a bloody good hiding!"

"I say shoot them."

"Don't be stupid—that's Rowland Sinclair."

"We'll shoot the others—we'll horsewhip Sinclair."

"A rich Red is still a Red."

Milton fell into silence. This was getting very dangerous.

A gunshot cracked the air. Instantaneously it quelled the mob. The sounds of engines and horns were now audible and the crowd parted as several motorcars and farm trucks approached in billows of dust. The Rolls-Royce Phantom stopped just in front of the smoking campfire, the tar only feet from its tyres.

Wilfred Sinclair stepped out.

Chapter Sixteen

Wilfred glowered. He was a man who did not even think to doubt his authority over everyone present. "What's going on here, Jessop?" He singled out one of the mob leaders.

"Just showing these Reds how we deal with their kind out here, Mr. Sinclair."

"I think you mean the Red, Jessop." Wilfred turned his eyes to the dripping Milton, whose head had been roughly shorn of its long tresses. "I believe you have made your point."

"We're not finished."

"I believe you are."

"Rowland Sinclair is a bloody Red lover."

The words of anger spat from one of the men who was restraining Rowland. The crowd rumbled its assent.

Wilfred's eyes flashed. "Weatherall, isn't it? You'll meet many Reds when you join the ranks of the unemployed."

Weatherall let Rowland go and stepped back. He didn't work on Oaklea, but then, Wilfred Sinclair did have that kind of power. "I didn't mean it, Mr. Sinclair…"

"You would all be well advised to leave my brother to me. Rowly, come here."

Rowland looked at his remaining captors, and they too dropped their hold of him. He stepped forward, but unsurely. He might have escaped the wrath of this mob, but Wilfred looked furious enough to shoot him. The vigilantes watched as Wilfred's livid blue Sinclair eyes locked the rebellious gaze of his brother's. "Leave," he said.

"I'm not going alone."

Wilfred motioned toward Milton and Clyde and they, too, were released. "We don't want them here, anyway. Now go, all of you."

Rowland nodded. He grabbed Edna's hand and Wilfred walked with them to the car. The crowd stood back, their certainty in their cause undermined by the presence of Wilfred Sinclair. Wilfred waited until the engine kicked over before he leant toward Rowland and whispered, "You wait for me at the Gunning Cemetery. Now, for God's sake, go!"

Rowland said nothing…Wilfred was beginning to scare him.

Gunning was a small, unremarkable settlement,

more a hub for the surrounding farms than a centre in its own right. The main street was deserted when they drove in, a couple of carts and an Oldsmobile parked by the post office. Rowland wondered whether all the good men of Gunning had gone to hear Charles Hardy speaking in Yass. They stopped only to refuel the Mercedes, and then drove out to the cemetery, parking under the shade of a large plane tree.

"Are you sure you want to wait, Rowly?" Clyde was worried. "We could just head straight home to Sydney. Wilfred looked pretty wild."

"I'm not afraid of Wil," Rowland rubbed the dust off the mascot of his car with the sleeve of his jacket.

"Perhaps you should be."

"Bugger Wil! Bugger him and his flaming lynch mob!" Milton shouted, taking off his once-cream jacket, now caked in fine Murrumbidgee mud.

"Don't be stupid, Milt," Edna snapped. "If it wasn't for Wilfred, they might have shot the three of you. Why can't you just learn to keep your mouth shut?"

"Last I heard we lived in a democracy." Milton snarled back at her. "No one expects Campbell or his Fascist cronies to keep their mouths shut, so why should we?"

"Because you might have got Rowly and Clyde killed. Don't you care about that?"

Before Milton could argue further, Wilfred's black Rolls-Royce pulled up, and he stepped out. Rowland could see McWilliamson and Maguire still inside the car.

Wilfred tipped his hat to Edna. "Miss Higgins."

"Mr. Sinclair." Edna looked at him openly, sincerely. "Thank you."

He nodded slightly. "Unnecessary. Rowly come with me." He turned and walked into the cemetery. Rowland followed.

Wilfred took them far enough to afford some level of privacy and then he turned on his brother, delivering a furious tirade as they stood among the headstones of Gunning's deceased. "You would do bloody well to remember that if the Communists get their way, we will lose everything and your arty hangers-on won't have any Woodlands House or Sinclair fortune to sponge on. You've always been irresponsible, Rowly—spoiled. Everything's been handed to you, and yet you will do nothing to hold on to it. You don't know the meaning of sacrifice. In your selfish headlong pursuit of your own pleasure, you're determined to undo what has been achieved by better men!"

Wilfred stepped closer, his voice shaking with

unmitigated anger. "What the blazes do I have to do to get through to you?"

Rowland had taken Wilfred's dressing down in stony silence; but by now his own fury had grown to match his brother's. "Go to hell, Wil. If you want to play tin soldiers, carry on, but don't expect me to sit calmly by."

Wilfred hit him, hard, and Rowland fell back against a headstone, too surprised to react.

Wilfred, too, seemed startled by his own action, and then embarrassed. He was not a man normally given to impulse, whatever the provocation. He offered Rowland his hand and helped him to his feet.

"Rowly," he said, "you're my brother, but I have responsibilities to more than just you. I can't do what I need to if you're running around making me look like a fool."

Rowland wiped the blood from his lip. "Milt's a mate, Wil. You didn't really expect me to just leave him, did you?"

Wilfred took off his bifocals and polished them with a handkerchief. "I suppose not." He looked up. "You'll have to go now. You can't come back here—for a long time, I imagine—though I don't suppose that will distress you greatly. It will be hard on Mother, though."

That reproach stung. "Look, maybe I could..."

Wilfred shook his head. "Just get in that… motorcar and go back to Sydney. I'll sort things out here. If I can." He met Rowland's eye. "Stay out of this, Rowly. Do you hear me? If you can't stand with me, at least don't stand against me. I wouldn't want to have to shoot you."

Rowland hoped his brother was joking, but there was no smile in Wilfred's words.

"I'll have your things put on the train," Wilfred continued as they began to walk back to the cars.

Rowland nodded. "Thank you, Wil."

Wilfred sighed. "You can thank me by staying out of trouble." They returned to the plane tree and, with no further farewell, Wilfred's Rolls soon pulled away.

Rowland sat under the tree and rubbed his face. Edna stooped down, and inspected the cut on his lip. Impulsively, she kissed the top of his head. "Don't let Wilfred worry you, Rowly," she said. "He'll get over it."

She left him to resume her squabbling with Milton.

Clyde sat down and snorted impatiently toward Edna and the poet. He and Rowland had often sat through the heated arguments between the two. Milton and Edna had known each other since they were children, and they bickered like brother and sister.

"Not the best day, Rowly."

"I don't know. Milt finally got a haircut."

Clyde laughed. "I guess it was worth it then." He got up. "Come on, mate, we better check the car to make sure we're good for the trip back." Rowland stood and opened the bonnet. Clyde busied himself checking oil and water. Among his long list of past occupations, Clyde Watson Jones had worked at a motor mechanic's garage. He knew what he was doing, and Rowland was happy to leave him to it. Instead he leant against the grill watching Edna and Milton. Clyde looked up and caught the direction of Rowland's gaze. He regarded him sympathetically. The Sinclairs had more money than God, yet the poor bastard was still in love with Edna. Clyde shook his head. They'd all been in love with Edna at some point, but loving her was like looking at the sun—it would send you blind in the end.

He closed the bonnet and stood next to Rowland. "You know, Rowly, Ed's never going to be a Kate."

Rowland smiled. He was well aware that both Milton and Clyde knew of the torch he carried for the sculptress. "And why would I want her to turn into my brother's wife?"

Clyde shrugged. "You know what I mean, Rowly."

"Yes, I do," he said. He was not defensive. There was no point. "Ed's fine just as she is."

Chapter Seventeen

NEW GUARD
SENT TO FIRE FRONT

Fire Fighters Annoyed

SYDNEY, Friday

A contingent of the New Guard left for Cuan Downs, where the bushfire is raging on a front of 50 miles.

A meeting of the unemployed and local bushfire volunteers called by the Mayor last night carried a resolution: "We view with disgust and contempt the action of the New Guard in sending a contingent to Cobar well after locals were good enough to give their labour to the small men on the land to put out bush fires."

The Sydney Morning Herald,
January 15, 1932

Rowland slammed the heavy oak door of Wood-lands House shut. He pulled off his jacket, tossing it fiercely at the coat stand in the tiled vestibule. He missed, but did not stop to retrieve it from the floor, storming instead into the main drawing room as he loosened his tie.

Milton looked up from behind a hand of cards. "Oh, it's you, Rowly…with all the banging I thought it must have been Ed."

Rowland stood at Milton's shoulder, and said to Clyde, "He's bluffing. He hasn't got a thing."

Milton grinned and twisted round to wink at Rowland, undermining any trust Clyde may have had in the surly revelation. As they continued to play their hand, Rowland dropped himself into an armchair.

"Rightyo, Rowly." Clyde dealt him into the next hand. "What's wrong?"

Rowland pulled himself up and moved over to the card table. "That man—Biscuit without the 's'—he's a damned idiot!"

Rowland had spent the morning trying to get some movement on the investigation of his uncle's murder. Inspector Bicuit had scoffed off Rowland's speculation about the "dark ghosts."

"The blithering fool is still convinced that Mrs. Donelly somehow masterminded murder to get hold of some valuable knickknack or other—he's going harass the poor old thing into her grave!"

"Want a drink?" Clive rose and went to the sideboard.

Rowland shook his head.

"Scotch." Milton checked Clyde's cards as soon as the painter had turned to pour.

Rowland carried on fuming. "The worst thing is that by the time the inspector realises what a colossal fool he is, it will be too late to find out who really killed my uncle! It's probably too late already."

"You told him Paddy was sure his attackers were New Guard, didn't you?" asked Clyde.

"He said the paranoid ramblings of a known Communist had to be viewed with suspicion." Rowland threw down a card in disgust. "Warned me not to associate with such elements…Condescending bloody pratt!"

"So, what are we going to do?" Milton asked expectantly.

"Us?" Clyde looked up. "What the hell can we do?"

"Well, if Bicuit won't uncover the culprit," Milton replied, "we'll have to."

"Don't be daft!"

"This won't be the first crime solved by informed amateurs."

"Oh, for pity's sake," muttered Clyde.

"We need to look more closely into the New Guard," Milton went on, his cards temporarily forgotten.

"Rowly, tell the man he's an idiot."

Rowland looked carefully at Milton, but said nothing.

"Oh, my God!" Clyde groaned. "Not you, too!"

"I'm not saying he's not an idiot," Rowland said slowly. "Obviously he is…but if we could find something to get Bicuit interested…"

Clyde dropped his forehead onto the table and moaned.

Milton raised a finger. "I am stung by the splendour of a sudden thought."

"Coincidentally, so was Robert Browning," Rowland noted.

"We need to get close to the New Guard." The poet didn't drop his finger.

"So why don't you join?" Clyde scowled.

"Not a bad idea," Milton stood to grab a newspaper from the sideboard. "But I've got a better one." He opened the paper, found the page he sought, and dropped it onto the table.

Rowland picked up the paper and held it so Clyde could see it too. "What are we supposed to be looking at, Milt?"

"The article on Buckmaster."

"Buckmaster?" Both Rowland and Clyde were perplexed. They skimmed the article: Ernest Buckmaster, the Victorian artist, was painting Sir William Irvine for the Archibald Prize. According to the article, Sir William was "honoured and thrilled" to be asked to sit for an artist of such reputation.

"Still have no idea what you're talking about," Clyde said flatly.

Milton sighed. "Stay with me, fellas." He sat back at the card table. "We're trying to show our friend without the 's' that there's a connection between Mrs. Donelly's dark ghosts and the New Guard, right?"

Rowland nodded. Clyde refused to give the poet any sort of encouragement.

"We know from what Paddy tells us that the New Guard has some kind of special unit that dresses up and assaults Communists."—Clyde remained unmoved, but Rowland was listening— "One has to assume they adopt this crazy getup because anonymity is so important to them that they are willing to look ridiculous…so finding out who exactly they are, might be difficult…even from the inside."

"Are you ever going to get to the point?" Clyde's fingers drummed an irritated rhythm on the table.

"My point is," Milton replied, "that to find out more about these blokes in black sheets and hoods, we need to get close to men a little further up the ranks."

Now Rowland was getting a little impatient. "So, precisely what has Buckmaster and the Archibald Prize got to do with that?"

"Nothing to do with Buckmaster." Milton smirked. "But everything to do with the Archibald. To find out what the New Guard's up to—and why they killed your uncle—you go straight to Eric Campbell, the commander-in-chief." He pushed the paper back toward Rowland. "Get him to sit for you…for an Archibald portrait."

Rowland whistled and rocked back in his chair as he considered Milton's proposition. Maybe the poet was right. Rowland had painted enough portraits to know that the artist often found himself cast as the sitter's friend, confidante, and confessor by virtue of his attention and his brush.

Clyde spoke first. "Assuming that Campbell even knows what happened to Rowly's uncle, don't you reckon he might be a bit suspicious if a second Rowland bloody Sinclair waltzes up and offers to paint his portrait?"

Milton shrugged. "Just use another name… he's never met you, has he?"

Rowland shook his head.

"Use Clyde's name," Milton suggested. "Then you could have Lady McKenzie as a referee. Or maybe her dog."

"You're not seriously considering it, Rowly? Are you?" Clyde was anxious.

"Campbell does seem eager to get his picture in the paper," Rowland said tentatively. "He probably wouldn't mind having his portrait painted as a distinguished Australian."

"That's my boy!" Milton slapped him on the back.

"Rowly, these people are dangerous," Clyde warned. "We've seen what they or their ilk can do…"

"What could happen?" Milton brushed off the concern. "It's not as if Rowly can't paint…The New Guard's a bit paranoid, but who's going to doubt a fresh-faced, up-and-coming artist?"

"The arts community hasn't exactly embraced the right wing," Clyde persisted. "Campbell will be suspicious."

"Which is exactly why Rowly will be all the more appealing in his three-piece suits. Campbell won't believe his fascist luck!"

Clyde turned to Rowland who had been conspicuously silent. Rowland shrugged. "It's worth a shot."

Milton hooted in triumph.

"Come on, Clyde," Rowland tried to talk him round. "Campbell could be interesting to paint."

"Interesting? He'll be bloody brilliant!" said Milton . "How many chances do you get to paint the crackpot head of an extremist political movement…in this country, anyway?"

"Actually, there seem to be a few around," Rowland admitted ruefully, thinking back to the meeting at Oaklea and to Charles Hardy.

"Look Clyde, if I can get the name of even one of the cowards responsible," his body tensed as his mind moved to how his uncle had died, "Bicuit will have to act."

Clyde sighed. "What if I go instead of you?"

"Thank you, old boy, but no." Rowland smiled. "I know this is a ludicrous plan, and I'm not going to drag you into it."

"Even in one of Rowly's suits, you'd look a bit like a bushie," Milton looked critically at Clyde's weathered face and his calloused hands.

"I don't have to call myself Clyde Watson Jones," Rowland added. "Any name will do."

Milton disagreed. "Clyde's been hung in a couple of galleries…If anyone checks, they'll find that Watson Jones is indeed the name of a local artist. Campbell isn't the kind of bloke to let himself be painted by a total unknown."

"But anyone who knows Clyde will know that I'm not him."

"And which of Clyde's mates is going to be mixing with the New Guard, exactly? The better question is whether any of their snooty upper-class members will recognise Rowland Sinclair?"

Rowland shrugged. "If they do, it won't matter what I'm calling myself, I suppose." He rubbed his chin thoughtfully. "I think I could risk it…I'm just going to paint Campbell, not contest his leadership."

"Use my name, Rowly. It's the least I owe you." Clyde said finally. "You know, we can't be sure that the New Guard had anything to do with what happened to your uncle."

"At the moment, it's all we've got to go on… I've got to find out, one way or another."

"So, how are you going to go about this?" Clyde resigned himself to what he considered an absurd plan.

"I'll need to borrow that letter of recommendation Lady McKenzie wrote, and any others you may have. I'll fabricate a few more, and then I'll just present myself at his offices."

"What do you mean 'fabricate a few more'?"

"I'll draft some letters from satisfied clients of appropriate social standing."

"That's a bit risky, isn't it? What if Campbell runs into the actual person?"

"Well, somewhat conveniently, the well-heeled have a tendency to take long tours of the continent, even in these times," Rowland replied. "I'll just forge the names of people I know to be abroad."

Clyde raised his eyes to the ceiling. "No wonder you Sinclairs are so bloody wealthy; you're common criminals."

"Hardly common," Rowland stood to search for a pen and stationery. He found what he was looking for and handed them to Milton. "Right, Milt, let's see you actually write something for once."

"That's deeply offensive, Rowly," Milton replied. "I'm a poet, a sculptor of words…not your flaming secretary." Even so, he proceeded to write effusive acclamations of the talent and professionalism of the artist Clyde Watson Jones using a variety of scripts, and signed with the names that Rowland supplied.

"You're a little bit too good at this," Clyde observed as he looked over the finished products. "You'd both better hope that Bicuit doesn't just decide to arrest us all for forgery and fraud."

Milton laughed. "Rowly can afford the best lawyers in town."

"Yes, I believe Campbell's one of them," Rowland noted as he folded one of Milton's letters of reference into an envelope. "I say, where's Ed?" he asked, realising that he had not seen her all day.

"Penrith."

"What's she doing out there?" Penrith was about thirty miles west of Sydney.

"A moving picture," Milton replied.

"Surely, she can see the film closer to home." Rowland gathered the forged letters into a neat pile. "Why go all the way to Penrith?"

"She's not seeing one," Milton corrected. "She's got herself a part in one—*On Our Selection*, it's called. She met some bloke called Ken who's the director or something."

"*On Our Selection?*"

"Ed says it's going to have sound."

"Apparently that eliminates the need for actors," Clyde said dryly. Rowland pulled in the cards and reshuffled the deck. They played several hands before they heard Edna talking to someone at the door. No one got up. They found it unnecessary to be introduced to every one of the sculptress' many gentlemen callers. But they played on silently, so they could eavesdrop on her farewell.

The other voice belonged, as they expected, to a young man whom Edna was calling "Kenny."

"You were brilliant, Edna darling," he told her repeatedly. "You'll be a smash!"

When she finally stepped into the drawing room, she was smiling broadly and her eyes sparkled with unbridled zest. She wore a long-bodied navy dress, which was now a little out of style, but in which she was nevertheless captivating.

"Well if it isn't Burwood's answer to Greta Garbo." Milton was the first to look up.

Edna glowed. "I'm going to be an actress."

"You had a good time, then?" murmured Rowland.

"Oh, Rowly, it was exhilarating. Inspired, actually." She threw herself dramatically onto the settee. "It's so amazing to be a part of someone's vision, part of the artwork itself."

"Really." Rowland was slightly put out. "New experience, was it?"

"For pity's sake, Ed!" Milton snorted. "It's a comedy about country hicks—hardly Shakespeare—I can tell you it doesn't quite count as art."

"It's a reflection of Australia's rural heritage told in the great comic tradition," Edna replied loftily. She smiled jumping up with an enthusiasm she could barely contain. "It was so exciting."

"Who did you play?" Clyde tried to show an interest.

"I was a member of the crowd in two scenes."

They laughed at her, rather rudely. She ignored them. Edna found promise and glory in the most surprising places—it was in her nature. Already, she could see a film career complementing the success she would eventually achieve through her sculptures. And when she so decided, nothing would diminish her joy.

After they grew tired of poking fun at her cinematic dreams, Rowland brought her into their plans. Edna shared none of Clyde's trepidation and approved of the scheme wholeheartedly.

"We should find out what the Boo Guard is up to," she said adamantly. "That trek of theirs out to Cobar…the one in the papers…was about a lot more than putting out fires. I'm sure of it."

"I suspect the only thing they put out was a few local noses," Clyde muttered.

The Guard's heroic charge to Cobar to fight bushfires had received substantial coverage in the press. Depending on the newspaper's leaning, it was either applauded as an act of altruism, or ridiculed as a grandiose display. Edna inclined at least to the latter view, though she strongly suspected the operation had a more sinister purpose.

"I'm not planning on becoming a general spy," Rowland pointed out before Edna's expectations became too militant.

"Why not?" she demanded. "Someone's got

to keep an eye on Campbell. Remember what happened in Yass."

"That wasn't Campbell's doing," Rowland reminded her, but Edna was not interested in the demarcation lines between the various far-Right movements.

"So how exactly are you going to become the court artist of the great Colonel Campbell?"

"I'll ring for an appointment," Rowland said casually. "Then, I'll just go see him with some of my work."

"Not the picture of Edna." Clyde smiled apologetically at the sculptress.

"Use the returned soldiers series you did last year," Milton suggested. "Campbell's a veteran."

Clyde nodded. "You'll have to change the signature."

Rowland walked over to rummage through the stacks of canvases piled against the studio wall. He found what he was looking for, and pulled out a number of portraits. They had been removed from their stretchers and so he lay them flat on the card table. Rowland had drawn the original sketches at the Anzac Day commemorations and, working from both his notebook and his memory, had painted the portraits in oil.

He took up his brush and carefully changed the signature to the name of Clyde Watson Jones.

"This might be the best work I've ever done." Clyde observed the wistful intensity Rowland had captured in a soldier's eyes as he leant against a post, watching a child place a wreath at the cenotaph.

"As long as I'm not destroying your reputation—as a painter, anyway." Rowland moved on to the next canvas.

He and Clyde painted in very different styles, but their professional admiration was mutual. Clyde's portraits were traditional and startlingly true to life. He posed his sitters in sparse settings and told their stories through the turn of their heads, the set of their shoulders, and the placement of their hands. And of course, unlike his friend, Clyde could paint trees. If anything, his landscapes surpassed his portrait work.

Rowland's brushwork was less defined; his work was more influenced by the Impressionist school and the tonal approach of the artistic renegade, Max Meldrum. His backgrounds were rich with context and movement. Rowland's particular talent was an ability to capture moments, fleeting expressions of the soul of which even his subject was often not aware, until they saw the completed work.

Once the reassignation of Rowland Sinclair's paintings was done, Milton poured everyone a drink and raised his glass. "To bringing the Fascists to justice."

"I just want to find out why my uncle was killed." Rowland refused to participate in the toast. "I don't really care about Campbell's politics."

"Sure you do," Milton insisted, "you just don't want to be a class traitor. We understand."

Rowland was startled. "What do you mean, you understand?"

"Wealth is seductive," Milton said, pouring himself another glass of Rowland's fifteen-year-old Scotch.

"We haven't all got Milt's stoic resistance to the finer things in life," Clyde interrupted dryly.

"Don't worry, Rowly." Edna's eyes were merry. "We don't expect you to lead the revolution."

For some reason, that irritated Rowland—not that he even remotely wanted to lead a workers' revolution, or any other sort, for that matter. But it rankled him to be dismissed, particularly by Edna.

She laughed when she saw his scowl. "Don't be silly, Rowly." She rubbed his arm fondly. "You are who you are. Given your gilded background, you could be insufferable, but you're not. I wouldn't have you be anything else."

Rowland gazed at her intently for a moment. Finally he reached over and placed the deck of cards before her. "Just deal," he said.

Chapter Eighteen

Deport Agitators

Eric Campbell's Advice

SYDNEY, Sunday

Eric Campbell, leader of the New Guard, told a meeting last night that while the United States deported 1,000 Communist agitators every week, Australia tolerated the presence of these alien dregs, and permitted them to indulge in their widespread propaganda to ferment unrest and create strikes.

He added: "The real voice of Australia is becoming more insistent—'Deport all foreign Communist agitators'."

The Canberra Times, January 18, 1932

Rowland climbed out of the taxi at Turramurra.

Though the New Guard kept offices in the city, Campbell had asked him to his home instead. Separated from both Woollahra and the city centre by Sydney's famous harbour, Turramurra wasn't in the most convenient of locations. Rowland had caught a ferry from Watsons Bay, then a train, and finally the motorcab to the architecturally pleasing Ku-ring-gai Close. Here the well-to-do lived on the fringes of parklands, with room for their horses.

He looked toward Boongala. Even here amid the opulent surroundings of Turramurra, the mansion stood out. Many considered it ostentatious, demanding more attention than was polite or tasteful among the discreetly grand houses of Sydney's Northern Shore.

Rowland hesitated at the porch, debating whether a painter should approach the front door, or go in search of a tradesman's entrance. In the end, he decided to knock and enquire—he wouldn't expect Campbell to answer his own door anyway.

The servant who greeted him wore a starched face to match her uniform. She led him into a small sitting room, indicating that Campbell was on the phone, but would be ready to receive him shortly.

The room was furnished in a traditional masculine style: chesterfield couches, oak paneling, and deep-piled maroon rugs. Gilded frames on the curlicued mantle held pictures of the world's most prominent Fascist leaders, most notably Mussolini. The bookshelves were crammed with leather-bound volumes and beside each chair was a Bakelite smoking stand. An Airedale terrier reclined in front of the hearth, padded over to him. Rowland patted the hound while he waited. He'd always been fond of dogs. He wondered absently, why he didn't own one himself.

A short while later, the door to Campbell's office opened, and Eric Campbell stepped out to greet the man who he thought was Clyde Watson Jones. The Airedale sprang up enthusiastically on sight of his master.

Campbell ruffled the dog's ears. "Down now, Paddy."

Rowland offered his hand. "Colonel Campbell, it's an honour to meet you, sir."

Campbell cut an impressive figure. He was a tall man of about forty years, broad-shouldered and immaculately dressed in a double-breasted suit of fashionably light fabric. He was bald on top with the remaining fringe cropped short in military style. His face was surprisingly soft, his smile broad under a small brush-like moustache. He addressed Rowland as "Clyde," though he did not invite the artist to call him "Eric."

Rowland made his case while Campbell flicked through the samples of his work. Milton had guessed correctly: the retired Colonel was clearly moved by the portraits.

"Last year's ANZAC Day commemorations?"

"Yes, sir."

"I was there, you know, with my regiment. I didn't notice you." Campbell studied the men marching in the background of one of the paintings.

"I'm an artist, Colonel Campbell," Rowland replied. "To record history, it's best that I'm not part of it."

Campbell seemed satisfied, but remained cautious. "I'm a busy man, Clyde." He unrolled the last canvas. "It is not in my nature to spend hours sitting still."

"That's not really the way I work, sir," Rowland assured him. "I prefer to observe my subjects as they go about their business; it gives the portrait context and atmosphere. The actual 'sitting still' time is minimal."

Campbell shuffled through the references Rowland had handed to him.

"Would you be so good as to wait here?" he asked as he took the documents into his office.

Rowland waited, nervous that any moment Campbell would spring out from behind a door screaming, "You're Rowland Sinclair!" He had no doubt that Campbell was checking his references. Surely he would be undone.

It was several minutes before Campbell emerged again. "It seems that tours abroad are all the rage this season." The colonel chuckled. "But Lady McKenzie couldn't sing your praises more highly. My contact at the Arts Council tells me that you have been exhibiting in a number of the smaller galleries very commendably…it is his opinion you could be an established name in a few years."

"He's most kind." Rowland made a mental note to relay the praise to Clyde. "The chance to paint a man of your standing would certainly be a step in that direction."

Campbell nodded. "Quite. I am inclined to accept your proposition, Clyde."

Rowland was more than relieved; he was almost incredulous, but replied calmly, "Thank you, sir."

"So how do you propose to run this?" Campbell looked again through the portraits.

"With your permission, sir, and at your convenience," Rowland started slowly, making it up as he went, "I'd accompany you on occasion, making sketches and getting to know what makes you Eric Campbell, Commander-in-Chief of the New Guard." Rowland tried to sound as though the title impressed him. "It will allow me to decide the best composition—how you are posed, what symbols I include in the background, that sort of thing. Only then do I paint."

"My correct title is General Officer, Commanding," Campbell informed him. "An Archibald Prize would be another affirmation of the movement's importance. You realise that, don't you Clyde?"

"I can't guarantee I'll win, sir." Rowland's response was a little alarmed. He hadn't actually thought as far as submitting the portrait.

Campbell took the nervousness in Rowland's voice as modesty. "I don't see why you wouldn't win, my boy," he said. "Of course, those trustees will have to get over their obsession with the Victorians."

The comment jolted Rowland, taking him back to his final rendezvous with his uncle when the old man had said something similar. His resolve to continue strengthened. "I'll try to do you justice, Colonel Campbell."

Without asking, Campbell poured them both whiskies and sat back in one of his generous leather armchairs. "Tell me, Clyde," he asked, "where did you go to school?"

Rowland smiled. He knew he'd have to deny the old school tie of Kings Parramatta. "Fort Street," he replied, aware the select government school would place him within a wide range of classes. "I travelled abroad, painting for awhile," he offered vaguely.

"I take it you're too young to have seen service?" Campbell was probing, almost sympathetic.

Service seemed to be a passport of trust in the circles of returned soldiers. "I had a brother who served in France," Rowland said carefully. He didn't like using Aubrey's memory in this way, but there was no point to what he was doing unless Campbell came to trust him.

"Had?"

"He didn't return."

Campbell nodded, warming visibly. It wasn't as good as actual service, but family sacrifice did evidence some sort of proximate patriotism.

"Tell me, Clyde," Campbell said, "with whom does a young man like you align himself in times like these?"

Rowland was prepared for this, but it was still uncomfortable. Considering the current tensions, and Campbell's position, it was only to be expected he would want to know the politics of those who wished to associate with him. "The Joneses are all Country Party men," he replied. "I'm from Yass originally."

Campbell seemed well pleased with this. Lady McKenzie had mentioned that the young portrait painter was a rural lad, a further confirmation to

Campbell that he could be trusted. "I'm from the country myself," he said. "Stout men, the men of the land. Not so susceptible to malcontent and insubordination as the labour forces in the city."

Rowland forced a nod. Campbell was nobody's fool, but it appeared that luck was with him.

With Campbell's permission, Rowland took out his notebook and sketched while they conversed. Campbell was surprisingly affable company. He seemed to accept, and be completely comfortable with, the focus of attention. He spoke of his wartime service and showed Rowland his Distinguished Service Order. Rowland looked curiously at the medal. He knew Wilfred had one too, but he had never seen it. Wilfred never spoke of his actual service, and never used his military title.

"Of course, we went as diffident boys," Campbell told him. "And we came back as men used to more responsibility and leadership than those who had remained—and were now our superiors—could ever have imagined."

Rowland's mind slipped momentarily, to the secret and not so secret armies that seemed to be arising in every quarter. Perhaps it was the natural tendency of Diggers accustomed to military command.

Campbell went on to denounce the Socialist agitators he saw as a mortal threat to both democracy and decency. He became more animated, his voice more strident

When their drinks and appointed time were finished, Campbell said, "I'm afraid I will be quite busy for the rest of the month." His face creased into self-satisfied smile. "I have to attend the Police Central Court where I'm charged with praising the Premier's bull."

Rowland knew what he meant. Eric Campbell had been arrested and charged with insulting Premier Jack Lang. Apparently he had publicly claimed to prefer Lang's bull, Ebenezer, to the Premier himself, for the simple reason that there was no law against shooting a bull. His arrest was probably an overreaction, and had in fact played straight into his hands. Now, Campbell could portray himself as a political martyr, a victim of a partisan police force.

"With your permission, sir," Rowland said, returning the smile, "I might attend."

"You may have trouble finding a seat, Clyde." Campbell winked broadly, as he showed his guest to the door. "Come early."

And so, Rowland Sinclair took leave of the man who had pledged to defend New South Wales from the insidious force of the "Red Wreckers." Paddy the Airedale followed them out and Rowland paused to make a fuss of the hound before he left. He liked dogs.

Edna, Milton, and the real Clyde were waiting anxiously back at Woodlands House to hear the news.

"So?" asked Edna as soon as he was in the door.

"He has a nice dog." Rowland dropped his hat on the couch. "An Airedale. We should get a dog. I don't know why I've never bought one…"

Edna slapped his shoulder. "Don't be an idiot, Rowly. What happened?"

"No, really…I want a dog."

"Are you painting our favourite Fascist, or not?" asked Milton.

"It wasn't all that hard to convince him." Rowland told them the details of the meeting, and his discussion with Campbell.

Milton let out a low whistle. "I can't believe it worked."

"What do you mean, you can't believe it worked?" Rowland demanded. "It was your flaming idea!"

"Yes, it was," Milton preened. "Damn clever, too."

"So, what now?" asked Clyde.

"He's agreed to allow me to follow him around, making sketches and so on, while he's being statesman, patriot, and hero of the people.

And he's got this trial next week. I thought I'd go and have a look."

"You can't," said Milton flatly.

"Why not?"

"Use your head, Rowly." Milton shook his own. "You've been dealing with the police as Rowland Sinclair. You can't just wander into the Police Central Court as someone else. What if you encounter Campbell and Bicuit at the same time? The game will be up. What on earth are you thinking, comrade?"

Rowland hadn't thought of that. "Right, so I'm a hopeless spy."

Clyde's face was a map of worry. "Actually, there's no guarantee that some New Guardsman won't recognise you at some point. But since you're determined to do this, I guess there isn't a lot we can do about that."

Rowland was not about to admit to being concerned. "It's my name that's well known," he said, "not my face."

"Still," Clyde exhaled, "you've been recognised once, already…remember the bloke at the Domain?"

Rowland was thoughtful. Henry Alcott had recognised him, true, but Henry had been Aubrey's best friend. "You're right," he conceded. "There isn't much we can do about it. I'll just have to make sure I see the Guardsmen before they see me."

"I still don't like it," Clyde grumbled.

"You'd best let one of us know where you're going at all times." Milton's dark eyes narrowed. "You know, in case you disappear."

Rowland laughed. "They're not gangsters, Milt. I don't think I'll end up in the harbour."

For a moment, a heavy silence prevailed as they all remembered that it was the murder of the elder Rowland Sinclair that had brought them into this business in the first place. Nobody mentioned it.

"So, Ed," Milton said, changing the subject, "when do you get to play something other than furniture?"

"I'm not playing furniture." She lifted her head indignantly. "I'm a full member of the supporting cast. You can't go straight into leading roles."

Milton feigned outrage. "One would think being the director's girl would count for something!"

Off the set, Edna had become a regular fixture on Ken Hall's arm. When the director came round, he claimed he'd found a new star, whom he was determined to nurture. The men who lived with the said star tolerated him, as they did all her suitors, but they hoped this latest infatuation, with both Ken and his film, would not last long. No matter what Edna claimed, it was just not art.

Chapter Nineteen

NEW GUARD CASE

Campbell Fined £2

SYDNEY, Monday

At Central Summons Court, New Guard leader Colonel Eric Campbell, charged with using insulting words near a public street, was fined £2 with 8/- costs, and in default, imprisonment with hard labour for five days.

The Chief Stipendiary Magistrate (Mr. Laidlaw), giving reasons for his decision, said that Mr. Campbell had publicly referred to Mr. Lang as a "nasty tyrant and scoundrel", as a "buffoon" and as "the hated old man of the sea". He also compared Mr. Lang to a bull. According to the magistrate, at least some of the words Campbell used about the Premier were insulting.

The Argus, January 19, 1932

Campbell's trial for breaching the Vagrancy Act lasted five full days. He was represented by two eminent barristers, both King's Counsel. The distinguished silks dealt with the prosecution by attempting to indict Premier Jack Lang for misgovernment. The government prosecutor responded with equally vehement attacks on Campbell and the New Guard. It was, as Campbell had hoped, a highly publicised event, attracting crowds of media and the curious public. On the third day of the trial, Edna and Milton managed to find a seat in the public gallery and later reported on the day's verbal stoushes. As they told it, the law had never been so entertaining.

"That Lamb bloke," Milton said, referring to Campbell's lead counsel, "is a pompous old bugger; but he's funny. It was some production. "

"And Campbell?" asked Rowland.

"He didn't get a speaking part," replied Edna.

"But he carried on from the dock like the romantic lead." Milton puffed out his own chest and strutted in imitation. "I thought Ed was going to swoon."

Rowland turned to Edna, his brow raised, "Campbell? Really?"

She shrugged. "He's very charismatic."

"For a Fascist lunatic," Clyde said, putting his feet up on the couch.

"The magistrate had to wait while Campbell posed for photographs," Milton sniggered. "He did everything but actually take a bow. That man's got style. If he wasn't trying to deport me, I think I'd buy him a drink."

"As long as Rowly paid for it," Clyde added testily.

When the trial had run its course, Eric Campbell was convicted and fined the princely sum of two pounds. Political martyrdom had never come so cheaply.

It was not until the following week that Rowland again visited Boongala. This time, he carried only his notebook; he was simply there to make sketches. Campbell accepted it as some form of artistic research. In reality, it was the men in bizarre black hoods, not their leader, whom Rowland planned to scrutinise. Spending time with Campbell would allow him to "look around" the movement, without actually enlisting in it.

It was a Saturday, so the New Guard's Commander was not going into his offices at Campbell, Campbell and Campbell. Instead, the day was devoted to New Guard business, and it was for this reason he arranged for Rowland to accompany him. Eric Campbell liked to control the way in which he was depicted, whether by journalists, photographers, or now, painters. He was not impolitic enough to tell Rowland what to paint, but he could influence how the artist saw him—an important consideration when one was carving one's place in history.

Campbell welcomed him into his study and offered coffee. A wide expanse of a man with an overlarge mouth in a heavily jowled jaw was sitting outside the door in the anteroom. He held his cigarette with chunky fingers, which seemed far too thick to have ever rolled the slim stick. He stood as they entered, and Campbell introduced him to Rowland as Herbert Poynton. Apologising that he had to make some urgent calls, Campbell retreated into his office, leaving the two men in each other's company.

Poynton was a gregarious individual and not at all unfriendly. Campbell had apparently spoken well of Clyde Watson Jones, the painter who would immortalise, if not legitimise him on canvas.

"So Jonesy," said Poynton, "you don't mind if I call you Jonesy…? What do you think of our Colonel?"

Rowland sipped his coffee. "He is certainly a patriot."

Poynton nodded vigorously. "Of course, you've only just made his acquaintance." He sat back, exhaling a dense cloud of smoke. "The Colonel and I have been close for a while…he's come to rely on me, if you like, and, of course, I am honoured to be a man he can rely upon."

"You work closely with Colonel Campbell?" Rowland was both intrigued and a little repelled by the man.

"I look after his personal security," Poynton replied. "The Bolsheviks would pay dearly to procure his demise, and we are called on to travel a great deal to meetings and rallies. I have some experience with this sort of thing, but circumstances prevent me from speaking about it…Suffice to say, I spend a great deal of time with the Colonel and have the privilege of his confidence."

"Indeed." Rowland took the notebook from his breast pocket. "You don't mind if I draw while we chat? It's a professional habit, I'm afraid."

"Be my guest." Poynton straightened his back as best he could, and lifted his chin slightly.

"The New Guard seems a colossal organization." Rowland opened the conversation as he sketched Poynton with dark, heavy lines. "I guess the Colonel must be very busy. It's very generous of him to allow me so much time."

"He is busy…very little happens without his input, on some level at least. Of course, there are different branches and specialised forces within the New Guard, like there are in any army. They may have special tasks," Poynton tapped the side of his nose conspiratorially, "under the authority of particular officers. Regardless, we all know who leads us."

Rowland travelled with Campbell from Boongala to visit various divisional branches. At each stop, Campbell spoke stirringly of the Communist threat to like-minded crowds who did not need convincing, but who nevertheless appreciated the eloquent echo of their own convictions.

Rowland watched with interest, filling page after page of his notebook with studies, not of Campbell, but of the men who made up his army. Of course it was futile. The New Guard was at least fifty thousand strong, and he didn't have a clue who he was searching for. It occurred to him, then, that this plan of Milton's was somewhat half-baked.

Poynton stood by him at each meeting, hanging on Campbell's every word with a kind of obsequious pride, applauding each time with the same zeal. Rowland found Campbell's bodyguard fascinating. In the Colonel's presence, he was almost militaristic, at pains to be useful and unobtrusive. When Campbell was absent, however, Herbert Poynton liked to talk. Mainly of his own importance both within the movement and to Campbell. With a great deal of gratuitous nose-tapping, he alluded to special assignments that Campbell entrusted only to him.

Rowland suspected Poynton was exaggerating his own significance; but still, the bodyguard knew a lot. Already he had told Rowland of the factional tensions within the movement, the men among them suspected of being either Communist or police plants, and the attempted blackballing of aspiring Guardsmen by business competitors who had already enlisted. All this came between Campbell's speeches.

When Campbell took lunch with some of his General Council, Rowland and Poynton went instead to a nearby hotel where Rowland heard much about Poynton's own plans. The bodyguard saw a great future for himself in the new order that he was convinced would come.

"Tell me, Poynton," Rowland said when the man finally paused, "you seem like a man of action. It must be immensely frustrating to stand by while the Communists, protected by both the law and Lang, openly talk of revolution."

Poynton wiped the white beer froth from his upper lip with the back of his hand. He grinned knowingly. "As I said, Jonesy, we have special troops to deal with the bludgers. Of course, I can't talk about it, but let us just say the law and the Premier are notably absent when the New Guard deals with the worst of the Communists."

"The worst? Aren't they all bad?" Rowland couldn't believe what he was saying. He resisted laughing at the idiocy of his own words.

"Well, yes, I guess they are, mate." Poynton nodded. "But some need to be taught a lesson, as an example to the others."

Rowland tried to be nonchalant. "And the Colonel decides who needs to be educated in this way?"

"Now, that wouldn't be wise. Colonel Campbell is, after all, a solicitor, an officer of the courts." He laughed into his beer.

Once Campbell had rejoined them, they spent the rest of the afternoon at a New Guard Smoking Concert. The programme was pleasant, inoffensive, and, to Rowland, somewhat bland. But it was not for the songs and piano recitals that the men of the New Guard had gathered. The concerts were all-male affairs, during which politics was discussed in a vague cover of cigarette smoke.

The Colonel worked the room, a hero among his people. Rowland wondered, briefly, if Campbell's back was bruised with all the slapping. The idea of their leader's portrait being hung with the other distinguished subjects of the Archibald met with considerable approval; and they generally assumed that an artist perceptive enough to make such a selection would be one of their number.

Rowland recognised the odd face because he noticed and remembered faces, but they belonged to acquaintances remote enough not to identify him as Rowland Sinclair, even if he seemed somewhat familiar.

<>◇<>

"Goodness, Rowly, you reek," Edna said when he arrived home late that night.

"Smoking concert," he said with a grimace.

"So how was it?" Clyde, who smoked himself, was less critical. "Are you aglow with the reflected glory of the great man?"

"You might say that." Rowland loosened his tie.

Milton sat forward. "Learn anything?"

"The Communists are amassing an army," Rowland replied gravely. "Apparently we are in danger of becoming a Soviet colony. Parliament House is about to be painted red and I think the Labor Party has been stealing babies and drowning puppies."

"Did you find out anything about the men in hoods?" Milton pressed.

"Come on, Milt, I could hardly just walk in and ask 'Who killed Rowland Sinclair?'"

"I suppose you're right." The poet was clearly disappointed. "So what did you do all day?"

"Mainly, I followed him around to branch meetings. I talked more to his bodyguard than to Campbell."

Clyde snorted. "I told you. Ridiculous bloody plan…"

"I don't know." Rowland was thoughtful. "This man, Poynton—the bodyguard—he seems to know rather a lot about the movement, or at least he claims to." Rowland filled them in.

"Hmmm, that is interesting." Milton was on his feet pacing the room. "Do you think you could get him to tell you more?"

"If he knows more, I don't think it would be too difficult," Rowland removed his jacket. "He's a forthcoming sort of fellow. A bit of a braggart, really."

"I take it no one recognised you?" Clyde frowned. He was yet to be convinced that what Rowland was doing wasn't completely foolhardy.

"There were a couple of chaps I'd met ages ago." Rowland shrugged. "But they didn't look twice. Apparently, I'm entirely forgettable."

Clyde shook his head, not comforted by his friend's flippancy. "Have you thought about what you're going to do if someone does recognise you?"

"Not really. They're not assassins, Clyde. If

they were, Lang would be dead by now. If I get found out, it'll be more embarrassing than anything else." He laughed. "Of course, Wilfred might kill me if he hears…"

Clyde wouldn't be distracted. "If someone recognises you as Rowland Sinclair, what are you going to do?" he repeated.

Rowland rubbed the back of his neck. Clyde was obviously not going to let this go. "I'll just keep insisting I'm you," he said. "I'll say I've never heard of this Rowland Sinclair."

"That's it? Rowly, that's just…"

"Get them to telephone here," Milton interrupted, his face intense with a new idea. "Anyone who recognises you will know you live at Woodlands—the telephone exchange will put them through. When you're out with Campbell," and at this point Milton adopted a very British accent, "it will be I who is Rowland Sinclair, gentleman and all round good chap. I'll be here, smoking pipes and drinking brandy with all the other jolly good fellows…pip-pip and all that."

"I don't speak like that," Rowland protested.

"Of course you do," Milton said, lightly punching his shoulder. He became serious. "Look mate, the charade'll create enough doubt to get you out of there in one piece. At the very least, it will let us know you're in trouble and we'll come get you."

"Brilliant, that's just smashing, wot." Edna supported the idea enthusiastically and added her own parody of his accent.

Rowland thought this plan more ridiculous than anything else Milton had come up with. For one thing, he did not speak like that…God, nobody spoke like that. But he had nothing else to offer Clyde and hopefully he would never need to rely on the poet's preposterous impersonation. "Okay, I'll tell Mary to hand all my calls to you… I'm not sure how I'm going to explain this to her. Good enough, Clyde?"

"Not really." He sighed. "But I guess there's nothing I can do but wait until you get tired of being me."

"Afraid so."

"Have you actually drawn anything yet?" asked Edna.

Rowland reached inside his jacket for his notebook and tossed it to the sculptress. "Pages of Fascists-in-training." He watched her flick through the sketches. "I'm a bit worried about the portrait, to be honest."

"Why?"

"I can't really produce one, can I?"

"Why not?' Milton looked over Edna's shoulder. "You don't have to like someone to paint them. And the Archibald rules require subjects to be 'distinguished' not 'sane.'"

"Oh, that's not the problem," Rowland replied. "I can't even say I dislike Campbell—he's quite congenial as far as aspiring dictators go."

"So?"

"Well, I've got to sign his portrait as Clyde… it might get tricky with the Prize trustees."

"Hopefully, you'll find out what you need to and be out of there before we have to worry about that." Clyde pointed at his friend. "Honestly, Rowly, considering what you're doing, the trustees should be way down on your list of concerns!"

"Are we still going to the races tomorrow?" Edna tried to change the subject. Clyde worried too much.

"Of course." Rowland, too, was relieved to talk about something else. The picnic races at Bowral were a highlight of both the racing and social calendar.

"We'll have to get up early to catch the train," Milton moaned. He was not at his best in the mornings and he hated trains.

"Why the train?"

"You can hardly drive, Rowly. If you and your car are seen together, it'll all be over. Bowral will be full of the Fascist classes in racing attire."

Rowland cursed. Milton was right.

"Though of course there's no reason why the rest of us shouldn't take the car," Milton added, pleased with the realisation. "We could meet you there with the food and refreshments…save you struggling with the load on the train."

Rowland glared at him. He didn't like anyone else driving his car. "Fine!" He conceded eventually, grudgingly. "Take the blasted car. Just be jolly careful."

"I'll take the train with you, Rowly," Edna volunteered, feeling rather a bit sorry for him. "You'll look a bit tragic going to the races on your own." And so it was agreed. The conversation turned to their plans for the next day, and to the most recent issue of *Art in Australia*, which was devoted to the work of Thea Proctor. Edna and Rowland had both studied under Proctor at the Ashton school. She had introduced them to linocut printing and was one of the founding members of the Contemporary Group, formed to encourage young avant-garde artists. These days, many considered her work dangerously modern, but she was a particular hero of Edna's. The sculptress had been taken by the strength and simplicity of her work. In this way, the intrigues of the New Guard were for a time forgotten, as they discussed the revolutionary movements of the artistic world.

Chapter Twenty

Edna adjusted the angle of her hat, securing it in place with the pearl-encrusted hatpin that had been her mother's. That done, she pulled on her gloves and checked herself in the mirror, allowing the gentle folds of her skirt to swirl about her as she swayed from side to side to critique the fall. The dress was new, a stylish creation of palest pink which had cost her everything she'd earned for the last six months. The Bong Bong Picnic Races had been well-attended by Sydney society since their inception. It was not an event for which one dressed carelessly, regardless of one's social class.

It was still dark outside. Edna and Rowland were to catch the early train to Bowral in the Southern Highlands. A motorised cab waited in the driveway to take them into Central Station.

Finally satisfied with her reflection, Edna went down to the dining room where Mary Brown had organised a pre-dawn breakfast. Rowland was already there, talking to Clyde while he drank his coffee. He had managed to find a suit free of paint. It was custom-tailored from the best English fabric; but then all Rowland's suits were such, regardless of how he treated them. They looked up as Edna came in. She was, like many beautiful women, accustomed to the glances of men, and so she barely noticed the admiration in their eyes.

"You look pretty, Ed," Rowland said as he returned to his coffee.

"Do you really think so?" She smiled in a way that made it difficult for him to swallow naturally.

"No, he doesn't." Clyde buttered his toast. "Rowly's just abominably polite."

"The taxi's here." Edna reached over and grabbed the toast from Clyde's plate. "Where's Milt?"

"Still asleep. We won't need to leave for awhile."

Rowland sighed, thinking of his car in Milton's hands. "We'd better get going." He rose from the table. "Just make sure Milt doesn't wear anything too ridiculous."

Milton's extravagant sense of style risked becoming a degree too experimental at times. And Bowral was a measure more conservative than Sydney.

Clyde snorted. "I'll do what I can."

They arrived at Central in good time and took their seats in the first-class carriage. The train was full. Despite the Depression, the Bong Bong Picnic Races were still popular among those more insulated from the downturn. Perhaps, more so.

Edna chatted about the technical difficulties of casting her latest sculpture. It was the largest piece she'd ever attempted. Rowland sat opposite her in their compartment and sketched, murmuring sympathetically on occasion, but not really listening.

Eventually, the train pulled into Bowral station and they disembarked into a crush of elegantly dressed bodies. Rowland grabbed Edna's hand to ensure they wouldn't lose each other in the crowd walking to the track. Men in shabby, worn jackets surged forward to carry hampers and bags for the well-to-do racegoers, in return for change. Rowland and Edna had no bags, but he slipped some coins into the hand of a man wearing a Returned Soldier's badge on an otherwise threadbare lapel.

"You have a good day, sir." Rowland looked from the badge to the haunted hungry face before him. The man checked his palm—it was more than change. He met Rowland's eyes and nodded with the very last of his dignity.

Edna and Rowland moved on with the crowd. Despite the fact that it was February, the Highlands were mild and so the walk to the track was no great inconvenience.

They were caught in the bottleneck of

racegoers heading into the grounds when Rowland heard the friendly shout. "Clyde!"

At first he did not turn.

"I say, Clyde Watson Jones!"

Eric Campbell stepped out of a nearby car, smiling. He signalled for them to come over as he assisted his wife from the backseat of the sedan. A handsome woman, she wore the very latest cinch-waisted style, complemented with a fur stole that the weather did not warrant. Mrs. Campbell sported a fitted cap adorned with a spray of peacock feathers, teased and tortured beyond reason. Rowland noticed Poynton in the front seat, beside the chauffeur. The bodyguard acknowledged him with a nod.

"Well, hello, Clyde." Campbell extended his hand. "I didn't expect to see you here. You've met my wife, of course."

"Pleasure to see you again, Mrs. Campbell." Rowland hesitated. "May I introduce Miss Edna Higgins, my…"

"Fiancée," Edna entwined her arm intimately in his.

If Eric Campbell had not been so captivated by Edna, he might have noticed the startled look on Rowland's face. "Clyde, you didn't mention you were engaged."

"Didn't you?" Edna looked up at Rowland,

pouting. "Clyde, how could you? I've been telling simply everyone."

Rowland was lost for words.

"I'm sure it's just that I didn't give him the opportunity," Campbell said graciously.

They conversed for a while longer, though Rowland said very little. Edna was charming and delightful. She was good at that. After several minutes' chatting, Campbell invited Clyde and his fiancée to join them in the members' stand. Rowland declined, saying, quite truthfully, that they were meeting friends.

"Then you must come for cocktails tomorrow," said Mrs. Campbell. "Eric will be home, for once, and we're having a small drinks party." She turned to Rowland. "We must hear more about your work; we're all so looking forward to seeing your painting."

Rowland glanced at Edna. He hadn't actually started the painting. Edna accepted the invitation to cocktails enthusiastically, for them both, and they said goodbye.

"You're a lucky man, Clyde," Campbell whispered as he shook Rowland's hand.

"Apparently," Rowland replied.

They watched in silence as the Campbells walked toward the restricted members' grandstand. Herbert Poynton followed the couple discreetly.

"What the devil are you playing at, Ed?" Rowland asked, without turning to look at her.

"I'm making you look more respectable." Edna was unrepentant. "And helping you get close to Campbell; nobody invites single men to parties."

Rowland groaned.

"Come on, Rowly." She hooked her arm through his. "We've been invited to cocktails. There'll probably be all sorts of New Guard people there—I can help you."

"This is not a game, Ed."

Edna refused to be chastised. "All the more reason I should come along."

Rowland started into the race ground. "We'd better find Milt and Clyde and tell them what you've done."

It took some time to find Clyde and Milton among the crowds now gathered on the grassy surrounds of the track. Some had set up their parties beside their motorcars, others were locals who had walked to the track, or Sydneysiders who had travelled by train. Edna caught sight of them first, reclining on a picnic blanket, enjoying a drink as they each leant against opposite sides of the massive hamper. She waved and led Rowland toward them, weaving through the other picnickers.

"Milt, you look so handsome!" she declared as

the poet stood to greet them. He smiled and turned slowly, so she could get the full effect of his finery.

Rowland looked at him carefully. "Isn't that my suit?"

Milton held open the jacket, so that they could see the embroidered label of Rowland's Macquarie Street tailor. "I don't think you ever wore it so well though, Rowly."

"You told me to make sure he didn't look ridiculous." Clyde poured drinks for the new arrivals. "All his own clothes are ridiculous."

Rowland took a glass and sat on the blanket.

"The car ran well." Milton filled his glass. "Took us no time to get here."

"Where is she?" Rowland looked around for his beloved Mercedes.

"Flat tyre." Milton grimaced. "Had to leave her at the local mechanic's. She's a bit too conspicuous to bring here anyway."

"Don't worry, Rowly," Clyde noticed the trepidation on Rowland's face; there were many mechanics who still refused to work on German cars, even all this time after the Great War. "I spoke to the bloke—he's all right…"

Rowland decided to be reassured. Clyde knew more about mechanics than he did.

"How was the train?" Milton opened the hamper, in search of food.

"Splendid," Rowland replied, draining his glass in a single swig. "Ed and I had a great time, and now it seems we've got to get married."

"What?"

Edna rolled her eyes and explained.

To Rowland's chagrin, the news was not greeted with any sort of alarm. Indeed, Milton was miffed that it was Edna who'd insinuated her way into what he considered some grand caper. Even Clyde wasn't unduly concerned.

"Well, as long as Ed remembers to call you 'Clyde,' and not 'Rowly', she might actually be useful."

"Even if she does accidentally call you 'Rowly,' you could pass it off as one of those ridiculous pet names that couples insist upon," Milton suggested. "Ed can talk to the women. Surely, one or two know something about what their husbands are up to."

Rowland thought of Kate, who seemed to have no notion of Wilfred's secret manoeuvring. He shrugged. "Maybe...perhaps they prefer not to know."

"You'll have to behave yourself, Ed," Clyde lifted a plate of sandwiches out of the hamper. "You can't be flirting with every man in the room if you're supposed to be engaged to Rowly, I mean

Clyde. You'll find the imperial classes are a lot less understanding about that sort of thing."

"You'd be surprised," Rowland murmured.

"I don't flirt!" Edna's protest was vehement.

"Like hell," retorted Clyde.

Rowland smiled. Edna's eye-fluttering claims of innocence bordered on the absurd. The sculptress was a siren of myth—she bewitched men; she couldn't possibly be oblivious to the fact.

"Well, you needn't worry," she declared. "I'll be utterly devoted. The Boo Guard will think Rowly the luckiest man in the world."

"Rowly is the luckiest man in the world," Milton said casually. "It's Clyde Watson Jones who has to be convincing."

"Well, it's done now." Rowland put his hat back on. "We'll just have to go along with it and hope it doesn't end badly. So, have you placed any bets yet?'

"No, I'm skint again, so is Clyde," Milton replied. "There's a Depression, you know. We were tempted to wager your car on a filly called Painter's Fortune, but we thought that would upset you…"

"Come on," Rowland got to his feet. "Let's find a bookmaker…Who do you like, Clyde?"

"Peter Pan," Clyde replied as he handed the form guide to Edna. She, too, chose a horse and Rowland and Milton set off to place the bets. With

Rowland's money, of course. But that was not something that concerned any of them.

The rest of the day passed pleasantly, companionably, and with no further mention or thought of Eric Campbell and his earnest men. Milton's horse won the cup and Edna considered how she could capture the speed and grace of a galloping beast in bronze. Clyde and Rowland discussed the work of William Dobell, who had recently emerged as a force on the Australian art scene. Rowland deeply admired Dobell's unique style; Clyde was more reserved. The excellent contents of the hamper were consumed and at some point Milton fell asleep for an hour. And so the day was spent.

Rowland and Edna returned to Sydney by train. Rowland was inclined to risk driving his car back, but Milton was insistent that he could not be seen in the flamboyant Mercedes—particularly with the New Guard's Commander in attendance. Rowland suspected it was more to do with the fact that Milton liked driving his car. He could hardly blame him, and gave in.

The train trip back to the Central Station was a little more subdued than the one they had taken out in the morning. The racegoers were tired after the rigours of watching, cheering, and celebrating. Rowland sketched the slightly dishevelled parties who continued drinking in the dining car, while

Edna poured tea for them both. In quick, sharp lines, he caught the drooping feathers that had begun the day in pert protrusion from fashionable hats, the loosened ties, and the wisps of hair that had escaped carefully coiffed styles.

Edna raised the Campbells' cocktail party, musing over what she should wear. Rowland murmured something unintelligible.

"I should probably have a ring," she said looking at her hand. "Is it proper to announce your engagement without a ring?"

Rowland glanced up at her. She was not looking at him, having pulled off her glove to consider how the said ring would look on her hand. A day in the sun had brought out just a few freckles across her nose.

"I'll buy you any ring you want, Ed," he said quietly. "But then, you really would have to marry me."

Edna laughed. Her eyes caught his, and her expression softened. "Don't be stupid Rowly," she said gently. "There's no reason to go that far."

He returned to his notebook with a faint smile. It was not as if he expected anything else. "Don't say I didn't offer."

"I have my mother's ring," Edna continued, pouring milk into her cup. "I'll wear that. It's not extravagant—just the kind of ring an emerging artist would give his love."

"Uh huh. Sounds fine."

Edna watched him draw, his eyes deliberately glued to the page. She bit her lip, aware that she was just a breath, an unguarded moment away from falling in love with Rowland Sinclair. Sometimes when they were alone like this, her art and her plans seemed trivial, they receded, replaced completely by him alone. It frightened her. She could lose herself in him. Unconsciously she shook her head and pulled back. The Bertie Middletons of the world were a less dangerous distraction—she could love them when she had nothing important to do. But still.

Chapter Twenty-one

There was already quite a throng at Boongala when they arrived. Edna was noticeably quiet. She tugged at the beaded fringing of her favourite gown. The dress had taken her weeks to make and she delighted in wearing it still, although now it was a couple of years old. Styles had changed quite dramatically in the past few seasons. Waistlines had gone up, and hemlines down. The men she lived with assured her she looked fine. But then, they were men. In the circles in which she usually moved, being a couple of seasons behind the latest fashion rarely warranted notice. Especially now. But of course, people like the Campbells did not need to show that kind of restraint. They would be dressed beautifully.

Rowland fiddled absently with the sleeve of his black dinner jacket. He had only just noticed a streak of crimson paint on the cuff. He couldn't remember painting in his dinner suit, but he must have done so. It didn't really concern him. It wasn't too noticeable and he was, after all, a painter. He turned to Edna, noting the way she glanced at the society women who were entering the house ahead of them. Her eyes were large, mildly panicked. He was surprised. Surely Edna could not be uncertain about the way she looked. "Ready?"

She nodded.

Unexpectedly, it was Eric Campbell himself who welcomed them warmly at the front door. Their host took them through to the manicured gardens, which had been laid out for a most elegant occasion. Nancy Campbell received them graciously, and after a barely perceptible pause, complimented Edna on her attire. "My dear, what a sweet dress. I used to have one quite like it."

"Thank you, Mrs. Campbell. Your home is just lovely."

Eric Campbell took Rowland with him, leaving his wife to introduce Edna to the ladies.

"De Groot," Campbell summoned a slim, slightly built gentleman, "I want you to meet Clyde Watson Jones, who will win the Archibald this year with a portrait of yours truly. Clyde, this is Captain Francis De Groot."

"Indeed," De Groot responded in an accent that was distinctly Irish. He shook Rowland's hand.

"May I say, Mr. Watson Jones, you have timed the selection of your subject well."

Campbell laughed. "We shall see, Frank, we shall see."

Rowland chatted with De Groot as Eric Campbell moved among his other guests. De Groot was a softly spoken retired soldier, now manufacturing period furniture and dealing in antiques. While he did not say so explicitly, Rowland gathered he was quite highly positioned in the New Guard hierarchy. De Groot's admiration for Campbell was clear.

Over De Groot's shoulder, Rowland saw Edna holding court among the ladies. The sculptress seemed to have overcome her earlier self-consciousness, and simply sparkled. Rowland sipped his drink, and watched as she engaged those around her with her gentle wit. She was not really his, but he was quietly pleased that the other men in attendance thought she was.

De Groot regained Rowland's attention with a polite cough, introducing him to another guest, a younger man, John Dynon, who described himself as a glass merchant. There was something about the man's demeanour that Rowland found disquieting—a grating slyness in his manner. Dynon immediately moved the conversation to what he called the "Red Terror," and the need for decisive action to squash the threat. Even here, among fascist sympathisers, Rowland suspected Dynon's politics were extreme. Having assumed Rowland was a Guardsman, Dynon did not temper his comments, declaring that things would not be right until Campbell was installed as dictator of the state, and every Communist expelled, one way or another. Initially, Rowland laughed, sure the man was joking, but he sobered hastily when he heard De Groot's cautious approval of the sentiments.

"You must encounter a few Bolsheviks in your line of work." Dynon addressed Rowland. "Filthy vermin, so-called artists with a preference for red, don't you think?"

"I tend to keep to myself," Rowland was non-committal.

"They're everywhere, I expect," Dynon continued, with contempt. "It's important to be vigilant, to keep an eye on people." He and De Groot exchanged a look, laden with a meaning to which Rowland was not privy.

"Didn't see you at the races, John," said De Groot.

"Met the boys for cards." Dynon winked theatrically.

The conversation was becoming laboured as De Groot and Dynon continued their parallel coded exchange. Rowland muttered something about paying his fiancée some attention, and excused himself.

"Jonesy!"

Rowland turned to the generous face of Herbert Poynton. He shook the bodyguard's hand, mildly surprised to find him here, among the guests, as opposed to outside.

"Poynton, are you working or drinking?" he asked, raising his own glass.

"Both," Herbert Poynton grinned.

"Surely the Colonel is safe in his own home?"

Poynton took a long drag of his cigarette. "I see you've had the pleasure of meeting our Mr. Dynon." He exhaled.

"You're acquainted with him?" Rowland noted the distaste that tightened Poynton's fleshy lips.

"Arrogant, self-important bastard!" Poynton spat. "Don't get involved with him, Jonesy. That would be my advice."

"Why not?" asked Rowland, though he had no thought of getting involved with Dynon.

At first, Poynton said nothing, and then, "I can't really talk about it…but maybe I'll show you one day. I like you, Jonesy." The bodyguard slapped him on the back. "The Colonel needs men he can rely on…there are big things happening."

"And Mr. Dynon's involved in these big things?"

"He thinks he is," Poynton smirked. "He's made a couple of blunders lately—he's impatient, fires without looking, if you know what I mean." He pulled a cigarette case from inside his jacket, and offered one to Rowland, who declined. "The New Guard is like any army, Jonesy—mostly good loyal men; but occasionally an idiot appears in the ranks."

Rowland chatted with the bodyguard for a while. He didn't mind Poynton; he wasn't the sharpest tool in the shed, and his faith in Campbell was almost childlike, but he wasn't unpleasant. For some reason Poynton had taken to him, a fact which made him a little uncomfortable. He was not by nature deceitful, but he couldn't turn back now.

There were now a number of men in the circle around Edna. Rowland thought that he'd best go act like a possessive fiancé, and made his way toward her. He was intercepted, this time, by his host.

"Clyde, over here," Campbell said from across the room. "There are some chaps I want you to meet." He introduced 'Clyde' to the New Guard's zone commanders.

Rowland gathered that they were his lieutenants. He was unsure whether Campbell was trying to impress him with the men who followed his command, or impress those men with the prospect that his picture would be hung alongside other eminent Australians in the Archibald.

As they drank, the talk moved freely to matters of membership and organisation. It seemed that Campbell, too, had forgotten that the artist was not actually a member of his movement, and Rowland was careful not to remind him. He listened as the Guardsmen argued over what they called A- and B-class men. Apparently, the A's were the younger, more able-bodied members of the Guard, the B's those who had some technical qualification. Rowland concluded that the C-class men, who were also mentioned in passing, were the more feeble-bodied Fascists, relegated to administration and catering.

"As you can see, Clyde," Campbell, turned back to him, "the New Guard is in position—ready and able to act as the circumstances demand."

"You certainly have a formidable organisation at your disposal, sir." Rowland replied.

De Groot joined them. He had heard the last exchange. "You should bring the lad along to Belmore, Eric," he suggested. "We can't dismiss the kind of publicity the Archibald could give us—Belmore will give Jones here a real taste of how history will remember the New Guard." He put his hand companionably on Campbell's shoulder. "After all, old boy, we wouldn't want him to paint you pruning your bloody roses!"

Instantly, Rowland wanted to paint Campbell in exactly that way.

"That's not a bad idea, Frank." Campbell tapped the side of his glass as he considered the logistics. "Clyde, perhaps you could meet my ferry on the thirteenth…about midday? I'll take you from there, myself."

Rowland agreed, intrigued. He glanced toward Edna, who in turn was trying to catch his eye.

"I think we should let you return to your charming fiancée," Campbell laughed. "I daresay she's feeling somewhat neglected."

Rowland looked again as several young Guardsmen jostled to stand about her. "She doesn't look too lonely."

He slipped in next to Edna, who grabbed his arm and introduced him. Rowland could tell, by the how firmly her hand was pressing on his wrist, that she was excited. He wondered what she had discovered.

The evening gave them no opportunity to converse alone. An elegant buffet supper was served, and afterwards the party segregated in the usual manner with the ladies retiring to the parlour for coffee, and the gentlemen in the library with snifters of brandy and cigars. Rowland didn't smoke. He didn't consider it a wise habit when he spent so much of his time surrounded with oil-based paint and highly flammable thinners. He had known artists who had accidentally sent their studios up in flames.

The congregation of men was in good spirits. The New Guard was at the height of its power, and the men in the room were its leaders. Most were ex-servicemen, proud that they were serving their country again.

Rowland put his brandy on the mantel, and took out his notebook. He sketched Campbell moving among his faithful officers, the men who hoped to follow him into history. For the first time, he became interested in the man artistically. He was caught by the camaraderie, the sense of noble purpose in the room. And then Campbell broke the spell, speaking without circumspect of the groups of unemployed the New Guard had broken up in the past days, and the Communists who had been taught a well-deserved lesson. He reiterated his pledge that Premier Lang would not open the Harbour Bridge, that the New Guard would do whatever necessary to deny him that privilege.

His words were met with cheers and postulating, reminding Rowland that this was no mere meeting of a local Masonic Club. These were men looking for revolution. As the hooting got louder, his drawings became darker, more conspiratorial.

He felt a man's breath in his ear. "Rowland Sinclair." Jolted, Rowland faced his accuser.

Chapter Twenty-two

Unconsciously, Rowland's hand went to his side, over the scar hidden beneath his clothes. He knew the bearded face well: Maguire, who had sewn his wound that night at Oaklea, and who may well have fired the shot that caused it.

They were interrupted briefly as another Guardsman introduced himself to Clyde Watson Jones. Maguire said nothing until the man had gone. Rowland was almost too panicked to wonder why.

Maguire smiled. It was a surprising thing on a face which seemed chiselled out of severity itself. "I see you finally decided to stand up and be counted," he said quietly. "Must say, I'm surprised Wilfred didn't tell me he planted you here, too. Still," he looked Rowland up and down, "it makes sense, I suppose. I'm glad you haven't let your brother down again."

Maguire did not seem to expect a response; he certainly didn't wait for one. He simply walked away, leaving Rowland sweating, but safe, on the sharp edge of exposure.

Clyde Watson Jones and his fiancée disembarked the ferry at Circular Quay. They farewelled the many others of Campbell's guests who'd taken the same trip, and headed for the waiting line of taxicabs. Rowland noticed a Riley on the other side of the road, stopped with its engine idling, although its seats were full. As they walked past it, he recognised the man behind the wheel from the cocktail party. For some reason, Rowland felt wary. He climbed into a taxicab after Edna, and gave the driver her father's address in Burwood. Edna looked at him questioningly, but he grabbed her hand and brought a finger to his lips before she could say a word. For all he knew, the man driving their taxi was a Guardsman, too.

Though Edna and Rowland didn't talk a great deal on the journey, the driver seemed happy to fill the silence with news of his day. He was a little tedious but far from sinister. Rowland was beginning to think the paranoia of the Guardsmen had rubbed off on him, until he caught sight of the Riley he'd noticed earlier. Every so often, he turned and saw the vehicle following at a judicious distance. It stayed with them until they pulled up at the house where Edna had been raised, an unassuming brick cottage. They alighted and paid the driver, trying not to be obvious as they watched the car drive past and out of the street, apparently satisfied that Clyde Watson Jones was, as he claimed, a resident of Burwood.

"What was all that about?" asked Edna.

"I think they were checking up on us." Rowland removed his jacket and placed it around her shoulders. "I gather that spying is standard practice in the movement."

The lights came on in the house.

"We're going to have to go in now," Edna warned.

"That's all right," Rowland stepped aside so she could climb the steps first to the small front verandah. "I rather like your father; and it's not that late; not for him."

Selwin Higgins taught philosophy at the university. He had often told Rowland that he would have been an artist himself if he'd possessed even a modicum of talent, but was forced instead to content himself with academia. He had spent several years in France where he'd seduced an emerging artist away from her hopes of greatness into becoming his wife and Edna's mother. He spoke of it with regret, a kind of guilt that he had clipped his Marguerite's wings. As a consequence, he encouraged his daughter's commitment to her own freedom, an unusual position for a father.

"You'd better take off that ring," Rowland knocked on the door, "or your father will kill me."

Edna slipped her mother's ring into her purse. Rowland was right. Her father was determined that she not abandon her talent for any man. He would not idly allow her to do for some "young buck" what her mother had done for him.

Selwin opened the door with surprise. He was still a handsome man, identifiably bohemian, despite his advanced years. Even at this hour, he wore a black beret. Rowland was aware that Milton had always coveted that beret. Fortunately, he thought, Selwin was attached to it, too. "Darling! What are you doing here? And Rowly Sinclair! Come in, come in."

The Higgins' home was in the middle bracket of Burwood houses which varied from the merchant-built mansions of the last century to the more recent low-cost railway housing. Despite a population of almost twenty thousand, the place still had a rural feel—or what Sydneysiders considered rural, anyway.

Inside, the house was a mess. Books were stacked almost anywhere but on the bookshelves, creating precariously skewed towers around which they had to weave. Just about every square inch of wall space was hung with artwork, many by Edna's mother, and a few by the sculptress herself. Several of Edna's early works balanced on randomly positioned book plinths. It had been a while since anyone had dusted.

Selwin Higgins moved some papers and a large grey cat from the couch, and invited them to sit while he went scrummaging for tea in the kitchen.

"Well, where have you two been in your Sunday best?" he called out, pouring tea into mismatched cups.

"At a party at Eric Campbell's," Edna blurted before Rowland could stop her. Selwin came out of the kitchen with such an instant look of horror and betrayal that they had no choice but to tell him the whole story. He listened without a word.

When they'd finished, he took off his spectacles and polished them thoughtfully with his tie. "I must say, I'm glad it wasn't your politics that led you to Campbell." He shook his head. "That would have been intolerable…simply intolerable." He looked intently at Rowland. "Even so, isn't this game of yours dangerous?"

"Well, sir," Rowland tried to explain, "there's no need for Ed to accompany me again. I don't think I'm in any real danger, either—the New Guard seems to be more talk than anything else."

"Didn't you say your uncle was beaten to death?"

"Yes."

"Rowly will be all right, Papa," Edna saw she needed to comfort her father. "You mustn't worry."

"You be careful, son," Selwin cautioned. "Men who take extreme positions are more likely to take extreme action."

"Oh, stop lecturing, Papa!" Edna stood. "We should get back, Rowly, or the others will worry. We'll have a bit of a walk to find another taxicab; it's too late to hop a tram."

Rowland drained his tea and stood with her. "I'll be glad when I can start using my own car again."

As Edna had expected, Clyde and Milton were up, playing billiards on the full-sized table in what had once been the ballroom. It was only then that Rowland remembered his suspicion that Edna had discovered something at the party—they hadn't really been able to speak freely since then, and he had of course been distracted by spies and the like. "So Ed, what have you been bursting to tell me all evening?"

She smiled, a little smugly, and launched into an account of her conversations with the ladies. "After they rabbited on and on about fashions, Mrs. Campbell asked me who made my dress, and

I told her that I had. At first I thought I'd made a real faux pas because, well, they seemed to be a little shocked. And then they all started talking about sewing."

"Sewing?" Rowland was surprised. Still, what would he know about the conversations of women.

"They started talking about their misadventures with their Singers. Mrs. Dynon told a story about how she made one of her husband's robes so tight he could barely walk…and then another woman, whose name I can't remember, said her husband was furious when she made a hood without eyeholes."

They all stared at her.

"A hood?" asked Milton. "Like a black, pointed hood?"

"I don't know," Edna shrugged. "They all laughed and then Mrs. Campbell changed the subject—I didn't want to seem unduly interested so I left it there."

"Probably a good idea," Rowland told them about John Dynon and his apparent lust for confrontation. And about Poynton's warnings.

"You need to get this fellow Poynton to tell you more." Milton chalked his cue.

"I'll try," Rowland promised. "Luckily, he's a talkative sort of chap. In fact, they're all pretty chatty—a bit of a contrast to Wilfred's lot," he added, recalling his brother's obsession with secrecy. He relayed the other conversations to which he had been privy, and mentioned the Riley that had followed them to Burwood. Finally he admitted that Maguire had recognised him.

Clyde's reaction was, as he expected. "You're pushing your luck, Rowly. You need to stop this now."

Rowland tried to reassure him. "Maguire's with the Old Guard, and he's apparently one of their spies in Campbell's movement. The Old Guardsmen who are shadowing the New Guard will simply assume I'm spying for Wilfred, too. They may even help me out if I'm exposed—this is a good thing, Clyde."

Clyde was dubious. "You're going to have to be ruddy careful, Rowly," he said. "If they find out you're anything but a sympathetic artist…When are you seeing Campbell next?"

"He wants me to go out to Belmore with him on the thirteenth."

"Why?"

"No idea. De Groot was worried that I'd paint his illustrious Commander as a gardener or something…not the right image, apparently."

"So what's at Belmore?" Clyde persisted.

Rowland sighed as he removed his bowtie. "More beware-the-red-terror speeches, I expect."

Chapter Twenty-three

NEW GUARD WOULD NOT TOUCH LANG'S CARCASE

Eric Campbell's High Words

SYDNEY, Saturday

"We are not going to interfere with Lang's carcase. Suggestions have been made that he should be kidnapped and hanged to the nearest lamp post, but we do not want to do anything like that," said Col. Eric Campbell, addressing a meeting of the New Guard to-night.

He added that if Lang was prepared to go to the people, the New Guard would see that he got a fair hearing.

"My desire is for peace," said Campbell. "We have been told that certain organisations are armed. The time is rapidly coming when the New Guard will be called upon to uphold the principle for which it stands."

The Sydney Morning Herald,
February 14, 1932

Rowland chewed the end of his brush as he scrutinised his work. He swatted impatiently at the fly that seemed intent on embedding itself in the wet paint on his canvas. It was the most irritating aspect of working outdoors. He wondered idly if Van Gogh had plastered insects into his masterpieces…perhaps the need to completely bury the odd winged intruder was what had inspired the impasto techniques of the Impressionist masters.

Rowland's easel was set up on the broad back verandah of Woodlands House. Edna sat at a small table in front of him, hand-building with terracotta clay. She chatted about her plans for the piece without lifting her eyes from what she was doing.

Clyde came through the French doors. He rummaged through the tubes of colour at the top of Rowland's paint box. "I'm out of burnt umber," he said eventually.

Rowland picked up a tube from the ledge of his easel, and tossed it to him. "Remind me to order some more; I'm low too."

"What are you painting?" It was not like Rowland to work outside.

"Me." Edna murmured, still focussed on her sculpting.

"Fully clothed?" Clyde walked round to have a look. Given Edna's reputation as a life model, it seemed a waste to paint her with clothes on. There were any number of models who could do that.

"This is for Selwin." Rowland stood back so Clyde could see the canvas.

"Surely your father knows that you…"

"Of course, he knows." Edna made a face. "Doesn't mean he wants to hang me on his wall in that fashion…he's still my father."

Clyde glanced at Rowland. He'd often wondered what Selwin Higgins thought of the life his daughter lived.

"Ed, hold your hands still for a moment," Rowland directed. He had left her hands till last so she could work while he painted her. "What do you think?" he asked Clyde.

Clyde saw a portrait of a sculptress absorbed in her clay. Her eyes were lowered and her face beautiful, deep in concentration. The sun bathed the piece she was sculpting and cast a gentle glow around the sunset colours of her hair. He looked at Rowland. "She's fatter than that, isn't she?"

Rowland smiled. "You're right—I'll get some more paint."

Edna responded fiercely without moving her hands. Her reputation as a model was well-deserved.

"Rowly, where are you?" The shout was Milton's and came from inside the house.

"Out here." Rowland returned to Edna's hands. He turned as Milton stepped out.

The poet grinned at him. "Brought you a present." He dragged on a rope so that what may once have been a greyhound emerged soon after him. It was a bedraggled animal, malnourished and dirty. All the bones of its ribs and hips were visible. Its muzzle was scarred. It shook, and it had only one ear.

"What the Dickens is that?" demanded Rowland.

"You said you wanted a dog."

"That's not a dog." Rowland leaned his head to one side and considered the shivering thing. "I'm not really sure what it is."

"Where did you get it, Milt?" Edna twisted her neck to see the creature without moving her shoulders or hands.

"At the track," said Milton. "He's not much of a runner and they were going to shoot him. I remembered you were looking for a dog."

"When did I say that?" Rowland squatted to

pat the poor frightened animal. He really did like dogs. It nuzzled his hand tentatively.

Clyde too bent down to show the dog some kindness. "You've let worse things move in."

"But the poor dog in life the firmest friend, the first to welcome, foremost to defend. Whose honest heart is still his master's own, who labours, fights, lives, breathes for him alone." Milton had apparently decided the hound's case was best presented by poetry.

"I think you'll find that Lord Byron was talking about an animal actually identifiable as a dog," Rowland said as the greyhound rolled onto its back and looked up at him. "What are we going to call you, mate?"

"I've already named him." Milton's smile was sly. "This fine fellow is Lenin."

Clyde called the poet an idiot, but Rowland didn't think Lenin was such a bad name. "Fine, Lenin it is. Milt can you go find someone to wash him…? But get Mary to feed him first."

Milton hesitated.

"For God's sake, Milt, Mary isn't going to hurt you…She won't approve, she'll probably sigh a lot, but she's not going hurt you."

Milton moaned and led the dog away. Edna complained her fingers were getting stiff.

"Very well, you can get back to whatever you

were doing," Rowland said, finally putting down his brush. He rubbed the face of his watch with a cloth to remove the paint, and read the time. "I'd better go or I'll be late for this thing at Belmore."

"You'll have to shower," said Edna looking at him. "Your hair's green." Rowland cursed. He'd been so careful not to cover his clothes in paint, but he hadn't checked his habit of running his fingers through his hair—mainly to keep it out of his eyes. Coloured hair was often the result.

"Go." Edna, stood and wiped her hands with a rag. "I'll clean up your brushes.

Rowland climbed into the backseat beside the Colonel. If Eric Campbell noticed the odd fleck of viridian green in the younger man's hair, he did not mention it. Instead, he introduced his driver, Hodges. Poynton sat in the front beside Hodges as he drove them to Belmore, in the south-west.

"What you will observe today, Clyde," began Campbell, "will give you an idea of what the New Guard stands for. We are no mere social club of like-minded men, but an army of patriots."

Rowland raised a brow. Just what was it that Campbell wanted him to see?

"Of course, what you will see today is not a public exercise."

"I understand."

They drove through Belmore, past the small shopping district. The area was semi-rural, a collection of small orchards and holdings. The houses were humble, mostly weatherboard. Empty paddocks fringed by natural bushland broke the built-up areas. To Rowland, Belmore seemed a great distance from the urban congestion of Sydney, or the gracious elegance of Woollahra.

Hodges pulled into the driveway of a large house on an orchard. Campbell mentioned it was the property of a New Guard member. De Groot strode out to greet them. "This way," he said, after the customary handshaking had been seen to.

They walked down a path that branched away from the fruit trees toward a paddock. Within minutes, what they had come for came into view. Standing to attention in military formation were hundreds of men each wearing an armband to affirm his allegiance.

Rowland stared, silent and stunned. His opinion of the New Guard as "rhetoric with cocktails" evaporated. This was something else altogether. It was eerie, unnerving—so many men in suits, bearing guns, standing in a suburban paddock, poised for battle. Campbell walked the lines with De Groot, inspecting his troops, stopping for a word with the occasional man. That done, he returned to stand next to Rowland and Poynton while De Groot shouted commands. The Guardsmen broke into units and drilled. They were a well-trained group, obviously some of the A-class men of whom Campbell had spoken previously.

On command, they dropped and advanced, manoeuvring, crawling, and preparing to fire.

Then began the vehicle drills. It appeared the New Guard had a fleet of motorcars at its disposal. The Guardsmen practised what Poynton called "lightning strikes." The exercises involved men jumping in and out of moving vehicles and riding on running boards as the motorcars moved at speed. Of course this was accompanied by a great deal of shouting and fist-waving.

Amazed, Rowland squinted through the billowing dust as armoured trucks, fitted with metal plating and makeshift gun turrets emerged from behind a rise. Good lord—the New Guard was preparing for a full-scale offensive.

"Well, Clyde, what do you think?" Campbell asked after they had watched the exercises for an hour or so. "This force of seven hundred is but a fraction of the men that I have at my disposal."

"It is an impressive display of firepower," Rowland chose his words carefully. He was starting to get more than a little worried that Campbell may actually manage to pull off his threatened coup.

Campbell patted him on the back. "I say, I forgot you didn't see service—it would seem like rather a lot of guns to you, I suppose. But the enemy is armed too, Clyde. Of course, we have no wish to shoot our fellow Australians…not unless absolutely necessary. Our boys have orders to use other weapons first."

"Other weapons?"

Campbell rocked back on his heels and opened his mouth to say more, but he was interrupted by the rumble of even more cars, a convoy pulling into the driveway behind them. He looked perturbed—it seemed the new vehicles were unexpected. Campbell strode over to alert De Groot.

"What's going on?" Rowland directed the question at Poynton.

The bodyguard moved to place himself in front of Eric Campbell as several men ran down the path from the cars toward them. They were armed, but with cameras—and for a moment, Rowland was blinded by the flashing bulbs.

"Reporters!" bellowed Poynton.

"This is private property," Campbell declared, pushing Poynton aside as the cameras continued to snap. "Leave now! You are trespassing on private property!"

De Groot shouted and two dozen Guardsmen broke away from the rest and descended upon the cameramen. The reporters held their ground, shouting questions at Campbell:

"Mr. Campbell, are you preparing for an offensive?"

"What is the New Guard planning?"

"Do you feel you have the support of the people, Mr. Campbell?"

"Get off this property now!" Campbell stood before a wall of Guardsmen, all wielding pick-axe handles.

But again the bulbs flashed. The Guardsmen responded by advancing, swinging their weapons without reserve. Cameras were smashed. Rowland blanched as shattered lenses and bulbs flew in all directions. At first the reporters resisted, and then as the Guardsmen fell upon them, they disintegrated into a panicked scramble in retreat. Their assailants were undeterred by the attempt to withdraw, the battle a welcome application of the preparation in which they had been engaged. Men threw punches in earnest and the pick-axe handles descended brutally. Eventually, Campbell ordered his men back. The reporters fled, hobbling and bloodied back to their vehicles, amid the deafening cheers of seven hundred men.

Rowland looked on, astounded, disturbed by the side on which he found himself.

The Guardsmen returned to their drilling with

increased vigour. "Bloody hell," Rowland muttered to Poynton.

The bodyguard grinned. "I wonder how the reporters knew we were here."

Campbell came back over, mopping the perspiration from his brow with a large handkerchief. "I'm afraid the boys run away with themselves sometimes," he said. "This is a covert exercise—spies of any sort are not looked upon kindly. Still, nothing more than a few sore noses."

Unsure, Rowland merely nodded. De Groot obviously didn't share his commander's nonchalance. He barked at his officers, demanding to know how their location had been leaked to the press. Eventually, he took Campbell aside to discuss the consequences.

Campbell tried to calm him. "I don't think any of the cameras, let alone the photographs, survived, Frank." De Groot looked anything but comforted.

After another hour's drill, Campbell addressed his men. His speech followed the usual themes—patriotism and preparation—but this time he included an additional rant about the threat posed by the Australian Labor Army, which he seemed to think was controlled by Soviet interests.

Rowland listened. For the first time he was beginning to believe that the New Guard could be dangerous on a large scale. Perhaps Milton was right, after all. Perhaps he was starting to care about Campbell's politics.

He leant over to Poynton. "John Dynon's not here?" he said.

"No." Poynton exhaled loudly. "He thinks his unit is too specialised for this nonsense."

Rowland decided to come out and ask. "What exactly does he do?"

"He runs the Legion."

Then, spotting Hodges heading toward them, Poynton put a finger to his lips. The show was over, and Rowland had no further opportunity to find out what this Legion actually was.

Because Campbell insisted on dropping him 'home,' Rowland found himself again calling in on Edna's father. He waved Campbell and his men off from the front gate then drank tea with a surprised Selwin Higgins before catching a tram into the city and another out to Woollahra. By the time he finally opened the front door of Woodlands House, he was hot and irritable.

He fell into the wingback armchair in his ordinary fashion, and loosened his tie. Mary Brown appeared with a pitcher of cold lemonade as if she had read his mind.

"Thank you, Mary," he said as he poured a glass.

"Master Rowly," the housekeeper started, after

a pointed sigh, "am I to understand that you wish that unkempt creature to continue having the run of your father's house?"

Rowland was amused. He knew Mary did not approve of Milton, but he had not heard her refer to him as a creature before.

"Milton…"

"Mr. Isaacs informs me that you wish to keep that animal as a pet."

Rowland smiled. The dog. He'd forgotten about Lenin. "Yes, Mary," he said pleasantly. "I seem to have acquired a dog."

Mary Brown sighed again, but said no more. She saw the dog as scruffy and as improper as the rest of Rowland's friends. Why, when he could afford a well-bred hound, he would choose to take in a mongrel from the streets, she could not understand. To her mind, he chose his friends in the same way. But it was not her place to say and she returned wordlessly to her duties.

Lenin bounded in with Milton close behind. Rowland suspected they'd both been waiting for the housekeeper to go. The hound had been washed and groomed somewhat, but had not improved much for it. He jumped into Rowland's lap. Rowland patted the one-eared head, wondering how even Milton could have found a dog so completely ugly. Lenin circled and settled down on him.

"We're going to have to fatten you up, Lenin, old mate." Rowland shifted so that the armchair could accommodate them both. "Those bones of yours are sticking into me."

"I knew you'd like him," Milton crowed.

"Rubbish—you just knew I wouldn't throw him out."

"Same thing really."

"Apparently."

Milton poured himself a glass of lemonade and added a generous portion of Pimms. "So, don't be coy. What went on in Belmore?"

Rowland told him.

Milton let out one of his low whistles. "You're joking. How many men?"

"Bloody hundreds." Rowland scowled. "I didn't really take them seriously before, but they looked like an army, Milt—they're organised, and armed. Campbell claims there are thousands more."

"That could be a problem."

"I feel like I should do something."

Milton laughed. "Rowly, I know you have connections, but you can't stop the New Guard by yourself."

"I was thinking more about going to the police." Rowland scratched Lenin's single ear.

Milton shook his head. "You wouldn't be telling them anything they don't already know. You can bet that Campbell's making sure that he's not doing anything technically illegal—otherwise the cops would have put a stop to it. He's a lawyer, remember."

Rowland knew Milton was right. The New Guard drill had been on private property. Gun licenses were not hard to obtain, and they probably all had one. Campbell would be particular about things like that.

"Anyway," the poet continued, "you can't blow your cover now."

Rowland apprised Milton of his conversation with Poynton. "He called it the Legion."

Milton was excited. "Look, Rowly, this man Poynton obviously knows a bit about this Legion. You just have to find out who's in it and then you'll have something to take to the police."

"Don't worry, Milt, I'm not going to back out now." He rubbed his brow. "I still can't imagine why these people would have a problem with Uncle Rowland. If he was a Communist, he was bloody quiet about it."

"Communists don't normally wander about announcing the fact—that's just me."

"I know," Rowland brooded. "But I was close to him, Milt. Why wouldn't he tell me? He told me far more shocking things...."

"I don't know, mate." Milton studied his

friend. It had been only a couple of months since the elder Rowland Sinclair had been murdered—it seemed a very long time ago now. "Maybe he assumed you knew...maybe something other than his political beliefs got him killed or maybe it wasn't the New Guard after all."

"Terrific! I've joined a band of lunatics for nothing." Rowland checked the time. "I say, where are Clyde and Ed?"

"Clyde's upstairs fixing something. You know what he's like. Some bloke came by and got Ed."

"Ken Hall?"

"No—apparently Ken really did think she could act. This one's someone new. Don't worry, she promised not to go anywhere public...the two of you being engaged and all."

"Very decent of her," Rowland replied. The thought did not help unsour his mood.

Milton refilled their glasses with something stronger than lemonade. Lenin watched, occasionally shifting position but otherwise happy to simply languish in the opulent circumstances in which he now found himself. It was hard to know whether the dog fully appreciated his good fortune, but he did seem content. Rowland, feeling under pressure far more than normal, didn't refuse when Milton repeatedly refilled his glass through the evening. While their conversation was initially inconsequential, anything but what was really on their minds, it became progressively less inhibited. Rowland could tell he'd had too much to drink. He was aware he was talking about Edna far too much.

"This thing you have for Ed," Milton said finally, "you're cutting a switch to flog yourself with, mate."

Rowland groaned. He knew. "What else can I do, Milt?"

"Look, Rowly," Milton leant forward and spoke directly, not caring that his tie landed in Rowland's glass, and Rowland not noticing. "I've known Ed since we were little tackers. There's no one like her, but she's single-minded about her work. With that French mother of hers—you should've met her…brilliant but too crazy for just about anybody but Selwin—Ed's trying to succeed for the both of them. Consider it a compliment that she won't give you a go. She only takes on men she's happy to walk away from."

"Great." Rowland took Milton's tie with two fingers and removed it from his glass.

"She ain't going to change, mate…and you can't keep waiting for her."

"I'm not waiting, Milt. I'm not stupid. But as you said, there's no one like her."

"There are other girls, though. You could have your pick." The poet raised his glass. "You're

Rowland Sinclair—you've got money, position, handsome friends." He swung his hands out, spilling gin in a wide arc. "Mate, you could choose from either side of the tracks."

Rowland laughed. "It's as easy as that."

Milton shrugged. "You're a hopeless romantic, Rowly. God, you'll be writing poetry next."

"One of us has to."

"You slander me, my friend." Milton smiled, unabashed, but added with gravitas, "The happiness of a man in this life does not consist in the absence, but in the mastery of his passions."

"I'm not completely sozzled, Milt. That's…"

"Yeah, all right…Tennyson."

Chapter Twenty-four

"Jock Garden"

Honour From Moscow

SYDNEY, Sunday

In the current issue of *The Worker's Weekly*, under the heading, "Moscow Correspondence", is a paragraph which states that the secretary of the New South Wales Labor Council, Mr. J.S. Garden, has been elected to the Fourth World Congress of the Red Internationale of Labor Unions and to the executive of the R.I.L.U.

The Argus, February 15, 1932

"Rowly! Rowly!"

Rowland shrugged on a dressing gown over his pyjamas. He was still half asleep. He would have been entirely asleep if Edna hadn't been shouting the house down. He opened his curtains and groaned. The sun was blinding. "I'm coming!" he called, wondering what could be so urgent. He and Milton had spent most of the night playing cards and drinking. He was a little hungover.

Edna was in the dining room with Clyde and Milton when Rowland came down. "What?" he demanded.

The three of them were huddled over a newspaper. "Have you seen this?" Edna said, holding up a copy of *The World*.

"How could I have seen it?" Rowland grumbled. "I was asleep."

"Look!" Edna thrust the paper at him.

Rowland scanned the front page. The headline read, "New Guard Assaults Reporters." A half-page photo showed Eric Campbell, his arm raised imperiously as he ordered the photographers off the property.

Rowland blinked, mildly surprised. He had thought that all the cameras were smashed. Apparently not. Still, he didn't think it warranted waking him.

"Is there any coffee left?" He looked hopefully at the silver pot on the sideboard.

"Look at the picture again, mate." Clyde pushed the paper back toward him.

Rowland did…and then he saw it. Behind Campbell, a number of men, Rowland Sinclair among them. "Oh." He poured the last of the coffee into a cup. "This could be embarrassing."

Clyde took the paper from him and looked hard at the picture. "It mightn't be so bad…It's not that clear and Rowly's just one of the chaps in the background."

"Does it matter?" asked Milton.

"Well, what if someone recognises Rowland Sinclair standing behind the Commander of the New Guard?" Edna looked over Clyde's shoulder at the image.

"Unless they know him well, they're unlikely to be surprised." Milton remained confident. "It's what you'd expect from the established classes. Besides, who ever notices the men standing in the background of a picture?"

"And if they do know him well?" Edna persisted. "Rowly does have one or two friends, apart from us."

"The people who know him well are hardly likely to talk to Campbell, are they?"

"You probably won't be welcome at Trades Hall for a while," Clyde said grimly.

Rowland drank his coffee. That was the worst of it, as far as he could see. The left-leaning art world, which had finally accepted him, would now regard him with suspicion once again.

"Rowly, are you going to say anything?" Edna demanded.

"Is there any more coffee?"

Edna considered the less-than-immaculate state of him. "You really shouldn't drink with Milt."

Rowland rubbed his face. "That's stating the flaming obvious."

Milton laughed, completely unaffected by the previous evening's consumption. But then, he was a far more accomplished drinker than Rowland.

"So, what are we going to do?" Edna tried to drain a few last drops of coffee from the pot.

Rowland stood. "I'm going to get dressed. What time is it?"

"Half past twelve."

Rowland cursed and then apologised to Edna, who couldn't have cared less.

"Are you late for something?" she asked.

"A meeting with Inspector Bicuit. At one." He swigged the half cup of coffee that Edna had managed to procure. "The incompetent fool told Mrs. Donelly not to 'leave town,' and as far as I can tell, that's the extent of his bleeding investigation."

"So what are you going to do?"

"I thought it might be time to throw some Sinclair weight around."

"This I gotta see." Milton's eyes brightened. "I'll come with you... There's no reason not to take the Rolls, is there?"

"I think we're pretty safe. It's the only way I'll make it on time, anyway. Have Johnston bring it around." Rowland departed to shower and dress.

It was just after one. Milton watched, entertained, as Rowland became a Sinclair. It was not so much what he said, but the way he said it—as if the entire police force worked for him personally. Milton was fascinated by the manner in which the officers responded, showing Rowland into the inspector's office as a matter of urgency.

Rowland Sinclair spoke to Inspector Bicuit behind closed doors. Milton waited outside. The voices were definite, but not raised. When Rowland reemerged, it was Bicuit who held the door open for him. To Milton, the inspector looked flustered, and distinctly unhappy.

"So?" Milton asked, once they were out of Bicuit's earshot.

"He hasn't got a shred of evidence on Mrs. Donelly. He's finally agreed to leave her alone... and maybe do a spot of actual police work."

Milton was impressed. "How did you manage that?"

Rowland smiled. "I told him I'd get Wilfred

to call the Commissioner. Essentially, it's a variation on the 'my father will thump your father' approach."

"Traditional," Milton nodded, "but clearly effective. Did you mention Campbell and his black-hooded men?"

"No. I didn't want to push my luck. I've already told him about Paddy Ryan, but that got me nowhere; I'll wait till I have some names."

They were just about to leave the building when Milton saw a familiar face, "Garden! What are you doing here?"

Harcourt Garden was a tall, solid man. Though barely out of his teens, he cut an imposing figure. It was hard to know precisely what he did for a living, but they knew he worked for the "Left." His father was Jock Garden, a Scottish immigrant and former Baptist preacher who had founded the Australian Communist Party, and who was now one of the fiercest supporters of Lang's faction in the Australian Labor Party, despite having been expelled from it at one time for his extremist views.

Rowland had come to know both Gardens through Milton. While he thought Jock was as mad as Eric Campbell, he did like his son.

Harcourt strode over to them. He wasn't smiling.

"How are you, Harry?"

Garden glowered at them before looking carefully about the room. The station was busy, despite it being a Sunday. "Outside," he said.

They followed him out of the station, to a small alleyway at its side. Rowland was uneasy. Harcourt Garden was, in his experience, a fairly upfront sort of chap. What business could he have with them in an alleyway?

Garden turned, his face clenched in a way that seemed to make speaking a strain. Still, he managed. "Well, Sinclair!" he spat. "Finally, you show your true colours!" Despite having been born in Melbourne, Garden's speech had a faint Scottish brogue—his father's influence—and it came out even more so when he was angry.

Rowland said nothing, realising that Garden had seen the photograph.

"I should've known it was too good to be true—the gentlemen socialist! What have you been doing all this time, Sinclair—amusing yourself by slumming with the lower classes? Or are you worse, some kind of Fascist spy?"

"Steady on." Milton stepped forward.

"I just stood behind him in a photo, Harry," Rowland said evenly. "That's all."

Garden swore at him. Rowland waited. On the face of it, Garden had a right to be angry.

While Rowland had never joined either the Communist or the Labor parties, the people he'd met had trusted him, as a friend of Milton's. He'd been to their rallies and even a few party meetings. His appearance with Campbell must have seemed a betrayal. He regretted that, but he knew its purpose, and they didn't.

Milton started to argue with Garden.

"Leave it, Milt," Rowland placed his hand on the poet's shoulder. What was the point? They couldn't tell Garden the truth.

Harcourt Garden looked at them both with an air of disgust. He leant in to Rowland, his breath hot. "Just you watch your back, Sinclair. Just you watch your back!" Turning, he stalked out of the alley and into the station.

"Come on," said Milton. "Let's go, before he returns with some mates."

The Rolls-Royce was waiting and they climbed in before Johnston could get out to open the doors. Rowland let his head fall back against the leather seat. Milton opened the drinks cabinet.

"Well, this is going to be awkward," Rowland said, declining the glass Milton offered him. He was still feeling a bit seedy from the evening before.

Milton poured himself a whisky. "Awkward's not the half of it, Rowly. Garden's mates don't mess around."

"Don't tell me you're worried, Milt?" Rowland replied a little amused. To date it had been Clyde who was the voice of caution, with Milton the provocateur.

"Rowly, we're not talking about Campbell's poncy bloody band of fairies. These guys know how to throw a punch, and now they think you're some kind of New Guard spy!"

Rowland sighed. "So it seems."

Milton downed his whisky.

Rowland spoke frankly. "Look, Milt, this is probably going rub off on you…maybe Clyde as well. You may need to keep your own heads down for a while."

Milton snorted. "Don't change the subject, Rowly. You heard what Garden said. They'll be looking for you."

Rowland shrugged. "Maybe. Not a lot we can do about it now—but I'll try to stay out of the paper in the future."

"That's not all you're going to have to stay out of." Milton refilled his glass. "Harry will put out the word that you can't be trusted…I could try telling them that you just happened to be standing in the background…."

Rowland laughed. "Good luck."

Johnston pulled the Rolls into the drive of Woodlands House and Mary Brown came out to tell them that Edna and Clyde were taking tea in the gazebo that overlooked the tennis courts at the back. It was a large octagonal structure, embellished with fretwork. A trumpet vine, now heavy with its orange conical blooms, insinuated itself through the frame of the roof. Lenin was tearing about the garden, chasing something that was visible only to him.

"How was Inspector Biscuit?" Edna asked as they walked up the stairs.

"As it turns out, he's the least of our problems." Rowland took a seat on the bench next to her. He poured himself a cup of tea and told them the latest.

"I knew this was a bloody stupid plan!" Clyde clipped Milton on the side of the head. "See what you've gotten Rowly into."

"It's not Milt's fault." Rowland came to the poet's defence. "I'm the one who got himself in the paper."

"That's right. It's all Rowly's fault," Milton agreed.

"It'll blow over," Rowland said. "Once I have the names I need, we can just tell Garden the truth, and hopefully he'll call his dogs off."

"And until then?" asked Clyde.

"I'll stay out of his way. You probably should too."

Clyde sighed. "There's nothing else we can do, I suppose."

"Have you started Campbell's portrait yet, Rowly?" Edna asked.

Rowland shook his head. "De Groot's insisting I attend the New Guard's Town Hall Rally before I decide on the composition…he rather likes to keep control of things, I think. I feel like he's commissioned me to paint the movement's next recruitment poster."

"If only he knew." Milton helped himself from the plate of Mary Brown's scones and the pot of her famous strawberry jam.

"Just be glad he doesn't," Clyde muttered.

"I have a piece to finish for the Life Exhibition first, anyway." Rowland decided to change the subject. The exhibition at the Fine Arts Gallery was to feature the nude in contemporary art. He had been gratified when he was asked to submit a piece; but of course he'd since been distracted by Fascists. He wondered, fleetingly, when his priorities would return to normal.

"Oh, yes, I forgot." Edna finished her cup of tea. "Do you want to start now?" She had promised to be his model.

"I probably should. I've left it a bit late."

Clyde looked at the sky. "You've lost the best light, Rowly."

"I know."

"Why don't we start tomorrow, early?" Edna suggested. "I'm free all day."

Milton lifted the lid of one of the box seats in the gazebo and took out several croquet mallets. The socialist poet rather enjoyed the civilised pleasures of the ruling classes.

Rowland glanced at the position of the sun. It was not like him to procrastinate with his work but the best light had indeed gone.

"Very well." He took a mallet. "We'll work tomorrow. Let's play."

Chapter Twenty-five

POLICE REPORT ON NEW GUARD

SYDNEY, Monday

After enquiries into a parade of the New Guard at Belmore, Sydney, on Saturday, detectives will today submit a report to the Police Commissioner.

The Canberra Times, February 16, 1932

Rowland had been up for some time when Edna emerged the next morning. He was showered, dressed, and already setting out his basic palette of colours. Edna had always found Rowland to be so. He approached his work with a professionalism not common among the artists she knew, whose work habits were more often…creative.

More surprisingly, Milton was also up. He sometimes watched Rowland work when he had nothing better to do.

Rowland used Milton to move the furniture around. "Back a bit...no, forward.... yes!" He wanted Edna backlit by the diffuse light coming through the window. Rowland changed Edna's position several times until he found a composition that pleased him, with her reclining on her side, her head resting on a hand propped up by her elbow, her eyes directly at him.

Edna had modelled for many painters of varying talent. Very few wanted her to look at them. Most had her glance away, lowering her lids and casting her gaze as demure or dreamy. Sometimes it was because the artist didn't have the confidence to paint her eyes, a notoriously difficult feature to capture. Others wanted to introduce an atmosphere of modesty to balance their unclad subject. Still others could simply not bear for the model to return their own scrutiny. This was not true of Rowland. No matter where he placed her arms or legs, he almost always had her look directly at him.

For some reason, on this day, she asked him why he did so. "Rowly, do you have all your models look at you?"

"Only the naked ones." He sketched in her

figure on the large canvas. In truth, he only used Edna for life work.

"Why?"

"Makes me feel important."

Edna wasn't sure if he was joking, but she didn't pursue it. She had been used by many artists whose reputations far exceeded that of Rowland Sinclair but she liked the way he painted her.

Milton sat in an armchair, getting his inspiration from the latest work of Conan Doyle while Lenin made a nuisance of himself by climbing up onto the chaise lounge with Edna, until he finally settled on the floor in front of her. Rowland toyed with the idea of including Lenin in the painting, but then the dog only had one ear.

He worked in absolute silence for a while, concentrating on getting the foundations of the piece right. Then he allowed Edna to stretch out before returning her to the same position so he could continue. Milton and Edna chatted to each other, but both knew the artist well enough not to try to engage him in conversation while he worked.

He let Edna go for a few hours in the middle of the day and worked on in her absence, relying on memory to create a likeness that was more than a mere image. Late in the afternoon, Edna took her place on the chaise again, and Rowland worked with what he could see once more. Clyde wandered in and out, as was his custom, often in search of colours. Rowland was always better stocked than he.

They heard a car pull up, and a knock at the front door. "Don't move," Rowland warned Edna. "Mary will answer it." He focussed on finessing the line of Edna's brow, expecting the housekeeper's tentative knock any moment. Mary Brown did not like being confronted with this aspect of his work. She would always knock and wait for him to come out.

And so, when Wilfred Sinclair opened the door and strode into the room, they were all startled. He turned immediately on his heel, and stood with his back to Edna. He took off his glasses. "For God's sake, Rowly!"

"Wil—what are you doing here?"

Edna cleared her throat.

"Oh, sorry, Ed," said Rowland. "Go ahead and move."

Milton looked up from his book, and tossed her a robe. Rowland put down his brush and wiped his hands on a cloth. This was distinctly uncomfortable.

As Edna slipped on the robe, she smiled at Rowland and spoke brightly to Wilfred. "Good evening, Mr. Sinclair. What a pleasure to see you again."

"Miss Higgins." Wilfred didn't turn around.

"What are you doing here, Wil?" Rowland asked again.

"We need to speak," Wilfred said curtly. "In the library." He walked out before Rowland could say another word.

"You'd better go." Edna flinched as Wilfred slammed the library door. "I'll take care of your brushes."

"Thanks Ed…sorry."

Rowland braced himself.

Wilfred looked more than a little agitated. "Close the door," he instructed.

Rowland did so. He had mixed feelings about the library at the best of times. On this occasion it was more than just the walnut panelling and stained glass windows that were familiar. Though Mary Brown kept it spotless, the library was now almost completely unused. When Rowland was a child, however, his father would summon him into this room. If the summons alone did not warn the boy that Henry Sinclair was seriously displeased, it would become clear soon thereafter. Rowland didn't remember the library fondly, but it amused him now that things had changed so little. "Are you going to hit me again?" he asked with the faintest smile.

"Don't be smart, Rowly," Wilfred didn't like being reminded of his loss of self-control.

"Are you going to tell me why you're here?"

Wilfred pulled a folded copy of *The World* from inside his jacket and threw it onto the mahogany desk. "I was called up to bloody Sydney to explain this!"

"Explain? To whom?"

"To whom do you jolly well think?"

"I have no bloody idea!"

"What in God's name are you doing with Campbell, Rowly? Your politics can't have changed—obviously your lifestyle hasn't."

Rowland sighed. "That was work, Wil," he said, holding up his paint-stained hands. "It's what I do."

"I don't care what you call it—just tell me why you've suddenly joined the New Guard!"

"I haven't joined."

Wilfred pointed to the picture on the front page.

"Since when do you read that rag?" Rowland asked. His brother would generally have regarded the sensationalist paper as beneath him.

"I don't," Wilfred replied. "But our people keep an eye on Campbell. It just so happened that one of them thought he recognised you in the picture. And then I spoke to Maguire."

Rowland was mildly comforted. He was counting on the fact that anyone who might recognise him would have sympathies either with the Communists or Wilfred's Old Guard, with neither likely to carry tales back to the New Guard.

Rowland studied his brother silently for a moment as he tried to find a way out of the conversation. He didn't see how he could do anything else, so he told Wilfred the truth.

Wilfred sat in their father's leather chair. His face was grim, incredulous, but he did not interrupt. When Rowland had finished, he took off his glasses and pinched the bridge of his nose. "Rowly, you're a bloody fool! What possessed you?"

Rowland found it hard to explain in a way that didn't sound ridiculous. So he said nothing.

"Do you have any idea what they'll do if they realise you're spying on them…if they find out who you really are?"

"What am I supposed to do, Wil? Nobody else was interested in who killed Uncle Rowland—that idiot Bicuit is still convinced Mrs. Donelly did it, somehow."

Wilfred's face softened just a little. "Look Rowly, I know you and the old man were close… but I think you've taken this miles too far."

"I'm just having a look around, Wil." Rowland made his case as rationally as he could. "I could truthfully be painting Campbell for the simple reason that he is an interesting subject. As soon as I find something to tie his men to Uncle Rowland, I'll leave the rest to the police."

"I'm not going to be able to talk you out of this, am I?"

"Don't think so."

Wilfred put his glasses back on. "Very well." He picked up the newspaper and studied the photo. "I'll square things with the chaps. Hinton can get a bit worked up where Campbell is concerned. Lord knows, we have our own people in the New Guard." He shook his head as he spoke, acting against his own better judgement. "I'll let it be known that my brother has gone abroad. It will confuse things a little, in case anyone else picks the photo." He turned back to Rowland. "If they think you're out of the country, they'll be likely to dismiss the resemblance."

"Thanks, Wil." Rowland was vaguely bewildered. He had expected a tirade; he wondered if he was missing something.

"Don't get me wrong, Rowly," Wilfred said sternly. "I don't approve of the company you keep, or the disgraceful way you choose to live your life, but I accept that Uncle Rowland was family. I suppose I shouldn't be surprised that of all of us you had some particular affection for the old reprobate.

And if Campbell's Boo Guard did have anything to do with the way he died, there will be hell to pay."

Rowland was relieved, but wasn't sure why. Perhaps there was a security in his brother's support, however grudging.

Wilfred hefted his briefcase onto their father's desk and unlatched it. "Look Rowly, there's something else." He took out a sheaf of documents and handed them across to his brother.

To Rowland, they appeared to be deeds, legal documents.

"It turns out that Uncle Rowland had an interest in some kind of nightclub. He was a silent partner…"

"The 50–50 Club!" exclaimed Rowland, staring at the paperwork in disbelief. The nightspot was notorious. "The wily old bugger!"

Wilfred looked over the top of his bifocals. "Needless to say, I want any connection to this foul establishment terminated."

"And you're telling me because…?"

"Because our blasted uncle left his interest in this dive to you, Rowly. Obviously, he thought you'd appreciate his less savoury pursuits."

A thought pierced Rowland's preoccupation with Campbell and his men. "Wil…do you think this interest in the club could have something to do with…?"

"His death? I hadn't thought about it…" He scratched his head. "Maybe. It's got to be far more likely than your crazy notions about the New Guard."

Rowland wasn't so sure. "I'll look into it."

"And while you're at it, divest your interest. Sell it or give it away—I don't care which. I don't want the Sinclair name connected with such a place any longer, silent or not. I would have sent our solicitors to do it, but apparently these underworld types don't do business according to the usual protocols. Frankly, I don't want it known that Uncle Rowland was even a patron, let alone an owner… The old fool—he's just as much trouble now as he was when he was alive!"

Rowland thought that nothing would have pleased his uncle more. The elder Rowland Sinclair had aspired to scandal. Why then, he wondered, had his uncle kept his interest such a secret, even from him?

Wilfred smiled slightly. "You know, Aubrey would have found this terribly funny."

Not for the first time, Rowland wished he'd had the chance to know Aubrey as Wilfred had.

The head of the Sinclair family got up from the desk and checked his pocket watch. "I'd better go," he said, straightening his tie. "I take it we understand each other?"

"I think so." Rowland shrugged. "I'll let you know if I find anything…and I'll do something about this." He held up the deeds.

Wilfred shook his head. "I'll let you get back to…to…"

Rowland grinned. "I was painting, Wil." He could understand how debauched it would seem to his brother but, in Rowland's world, painting from life was very ordinary.

Wilfred put out his hand. "Why can't you just drink too much like everybody else's wayward brother?"

Rowland laughed. It was the first warmth he'd heard from Wilfred for a long time. "I'll make sure I'm totally under the table next time you see me."

"It would make your actions far easier to explain." Wilfred snapped his briefcase latch closed, but he seemed more resigned than angry.

Once Wilfred had left, Rowland returned to the drawing room. Edna, now dressed, had cleaned his brushes, and Milton had returned the furniture to its usual positions. They sat together on the couch, Edna with a cup of tea, Milton with a Scotch, laughing.

"Not hard to guess what you two were talking about." Rowland took the armchair.

"Sorry, Rowly," Edna said hastily. "Was he very cross?"

Rowland smiled. "Don't be sorry. It was pretty funny."

"What did he want?" Milton asked.

"He'd seen the newspaper, of course, but then there was this..." Rowland handed him the sheaf of legal papers. "It came to me in Uncle Rowland's estate."

Milton was wide-eyed as he shuffled through the papers. "My God!" he almost squealed. "Rowly, my boy, I knew you'd come good in the end. The 50–50 Club! You're a bloody proprietor of the 50–50 Club! I could kiss you..."

"Please don't."

Edna snatched the documents out of Milton's hands to look for herself. The club was an establishment of very dubious reputation—a sly grog den where prostitutes plied their trade, a house of assignation frequented by Sydney's razor gangs and underworld. And now it belonged, in part, to Rowland Sinclair.

"I've got to get rid of it...or at least my interest in it."

"But why?" Milton sounded like a thwarted child being deprived of his toys. "You can't..."

Without taking her eyes from the documents, Edna reached out and whacked him. "How exactly are you going to get rid of it, Rowly? Do you even know who your partners are?"

"Doesn't it say in there?" He waved toward the papers.

"Not really," she replied. "You seem to hold the deed to the premises, but there's nothing I can see about any partnership." She got up and moved over to sit on the arm of his chair. "Rowly, it's been four months since your uncle died. Maybe you're better off just forgetting about it...The 50–50 Club seems to be operating quite happily in your absence...And I don't know that you want to risk upsetting these people."

"If it was just that, I probably would," he said, keenly aware of the rose scent she wore. "But I'm starting to wonder if our theory about the New Guard is just a wild goose chase. It appears my uncle was involved with some very dangerous men."

Edna took a deep breath. "Rowly, you can't go digging around the 50–50 Club the way you have the New Guard. Milt and I grew up with people like this. We're not talking about polite disagreements. These men really hurt people."

"What happened to Uncle Rowland was more than a polite disagreement, Ed," Rowland said quietly. "I'm not going challenge them. I'll offer them the deeds in exchange for what they know about Uncle Rowland.

"You can't just walk into a place like the 50–50 Club and ask to speak to the owner!"

"Why not?'

Milton interrupted them. "I know a bloke who knows some blokes. He could set up something."

"What? Who?"

Milton looked at Edna. "Remember Reggie Jones?"

"That idiot who used to shoot at the ceiling whenever he got excited?"

"Yep. The doctor."

"He went to England, didn't he?"

"He came back...has a practice in Canterbury. Calls himself Stuart-Jones now. I caught up with him at the track. He runs a few dogs, among other things."

Rowland listened, intrigued by what was unspoken between Edna and Milton. "And this doctor knows people connected to the 50–50 Club?"

"The Doc isn't your conventional medical practitioner," Milton chose his words carefully. "Most of his patients are girls in trouble, if you understand me, Rowly."

Rowland did. Polite company did not talk of such things, but it was a sad reality of the times.

"That's not why I knew him, Rowly." Edna reached for his hand. "Milton introduced us, and he asked me to the theatre a couple of times."

It wouldn't have occurred to Rowland that Edna might have sought Jones' unhappy medical skills for herself. Even if it had, he would never have asked but, admittedly, he was relieved. He rubbed her arm.

"I didn't want you to think…"

"I don't."

"Anyway." Milton ignored the exchange "The Doc knows people. I'll sound him out—see if he can get us a meeting with whoever runs the show there."

"Why don't you take care of it all, Milt?" Edna suggested. "Rowly doesn't need to go—I don't trust Reggie Jones."

"I'm not a child, Ed." Rowland's voice was gentle, but it was firm. "I know what goes on at the 50–50. I don't need to be protected from it."

"I think you probably do." Milton smiled. "But I don't think they'd deal with me. You're the man with the deeds." He placed his arm about the sculptress' shoulders. "Don't worry, old girl; I'll look after him."

"How dangerous can it possibly be, Ed?" Rowland could see that Milton had not settled the disquiet in her eyes. "I'll be giving them back the title to their damn club. And I'm not going to accuse anyone, just ask…just in case they know something."

Milton nodded. "I'll call in on the Doc tomorrow and see what can be arranged. For the record,

Rowly, I still think this is down to Campbell's men, not these jokers."

"Why's that?"

"These blokes…if they wanted your uncle dead…they wouldn't put on fancy dress to do it."

Chapter Twenty-six

SYDNEY BY DAY

SYDNEY

It is gratifying that Inspector MacKay, the new head of the detective force, believes he cannot merely suppress but must abolish the razor and other gangs. If he achieves results, he will win public plaudits.

The Argus, February 18, 1932

The 50–50 Club was essentially a large hall in a part of Sydney where the Depression had hit hard: Darlinghurst, just up from Kings Cross. Very little expense had been incurred in its décor, which consisted of a collection of tables of varying shapes, all draped in yellowing linen, and circled with bentwood chairs. There was a grand piano in the corner, at which sat a pale young man who played

without pause. The bar ran along one wall. And that was really the extent of the celebrated salon in which Rowland had inherited a share.

It was nine in the evening. Legal liquor sales had concluded at six, and clubs like the 50–50 now divided up the market among themselves, plying their trade in sly grog. It was a thriving, profitable industry.

Milton had procured the password and they had been admitted to the crowded premises. After claiming a table, they ordered drinks. It was not the first such establishment at which Rowland had found himself. The sly grog trade was integral to the social lives of the bright young things of the era. Many clubs had become quite chic, ignored by the police and frequented by the supposedly respectable. This enterprise, however, made no pretensions toward any form of refinement. Milton, of course, seemed entirely at home.

"So where is he?" Rowland loosened his tie just a little. The hall was badly ventilated and packed with patrons. Cigarette smoke cast the space in a blue-grey haze.

"The Doc will be here, Rowly. Relax."

Rowland started as a hand fell on his shoulder and trailed up his neck. The woman stooped to whisper in his ear. She was passably pretty, but her nostrils were dilated and her eyes showed the unmistakeable signs of the drug they called Angie. Her breath reeked of poor hygiene, cigarettes, and cheap gin. Rowland sipped his drink purposefully, saying nothing while she proposed various obscenities and called him "lover."

Milton waved her away. "Forget it, sweetheart. He can afford someone a lot prettier than you."

The prostitute swore at them both and stomped off to another table.

"Bloody hell, Milt." Rowland muttered.

"What? Were you interested?" Milton was surprised. Despite his torch for Edna, Rowland had not taken holy orders. He enjoyed the company of women, but girls on the game were not his style.

"Of course not," Rowland replied. "But there was no need to insult the poor wretch."

Milton sized him up for a moment, and then laughed. "Look at her, Rowly." He pointed ever so subtly. "Notice the scar across her cheek; probably slashed by a razor. And the bruises on her arms? See her eyes? The girl's chock full of Angie…She's a rough piece who's had a rough life. Me telling her she's not pretty enough for you isn't going to upset her much in the scheme of things. You're really going to have to let go of this excessive civility of yours."

Rowland did not reply. The ruthlessness of the city, of the Depression, and the people who felt it most, seemed concentrated here, intense. The faces around them were hard, prematurely aged, and scarred by violence and life in general. The laughter was false and harsh, and the language, vulgar. Patrons huddled around the tables over small bowls of white powder, snorting and hooting.

Rowland took out his notebook to draw the confronting coarseness. As he had once told Wilfred, it helped him see. At Milton's insistence, he kept the book on his lap under the table and away from hostile eyes.

It was at least a half hour later that a stocky man approached the table. He was well dressed, his tie matched exactly by the silk handkerchief that protruded from the upper pocket of his expensive pinstriped jacket. His patent shoes were polished to a sheen that was matched by that of the dark hair slicked back from his high forehead. He clenched a cigar between his teeth. He was not an old man, by any means. He had, however, a certain dissolute worldly air that made it hard to call him young, though he may well have been.

"Milton Isaacs," he boomed, putting out a manicured hand. "Sorry, I'm late." He pulled out a chair and, turning it around, straddled it from behind.

Milton introduced Dr. Reginald Stuart-Jones to Rowland Sinclair. "Well, well," said the doctor as he shook Rowland's hand. "So old Sinkers had a nephew! And another Rowland, at that. Full of surprises, that fellow."

"So you knew him?" Rowland asked uneasily.

"Of course…He came to the track every other day. Had a good eye for the dogs when the race was fair."

Milton ordered a drink for their guest, and another for himself. Rowland had hardly touched his glass.

"So, Sinkers left you his interest in this fine establishment?" Stuart-Jones took a whisky from a passing waitress' tray and swigged it.

"It appears so," Rowland replied. "Milt informs me that you can introduce me to my uncle's partners."

"That I can." The doctor's smile was broad, revealing a gap between his two front teeth. "And I will." He glanced at his gold watch, breathed on the face and polished it with his handkerchief. "In fact, Snowy should be here in a few minutes."

Milton and Stuart-Jones fell into conversation about the shortcomings of some greyhound for which the doctor claimed to have paid a substantial sum. Rowland continued to sketch. Every now and then, girls would call by the table to offer their services suggestively, sometimes explicitly. Stuart-Jones joked with them, using double entendre to an extent that Rowland considered excessive, and a little juvenile.

Harold "Snowy" Billington was a big man. He arrived at the 50–50 with a simpering young woman on each arm and a few swishing behind. A thin, dark-featured man ran ahead of him, loudly organising chairs and drinks for "the Boss." It was an entrance calculated to impress.

Rowland and Milton stood.

As Stuart-Jones made the introductions, Billington regarded Rowland suspiciously. "Sinkers never mentioned a nephew."

"He didn't mention an interest in the 50–50, either." Rowland's voice was even.

"And what's it to you?" Billington sneered, biting the tip off a cigar and spitting it onto the floor.

"I appear to have inherited his interest."

Billington laughed—the harsh, scornful kind of laugh that Rowland noticed earlier. "That's not the way we do things, Mr. Sinclair. My agreement was with Sinkers—and it died with him."

"Perhaps, Mr. Billington. The thing is, my uncle didn't just leave me his interest in your club… he left me the deeds to these premises. I appear to be your landlord."

"Rowly!" Milton whispered in warning.

The man who entered ahead of Billington, now standing beside him, put his drink on the table, and in a move so quick that Rowland missed it, he pulled out a razor. The straight-edged blade was at Rowland's cheek before he had time to flinch. The 50–50's patrons went about their business, laughing and snorting and hooting.

"And just who do you plan to leave those deeds to, Mr. Sinclair?" Billington asked with a cold smile. "We might need to contact them…let them know of their windfall…if you catch my meaning."

Rowland looked calmly down the arm holding the razor, to the face of the man who held it, and then to Billington once more.

"The Salvation Army, actually."

The silence was heavy, palpable. Stuart-Jones looked nervous, Milton somewhat panicked. Rowland did not move his eyes from Billington, despite the blade resting against his face.

And then, suddenly, the other man laughed and flicked the razor shut, before returning it to his pocket. "He's got you, Snowy." His voice was clipped, the accent an antipodean mutation of its original Cockney. Billington's razor-wielding thug was wiry, his face cunning, and his manner restless. His features combined to give an impression of volatility. He pulled out a chair and sat opposite Rowland as he waved for Billington to follow suit. "Sit down, Sinclair."

Rowland did so slowly, a little confused by the

abrupt switch in authority from Billington to this thug. The doctor straddled his chair as before, but Milton remained standing behind him.

"Now, Mr. Sinclair, what is it that you're wanting?" The question was direct and delivered coldly.

Rowland glanced uncertainly at Billington, who was sitting attentively with a girl in his lap, as well as one at each shoulder.

The other man noticed the glance. "I am Phil Jeffs," he said. "Sometimes Phil Davies, sometimes 'The Jew.' This…"—he waved his hands widely—"is my joint. Snowy here's my cover. Welcome."

"Am I to understand that you were my uncle's partner?"

Jeffs nodded.

"I want to know who killed him, and why."

"And in exchange?'

"I'll give you the deeds and make no further claims."

"Your claims don't worry me, mate," Jeffs replied. "Where are the deeds?"

Rowland smiled, barely. "With my lawyer," he said. "I can have them sent to you tomorrow."

Jeffs glared at him. Milton stepped forward, ready for something, but unsure what. One of the girls draped over Billington began to inhale Angie from a bowl that had appeared on the table.

Then Jeffs grinned. "Sinkers wasn't

stupid...'Spose I shouldn't be shocked that his nephew isn't either. First tell me, Sinclair, why'd you think I'd even have a clue about what happened to Sinkers?"

Rowland looked around him at the degenerate clientele of the 50–50, the drug addicts, the prostitutes, and those who profitted from and used their services. A fight had broken out on one of the far tables and a lone couple dragged a drunken Charleston on the scuffed dance floor.

"It seemed like a reasonable guess," he said, as a woman stood and screamed slurred obscenities at the man who drank beside her.

Jeffs looked carefully at him. "I can't help you. I have no idea who killed him. If I did, the bastards would be dead!"

"He was beaten to death in his home."

"You think Phil 'The Jew' doesn't know that? If it had anything to do with the club, I would've heard about that, too...it's not the way we do things."

"But it is to your advantage that he's dead."

Jeffs' eyes grew flinty, dangerous. Rowland regarded him warily, watching for the razor.

"I had no beef with Sinkers," Jeffs said finally. "He knew what it meant to be a silent partner... and he was very useful in matters of cash flow...In fact, if I thought you were half the bloke old Sinkers was, I'd tell you to keep your deeds and we'd talk business ourselves."

Rowland stood. "I'll have the deeds sent over tomorrow." He held out his hand.

Jeffs took it. He shot a glance at Milton, and sneered. "I should have you both given a bloody good hiding, coming in here all bloody high and mighty," he said, "but for Sinkers' sake, I'll lay off yer." Jeffs pulled Rowland closer. He spoke quietly. "If you find out who did Sinkers in, let me know— I'll even the score for both of us."

Wisely, Rowland chose not to reply. He did not want Jeffs doing him any favours.

Jeffs tipped back in his chair, suddenly amiable. "You should enjoy our attractions while you're here." He gestured expansively at the hall. "Or take some girls with you... They're Tilly's girls—perfectly legal."

Tilly Devine was nefarious in Sydney. Madame of the city's most successful brothels, having slipped through a loophole in the law which made it illegal for men to profit from prostitution, but which was silent on the subject of women. Tilly's girls were not criminals by virtue of their occupation, at least, and probably at best.

Rowland declined, but politely.

"Are you sure?" Jeffs grinned lewdly and flicked his head toward a tall ginger-haired girl who sat near the piano. "Sinkers took young Gracie home when the spirit took him."

For the first time in a long while, Rowland thought of the fishnet stockings found in his uncle's house. He shook his head. "Thank you, but no."

Johnston was waiting in nearby William Street with the Rolls. The chauffeur did not bother to open the doors; the younger Mr. Sinclair always climbed in before the old driver could get out to observe the proprieties.

"Well, that's done then." Rowland watched as Milton opened the drinks compartment.

"For the love of God, Rowly, the Salvation Army? You threatened Phil The Jew with the Salvation Army!"

Rowland smiled. It was all he could think of at the time. "It worked, Milt."

Milton handed him a glass and raised his own. "You're either tougher than I thought, or a bloody idiot!"

Rowland drank. "Probably both." He had not found the 50–50 a pleasant experience. Razors and criminals aside, it disturbed him that his cheerful, doting uncle could have bankrolled something so seedy. He wondered if he should trust Jeffs' word that the attack had had nothing to do with Rowland Sinclair's connections at the 50–50.

"You all right?" Milton asked.

"I'm fine. Just wondering where the hell tonight leaves us. Beating a man to death still seems more like Jeffs' style than Campbell's to me."

Milton said nothing for a moment. "If I was you, mate, I'd take Jeffs at his word."

Rowland looked sceptical.

"Don't get me wrong," Milton went on. "The man's the worst kind of criminal and liar, but I think if he did have your uncle killed, he would have told you to your face—if only to make sure you toed the line. His kind don't take people out in secret…it doesn't serve their purpose."

"I suppose so," Rowland conceded. It was true that the gangland figures of Sydney did have a tendency to just walk up and shoot people. Disguises did seem out of character.

"Anyway, I think he was sincere about his regard for your uncle."

"Why's that?"

"He could have given us a good kicking… he's bashed men for a lot less than what you said to him."

"So that was him being sentimental?"

"Believe it or not Rowly, I think it was."

Chapter Twenty-seven

New Guard
Statements Against Police

Minister Refutes

SYDNEY

The Chief Secretary (Mr. Gosling) said to-night that he had received from Mr. E. D. Irving, the acting Metropolitan Superintendent, a report replying to a statement made by Mr. Campbell in the Town Hall last night.

The report said: "A statement by Campbell that a detective officer was promoted, and another derated over the insulting words case is incorrect."

The report also challenges many other statements by Campbell and denies that a transcript or notes was taken by police at a meeting held at St. George's Hall, Newtown, on January 31, when Kavanagh, a

Communist, is alleged to have insulted the
King.

The Daily Telegraph, February 19, 1932

Rowland pushed his necktie into place and buttoned his jacket. He slicked his hair back and
promptly dishevelled it with a careless drag of his
hand. Even so, he was the picture of the young
conservative gentleman. No one would suspect
that he had just divested himself of a part-interest
in the city's most disreputable nightclub.

He could hear the motorcab idling in the
driveway. He touched the outside of his jacket
pocket to check he had his notebook, and grabbed
his hat as he headed out the door. It was early evening. The New Guard was gathering at the Sydney
Town Hall, or at least a representation of the New
Guard. The Hall would hold a maximum of three
thousand men, so only a few delegates would be
allowed from each locality.

In the pocket of his trousers, Rowland carried
the khaki armband he had been issued. He'd take
it out to slip over the sleeve of his jacket when he
got there. He certainly wasn't going to wear it in
the street.

Traffic clogged the main roads of the city

centre, and so there were several minutes between the moment Rowland spied the clock tower of the Hall, and when they actually reached the building. Eventually, his motorcab dropped him at the porte cochere that had been constructed in front of the entrance for the comfort and convenience of the city's wealthier citizens. As he alighted, Rowland paused briefly. The Town Hall was looking a little worse for wear. The construction of the railway station beneath the building had caused significant cracking. Even the porte cochere had to be reinforced with temporary supports, and wooden scaffolding had been creeping up the sandstone tower, following the progress of the cracks. Still, this was the Sydney Town Hall, majestic, even if its foundations were compromised and the stability of its tower in doubt. To Rowland, it was the perfect place for the New Guard to meet.

He paid the driver through the window and pulled on his armband, ready to be marshalled by the staff officers who were on duty to ensure a quick and orderly entrance into the venue.

"Hello, Jonesy." It was Poynton. "Wrong arm, mate." He pointed to the armband. "Goes on the other arm."

"Thank you." Rowland moved the khaki strip to his left arm.

"You're to come with me," Poynton said. "The Colonel wants you up front."

"Lead on." Rowland suppressed any sign of his reluctance. He had hoped to slip into the back unnoticed.

He saw the hall was beyond full. Poynton informed him that, by crowding, the organisers were aiming to squash in a force of double the standard capacity. The men were seated in groups, their units distinguished by the colour and markings on their armbands. Poynton escorted him down the left-hand aisle and toward the steps leading up to the stage.

"We're just here." The bodyguard turned into the first row.

Rowland followed him, looking up at the stage. Several chairs had been placed in a wide arc behind the podium. Cables ran across the wooden boards and microphones had been set up. Campbell's address to the New Guard was to be broadcast over the wireless.

Rowland sat down, pressed against Poynton on one side, and another Guardsman on the other. The seats on the stage now started to fill, with several faces he recognised from the party at Boongala. De Groot sat up there with the other zone leaders and nodded primly when Rowland caught his eye.

John Dynon was in Rowland's row, a few seats

down, talking to a young Guardsman. Rowland stared; he knew the man Dynon was talking to. Their dealings had been brief, but he rarely forgot a face. If the recognition was mutual, Clyde Watson Jones could be in serious jeopardy. He shifted, hoping the bulk of Poynton would be enough to keep him from the man's sight.

Every seat was now spoken for, and the temperature was rising. The air was charged with a kind of reverent expectancy as the men of the New Guard waited for their leader. When Campbell finally walked down the aisle with all the ceremony of a bride, the hall rose as one and exploded into a spontaneous ovation. Two standard-bearers walked behind Campbell, holding aloft the Union Jack and a five-coloured pennant with purple tassels which Rowland had become aware was the New Guard's own flag.

The noise had not yet subsided when Campbell stepped onto the stage and handed a carbon copy of his address to each of the men seated at the press tables.

The strains of the grand pipe organ eventually overshadowed the applause as the meeting opened with "O God Our Help in Ages Past." The sound of close to five thousand male voices, raised in fervent song, was slightly more tuneful but no quieter than the reception that had greeted Campbell.

After the chaplain dedicated the colours, Campbell rose again to thunderous applause.

Rowland took out his notebook and made a few sketches of Campbell at the lectern, more because De Groot was watching than anything else. He didn't so much listen to the words as to the tone, and it sounded like it was the standard mix of fiery rhetoric, patriotic zealotry, and ruling class paranoia he was hearing far too often for his liking. The men around him, however, hung onto every word as if Campbell was some kind of holy prophet. When his message was delivered, the audience stood and roared with unrestrained adulation.

Campbell called for silence and with him, five thousand men raised their right arms in the Fascist salute and took the affirmation of the New Guard:

"I solemnly and sincerely affirm that I will by every means in my power and without regard for consequence, do my utmost to establish in the state of New South Wales the high principles for which the New Guard stands. I will not consider my oath fulfilled until Communism has been completely crushed and until an honourable government has been established. I make this affirmation in the name of God and the King and in memory of my countrymen who lost their lives in defence of the same principles. So help me God."

Rowland avoided the salute and the affirmation by drawing furiously and obviously.

The affirmation was followed by a bombastic rendering of the "Song of the New Guard," a painstakingly rhymed ballad which declared the Guardsmen to be both ready and steady, and which finished with the cry "God save our King."

Then the hall rang with "Advance Australia Fair,"

"Land of Hope and Glory," and the national anthem. Just when Rowland was beginning to feel he was caught in a never-ending patriotic sing-along, the congregation finished with "For He's a Jolly Good Fellow" and the rally concluded.

The Guardsmen began to file out of the hall. Campbell remained at the lectern, shaking hands and accepting congratulations. Once again, there was a flurry of backslapping. Poynton stood and after stretching, ushered Rowland up the stage steps.

De Groot met them first. "Jones," he said, ignoring Poynton, "I trust we managed to impress the nature of our organisation upon you." His eyes fell meaningfully on the notebook Rowland was still holding.

Rowland smiled. "I did make a few sketches," he said, "though I hope you didn't do all this just for my benefit."

De Groot looked at him sharply, and then laughed. "Very good, very good."

"De Groot!" John Dynon was making his way toward them. Rowland closed his eyes for a moment, sure now his game was up.

Dynon was bringing with him the man Rowland had recognised earlier. If he was going to be exposed, this was probably the worst possible time for it to happen. Dynon shook hands with De Groot. Rowland met the eyes of Constable Delaney, who had told him his uncle was dead, and who had watched him identify the body. Delaney's face was startled and Rowland knew he had been recognised. His own precarious situation meant that he did not pause to wonder what a serving member of the New South Wales police force was doing in the New Guard.

"You've met Poynton and Jones," De Groot said to Dynon. "Jones has found tonight's meeting useful as a background for his painting of the Commander."

Rowland didn't take his eyes off Delaney as he waited for disaster to descend.

Dynon returned the formality. "Allow me to introduce Jack Harris," he said. "Harris has recently joined the Guard, my own unit. He'll be joining us for cards in the near future." Dynon winked and De Groot cleared his throat.

"What line of business are you in, Mr. Harris?" De Groot asked.

"I'm a printer, sir."

They stood in stilted conversation for a while.

Finally Poynton edged Rowland aside. "Jonesy, I'd love to offer you a lift home, but the Colonel needs me tonight."

"I'll give you a lift," Delaney volunteered, before Rowland could respond. "I have my car parked down the street a short way."

"I wouldn't want to trouble you," Rowland replied, bewildered by both the man's presence and his failure to expose Clyde Watson Jones as a fraud.

"I insist." Delaney's tone made it clear to Rowland that he was in fact insisting.

They spoke relatively little until they reached Delaney's black Ford Tudor. Rowland climbed into the front passenger side seat, and Delaney started the car. "Right, Mr. Sinclair," he said, "what the hell are you up to?"

"And who exactly would I be telling? Jack Harris or Constable Delaney?"

Delaney put the Ford into gear. "Actually it's Detective Constable now. We're going to make a small detour before I drop you home."

"Why?"

"I think we may need to better understand

each other, Mr. Sinclair." Rowland didn't see he had any other option.

When they arrived at police headquarters, Delaney took him into the building through a back way, and left Rowland in a small office, alone.

A few minutes later, Delaney returned to wait with him but was unwilling to say anything more. Half an hour passed and Rowland began to pace impatiently.

There was no knock at the door. It was simply opened and a large man strode in. He was dressed in white tie and tails; apparently, he had been dining when he'd received word from Delaney. Consequently, he was not in the best of moods.

"Mr. Sinclair," he said in a thick Glaswegian accent as he offered Rowland his hand. "I believe we have a situation."

The newcomer's belligerent jaw and barrel chest exuded a kind of pugnacious strength but his face was otherwise round and unexpectedly boyish.

"I don't believe we've had the pleasure." Rowland took his hand.

"Superintendent MacKay, Criminal Investigation Bureau." Rowland had read of MacKay in the papers.

"Detective Constable Delaney tells me that you have found yourself involved with the New

Guard, but that you do so under the name of Jones."

"In that respect, Superintendent, Detective Constable Delaney is telling the truth," Rowland said carefully.

MacKay's face flushed a little. "Just suppose, Mr. Sinclair, that you tell us why Mr. Campbell and his colleagues know you as Jones?"

Rowland looked slowly from MacKay to Delaney, and then back to MacKay. He wasn't sure if his actions to date were illegal, but he doubted it. He told them what he was doing and why, though he omitted mentioning the forged references.

Delaney raised his eyebrows, and the line of MacKay's mouth tightened considerably.

"Mr. Sinclair," said the Superintendent tersely, "while I commiserate with your loss, you are interfering in matters best left to the police. You are not only putting yourself in danger but jeopardising a police operation."

"About that…" Rowland tried to be pleasant. "Am I to understand that Detective Constable Delaney here has insinuated himself into the New Guard as a spy, under the false name of Jack Harris?"

"That is not your concern."

Rowland carried on regardless. "If that is the

case, it seems you require my discretion as much as I do yours."

Delaney winced in the brief moment of silence before MacKay exploded—he was not going to be blackmailed by some well-heeled upstart. Rowland stood his ground. Indeed, despite his accent, MacKay's remonstrations took a tone similar to that of Wilfred's, and Rowland became instinctively stubborn.

"I am afraid, Superintendent," Rowland said firmly, "I have every intention of finding out who killed my uncle. I don't see why that should be a problem for you."

In the end, MacKay slammed his fist on the desk in disgust. "I would like nothing better, Mr. Sinclair, than to march you up to Mr. Campbell's door and tell him he's been played for a fool...." He glanced at Delaney. "However, the operation the Detective Constable is involved in is crucial to the security of this state, so I will have to tolerate you despite my better judgement."

"Very good of you." Rowland held back a smile.

"Get him out of here!" MacKay barked at Delaney as he stormed out the doorway back to whatever was left of his dinner party.

Delaney took Rowland back to the car. When they were safely away, he grinned.

"I'm afraid the Superintendent's not very happy with you, Mr. Sinclair. I'll venture you've spoilt his evening."

"I'm sure he won't starve." Rowland gathered that the Superintendent was a formidable man to work for. "Look Delaney, there's no reason we should be enemies—we may even be able to help one another."

"I was thinking that too, sir."

Now that the subject had been broached, the two exchanged information freely. Delaney, posing as Jack Harris the printer, had joined the New Guard to gather intelligence for the police force. He was looking for any signs that Campbell was inciting revolution. While he did not say so explicitly, he intimated he was not the only police agent who had infiltrated the movement.

"Why is Dynon so obsessed with playing cards?" Rowland asked, remembering the Guardsman's cryptic allusions and the winks that went with them.

"It's a code but I'm not sure what for." Delaney frowned. "Dynon's paranoid about spies, so he keeps you in the dark until you're standing in it. Seems he gets a fair bit of churn in his unit. He regularly chucks people out for disloyalty."

"All things considered, his paranoia's probably not unwarranted." In turn, Rowland told Delaney everything he had already passed on, but unlike Inspector Bicuit, Delaney did not dismiss it.

"You may be onto something, sir," he said. "I'll keep a lookout…let you know if I find anything."

"Thank you, Delaney…I mean Harris," Rowland corrected himself. "You don't think Campbell's really planning a coup, do you?"

"That's what we want to find out." Delaney shrugged. "They seem ready to fight, but it's hard to know what they'll do when they're faced with it. It's easy to march around and shoot when there's no one shooting back…They may just be in it for the parades. I certainly hope so."

Chapter Twenty-eight

SYDNEY BY DAY

SYDNEY

A feature of the ball in the great hall at the showground will be ultra-modern and old-time dancing by Lady Anderson Stuart with a professional partner. Lady Anderson Stuart won praise in English society competitions for her foxtrot and waltzing.

The Argus, February 19, 1932

The gramophone was playing a swing recording when Rowland walked into the drawing room. The furniture had been moved to the walls and Milton was collapsed on the couch, clutching his ribs and laughing. Clyde and Edna stood in the middle of the floor, the latter scolding Milton, and the former looking mortified. Lenin sat watching them, his head tilted at an angle that accentuated the fact that he was missing an ear.

"What's going on?" Rowland shouted over the racket.

Edna led Clyde in a stumbling swirl over to the gramophone and lifted the needle. "I'm teaching Clyde to foxtrot," she said. "Can't you tell?"

Milton started to laugh again and Clyde strode across and cuffed him.

"Why?" Rowland asked. Milton and Edna had always kept up with the latest dances, but Clyde?

All eyes turned expectantly to Clyde. Clyde stuttered for a moment and then, with the sigh of a man defeated, admitted, "I met a girl."

Milton started laughing again.

"So why do you need to foxtrot?" Rowland was still a little perplexed.

Clyde glowered at Milton. "I'm told it's necessary."

"Whatever for?"

"My point, exactly," Clyde grumbled.

"Because," Milton intervened, "if one is to court a girl, one must be able to take her to a dance—it's how things are done…unless she's a Methodist."

"Oh." Rowland removed his jacket. "How's it going then?"

"Clyde should consider becoming a Methodist."

"Be quiet, Milt. You're not helping," Edna said crossly.

"If he must dance, Ed, why don't you teach him to waltz?" Rowland suggested. "It's easier and, trust me, the foxtrot will never catch on."

"How long has it been since you went out dancing, Rowly? All the bands are playing foxtrots now. And Clyde needs to make a good impression."

"You'd better get back to it then." Rowland turned. "I'm going to find something to eat."

"Wasn't there a supper after the meeting?"

Rowland laughed at the image of five thousand Guardsmen arriving with plates of sandwiches dutifully prepared by their wives and mothers. "No. No supper."

"What happened?" Clyde was clearly desperate for any reason to postpone his dancing lesson.

"See for yourself." Rowland tossed his notebook over to him. "I won't be long."

He returned shortly, with a tin of Mary Brown's highland fruitcake. He shoved Milton, and the poet made room for him on the couch.

"What's going on here?" Clyde pointed to the drawing of men with their right arms raised in the Fascist salute. "Who are they waving at?"

Rowland told him about the pledge.

"I didn't realise we went to war to crush

Communism," Milton muttered. "Thought it was the Huns."

"It was like a Masonic meeting gone mad—I was expecting someone to come up with a secret handshake." Rowland broke off a hunk of fruitcake and told them about Jack Harris who turned out to be Constable Delaney.

"They have someone investigating your uncle's murder from within the New Guard."

"No," Rowland replied. "Delaney is working directly for Bill MacKay, not Bicuit. He's more interested in whether Campbell's really going to lead a coup any time soon."

"What do you think, Rowly?" Clyde decided to help his friend finish the cake. "Are these people serious about revolution, or is it all talk?"

"I don't know…maybe." Rowland frowned. "You'd feel a bit of a fool with all the drilling and saluting and singing, if you weren't serious, don't you think? If they don't do something soon, they run the risk that history will remember them as clowns, and I'm pretty sure Campbell would declare war just to avoid that."

"What about MacKay?" Milton asked.

"Looks good in tails…a jolly, determined sort of chap." Rowland fed the remains of the cake to a grateful Lenin. "According to Delaney, MacKay's got spies and informants everywhere, and not just with Campbell's men."

"Well, that's comforting," said Edna. "But you don't think this is getting too dangerous, do you, Rowly? You were nearly found out today."

Clyde snorted triumphantly, but said nothing.

Rowland smiled. Compared to the 50–50 Club, the New Guard seemed very tame indeed. "No, I think it'll be all right," he said. "Although, I'm probably bloody lucky not to have run into someone else who knows me."

Milton chuckled. "We could always call your brother to ransom you if things go really wrong."

"I'm not sure his lot is all that different than Campbell's, you know…they're just quieter." He wrinkled his nose. "All this fanfare is very bourgeois."

"Marvellous," said Milton. "All we have to do is manoeuvre between the ruling class and the really ruling class."

"Rowly…" Edna took down a frame from the mantelpiece. She studied the picture of the young man who looked so much like Rowland Sinclair. "Was Aubrey like Wilfred?"

The question was unexpected, but Rowly wasn't surprised that Edna would ask it. The sculptress had a very direct way of dealing with anything that caught her attention. "I was barely ten when I last saw him, Ed—even Wilfred wasn't like Wilfred back then."

"Would Aubrey have joined the Old Guard?"

"I don't know that Aubrey ever took things as seriously…I vaguely remember him calling Wil, 'Lord Wilfred Properly of the Colonies.' I had a couple of his letters from the front, before he died…he probably would have come back changed. Wil did. Most people did."

"Why the sudden interest in Rowly's brothers?" Milton asked.

"I was always interested." Edna returned Aubrey's picture to its place. "Just haven't asked before."

"We just missed it." Clyde spoke wistfully. "…the war…if we were a year or two older, we would have gone, too."

"Of course Rowly would have got a commission," added Milton. "You and I would have joined the rest of the proletariat in the general infantry."

"But we would have seen service, all the same." Clyde's eyes were distant.

Rowland was unsure whether it was regret or relief, but he thought he understood how Clyde felt. They were all of a generation who could not possibly have seen war service, but who were marked by the lack of it, all the same. Certainly, he was aware it lessened him in Wilfred's eyes. Perhaps

Clyde felt it even more keenly. A couple of years his elder, Clyde had finally managed to make himself look old enough to enlist, but he was too late…the war was won by then. Milton, too, would probably have volunteered as soon as he could, although Rowland suspected the poet would have been shot for insubordination before long.

"We've dodged that bullet." Milton was unusually reflective. "I don't know if the Great War was the war to end all wars—it probably wasn't— but there won't be another one in our lifetimes."

Clyde snorted. "What about Campbell's revolution?"

That had crossed all their minds.

"So, Rowly, have you finally started Camp-bell's painting?" Edna intervened before the mood became too sombre.

"Tomorrow," Rowland replied. "Really."

"How are you going to paint him?"

"I'm tempted to paint him pruning his roses… or sitting in the sun with a big fluffy cat in his lap." Rowland laughed. "But I won't…I'll paint him as King Campbell surrounded by his Fascist legions."

"Just paint slowly," Milton warned. "The way you usually work, you'll be finished in two days and you'll have no reason to hang around."

"You have a point," Rowland sighed. "But I'll have to show them something soon."

"Do some large preliminary sketches." Clyde flicked through Rowland's notebook. "It'll make him think you're working and allow you to waste a bit of time."

"That's not a bad idea." Rowland closed the empty tin. "I'll take some in for our next sitting date…Now, shouldn't you be learning to dance?"

Clyde cursed and complained, but allowed himself to be dragged back to the makeshift floor by Edna. Within minutes, Milton had resumed laughing. Rowland watched more politely, but even he had to struggle not to smile. Frustrated, Edna bid Clyde to watch and grabbed Milton to demonstrate. A very accomplished dancer, now with an audience, Milton incorporated the flamboyant moves of a skilled exhibitionist. He dipped and twirled and flourished with aplomb. Clyde laughed and made some quite unnecessary aspersions about the poet's masculinity. In the end, Edna used Rowland to show Clyde how normal people danced.

A few evenings later, Rowland stood at his easel working on a series of drawings to present to Campbell as drafts for his portrait. It was late, but the quiet in the house allowed him to concentrate. Until the front door burst open, and Clyde charged in.

"Where's the fire?" Rowland didn't look up.

"Bankstown. We've got a problem, Rowly… Milt's been arrested."

Rowland put down his pencil and grabbed his jacket from the back of the couch. "What for?"

"Riotous behaviour."

"In Bankstown?" said Rowland, as if the location was more surprising than the charge.

They walked briskly toward the stables. "What was Milt doing in Bankstown?"

"We were both there," Clyde replied. "At a Party meeting. The New Guard arrived to break it up."

"I see."

The New Guard had been making it their business to break up left-wing meetings.

"I'd better drive." Clyde slipped in behind the Mercedes steering wheel. "That way, you can duck if we happen across any Guardsmen…which we might."

"So, what happened?"

"The Fascists turned up—about twenty carloads. They fronted the meeting and started singing 'God Save the King' at the top of their lungs. Of course the Party faithful hit back with 'The Red Flag.'" Clyde shook his head. "It was kind of ridiculous."

"There's a lot of that going around."

"Well, after a while, the singing—if you can

call it that—turned into a general rabble…people only ever remember the first verse anyway, and anything after that is mumbling guesswork. So, we're all standing there, tunefully abusing each other when things start to get a bit interesting. Someone clocked a Guardsman with a garden stake, and then it was on…and you know Milt, he made sure he was in the thick of it."

"Is that when the police…?"

"No. The Labor Party was holding some big do across the street, in aid of the unemployed, so they raced over and joined in and, all of a sudden, there was brawling in the streets. The Guardsmen got back into their cars and drove around in circles, shouting threats."

"But how did Milt get arrested?

"The police did finally turn up and they arrested a few people—Communists, of course, not Guardsmen. And Milt, the bloody fool, just couldn't keep his mouth shut, accusing the police of being in league with the Fascists. He's lucky they didn't shoot him."

Rowland sighed. "I guess it's part of his charm."

"Listen, my cousin lives near the police station," Clyde said as they got close to Bankstown. "We'll park at his place; posh cars aren't too popular out here right now."

Rowland nodded, giving the dash a comforting pat.

Bankstown was one of the suburbs on which the Depression had settled. Many of the businesses down the main street had been shuttered for months, the weatherboard cottages had not seen paint in far too long, and fences were dilapidated. Windows were broken and boarded up and the remnants of barbed wire flagged those houses that had been the subject of eviction sieges. Vacant blocks were piled high with the trash, and though the recent public works schemes had seen sewerage extended to the area, the air was tainted since sanitation mostly still relied on poorly maintained outhouses. Bankstown had more than its share of unemployed, and it had become a stage for riots and unrest as political extremes collided.

Clyde pulled into a large block and drove the Mercedes right down the back. The motorcar's headlamps caught the glow of startled eyes as several rabbits hopped out of its path.

"Bankstown roast," Clyde pointed to the hopping rodents. He hadn't eaten rabbit since he moved to Woodlands House.

Lights came on in the cottage and the tenant emerged shortly thereafter, still in his nightshirt, but ready for a fight. "Put the cricket bat down, Mick," Clyde shouted by way of greeting.

"Clyde! What the hell…?"

Clyde calmed him and introduced Rowland.

"We need to get someone out of gaol, but we don't want to risk the car."

Mick seemed somewhat confused. He scratched the thinning hair on his head as he gazed at the immaculate yellow tourer. "Yeah, all right, I'll keep an eye on 'er."

"Thank you." Rowland offered Mick his hand.

Mick shook it, still a little vague. He had, after all, been woken in the middle of the night. "Do yer mind if I bring the young fella out to have a look at it?—He'll be living the life of Riley."

"Certainly," Rowland replied. "We'll drop by and take him for a ride one day, when things have calmed down. Hopefully, we won't be too long tonight."

"Yeah, if they haven't already hanged him," Clyde added.

Having ensured the Mercedes was defended, they made their way to the Bankstown Police Station. It was well after midnight and though the station was active, calm had returned to the streets. As they walked in, they could hear a rowdy chorus of "The Red Flag" being sung from behind the door that led to the cells.

"… *Then raise the scarlet standard high, Within its shade we'll live and die…*"

Rowland approached the desk sergeant and informed him that he wished to secure the release of a man who had been arrested earlier for "riotous behavior."

The officer's thick moustache bristled. "Would that be one of the Messrs. Eric Campbells, or one of the Messrs. Francis De Groots?"

"I beg your pardon?"

"Nine men were arrested at the, ah, events." The sergeant checked the numbers off his charge sheet. "Five have given their names as Eric Campbell, the other four as Francis De Groot. For which of these men do you wish to pay the fine, sir?"

Rowland heard Clyde laugh behind him.

"How about I just pay all the fines?" Rowland pulled out his chequebook.

"Then I would thank you...Damn infernal noise!"

"The Red Flag" rang through the station yet again. "...*Though cowards flinch and traitors sneer, We'll keep the red flag flying here...*"

And so, Rowland Sinclair secured the release of nine men who had been arrested, rightly or wrongly, for riotous behaviour during what the newspapers would later report as the "Battle of Bankstown."

Milton was in extraordinary spirits for a man who had spent the last several hours incarcerated, as were all the men who emerged from the cells. Rowland and Clyde politely declined invitations to celebrate the mass release, and returned to the car with a slightly reluctant Milton. The poet was exhilarated by his own minor martyrdom, and he subjected his friends to solo renditions of the Communist anthem on the walk back.

They found Mick sitting in the Mercedes, with a cricket bat in his lap, while his young son sat awestruck behind the wheel. They thanked him, threatened to assault Milton if he didn't stop singing, and returned to Woodlands House. It was still a few hours before dawn.

Rowland flung his jacket at the coat stand, loosened his tie, fell into the couch and looked at Clyde and Milton, who had taken to the armchairs in a similar fashion. He started to laugh. He had maintained his composure as he bailed the multiple Eric Campbells and Francis De Groots and ushered the same improbably named group out of the station as they triumphantly sang "The Red Flag." But now, he laughed.

Milton grinned, relieved. They had driven back with the top down, making conversation impossible. He had been a little unsure of how Rowland felt about personally signing for the release of nine Communists accused of riotous behaviour. As he watched him laugh, he was reminded of what an uncommon man Rowland Sinclair was.

"Thank you, Rowly." The poet was sincerely grateful. "I didn't expect you to bail the entire party."

Rowland sat up. He wiped his eyes. "God, it was worth it!"

Milton stood and poured drinks, and as was often the case when he had a glass to hand, he was moved to poetry. "Thou who art victory and law, when empty terrors overawe; From vain temptations dost set free, and calm'st the weary strife of frail humanity!"

"Wordsworth," groaned Rowland. "And very tenuously relevant."

"I'll give you bloody frail humanity," Clyde muttered.

"We'd better toast the freedom of Eric Campbell then." Milton was undeterred. "To Eric Campbell—any one of them!"

"To Rowland Sinclair," corrected Clyde, "who, it appears, has released the Red Army from the Bankstown watch house."

Rowland laughed again and shook his head. "The whole state's gone mad…we're all following lunatics into revolution."

Chapter Twenty-nine

CLASH WITH COMMUNISTS

New Guard in Sydney
POLICE RESTORE ORDER

SYDNEY, Friday

There were wild scenes in Thompson Park, Bankstown, tonight when a detachment of the 200 New Guard in 37 vehicles clashed with Communists holding a rally.

Earlier in the night members of the New Guard broke up a meeting of the Unemployed Workers Movement at Newtown, at which revolutionary statements were alleged to have been made.

Large detachments of police were hurried to Bankstown and, after a number of arrests, order was restored.

The Argus, February 28, 1932

They had all slept late the next morning, and so it was over luncheon that they exchanged the various morning papers which reported the violence from the night before. Edna was the last to emerge and came in to find Mary Brown's elegant meal buried under the open broadsheets.

"What time did you get in last night?" Milton remembered her absence.

"I didn't." She poured lemonade from a large jug.

"Oh, that's all right then."

No one enquired further; they were none of them the sculptress' keeper, and nor were they monks themselves. In any case, only Rowland really cared, and he kept that to himself.

"*The Herald* has the Guardsmen victorious," Rowland said, calmly moving the conversation back to the reports in the newspapers.

"*The Workers' Weekly* says the people taught the Fascists a lesson they'll never forget," said Clyde from behind that paper. "Apparently they thrashed the Guardsmen and then attacked their cars."

Rowland winced. Damaging cars was uncalled for.

"They're calling it the Battle of Bankstown." Milton peered over Clyde's shoulder, clearly pleased with the epic nature of the title. "Here...'several rowdy men were arrested and fined for riotous behaviour'…that'd be me."

"You were arrested?" Edna looked up, alarmed.

Milton told her what happened, with more embellishments than even *The Workers' Weekly*, when it came to his own involvement.

"Perhaps now you won't have to look over your shoulder for Harcourt Garden's mates." Clyde was hopeful.

"I wouldn't count on it," Milton warned. "Harry doesn't let go of things that easily."

"I'd like to be a fly on Campbell's wall right now." Clyde searched under the newspaper for his plate. "Do you think he knows he was arrested last night—several times?"

"I don't think the New Guard is as friendly with the police as Campbell has the world believe." Rowland stirred his coffee. "And that's the only way he'd know."

Rowland spent the next few hours finishing his 'statesman' series of drawings—Campbell among the New Guard in salute, in the midst of a fiery address, and being backslapped by his minions. After rolling up the large sheets into a manageable parcel, Rowland left for Boongala, where he was due at four o'clock. The Colonel had a military obsession with punctuality.

The Commander of the New Guard was

pleased with the sketches. It seemed to him that Jones had benefited from his attendance at Belmore, and the Town Hall. He did wish that he still had a full head of hair, but perhaps he could get Jones to paint him in a hat. De Groot would be satisfied anyway; he was sure of it.

Rowland had expected to make arrangements for Campbell's first formal sitting that day, but the Colonel was called away to talk to the papers about the "Battle of Bankstown." He sent Herbert Poynton to deal with the artist who waited for him in the sitting room outside his study.

"Afraid the Colonel's not going to be finished for a while, Jonesy," the bodyguard said, taking the armchair beside Rowland and placing two glasses of whisky on the side table between them. Rowland left the drink.

"He's very happy with your sketches…got us both thinking you're the man to help us with a little job."

"Oh?" Rowland doubted very much that Campbell consulted with the bodyguard on such matters. It was more likely that he simply instructed Poynton to engage Rowland…Still, he was intrigued.

"Yes, a man of your artistic talents is just what we need…," Poynton swirled the whisky then held the glass up to the light. "What do you say, Jonesy? Shall I pick you up tomorrow?"

"What exactly do you want me to do?"

"Well, I can't really tell you more until I know you're in." Poynton tapped the side of his nose. "Let's just say, you'll need your pencil."

Rowland relaxed. For a minute, he thought he was going to be asked to do something illegal. They just wanted him to draw some other fist-waving Fascist; he wondered who it was.

"Very well. I'll do it...whatever it is."

"I'll pick you up tomorrow at nine." Poynton finally took a sip. "We'll be away overnight, so bring what you need."

"Where are we going?"

"Need to know, Jonesy," Poynton replied. "I'll fill you in on the way."

Rowland wondered whether he should have been so quick to agree, but the time to back out gracefully had passed.

◇◇◇

"I don't know, Rowly." Clyde was clearly troubled. "It's a bit stupid to go off with no idea what they're expecting you to do. What if they want you to assassinate Lang?"

"With a pencil? I'm not much of a shot even with a gun," Rowland replied. "No, they'll just be wanting me to paint someone."

"So why all the secrecy?"

Rowland shrugged. "I gather Herb Poynton gets a bit carried away with his own importance."

"We'll have to go with you," Milton decided.

"How do you plan to do that? Poynton's picking me up."

"We'll follow."

Rowland laughed. "In my car? I don't think so, Milt—she's not exactly discreet."

"He's right." Even so, Clyde was not happy

"It'll be all right," Rowland assured him, smiling. "Poynton's not a bad chap really…he's just fallen in with a bad crowd."

"I'm glad you find this amusing," Clyde muttered.

"What do we do if you…disappear?" Milton pulled a coin from his pocket and made it vanish.

Impressed though he was by the poet's sleight of hand, Rowland didn't think that his own disappearance was likely. "Get in touch with Constable Delaney," he said. "And phone Wil."

Edna, when she returned, was more intrigued than concerned. "I wonder where he could be taking you."

"I'll find out tomorrow."

"If you had a less ostentatious car, we could follow you." The sculptress sighed.

"Ostentatious!" Rowland was affronted. "I think you mean distinctive."

"Yes, of course, that's what I meant."

They passed the evening in their usual fashion. Clyde departed early to attend the charity twilight dance for which he had been practising. Rowland offered him the Mercedes, but the painter declined.

"I don't want to raise the poor girl's expectations," he said resolutely.

"After dancing with you for a while, she's unlikely to be able to walk far," Milton said as he dealt hands to Rowland and Edna. "You should take the car." Clyde might have responded rudely, but there was a great deal of truth in what the poet said.

"You look very handsome, Clyde." Edna kicked Milton under the table. "Any girl would be lucky to be on your arm."

Milton snorted, but Clyde looked a little less nervous.

"Just remember not to count out loud," Edna added helpfully.

"Why don't you come along, Rowly?" Clyde stopped at the door. "There are plenty of girls at these things. I could wait while you…"

Rowland laughed. "And just which one of us would be Clyde Watson Jones?" he asked. "It could be a bit confusing for your young lady."

"Right, I forgot."

"Take the car," Rowland said, rearranging his

hand. "You can lower her expectations once she's agreed to marry you. That's how it's usually done."

"I'm just taking her to a dance," Clyde muttered uncomfortably; but in the end, he took the car.

Rowland and Milton played poker with Edna, while Lenin lay under the card table between them.

Early next morning Rowland arrived at the house of Selwin Higgins in Burwood. Edna's father had now become accustomed to Rowland's unexpected appearances, and was more than happy to accommodate the young man's need for a humble address.

They heard Poynton's horn blast on the dot of nine. Rowland climbed into the front of the blue Buick, tossing his small carpet bag onto the backseat. "Where are we off to?" he asked.

Poynton kept one hand on the steering wheel and removed his cigarette with the other. "Berrima."

Rowland nodded. Berrima was only a couple of hours south of Sydney, not far from Bowral. "Why?"

"Reconnaissance…time well spent, you know."

"For what?"

"As I've told you, Jonesy, there are big things happening. We're going to see about accommodating some of those big things."

"And how do I fit in?"

"The Colonel needs a plan of the facility

drafted…so he can assess what has to be done… where to put men, weapons that sort of thing."

Rowland was becoming quite alarmed. "Look, Herb, you're really going to have to tell me what this is all about."

Poynton smiled smugly. "In times of war, Jonesy," he said, tossing his cigarette butt out of the window, "it's necessary to have somewhere to hold the enemy…prisoners of war, and all that."

"What war?" demanded Rowland coldly.

"The one we're about to start, Jonesy."

Chapter Thirty

Poynton's Buick pulled up at the gates of Berrima's former gaol and, after a few knowing nose taps, they were waved through into the complex of imposing stone buildings. The site hadn't been used as a criminal prison for decades; so-called enemy aliens had been interned there during the war, but it had since fallen into disuse. As Poynton parked, two men walked out from one of the buildings to greet them. He introduced them as Gerald Clarke and John Winslow. The younger man, Winslow, was the current lessee of the facility, and both were stalwarts of the New Guard.

"We'd better let you gentlemen get on with it," Winslow said, pulling a cigarette from a slim gold case. "I've already prepared a summary for you with the position of dark cells and suitable places for officers' quarters, cookhouses, latrines, and the like." He opened an enamelled lighter, and held the flame to his cigarette.

Rowland studied Winslow's face. It was narrow, sculpted with high cheekbones. It might have been a cruel face if the man's eyelashes had not been ridiculously long, giving him a feminine and theatrical air. "I think we can more than accommodate the numbers the Commander has in mind," Winslow concluded.

"And, once you're finished here, gentlemen, we shall expect you at Sunbury," said the flame-haired and freckled Gerald Clarke. "It'll give you a chance to meet the Princess." He beamed proudly.

Rowland was startled by this latest revelation. What princess? Was Campbell planning to install his own monarchy? Winslow rolled his eyes, almost imperceptibly.

Clarke and Winslow took them on a brief tour of the facility, showing them the general cell blocks and other accommodations. When they came back into the yard, Winslow pointed to the roof. "With a few minor modifications, you could mount machine guns there…there…and there."

"Machine guns?" Rowland exclaimed, before he could check himself.

"The Commander's made it clear that escapees will be shot." Winslow now regarded Rowland with suspicion. "You don't have any war service, do you, son? If you had, you'd know this was no time for half-measures…you'll learn that, if you're lucky."

Rowland bit back a response, and decided that he did not like John Winslow. Their guides then left them to attend to some business of their own.

"I'll book a call through to Eric," Clarke said over his shoulder. "Let him know you have the job in hand."

"Right," said Rowland once he was alone with Poynton. "What the hell are we doing here, Herb? Just who is the Colonel planning to imprison here?"

Poynton smiled in his broad, simple way. "Settle down, Jonesy...you're gonna love this." Poynton spread out his arms. "This illustrious facility is soon where we'll be holding the very bastards who are destroying this great nation."

"The Communists?" Rowland was incredulous.

"No, the Premier...the Big Fella himself."

"You're going to imprison the Premier?"

"Not just the Premier, Jonesy, the entire State Cabinet—all Lang's partners in crime. The Colonel says they've had their chance; our hand has been forced. If we don't act soon, the Reds will take control. First it'll be this State, then the nation. A nation under the Reds...imagine it, Jonesy. It'd be the end of everything we know and love."

Rowland stared at him, staggered.

"So we have to make sure that this place can be made absolutely secure." Poynton flung a friendly arm about his shoulders. "That's where you come in. You're going to draw up plans, a layout, so we can do what's necessary to defend it."

Rowland was at a loss. These people were truly insane. He thought quickly—he'd have to go to the police with more than the refurbishment of an old gaol. "So, exactly how long have we got before you, er, kidnap the Cabinet?" He kept his voice as even as he could, a struggle in the circumstances.

Oblivious to the tension in Rowland's voice, Poynton tapped the side of his nose. "All in good time, Jonesy. For now, we need to draw the plans of this place so the Colonel can make his decision."

"Decision?"

"Whether this is the best place to hold the enemy. We have a couple of options, you know. The Colonel will choose after he's seen your drawings."

Rowland took a deep breath and extracted his notebook. He began to make drawings, first sketching the buildings in elevation and then a rough plan of each. It was an involved and time-consuming process. Rowland had an artist's eye, trained for proportion and detail, but it was also necessary to work out the internal configuration of each cell block and the relative placement of each structure to the others. He didn't usually work with this level of precision. Poynton asked him to take special note of access routes, ventilation, and vantage points for guards. Rowland did this work meticulously. He'd thought of making intentional mistakes but knew he had to keep Poynton's trust.

Somehow—he had no idea how—he would have to make sure this plot to capture and incarcerate the New South Wales Cabinet failed, but simply producing a sloppy plan would not do that.

By the end of the day, Rowland's head throbbed and he had to force his eyes to focus. He must have made a hundred drawings and as many pages of scribbled notes, but had no idea what he was going to do. "I'll have to draw these up onto larger sheets," he said, as he flicked through the pages.

"You can do all that at Sunbury—Clarke will make sure you have everything you need," Poynton replied. "He's one of the movement's finest."

Sunbury, the Clarke estate, was a sprawling homestead a few miles out of Berrima on lush irrigated lawns. Poynton turned the blue Buick into the sweeping driveway.

Gerald Clarke met them as they crossed the tiled verandah. "I say, good of you to come," he effused as if they were making a social call. He clapped them both on the back, clearly excited. "Come along, gentlemen. You'll be wanting to meet the Princess."

Rowland caught Poynton's eye, but the Colonel's bodyguard gave no sign he was perturbed in any way by the proposed audience. Clarke led them on a long walk…around the back of the house, through the gardens, and toward a cluster of barns and sheds. When they reached the largest, he opened the doors.

"Here she is, gentlemen, a bonny lass, is she not?"

Rowland gazed at the gleaming Tiger Moth. He laughed. This was darn sight better than an audience with the bunyip aristocracy. Rowland walked past Poynton to inspect the aircraft more closely.

"You'll not see a more beautiful thing in the sky," Clarke said, stroking the plane.

Rowland was inclined to agree. She was, to his eyes, a magnificent machine.

"Gentlemen, the Princess is at your disposal… she'll be perfect for the Bunnerong mission."

Rowland's attention sharpened at the mention of Bunnerong. South of the city centre, it was the site of the power station supplying Sydney with its electricity.

Poynton nodded. "She could be bloody useful, Mr. Clarke."

"Let us use the modern technologies of the Empire to safeguard her, gentlemen." The grazier's voice was solemn.

"Do you pilot her yourself, sir?" Rowland made no attempt to hide his envy.

"Indeed, I do, young man…Served with the Royal Air Force last year of the war, you know. Of course the Princess is a ways ahead of the old crates we flew back then…but still, once a man has flown, it's hard to ground him again."

Rowland nodded. He'd never flown, but standing beside the Princess he was stirred by the very idea.

"You wouldn't get me up there, I'm afraid," said Poynton, as he lit a cigarette. "Too fond of solid ground, I am."

"It's not for everyone." Clarke was sympathetic. "Take Charles Hardy…I took him up a couple of times, when he was marshalling the country against the Reds. Poor chap never took to it, either…white knuckles the entire way and had a jolly job cleaning her out afterwards."

Clarke could see the glint in Rowland's eyes and the old airman was gratified. "Would you like to go up?" he asked. "I could take you out in the morning."

"I'm afraid Jonesy still has work to do," Poynton said before Rowland could respond. "And the Colonel wants those plans as soon as possible. We can't be holding up the mission for joyrides, can we Jonesy?"

"I suppose not." Rowland would have been

perfectly happy to hold up Campbell's plans for a ride, or for anything else, if truth be told.

Clarke gave them the run of the guesthouse, situated directly behind the homestead. Rowland commandeered a small oak table and began to draft his notes onto detailed layouts and plans, working solidly until they were summoned for dinner at the main house.

Gerald Clarke and his wife had three daughters, all unmarried. Attractive girls, well-schooled in the social arts, they brought a certain civilised frivolity to the meal. Rowland found himself having to be cautious in how he responded to their conversation. While Clyde Watson Jones was from a good family, his background and means were far more humble than either their hosts' or his own. Consequently, he chose to remain a little subdued, feigning a sense of polite awe. The Clarke girls interpreted his reserve as a charming shyness, and redoubled their attentions in an effort to draw him out of it. It wasn't every day they had a famous artist in their very dining room. They'd never heard of him, of course, but their father had told them he was going to win the Archibald Prize, and the whole world knew about that.

The subject of Berrima Gaol didn't come up until the ladies had retired and the men retreated to Clarke's study for brandy. Poynton and Clarke did most of the talking. Rowland listened, now aware that as mad as kidnapping the State Cabinet sounded, it was only half of the New Guard's crazy plans. Secure he was one of them, his companions spoke without reservation in his presence. Clarke, like Poynton, had the utmost admiration for Campbell and saw the Guardsmen as defenders of the faith, the King and the Empire—in Australia at least. They spoke eagerly of the "Bunnerong mission."

From what they said, Rowland pieced together that the New Guard planned to lay siege to Bunnerong Power Station in order to plunge the city into darkness. Under the cover of this orchestrated blackout, they'd take Parliament House, and imprison the State's highest-ranking elected representatives at Berrima. It occurred to Rowland that, given the time of year, and the fact that it was light till late, Parliament was unlikely to still be sitting after dark. The outcome of the mission could well be the abduction of Parliament House's cleaning staff. He said nothing, however. The last thing he wanted to do was help the New Guard improve their plans for revolution.

"When exactly, will we be moving on the Cabinet?" Rowland asked tentatively.

"We haven't decided." Clarke was pleased to let the others know he was one of the inner core. "We can't let Lang open the new bridge...given Eric's public pledge that he won't, it would be humiliating if we didn't deliver, so I think you'll have your chance to fight within the month, my boy."

Rowland tried to look pleased.

"Houghton will be relieved," Clarke added. "Poor chap has been stationed outside Lang's farm for the last six weeks, keeping an eye on the Lenin-loving blaggard. He's heartily sick of living rough."

"We've dressed Mr. Houghton as a swaggie," Poynton explained to Rowland, "so he can keep an eye on the Premier without arousing suspicion."

"Actually, he enjoyed it at first," Clarke laughed. "But after a month of flies and being charged by Lang's bloody bull, I think he'll be rather happy to get back to his practice."

"He's an accountant," Poynton added helpfully.

Rowland elected to say nothing. What could he say to people who would dress as hoboes and oust a democratically elected government in the dead of night?

Gerald Clarke filled their glasses and stood. "To Eric Campbell, gentlemen, and the right-thinking men who follow him. With a little luck, we will soon be running this State."

Chapter Thirty-one

AT AN END

Lyons-Lang Letters
STATE PREMIER'S BROKEN
PROMISE

CANBERRA, Wednesday

After repeated efforts to obtain the amount of £958,763 representing interest payments to overseas bond holders which the Government of New South Wales failed to meet when it fell due between February 1 and 4, the Commonwealth has decided to cease negotiations with the Premier of New South Wales (Mr. Lang) in regard, to the matter.

Action under the new Financial Agreement Enforcement Bill will probably be the next step.

The Daily Telegraph, March 3, 1932

Clyde came out of the sunroom he used as a studio. "Rowly! You're back…What's wrong?" he asked as Rowland threw his notebook at the wall in disgust.

"Those idiots are planning to kidnap the State Cabinet!" Rowland walked to the phone in the hallway and rang through to Sydney Police Headquarters. He asked for Detective Constable Delaney.

Clyde picked up Rowland's notebook and started flicking through it.

"Delaney, it's Rowland Sinclair. I need to speak with you….It's rather urgent. Could you come here? An hour, then."

As he hung up, Milton emerged from the conservatory and Edna came down the staircase. Rowland motioned them all into the drawing room.

"Since when did you become an architect…?" Clyde started. He'd never known Rowland to have any interest in buildings.

"You're not going to believe what those clowns are up to." Rowland rubbed his temple becoming aware that he had a headache. He told them the whole story.

Milton exploded, and stormed toward the door. Rowland grabbed his arm. "Where the hell are you going?"

"To tell Ryan and the boys," Milton spat

angrily. "Those bloody Fascists'll get a fight before we let them take over."

Rowland held his arm. "No. We're not going to start a flaming war."

"We wouldn't be starting it."

"Milt, sit down! Listen to me. If you tell them, they'll go after the Guard...it'll give Campbell the very excuse he needs to justify his revolution, and the Fascists just might win."

"Rowly's right," Clyde agreed. "This could get really ugly."

"So what do you plan to do?" Milton demanded.

"I've just called Delaney. He'll be here within the hour. The police might be able stop this quietly...."

"That's it? That's all? Leave it to the bloody useless coppers?"

Rowland held his gaze. "I'll call Wil."

"For God's sake, Rowly—you're planning to stop one Fascist army with another?"

Rowland stood. He was tall, but it was a fact that was not always noticed. "Milt, sit down," he said calmly. "We may well be the only people in this State who are not completely mad. We are going to be careful."

Milton stared at him, mutinously at first, and then he seemed to realise: this was Rowland Sinclair...he was not the enemy—perhaps he was wrong, but he was not the enemy. He sat down. "I hope you know what you're doing, Rowly."

"I have no idea, actually." Rowland was truthful. "I'm just making it up as I go."

Edna giggled. "Did you really just say we were the only people who weren't mad?"

Rowland smiled at her. "It's all relative, Ed."

True to his promise, Detective Constable Delaney arrived within the hour. Mary Brown answered the door and took him straight to the drawing room as she had been instructed, where he found them all waiting for him. Lenin jumped from the couch to greet him. Delaney leant back from the mangy, one-eared creature and its excessive tail. "What's that?" he asked, surprised to see something so ill-bred in Woollahra.

"That's my dog…Lenin."

Delaney patted the dog, carefully. "Sure is ugly."

"Afraid so," Rowland replied, "but he grows on you."

"Unlike the real Lenin," Delaney wagged his finger at Milton. Rowland was startled—he'd not known that Delaney was acquainted with the poet. "Have you met…?"

"Oh, Mr. Isaacs is well known to the Force." The detective smiled quite congenially at Milton. "Haven't seen you in a while, though."

"I've been busy."

Rowland decided to leave it. "Right, Delaney, you might need to sit down…." He unloaded all the details of his trip to Berrima, to Clark's property, and what he had learned of the New Guard's audacious plans. He described the old Berrima Gaol and how it could be fortified with men and guns to make it a very defendable prison.

He ran his hand through his hair, almost embarrassed by his own tale. "Look, Delaney, I know all this sounds ridiculous, but I rather think they're serious."

Delaney tapped his fingers on the arm of the couch as he thought. "It fits. We know Campbell has called for the Guardsmen to be ready for mobilisation within the month. He's issued instructions for street fighting and told his men to pack a day's provisions when they're called."

Milton swore. He was taking this latest plan of the New Guard very personally.

"Do they have any idea that you're not really one of them?" Delaney asked Rowland.

"I doubt it. They wouldn't have told me…"

Delaney nodded. "True. Perhaps this is the time for you to call it quits. The stakes are getting much higher now."

Rowland shook his head. "No…not yet. Not

till I find out if it was these traitorous idiots who killed my uncle."

Delaney didn't look surprised. "Fair enough. I'll take your information to the Superintendent."

"That's all you're going to do?" Milton was unable to keep quiet any longer. "Someone's got to stop those morons, and if you won't…"

"Rest assured, Mr. Isaacs, they will be stopped—but we've got to tread carefully."

"So I've been told," Milton glanced at Rowland.

"There are rather a lot of Guardsmen," Delaney tapped his fingers again. "We're better sabotaging the plan, undermining it, rather than opposing it openly."

"And how will you do that?" Clyde asked.

Delaney beamed. "MacKay's infiltrated a few men into the Guard, and the intelligence Mr. Sinclair's just given us will give us a good start. We'll stop Campbell and make him think it's his idea."

"They couldn't really…they can't just…" Edna sounded unnerved.

"The New South Wales Government has many enemies, Miss Higgins—more than just Campbell and his cronies. To tell you the truth, anything could happen right now. We're in uncharted territory. "

"What enemies…who else?"

"The Commonwealth government, for one,"

replied Delaney. "This latest wrangle over funds is getting bloody nasty. There are some who think that Canberra will move on Lang before Campbell does."

Depending on the publisher, the newspapers had either decried or applauded Lang's repudiation of foreign loans, and the Commonwealth's consequent attempts to garnishee the State Treasury in its determination that New South Wales would not damage the entire country's financial position.

"Move? How? With the military?"

"Some say Canberra will use the Old Guard."

Rowland looked up sharply.

Delaney raised his brows. So, Rowland Sinclair was aware of the Old Guard—the Detective Constable had thought as much. "Unfortunately, we don't know a lot about them." Delaney played his cards close to his chest. "They're secretive, unlike Campbell's show ponies, but we believe their numbers dwarf Campbell's and that they, too, are amassing."

Rowland chewed his lower lip. So the Old Guard was mobilising; Wilfred had said nothing of this. He brought his mind back to the matters at hand. "Your turn, Delaney…have you heard anything from Dynon…about my uncle?"

Delaney looked warily at Rowland's house-guests, and nodded slightly. Rowland saw his hesitancy. "I've already told them," he admitted. "You'll have to trust them."

Delaney sighed, studied Milton for a moment and then continued. "All I've got so far is that Dynon wants to induct me into the Legion…it's some kind of special force within the New Guard itself. He hasn't told me much at this stage. I know the Legion's entire membership is kept tight, under fifty, but I haven't been to a meeting yet. I think this Legion might be the key to your 'dark ghosts.'"

"You'll tell me if you find out anything?" Rowland looked for Delaney's word.

After a moment's pause, the detective nodded. "Yes, I'll tell you…but this particular arrangement stays between us, right?" He looked pointedly at Milton again. "I'll be lining up for the Susso myself if MacKay ever finds out."

Rowland nodded. "Done. Thank you."

Delaney stood, and rubbed his chin thoughtfully. "I think you should come with me, Sinclair. MacKay may have some questions for you. What do you say?"

"I can't be seen wandering into Police Headquarters."

"I'll take you in through the back—no one will see us. Anyway, if they did, there's no reason at all why Clyde Watson Jones and Jack Harris shouldn't be seen together."

Rowland stood. "Good enough."

Delaney turned to the others. "And you lot watch yourselves—someone's bound to figure this out soon. As I said, the stakes are getting higher."

"You be careful, too, Detective Constable," said Edna earnestly. Delaney smiled at the beautiful sculptress who thought to be concerned for his safety. Milton rolled his eyes. Rowland looked amused.

"I'll do that, Miss Higgins."

He and Rowland made their way out. Delaney paused outside the front door. "You know you're being watched don't you?"

"By whom?" Rowland was genuinely surprised.

"Them." Delaney pointed his hat toward a black Oldsmobile parked across the road. "You haven't noticed…? They're not exactly subtle."

Rowland hadn't noticed. "Who are they?"

"Federal agents, I'd say—if they were us, I'd know." He smiled, "They're not dressed up as hoboes, so they can't be Guardsmen."

Rowland squinted until he made out the men, all in suits, sitting in the Oldsmobile. "A swaggie might stand out in Woollahra," he said dryly. "Should I be worried?"

Delaney shrugged. "Depends what you've been up to."

Rowland's mind flew back to the 50–50 Club.

"Do you think they know about my links to the New Guard?" He kept his eyes on the surveillance vehicle.

"You're assuming it's you they're watching, Sinclair."

"Aren't they?"

"Maybe," Delaney glanced over his shoulder back into the house. "But you keep some interesting company. The Feds are out watching Communists, Guardsmen, and a few lots in between at the moment. Got their hands pretty full."

Suddenly Rowland remembered the Oldsmobile that had been parked outside Oaklea. It was black, too. He had vague recollections of seeing black Oldsmobiles on several occasions since. Was it something to do with Wil? Could it be that the car was waiting in case his brother returned to Woodlands House? He said nothing.

The young officer manning the desk outside MacKay's office looked up in alarm as they passed. "Detective Delaney, the Superintendent is—"

"Expecting me." Delaney strode past and pushed MacKay's door.

Rowland came in behind him. The office was large and functional; no mementos, photographs, or personal touches at all. Bill MacKay stood as they entered.

"Delaney! What the blazes…?"

Delaney stopped. Rowland heard him swear under his breath. "I'm sorry, sir, I didn't realise…"

MacKay was not alone. A second man, in one of the visitors' chairs, sat with his legs stretched out halfway across the office. Rowland needed no introduction. The jutting lower jaw and the drooping moustache had been caricatured for years by countless cartoonists and poster artists.

Delaney was mortified. "Premier Lang, I'm sorry to disturb you, sir."

"Not at all, Delaney…" Lang smiled. "You're one of Bill's men inside the New Guard, aren't you?'

MacKay was not so easily placated. Rowland could almost feel the rush of air as he roared, "Sinclair, what the hell are you doing here? Delaney, have you lost your mind, boy?"

"Mr. Sinclair has some valuable information on the New Guard's latest plot, sir. Very significant information," Delaney replied. "But we can come back…"

"Another plot!" Lang interrupted. "What on earth is Campbell up to now? I've only just hunted out the bloody Guardsman they had under my sister-in-law's floorboards. I thought she had rats!" He slammed his hat down on the desk in frustration. "They're more trouble than the flaming Communists!"

An awkward silence followed as Delaney waited for MacKay's direction.

The Superintendent spat, "You heard the Premier—get on with it!"

Delaney introduced Rowland Sinclair. Premier Lang stood and shook his hand. "You're not a member of the force then, Sinclair?"

"No, sir. I have my own reasons for looking into the New Guard's activities."

It was Lang, not MacKay, who offered them both a seat. "So Mr. Sinclair, what cockeyed scheme has Eric concocted now?" MacKay's face was thunderous.

Rowland recounted his excursion to the Southern Highlands, the New Guard's astonishing plans for Berrima Gaol. Again he felt like he was telling some ludicrous fairytale.

When he'd finished, Lang sat back, his fist placed thoughtfully on his lips. Suddenly he laughed. "A swaggie, you say. I've seen the poor fool running for his life through the paddocks...capital bull that Ebenezer." He held his hands about four feet apart, "Horns on him like that!" He laughed again.

MacKay turned to Rowland. "Did Campbell send you to Berrima?"

"Not exactly. Poynton filled me in…He said it was at Campbell's request."

MacKay shook his head. "He's set up this Poynton to take the fall…Campbell will claim to know nothing, should it come out."

"MacKay, I want this swaggie arrested for interfering with my bull," Lang declared. "Exposure to an accountant could affect the yield this season."

"Premier, we can't let them instigate the plan, however ridiculous it is," MacKay looked up at Rowland. "Thank you for your information, Mr. Sinclair. We'll take it from here. Delaney, escort Sinclair home."

Rowland stood, a little annoyed at being dismissed in so offhand a manner.

Lang stood also, and stuck out his hand. "Pleased to meet you, Mr. Sinclair. I could use a man like you."

Rowland smiled. If anything would make Wilfred shoot him…"It's been a privilege, sir. I'll leave you gentlemen to defend democracy."

"Well, if you're ever looking for work…" the Premier replied, beaming beneath his famous moustache.

MacKay cleared his throat and looked hard at Delaney, and with that, Rowland Sinclair and the detective departed.

"So, what did you think of our beleaguered

Premier?" Delaney asked as he drove Rowland back to Woodlands House.

Rowland laughed. "Seems rather more fed up with the Communists than I expected," he said, intrigued that the perceived champion of the Bolshevik cause, could be so.

"Oh, he hates them," Delaney replied. "Always ranting about Jock Garden."

Rowland found Milton pacing the floor. Clyde was sketching Edna onto a large sheet of drawing cartridge as she lay on the couch with Lenin.

"Problem?" he asked, as Milton all but walked into him.

"Call me difficult, Rowly, but I'm a little uneasy about leaving this situation in the hands of the police."

Rowland ran them through his meeting with MacKay and the Premier.

Milton was in no way appeased. "Lang hasn't been able to do a single thing about the New Guard to date."

"I did say I'd call Wil." Rowland was now starting to doubt the wisdom of doing that.

"Hold off, Rowly," cautioned Clyde. "With due respect to your brother, his lot don't sound a great deal more rational than the Boo Guard...

They may even think kidnapping the Cabinet is a good idea, and then we'd just be giving Campbell more allies."

"Wil's adamant that the Old Guard is purely defensive, but who the hell knows?" Rowland conceded.

"I still think we should make the Party aware of Campbell's plans," said Milton. "We'll need to be ready."

"No. Rowly's right." Clyde was firm. "That would only start a war—which is exactly what Campbell wants, I reckon. Let's face it Milt, the Left is as organised as a traffic jam on Pitt Street—not like the Fascists. I'd never shirk a fight—you know that—but right now, we'd lose. It'd be pointless."

"Listen to him, Elias." Edna's voice was hard and low. It was not a request.

Milton shot her a dark look. Edna didn't often use his real name. He had been called Milton since he fashioned himself into a poet. "I won't say a thing," he sighed. "But, Rowly…"

"If Delaney doesn't pull it off, we'll tell anybody who'll listen," Rowland said, anticipating his friend's comment. "At the moment it's just a plan."

Milton was sullen; persuaded but not entirely convinced. "I hope we're doing the right thing."

"God, I do too." Rowland was equally unsure.

◇◇◇

Rowland did phone Wilfred that day. The call was unsuccessful, but not entirely so. He had hoped to find out what the Old Guard was up to. Of course, he knew that Wilfred would tell him nothing, but he wanted to ask all the same. He spoke briefly to Kate who told him that the elder Sinclair was in Canberra.

"What's he doing there, Kate?" Rowland asked.

"I'm not really sure, Rowly. Ernie…Shh!… Oh, all right, I'll ask…Rowly, would you mind saying hello to Ernie?"

"Sure, put him on."

"Uncle Rowly!" Ernest bellowed into the phone.

"Hello, Ernie. No need to yell, mate. I can hear you."

"Daddy's in camera."

"I heard."

"Daddy's very important."

"I'm sure."

"He's meeting the Pry Minster."

Suddenly, Kate was back on the line. "You mustn't listen to Ernie." She was obviously flustered. "He says the most nonsensical things."

"Don't be cross with him, Kate," said Rowland. "I won't mention anything to Wil."

After hanging up, he walked to the window from where he could still see the black Oldsmobile parked on the other side of Woodlands' wrought-iron gates. What business did Wilfred have with the Prime Minister, he wondered.

Milton came into the drawing room and looked out the window with him. "Any luck?"

Rowland shook his head. "He's in Canberra. With the Prime Minister."

"Social visit?"

Rowland smiled. "I don't think so, but who knows? Every man's got to have friends, I guess."

"Our friends are still out there, I see." Milton tapped the window. "It's quite flattering really…"

"I wonder who they're watching?"

"Good question. Why don't we ask them?" Milton moved toward the drinks cabinet. "They'd be whisky men, don't you think? Policemen always drink whisky…" He poured two quite generous glasses.

"Milt you can't…"

"Why not?"

"I don't think we're supposed to know they're watching us."

"You think they'll be offended?"

Rowland groaned. "Just don't give them a reason to shoot you!"

Milton put the glasses on a silver tray and

Rowland watched from the window as he strode out of the house and leant against the car before passing in the whisky. After a few minutes, he came back in, with the silver tray under his arm.

"Well?"

"They swore a bit, but they liked the drinks." The poet shook his head sadly. "It's not me they're watching. Damn luck…thought I'd be able to dine out on that. Don't tell Clyde, but they had no idea who I was…"

"Well, who…?"

"They said they weren't watching—told me to bugger off. They were kind of tetchy."

Rowland glanced out the window again. "They're going." He watched as the Oldsmobile pulled away.

"You're kidding!" Milton looked out himself. "Ungrateful bastards!"

"What? You wanted to be watched?"

"They've got your bloody glasses!"

Chapter Thirty-two

Punishment for Default

Commonwealth Move To Bring
Mr. Lang To Heel

CANBERRA, Wednesday

Close secrecy is being observed concerning the details of an important bill to be introduced into the House of Representatives, the object of which is to enable the Commonwealth Ministry to compel the Lang Government to adhere in future to the provisions of the Financial Agreement.

The Canberra Times, March 10, 1932

Rowland stood on the flagstoned courtyard outside what had once been a tack shed at Woodlands

House. It hadn't been used as such for years, since the Sinclairs had moved to motorised transport.

Nowadays, it was Edna's studio, where she worked on the larger pieces that couldn't easily be moved. He knocked.

"Come in."

He pushed open the door and entered. The walls inside were extensively shelved. Originally they had held the saddles and harnesses, which were now stored in the building's loft. The shelves were packed instead with various kinds of clay, chisels, bags of plaster, and the other tools of the sculptress' trade. There was only one small window to light the room, but Edna claimed the dimness enhanced the texture and movement in her work by forcing her to rely on her hands and her heart more than her eyes.

The sculptress was working on a piece that was as tall as she, the first on this scale she'd attempted for a while. Before the downturn she had received several commissions for cenotaphs and memorials, with every town and community across the country seeking to honour their servicemen. Even now, Edna Higgins was occasionally approached to produce a soldier in bronze for a park monument. Though the work was largely traditional, it had always moved her, and it paid what bills she had. Edna's natural sensibilities were with the Modernist movement, and it was in one of these conceptual pieces that she was now engrossed.

As Rowland entered her studio, Edna was burnishing, working the leather-hard clay in circular movements with the back of a teaspoon, to crush the silicates and smooth and polish the surface.

She kept going as he watched. The sculptress wore overalls, her hair tied up in a cotton scarf. Her arms were covered to the elbow with a fine film of dark clay. This was messy work.

"Well," she said, without looking up, "what do you think?"

Rowland studied the sculpture. To him, it looked a little like a tree, with two intertwined trunks emerging from a common base. They wove in and out of each other with a fluidity and urgency that made it seem that each was repelling, attempting to escape the other. And yet, he could see that the branches were codependant, supportive. If either branch were removed, the structure would be unstable. "It's remarkable, Ed. Are you going to be able to cast it?"

"I'm not sure…I might have to cut it up to bronze it in a few pieces and then weld them back together."

Rowland stepped closer and ran his hand over the sculpture, tracing the smooth flow of the clay—Edna's creations always begged to be touched. "What are you calling it?" he asked.

She smiled. "Brothers in Arms."

"Very funny."

"Not at all," she said. "I've sat for you so often, I thought it was time you modelled for me."

"It's not a commission, then?"

"An indulgence."

"Will you let me buy it?"

Edna laughed. "No. But I will give it to you. If you like it."

"I like it."

"It's settled then." She put down the teaspoon.

Rowland picked it up and turned it over. "Mary told me the silverware was disappearing," he said, smiling. "I'm sure she thinks it's Milt."

Edna giggled. She'd always used cutlery, even with the array of clay-working tools she'd acquired over the years.

"I have to go to Pyrmont this afternoon to check on some of my castings." She scrubbed the clay off her hands in the corner trough. Edna had most of her pieces cast into bronze at the Rose Foundry, in the dockside suburb. "Come with me...we can have tea somewhere."

Rowland agreed and Edna disappeared to change out of her overalls into something more befitting an afternoon in the city.

They jumped onto a tram to Darling Harbour and walked across the Pyrmont Bridge. It was a warm day but the harbour breeze was cool, helping to disperse some of the pungent odours from the docks and factories nearby. They strolled along Union Street, where the spewing smokestacks of the small, closely set factories declared which among them had not yet closed. Brick walls were papered with layer after layer of political posters, some in support of Communism and others railing against the Red Terror.

Rose & Rees was a commercial iron foundry, but with the lack of industrial work around, it also accommodated sculptors. Familiar with this part of the city, Edna and Rowland, deep in discussion, were oblivious to the men who had fallen into step behind them. Neither did they notice the motorcars that slowed as they passed by. It was not until they crossed one of the side lanes between two warehouses that Rowland noticed the heavy steady footfall. He glanced over his shoulder.

Half a dozen of them, big men…and he recognised the man who walked at their fore: Harcourt Garden.

"Ed," he said quietly as he took her hand. "Don't turn round, and when I give the word, we're going to run."

"Who is it?"

"Harry Garden…run, now!"

They took off, pelting down the alley into the next street. Garden and his mates were startled for only a second before they were hotly in pursuit, shouting taunts and threats. There were other pedestrians around but the roads weren't particularly populated, and it seemed such skirmishes had become so commonplace that no one sought to interfere.

Rowland made his mistake early on. He cut through another side lane in the hope of getting back to the main street but a gate barred the way through. He and Edna turned, but Garden and his gang blocked their way out.

Rowland glanced at Edna. He didn't think they'd hurt her.

"Sinclair, you bloody two-faced traitor!"

Rowland noticed the short length of pipe in Garden's hand. Obviously, the Queensbury Rules weren't going to be much use to him.

But women were different. "Let Ed out of here first, Harry," Rowland was backed against the wall.

Garden nodded. "Go," he said to Edna, pointing to the street with his pipe.

"Like hell!" she replied.

Garden shrugged. "Then you'll have to watch what we do to spies." He lifted the pipe above his head.

"Harry, no!" Edna screamed.

Garden hesitated, not because of Edna, but because of the horns and shouting from the motorcars that screeched up to block the mouth of the alley. He turned as a dozen men, with pick-axe handles held high, burst out of the vehicles and laid siege to the lane. Rowland recognised them, too.

"Jones, get your girl out of here!" one of the Guardsmen shouted. "We'll show these Red mongrels not to take on one of ours." He swung his weapon at Garden who blocked it with his pipe and retaliated. The brawl was on.

Rowland grabbed Edna's hand. More dangerous than Garden's mob, was standing between the Communists and the New Guard. Especially, while he was both Rowland Sinclair and Clyde Watson Jones.

Chapter Thirty-three

BLACK HOODS

SYDNEY, Wednesday

A New Guard official today, referring to
the existence of the black hoods and gowns,
declared that talk of the Fascist Legion was
"all bunk" but added that he knew of six
such hoods.

The Sydney Morning Herald, March 17,
1932

Rowland used raw sienna to mark in the basic
shapes of the large work. Eric Campbell stood
before him, posed in a manner that, by itself,
seemed a little bizarre. The Colonel had insisted
on being painted with his hat on for some reason,
but Rowland had managed to accommodate the

request. Campbell stood with one arm raised triumphantly and the other grasping the empty air. On the canvas Rowland would later add figures into the scene with whom the painted Campbell would interact. That was the plan, anyway. Right now he used his brush to knead the shapes he'd marked, so that very quickly he found a sepia shadow of his subject.

Campbell chatted amiably as Rowland worked, unguarded in his conversation. Clyde Watson Jones had proved reliable.

"I'm afraid your plans of the Berrima facility, outstanding as they were, will be for naught, Clyde," he said, speaking gently in an attempt to soften the blow.

"Has something happened, sir?"

"What hasn't happened?" Campbell sighed. "The man we posted at Lang's farm was picked up for vagrancy...Winslow's lease on the gaol has been terminated...unlawfully, but that will take an age to fight...and they've started bloody roadworks outside the Bunnerong power station, so the access routes are completely compromised. I've recommended that the Council of Action votes to stop."

Inwardly, Rowland cheered for Delaney. "I'm sorry to hear that, sir."

"Me, too, Clyde. Still, it's a delay not an end."

Campbell went on to talk, in more general

terms, of his plans for the state, the benefits of government by commission and, of course, the scourge of the Communists. Rowland worked quickly, pulling pigment into a tonal representation. After an hour or so, he let Campbell leave but continued to paint in the sunny sitting room at Boongala, which his subject had designated a studio.

Poynton wandered in a little while after Campbell had returned to his office, and sat smoking, watching the artist at work. "John Dynon is furious."

"Why?"

"Stupid bastard thinks someone's leaked the plan…But if that were true, we'd have a bloody sight more problems than roadworks." Poynton exhaled a large cloud of smoke. "Dynon's on some kind of quest to find this spy. Good luck, is what I say."

"This unit that Dynon heads…you called it the Legion…what is it, exactly?"

Poynton grinned. He got up and shut the door to the room. "The Fascist Legion," he said, lowering his voice. "Special forces—assassins, of sorts—but they don't go that far…they deal out a hiding when it's called for."

"They've never been arrested?"

"They're pretty hard to identify…only Dynon knows who they all are."

"How do they manage that?" Rowland continued to dab paint as he spoke.

"They do everything in disguise—meetings, operations, the lot. They don't use names, their membership changes regularly...it's kind of hard to explain."

"So these people they deal out hidings to— who decides who gets it?" Rowland tried to ask the question without weight. "The Colonel?"

"God, no!" said Poynton. "I suppose if the Colonel had a request, Dynon would take care of it...but he doesn't involve himself in that level of detail. He's a busy man."

"Who, then?"

Poynton shrugged. "Dynon and the Kings, I guess" Rowland put down his brush.

"The Kings?"

"Dynon's men," Poynton kept his voice low. "Not a nice bunch—cut from the same cloth as Dynon—the numbers just do as they're told."

Rowland stared at the bodyguard. "The numbers?"

Poynton smiled. "The Legion never uses names, so they've all taken a card as identity—a deck of forty-nine."

"There are fifty-two cards in a deck," Rowland pointed out.

"Well, naturally nobody wanted to be a

Queen, so that's forty-eight." Poynton sniggered. "And Dynon made himself the Joker."

"Naturally," agreed Rowland. Apparently, men who dressed up to assault innocent citizens drew the line at being called "Queens."

"Why are you so interested in the Fascist Legion, Jonesy?"

"You've got to admit they're a bit odd," Rowland said casually. "I'm just curious."

Poynton's grin returned. "Do you want to go to a meeting?" he asked slyly. "You know, see how they work?"

"But how...surely they don't allow spectators?"

"We wouldn't go as spectators." Poynton motioned for Rowland to take the chair next to him. "As I said, they go to the meetings in disguise—the numbers don't really speak—they just hold their card. There's forty of them currently and they don't all come to every meeting."

"So, what are you proposing?" Rowland asked, trying to get past the absurdity of the deck of cards.

"I'll find out who isn't going to be there—we'll go in their place. Robed up we won't be recognised...It'll be a lark."

"Where do we get the robes?"

Poynton looked a little embarrassed. "I have my own set," he admitted. "I was in the Legion before Dynon decided I wasn't made of the right stuff—I'll just get my old mum to run up a set for you…She's amazing with a sewing machine, my mum…and the robes aren't exactly high fashion."

Rowland hesitated. "It sounds a bit risky."

"Come on, Jonesy!" Poynton was excited now. "What could happen? It's just a bit of a joke. You're the Colonel's blue-eyed boy at the moment—even Dynon's not going to mess with you."

Rowland smiled. "Fair enough. So, when?"

"I'll let you know," Poynton said as he predictably tapped the side of his nose. "When are you next coming back to paint?"

"Day after tomorrow."

"Perfect—I'll have your robes by then and I'll know when and where, and whose cards we can carry…" The bodyguard was clearly relishing his plan.

Back at Woodlands House, Rowland shrugged off his secret life as Clyde Watson Jones, and began preparing canvases for another series that he'd been mulling over since the evening at the 50–50 Club. There was something about the grittiness, the debauched misery of the place. It was raw, a shocking base reality. Women who—even fully clothed—reeked of depravity in a way that his nudes never did, and men who were completely indifferent to the law. The unselfconscious ugliness of it all intrigued him, challenging him to capture it in paint. It was a stark contrast to the carefully orchestrated, lyrical image he was painting of Campbell; and it interested him far more.

It was only when he had stretched a half dozen canvases that he remembered his paint box was still at Boongala. He cursed, frustrated. Clyde was home, so he was able to cadge a basic palette and a couple brushes, at least, to begin while the muse still had him. Having not been at the 50–50, Clyde watched while the other painter played with compositions of prostitutes and patrons. Rowland spoke to his friend of the Fascist Legion, the pack of cards without Queens, and Poynton's plan.

To his surprise, Clyde wasn't overly concerned. "You and Milt walked in and out of a confrontation with Phil The Jew." Clyde stretched out on the couch. "If you can get away with that, nothing you do with the New Guard is going to worry me again." He glanced at the ceiling. "It's obvious somebody up there's looking after you."

Rowland grinned. "Maybe."

"So, are you back to thinking the New Guard is responsible for your uncle's death?" Clyde asked.

"I don't know, really." Rowland squeezed titanium white onto his palette. "Jeffs could be lying...I guess I'm just trying a process of elimination."

"What?"

"Well, if it turns out the Fascist Legion has nothing to do with Uncle Rowland, I'll start looking at Jeffs and the 50–50 again."

"What are you going to do…Offer to paint The Jew?"

"I could," Rowland laughed. "I'll worry about that if I turn out to be wrong about the Legion. For the moment, I think I believe him…It sounds like Uncle Rowland was a source of funds that asked no questions."

"Does it bother you that your uncle was so involved with these people?"

"It didn't, till I met them."

"And now?"

Rowland continued painting. "How could it not bother me?"

"Well you're rid of it now." Clyde had no doubt that the squalid unattractive amorality of the 50–50 troubled his friend. Rowland had chosen a more libertine life than that to which he was born, but it had been sanitised by his name and his wealth.

Poynton did not disappoint. The bodyguard entered the makeshift studio after the Colonel had finished his session and thrust a parcel at Rowland.

"Your uniform," he said tapping the side of his nose in his fashion.

Rowland took the package as Poynton pulled a playing card out of his pocket. He handed the artist the three of hearts. "Don't lose this," he said. "You're going in for Bob Russell. I'm going to be Mal Marshall—he's the deuce of clubs."

"Why aren't they going?"

"Bob's got some business out of the city, and Mal's wife won't let him go. Anyways, they both think I'm relaying their apologies to Dynon, so nobody will be surprised to see their cards."

"When?"

"Couple of hours. The King of Diamonds has been abroad, so they haven't met for a while. They're gathering at one of De Groot's warehouses in Rushcutters Bay."

"Is De Groot in the Legion?"

"I doubt it," Poynton replied. "I can't see him as one of the numbers kowtowing to the Kings."

"Give me a minute to clean up."

Poynton was making a night of it. The actual meeting was for late in the evening, so he took Rowland to a nearby hotel for a meal. Rowland decided he quite enjoyed Poynton's company. Talking to the man, he could as easily have been a Communist as a Guardsman, or anything in between. Poynton just had a need to belong to something, to be a part of what was happening. It just so happened that he found the New Guard first, and brought to it all the enthusiasm of a child allowed to join his big brother's gang.

They caught a train from Turramurra and then a ferry from Milsons Point to Circular Quay. From there, they hailed a motorcab, which let them out at Rushcutters Bay to make their way the few blocks to De Groot's premises. As they approached the warehouse, Poynton took them into an alleyway. "Here's where we put on our uniforms, Jonesy," he said. "Legionnaires have gotta arrive in robes to maintain secrecy...wouldn't want to be recognised."

Rowland watched Poynton and then pulled on his own long black robe and hood, courtesy of the bodyguard's mother. He felt utterly ridiculous.

As they skulked out of the alley and into the grounds outside the warehouse, Rowland could only hope that they wouldn't be noticed or, worse, arrested for wandering Rushcutters Bay in such bizarre outfits. Under the hood he winced with embarrassment at the mere thought. How would he explain it? He'd have to shoot himself...it'd be the only honourable way out...If it hit the papers, Wilfred would shoot him anyway.

Fortunately, they encountered no one until they were within the warehouse grounds. Rowland followed the detailed instructions Poynton had given him about how he should conduct himself. He held the three of hearts in front of his chest at all times, lifting it before his face in some kind of peculiar salute every time they came across another Legionnaire. Nobody said a word. Every now and then Rowland wanted to laugh, but suppressed it. He did wonder what Phil The Jew would think of this.

The warehouse had been readied for the Legion's meeting. Dynon, who was unhooded, and who held the Joker before him, called everyone to order. He stood on an elevated stage, the four Kings seated behind him facing the lesser royals and the numbers who sat on chairs set out in rows. The Kings, too, had removed their hoods. Rowland stiffened. Henry Alcott, Aubrey's old friend, held the King of Diamonds.

The meeting began and it soon became apparent why the Joker and the Kings were unhooded. It was for them, and them only, to speak. The hoods would have muffled any discourse.

The Legion was organised into four units—the playing card suits. Rowland listened as the Kings and Dynon spoke of their plans for future operations. It seemed that when a King proposed an operation, another King and his suit were given the responsibility for executing it. Convoluted, but

Rowland supposed this was to do with maintaining secrecy.

The Kings were debating a proposal, put forward by the King of Spades, to kidnap the Premier and bring him to the Harbour Bridge Opening, dressed as a beggar. Clearly, the Fascist Legion was somewhat obsessed with fancy dress. The logistics were tortuous, involving an ambulance and several umbrellas, and the other Kings were less than impressed.

"Bloody hell, McCreagh, it was your men that botched the Sinclair job—what makes you think you can handle this?" said Henry Alcott, the Diamond King.

That was the one moment Rowland was relieved the hood obscured his face. Despite his long-held suspicions, this specific reference to his family, this admission that these men were involved in his uncle's murder, outraged him.

"That was more to do with your supposed information than anything we did!" McCreagh bit back.

Alcott raised his voice. "He was a bloody decrepit old man…You'd think it was bleeding obvious when he opened the door!"

"He was your target. You suggested it!"

"Gentlemen!" John Dynon demanded silence.

"The incident was unfortunate, but I won't let it inhibit our work."

"That's all very well, but the original matter remains unresolved," protested Alcott.

"Perhaps you and McCreagh could work together to resolve it then?" Dynon said to end the matter. "It might return some self-respect to both your suits. Shall we move on?"

The Kings of Diamonds and Spades nodded begrudgingly, and the topic moved to Jock Garden and other prominent Communists.

Rowland's mind worked at speed. Henry Alcott, who had served with his brother, and been Aubrey's best friend, had made the nomination that had seen his uncle killed. Why? He doubted Henry had even met the old man. Had Alcott discovered something about his uncle's ownership of the 50–50? But why would the New Guard care about that? And why was the job botched…could it be true they hadn't intended to kill him? He was getting very hot, and quite claustrophobic, under the hood.

The Kings went back to the plan to kidnap Lang. Eventually the location, timing, and props were agreed, though this time without umbrellas.

"I'll have to take this to the Colonel," Dynon said finally. "Something involving Red Jack needs his approval…and we'll have to coordinate with whatever De Groot is cooking up for the bridge opening as well…"

They ended the meeting with "God Save the King," for which it seemed the code of silence for the lesser cards was relaxed.

The Legionnaires left the warehouse and disappeared into various alleys and buildings to transform back into ordinary citizens once again. Rowland rolled up the robe and hood and stuffed it under his jacket.

Poynton grinned at him. "Well, Jonesy, what did you think?"

"The Sinclair job…what was that all about?"

Poynton shrugged. "I was out of the Legion by then…all I know is some fella died and it was a major cock-up—the Colonel was furious. I think that's why Alcott had to make himself scarce for a while…Something wrong, Jonesy?"

Rowland closed his mouth and focused. "No…It was hot wearing that hood; it's just made me a bit light-headed…We should go. Two men loitering in a dark alley can't look good."

Once again, Rowland called Delaney as soon as he reached home. To his surprise, despite the time of night, the detective had just come into the station. "I'll be right over, Sinclair."

While he waited for him, Rowland recounted

the meeting of the Fascist Legion to his house-guests, who had been waiting for his return.

"So Alcott sent these lunatics after your uncle?" Edna was shocked. "But why?"

"I honestly don't know."

Clyde frowned. "What did he mean that the matter was unresolved?"

Milton stood and started to pace the room. "Was there something at your uncle's house that they wanted? Perhaps Mrs. Donelly interrupted them before they could find it."

"That'd fit," Rowland said slowly. "But what would Uncle Rowland have that they would want?"

"Maybe they were after the deeds to the 50–50?"

"What would the Legion want with a sly-grogerie?"

Milton's brow furrowed. "Who knows? Maybe it was something else. The important thing was that they were after something that they failed to get."

"Why is that important?"

"Because they might come back for it...to resolve the matter."

Rowland looked at him in silence. The poet was right.

Delaney arrived at that point and Rowland started to tell his tale. "I know," the detective interrupted. "I was there." He drew the five of clubs out of his jacket pocket.

"Then you heard what they said about my uncle's murder." Delaney sat on the sofa next to Milton.

"I'm sorry Sinclair…they didn't really say enough for an arrest. We could take them in for questioning, but that would alert them…MacKay wouldn't be happy if I blew my cover for that. Not yet."

"What do you suggest then?" Rowland's tone was icy.

"They want to finish what they started…or that's what it sounded like. Your uncle's already dead so maybe it was something else that took them to his house." Delaney had obviously made the same deductions as Milton. "I'll see if I can get men watching his house…It'll be difficult; most of our men are tied up with the bridge being opened and all…but I'll try."

"What about the plan to kidnap the Premier?" Rowland asked. "Surely you can arrest them for that."

"Probably," Delaney conceded. "But the Super's got other ideas. We've got men looking after the Premier…but they won't go that way. Campbell will knock it on the head. They'll go with De Groot's plan."

"And you'll stop that?"

The detective shook his head. "No. De Groot's plan is bloody daft. We're going to let him do it…it'll be a publicity disaster for the New Guard and it'll give us something concrete to go after them with."

"What exactly is he planning?"

Delaney grinned. "You'll see on Saturday… but make sure you get there early so you can get a good vantage spot."

"And what about my uncle?"

"A watch on his house is the best I can do for the moment, and I may not even be able to spare that. I'm sorry, Sinclair. We're stretched right now."

Rowland was angry. It seemed to him that his uncle's death was being afforded the lowest of priorities. It was not something to which the Sinclairs were accustomed.

"Look, Sinclair," said Delaney. "I won't let this go. All I need to do is find one weak link in the Legion, who'll turn and dob in the others. I've got my hood now…it's only a matter of time."

Rowland was not particularly comforted, but he accepted it. As soon as the detective's car had left the driveway, he stood and grabbed his hat.

"Where are you going?" asked Edna.

"Delaney won't be able to organise men tonight," Rowland replied. "I'm going to keep an eye on my uncle's house."

"I'll come with you, Rowly," Milton grabbed an iron from the stand by the fireplace, testing its weight as a weapon. "My strength has the strength of ten because my heart is pure."

Rowland rolled his eyes. "Tennyson," he muttered as he led the way out.

At his uncle's house, Rowland gave the domestic staff strict instructions not to answer the door. He and Milt retired to the sitting room with their fire irons. However, the easy comfort of the old man's sofas was not conducive to vigilance.

It was nearly midnight when Rowland was jolted from the stupor into which he had fallen. Milton was stretched out on the couch. A motorcar had just pulled up in the driveway.

He shook Milton awake as he walked to the door with his fire iron in hand.

There was a knock.

He waited until Milton found his weapon. The knocking became more insistent.

They positioned themselves in the vestibule on either side of the door. Rowland was uncomfortably aware that this was precisely where his uncle had died. In similar circumstances.

The knocking was now a pounding.

Milton stood battle-ready, fire iron raised. Rowland reached for the handle, undid the latch, and flung the door open.

Chapter Thirty-four

What are you doing here?" Wilfred demanded, shocked to see Rowland and his Communist friend at all, let alone wielding weapons. "Where the hell are the servants?" The elder Sinclair glared at Milton, who smiled and lay down his fire iron.

Over a drink, when Wilfred had calmed a little, Rowland told him everything.

Wilfred's reaction was measured, thoughtful. "Your Detective Constable is right, Rowly—it's probably not enough to arrest them yet..." He shook his head. "Henry Alcott...what would Aubrey say...?"

"That's what I can't figure out, Wil," Rowland poured another sherry for himself and Milton. "Even if Henry is in the New Guard, what on earth could he have against Uncle Rowland?"

"Who can say? We both know the old fool could find trouble anywhere. Perhaps he offended Henry somehow—he offended a lot of people, you know."

"Henry didn't just drop him from an invitation list, Wil—he had him killed."

"You said yourself that they didn't intend to kill him...I'm sure the police will find the answers now that you've put them on the right path. At least you can stop this insane charade you're playing with Campbell."

Rowland was conspicuously silent.

Wilfred stared at him, waiting for confirmation he had finished with his subterfuge.

"I have to get my paint box back first," Rowland muttered, before he changed the subject. "Why are you in Sydney, Wil?'

"The bridge opening." Wilfred shrugged, a little embarrassed. "The A.I.F. veterans are marching in the pageant."

Rowland refilled his brother's glass. It wasn't like Wilfred to march; he had never done so in all the years since the war. His brother wore his patriotism proudly, but he kept his service private.

"Kate insisted," Wilfred continued uncomfortably. "She thinks I should march for Ernie's sake....They came up with me."

"The opening will be a big show, Wil," Rowland replied, "and Ernie's very proud of you. Every boy wants to point out his father in the parade."

Wilfred drank his whisky. "Mick Bruxner's arranged for them to be admitted to the area reserved for the Country Party, right at the head of the bridge," he said. "I intended to phone you tonight...I want you to escort Kate."

Rowland nodded. "Of course."

Lieutenant Colonel Michael Bruxner, a decorated veteran and old friend of Wilfred's, had recently won leadership of the United Country Party. Presumably Premier Lang had offered the members of the opposition and their families the courtesy of proximity, to view his moment of triumph. Rowland did have his own plans for the opening, but he would change them.

"Where is Kate?" he asked, becoming conscious of his sister-in-law's absence.

"She and Ernie are staying with her sister in Mosman tonight. I had some business to attend to in the city," Wilfred replied. "They'll catch the first ferry tomorrow morning."

"I'll meet the ferry," Rowland promised.

They remained in conversation for a short time, and then Wilfred urged them to go.

"I have no intention of admitting any late-night callers," he said. "Mrs. Donelly, bless her, doesn't seem to hear anything after eight o'clock." He pulled a handgun out of his hip pocket and laid it on the occasional table beside him. "You needn't be concerned, Rowly."

"I really have to get my paint box back from Campbell's." Rowland and Milton walked into the drawing room at Woodlands House.

Milton didn't react. In his experience, artists were obsessive about their favourite brushes and pigments, so he was not surprised that Rowland was pining for his paint.

"I'm thinking I should retrieve it tomorrow."

"There is the small matter of the bridge opening," Milton reminded him. "You're going to have bugger all time to get to Turramurra. It'll keep, Rowly—just use Clyde's stuff."

"Someone's bound to recognise me at the bridge opening, Milt—it'll be difficult to explain what Clyde Watson Jones is doing in the official party and somewhat awkward to claim my paint box from Campbell's house, once they think I'm either a spy or a turncoat."

"Forget about the box, then. It's just paint, mate…I know you and Clyde have lucky brushes and all, but you can easily afford to replace them."

"It's not that." Rowland grimaced. "I only remembered, when Wil took out that gun, I never did return the revolver he gave me in Yass. It's still in the bottom of my paint box."

Milton choked. "Good God, Rowly, how could you forget something like that?"

"Well, I did."

"Don't worry about it—it's probably clogged with paint and utterly useless by now."

"I'm not completely daft," Rowland said defensively. "I wrapped it in a rag."

He looked critically at the half-finished work on his easel. "It looks like I need to get my lucky brushes back before this is completely beyond redemption."

Clyde and Edna came into the drawing room with cups of tea and a plate of biscuits. They were both wearing dressing gowns, having apparently tried and failed to sleep. They had encountered each other in the kitchen when hunting for a late night snack.

"You're back!" Edna exclaimed.

Milton told them why he and Rowland had returned so soon.

"So what now?" Clyde dunked a biscuit into his steaming cup. "Are you going back to being Rowland Sinclair on a permanent basis…or have you become attached to my name?"

"I may not have a choice after tomorrow… but the police seem focussed on other things at the moment. I have half a mind to call on Henry Alcott!"

"That's just going to warn him," Milton objected.

Rowland sighed, irritated. "I still have no idea why Alcott nominated Uncle Rowland."

"Enough!" Edna put down her cup. "Whatever you do the day after, tomorrow you're just our Rowly, and we're all going to the opening." She was excited by the planned festivities. It was probably why she couldn't sleep. For a day, at least, the Depression would be forgotten as the whole of Sydney celebrated its bridge.

"About that…" Rowland looked at Milton for help. "Wil needs me to accompany Kate and Ernie to the ceremony."

"Rowly, no!" Edna's face fell. "There won't be another opening day. Not ever."

Sydney had been preparing for months and the mood was now almost euphoric. The residents of Woodlands House had long planned to spend the historic day together, attending the extravagant celebrations, both official and otherwise.

"Don't whine, Ed," Milton admonished. "Rowly can't really say 'no,' and we can have an even better time without him."

"Steady on!" Rowland shoved him.

"I'm trying to help you, comrade."

"I can still get to the Venetian Carnival," Rowland offered, not entirely happy with Milton's help.

The Venetian Carnival scheduled for the evening promised, in any case, to be the most magnificent of the celebrations. They had invitations to a number of private parties being held on the foreshore in view of the spectacle, including an outdoor masquerade ball, for which Edna had organised their costumes. Eventually, albeit reluctantly, the sculptress accepted the disruption to her plans, and they retired in anticipation of the next day.

As he had promised, Rowland met his sister-in-law and nephew early the next morning. He had travelled in the Rolls-Royce, an unconscious concession to his brother's feelings on the choice of motorcars.

Ernest saw him first and raced over. "Hello, Ernie. Don't you look the gentleman." Rowland greeted the boy, immaculate in suit and tie, and ruffled his hair.

Kate, now quite obviously pregnant, hurried up behind her son and immediately began to smooth the curls, while Ernest struggled to duck away from her hand. Rowland kissed Kate and winked at Ernest.

"Unhand him, Kate—no man likes to be groomed in public"

"Rowly, isn't this exciting?" she said. "Did Wil tell you he was marching? Colonel Bruxner's been so kind to invite us to stand with him. It's so wonderful that you're with us, too. What an historic day…"

Rowland helped Kate into the Rolls while she enthused. Johnston drove them to The Rocks and they went the rest of the way on foot, slowly. It seemed like every man, woman, and child from the whole state, if not the country, had converged on Sydney. Rowland was glad Wilfred had asked him to accompany Kate and Ernest; navigating through the crowds today was no task for the faint-hearted. The streets were thick with people. Delighted, excited people, street jugglers hoping to make a few pennies, and vendors hawking memorabilia with pictures of the bridge. The route Rowland had expected to take was cordoned off for the movement of dignitaries and officials. He hoisted Ernest onto his shoulders for fear of losing him, while Kate clung to his arm. For what would normally have taken ten minutes, it was over an hour before they could take their places at the head of the bridge.

"Rowland Sinclair." Michael Bruxner, the new leader of the Country Party, their host for the day, shook his hand. "Good to see you. But I thought Wilfred said you were abroad?"

"Just returned," Rowland lied. "Wouldn't miss this for quids. And let me introduce…"

"Kate, and young Ernest. So good to see you both again."

Their situation afforded an excellent view of the proceedings. The official silk ribbon, which stretched from one side of the bridge to the other, was just a few yards in front of them, awaiting the Premier's scissors. The man himself was nearby, talking to his colleagues in the government, standing a balding head above the height of most men. The press was out in force, well aware of Campbell's threats to disrupt the ceremony. Rowland noted the Premier's three-piece suit; the plan to bring him dressed as a beggar had obviously been foiled. Photographers and a Movietone News camera were positioned by the festooned dais. The New South Wales Police Force was present in large numbers. Rowland caught sight of both MacKay and Delaney standing unobtrusively, but close to the official parties. More dignitaries began to arrive, heralded in by marching bands and a flurry of flag waving.

When the Governor-General, Sir Isaac Isaacs, was escorted in by the Royal New South Wales Lancers, Ernest tugged on Rowland's jacket. "Can you draw the horses?"

Rowland took out his notebook and obliged; he had in any case been itching to capture the pageantry. And because he was drawing, focussing on the details, he saw what everyone else was missing.

A horse at the tail end of the mounted escort somehow seemed wrong. It was clearly no military charger. The chestnut gelding was too overweight for that. The rider, too, was out of place; though on first glance he blended with the others. His uniform was not quite right; it seemed too big for him. As the Governor-General's escort approached the dais, closer to where Rowland's party was standing, he saw that unlike the other Lancers, the odd rider's sabre was tucked behind his belt rather than attached to his saddle. As the horseman's face came into view, Rowland's pencil lost momentum and dropped to the ground.

It was Francis De Groot.

Almost mesmerised, Rowland slipped his notebook back inside his jacket. Ernest tugged on his sleeve and handed him his pencil. "Can I see the picture?"

"Sorry...here." Rowland gave him the book, while his eyes searched for MacKay and Delaney. They were not far from De Groot, who had stopped his horse behind the Movietone camera stand, and they were looking right at him. Delaney had an expectant smile on his face. MacKay's betrayed no emotion, though his hand was held in what Rowland guessed was a "hold firm" position at his waist. If it was a signal, it was a subtle one.

The State Governor Sir Phillip Game opened

the official proceedings with a message of congratulations from King George V. Rowland removed his hat for the national anthem and then Lang made his speech. The Premier stepped from the dais to cut the ribbon.

Rowland's eyes were fixed on De Groot, who was now inching his mount through the police lines. The constabulary moved out of the way to avoid his horse, but did nothing to stop his progress. Without realising he was doing so, Rowland stepped forward, toward the advancing steed. De Groot reached the ribbon before Lang and spurred his horse forward. The animal baulked at the crowd and reared. De Groot drew his sabre and attacked the ribbon valiantly with two upward cuts. The crowd gasped as one, women screamed, but the ribbon was unharmed. Undeterred, De Groot dropped his reins, seized the ribbon and started sawing through it. Eventually the silk gave way, and turning to face the cameras, he held his sabre aloft in elated triumph. "I declare this bridge open, in the name of the decent and respectable citizens of New South Wales!"

It was only then the police surged toward him.

"You can't touch me. I'm wearing the King's uniform!" De Groot shouted at the clamouring officers.

At that moment, MacKay entered the fray,

grabbing De Groot by the heel and propelling him bodily out of the saddle. With his other foot caught in its stirrup, De Groot remained half-suspended, hopping on a single leg. His horse began to panic. But with the police officers focussed on trying to free him from the stirrup, the horse's distress was missed. Afraid the animal may bolt and drag De Groot through the crowd, Rowland jumped out, grabbed the dangling reins and tried to calm the beast.

He was there for less than a minute before MacKay took the reins from him, but it was time enough for De Groot to recognise him, and to hear the Superintendent say, "Well done, Sinclair!"

As De Groot was bustled away, the crowd cheered, though Rowland was unsure as to whether it was for De Groot or for his exit. The violated ribbon was re-tied and Lang cut it, this time in a fashion more sedate, though somewhat more efficient than that of De Groot.

Delaney approached Rowland. "Glad to see you got a good spot, Sinclair," he said. "Quite a show."

"It was rather…though it looks like my cover's blown."

"Probably," Delaney agreed. "De Groot won't be telling tales for a while, though; MacKay's going to have him committed." He laughed. "Campbell will have his hands full, trying to get his Irish mate out of a straitjacket!" He looked at Rowland, his face suddenly pensive. "You'll need to be even more careful now, Sinclair. Dynon's dangerous and there were Guardsmen in the crowd. I'll organise a detail for your house tomorrow."

Rowland shrugged. In the bright light of day, among the crowds, the Legion seemed more silly than threatening.

The pageant parade which followed the official opening was over a mile in length, a vast cavalcade of floats and bands and marching groups. Rowland lifted Ernest onto his shoulders as Wilfred's regiment passed, so the boy could see his father as the war hero he was. Once the pageant had crossed the bridge, the public followed, and Rowland walked with his sister-in-law and nephew across the length of the deck. At the other end, they met Wilfred as arranged and enjoyed Colonel Bruxner's hospitality for lunch, an elaborate sit-down affair in a marquee on the harbour foreshore.

It was past six when Rowland finally parted company with his brother's young family. It took him well over an hour to battle the traffic and so he returned to Woodlands House long after the others had left for the Carnival Ball. He showered quickly and struggled into the eighteenth-century costume that Edna had left for him. He checked his reflection before donning the mask. He might have felt silly, but only a day ago he was wearing a black hood and robes and waving a playing card around—it was all relative.

Johnston drove Rowland to the ball before he, too, went to some opening celebration. The foreshore had been decked out with lanterns and decorated tables, transforming the area into a magical glittering setting. Hundreds of softly lit boats floated nearby, creating an ethereal backdrop for the masquerade.

Despite appearances, this was not a party hosted and funded by the wealthy, but by the arts community. The decoration, the costumes, and the atmosphere had been conjured by the resourceful talents of artists, poets, and performers and a few of their benefactors, who had united to celebrate the opening in a style that defied the economic times.

Rowland felt easy here, not just for the fact that everybody present was as ludicrioiusly dressed as he, though it helped. Milton had been custodian of the tickets, but Rowland was recognised and waved through. The party area was not enormous, but as he tried to find his friends, he encountered many people he knew, who were already well-lubricated and all keen to discuss De Groot's display. When he reached Edna, he'd found a glass himself. She and Clyde were on the dance floor.

"Rowly!" Clyde shouted when he saw him. "For God's sake, cut in."

Rowland obliged. "Where's Milt?" He took the sculptress in his arms.

"He went back to get the tickets," Edna replied. "He left them behind…they let us in anyway, but he'd already gone."

"I must have just missed him," Rowland said as he and Edna cut across the floor.

Chapter Thirty-five

GET OUT OF THE WAY

Hitler to Hindenburg

BERLIN, Wednesday

Addressing 70,000 followers by means of loud speakers, Hitler deplored the loss of the pre-war system of government, which had made Germany the world's greatest nation. The post-war system had destroyed everything.

He honoured President Hindenburg as a field marshall, but was now compelled to say: "Worthy old man that you are, get out of my way."

The Canberra Times, March 20, 1932

It was Edna who first thought to be concerned by

Milton's prolonged absence. Both Rowland and Clyde were initially inclined to believe he'd simply become distracted, as Milton was often.

"Where could he go, dressed like that?" Edna argued. Milton had been gone three hours.

"I'll go back and find him," Rowland volunteered.

Clyde drained his glass. "We might as well call it a night and come with you. Otherwise, Ed's only going to start worrying about you five minutes after you go."

When they got to Woodlands House, it looked deserted. The staff had all been given the day off for the bridge opening. Wilfred would probably have kept at least one person on duty, but Rowland tended to be more relaxed in the management of his servants.

Clyde unlocked the door. "Milt! Where the dickens are you?" There was no response.

They made a quick search of the house, and found the tickets to the Carnival Ball still on the sideboard. It seemed Milton had not made it back at all.

Lenin was barking incessantly out the back— Milton never left him outside. Rowland walked out to the rear verandah and called out to the dog. Lenin continued to bark. Though it was late, there was enough moonlight for Rowland to make out the hound at the farthest end of the hedgerow. Obviously the neighbours were all out enjoying the festivities, or else the din would have brought complaints by now.

He called again, but it made no difference. "Clyde, grab a torch and get out here!" Rowland was suddenly suspicious.

Clyde emerged with torch in hand. "What's wrong with the dog?"

"Let's find out," Rowland glanced back at the sculptress as she came out onto the veranda. "Ed you stay here."

She nodded, too worried to quarrel.

Rowland and Clyde moved quickly toward Lenin. As they neared, the dog came to them, but he kept barking. Clyde scanned the torch beam across the hedges and garden beds.

And then they heard it. A groan. "Aah! Shut up you useless bloody mongrel!"

Clyde moved the beam toward the voice. Milton lay facedown on the ground, almost completely obscured by English box and dahlias.

"Milt, are you all right, mate?" They turned him over gently, tentatively.

Slowly, Milton sat up. "Bastards jumped me." Gingerly, he wiped his bleeding lip.

"Come on, we'll get you back to the house." Rowland put his arm around Milton's back and helped him stand. They took him in through the French doors. Once in the light, they could see the shocking state of the poet.

"Clyde, send for a doctor," Rowland said grimly. Edna ran to fetch a basin of water and cloths from the kitchen.

"Lock the doors," Milton closed his swollen eyes.

"Why?

"They might come back." Rowland bolted both doors.

"Stop looking at me like that!" Milton grimaced as tried to sit up. "I've had plenty of fat lips and bloody noses before this."

"Milt, your forehead…" Edna put down the basin.

Milton put his hand to his brow. "Oh that… queer bastards held me down and painted something on my face."

Clyde came back in. "The doctor will be here in…" He stopped mid-sentence, then swore. He stepped forward and peered at the poet's forehead and swore again.

"What!" said Milton. "What the hell is the problem?"

The poet's forehead was blazoned with the word "Red" in purplish black letters. They told him.

Milton was not particularly concerned. "Bloody gutless," he muttered. He grabbed a wet cloth from Edna and wiped it across his face. The cloth took off nothing but blood. The word "Red" remained.

Now Rowland started to curse. He knew what this was, so did Clyde and Edna. As artists, they had worked with photography. They recognised the effect of the developing chemical that turned the skin purplish-black on contact. Milton had been effectively branded.

"What?" demanded Milton again.

"The bastards have used silver nitrate, Milt. It's not going to come off."

Milton was silent. Edna sat next to him, stroking his arm. Clyde poured him a large brandy and put the glass into his friend's hands. "What happened?"

"Rowly's Legion mates," he said finally. "They jumped me as I got back to the house—they were on the verandah." He looked at Rowland. "They thought I was Rowland Sinclair."

"Me? Why didn't you tell them?" Rowland felt sick.

"I didn't know whether you'd already come back," Milton replied. "I thought you could turn up any moment. They did this to me just because to them I was Rowland Sinclair. Hell, if they knew you were also Clyde Watson Jones..." He shook his head.

"They thought they were attacking Rowly?" Edna's sympathies were now for both men. She could almost feel Rowland's horror, and guilt, over the beating Milton had taken for him.

"I'm afraid they know I'm not you now." Milton gulped his brandy, sputtering a little as it went down. "After they did this," he touched his forehead, "another couple of cars pulled up and more hooded idiots piled out. One of them took a look at me and started screaming they'd got the wrong man again."

"He recognised you?" Clyde asked.

"He recognised that I wasn't Rowly."

Rowland spoke, stricken. "Again? He said 'they'd got the wrong man...again'?"

Milton nodded.

Rowland rubbed his face in his hands, "God, Milt, I am so sorry."

Milton looked at him. "None of this is down to you, mate. Not this, nor your old uncle."

"They killed your uncle because they got the wrong Rowland Sinclair?" Edna was aghast.

"I doubt they meant to kill him, Ed...just teach him a lesson." Milton's concern furrowed the brand on his forehead. Rowland had always been slow to anger, but he was truly livid now. The poet could see it in his eyes—it worried him.

"But why?" Edna asked. "You hadn't done anything."

Rowland stood. "I'll just go ask Campbell, shall I?" The ice in his voice chilled the entire room. "I'm going to change into something more suitable for visiting. Clyde, would you call the police?"

Edna picked up the voluminous skirt of her costume and followed him out.

"Where are you going?" Clyde asked her.

"I'll get changed and go with him," she replied. "Rowly won't do anything stupid if I'm with him. You look after Milt, and call the police."

"Well, maybe I should come…"

"No, Clyde." Edna was adamant. "Rowly needs someone to calm him down now, not another set of fists to help him get into real trouble. These men are dangerous—they've already killed one man and attacked Milt, just to get to Rowly."

"Let her go, Clyde," said Milton, shifting himself painfully on the couch. "Rowly might listen to her."

It took neither Rowland Sinclair nor Edna Higgins long to change. They argued for a while. Rowland did not want her to come, but she wouldn't give him any option. With Clyde and Milton backing her up, Rowland relented. He wasn't really sure what he planned to do, anyway. He wanted to shout at Campbell—to tell him what his insane followers had done. He wanted to hunt down Henry Alcott and break his neck.

They left just as the doctor arrived to see Milton. Edna whispered to Clyde as she walked out, "Call Wilfred."

Rowland had barely driven out of the gate when Edna started to harass him to leave it to the police. On some level, he knew she was right. Still, for the most part, he ignored her. He hardly noticed this first time to drive his car over the Sydney Harbour Bridge.

"Rowly, you can't just barge in and attack Campbell," Edna pressed, wondering if he was even listening.

"I'm not going to do that Ed," he said, smiling faintly. "The man carries a gun."

"How do you know that?"

"He showed me—he's quite proud of it."

"Then what are we doing, Rowly?"

"I just want him to know, Ed. To know. He's so bloody convinced he's right; he doesn't care what he's unleashed. These men—Alcott, Poynton, De Groot—they all talk about him like he's God. They do all this in his name. I want the names of the men who killed Uncle Rowland and attacked Milt, but frankly he's as guilty as they are!"

"Couldn't the police do this, Rowly?"

"Probably," he replied. "But I need to get my paint box."

He pulled into the driveway at Boongala and the guards posted at the gate waved them through, recognising Rowland as the Colonel's artist.

The house was quiet.

"Rowly, it's nearly midnight—they'll be asleep."

"Campbell will have been out celebrating De Groot's efforts on the bridge. If he's in bed, it won't have been for long—and, honestly, I don't care."

Edna hurried after him as he stalked to the front door and knocked loudly. The housekeeper answered.

"Mr. Watson Jones!" she said, surprised, tying her dressing gown around her waist. "Was Colonel Campbell expecting you this late?"

"I'm afraid not, but I must see him on a matter of some urgency."

"I'm afraid he and Mrs. Campbell are not back yet, sir." Rowland's face did not show his disappointment. He was starting to calm down a little now, to think more clearly. He was still angry, but it was becoming a more thoughtful anger. "I've left some equipment in the studio," he said smiling sweetly, as if it was perfectly normal to bang down a man's door at midnight to collect some paints as if your life depended on it. "I might just retrieve it while I'm here."

The housekeeper seemed happy to admit them. The young artist was trusted by the Colonel, and she was anxious to return to bed.

"We'll let ourselves out," Rowland assured her. "I'm sorry to have got you up."

The housekeeper let them make their own way to the studio. Rowland found his belongings were exactly as he had left them. He opened the paint box and rummaged under the tubes of paint. The revolver was still there. Double-checking that the safety catch was still on, he returned it to the paint box and closed the lid.

Edna was staring at him. "Rowly, we didn't come here to get that, did we?"

He looked up. "No…God, no! I'm not planning to use it, Ed. I remembered it the other day, that's all, and I didn't want to leave it here. Who knows what these lunatics could do with Wil's gun. It could get him in all sorts of trouble."

They heard voices outside the room. Perhaps Campbell had returned. Rowland stuck his head out and looked down the corridor. The housekeeper was again at the front door, not with Campbell, but with Henry Alcott and several other men who Rowland had not seen before. She gestured back toward the studio and Alcott looked his way.

Rowland pulled his head back and moved quickly. He pushed Edna behind the couch. "Stay here. Don't make a sound! Don't let them know you're here. I'll be all right."

Edna nodded, frightened. She could already hear the heavy footfalls in the corridor. The door flung open. Flanked by four others, Henry Alcott walked in. Rowland stood his ground. "Hello, Henry."

"If it isn't the elusive Rowland Sinclair."

"Have you been looking for me?"

The scarred right side of Alcott's face twitched. "So Dynon was right...we do have a spy in our midst. Reporting to your filthy Communist mates—you're a disgrace to your brother's memory, Sinclair."

"Go to hell, Henry! Aubrey loved Uncle Rowland. If he knew what you've done..."

"How was I to know those idiots would get the wrong Rowland Sinclair?" Alcott's eyes bulged as he stepped toward his best friend's brother. At that moment, Rowland understood that Alcott's mind was no longer right. "They were only meant to teach you a lesson, Sinclair, to get you to walk the right line...Don't you see...? I had to turn you around...for Aubrey. But it's too late for all that now. Turning up to a Red rally at the Domain's one thing, but now...now you're a damn spy for them!"

One of the men behind Alcott quietly sidled

up to the fireplace and took a fire iron. Rowland cursed himself for not thinking to take the weapon first. "This is Campbell's home, Henry," he said, his voice deceptively calm.

"We'll clean up the mess." Alcott shook his head slowly, suddenly tearful. "Good Lord, you look like Aubrey—you could have been Aubrey." He motioned, and two men leapt forward and seized Rowland by the arms.

Alcott hit him first. In rage, Rowland struggled but couldn't wrest out of their grip. Then the beating began in earnest. The fire iron struck hard against his ribs, winding him, but mostly it was Alcott's bare fists and his fury, a fury that was about so much more than Rowland Sinclair.

Edna crawled out from behind the couch. Alcott and his men did not seem to notice her, but Rowland did. He insulted Campbell, King George, and every right-wing bastion he could think of, desperate to keep their ire and their attention on him. He hoped she would run for the door.

Instead, Edna opened his paint box, fumbled for the gun he had placed back in there, and unwrapped it. "Stop!" She held the weapon in shaking hands, crying already. "Leave him alone!"

His breath heaving, Alcott stopped. "You brought a girl with you?" he sneered. "My, you are getting cocky, Sinclair."

Edna pointed the gun above her to fire a warning shot, as she had seen done in the cinema. It clicked uselessly. Alcott laughed and sent his fist flying into Rowland's stomach again.

Dismayed, Edna remembered the safety. She had seen Rowland flick it. She pushed it the other way. They were ignoring her. Rowland was barely fighting back now. They were going kill him—she was sure of it. With both hands, she held the gun in front of her and pulled the trigger. The sound seemed to stop her heart for a moment, and the gun kicked her back. Hysterical and terrified, she fired again with no idea where the bullets were going.

The Guardsmen were swearing as they scrambled for the door. Edna fired again. Though her ears were ringing from the blasts, she could hear glass breaking, and then sirens.

"Ed, stop!" Rowland gasped from the floor. He tried, but couldn't get up to reassure her, to stop her. A dark spreading stain on the patterned Axminster grew inexorably outwards. "Ed!"

Edna heard him. She looked down to where he had dropped. She saw the blood and realised she'd shot him. The gun became red hot in her hand. She dropped it, screaming.

Chapter Thirty-six

NEW GUARD PLOTS

SYDNEY, Sunday

Mr. Eric Campbell, in a statement today, denied that Fascist tactics formed part of the New Guard policy. He declared there was no such thing as a Fascist Legion in the New Guard and to talk of black hoods was arrant nonsense.

Mr. Campbell said that the evidence in the assault case yesterday showed that a number of decent and thoroughly loyal New Guardsmen had set out on their own account to do a job they considered in the public interest, and if the public approval which rent the air outside the courthouse were any criterion, they did so thoroughly.

The Daily Telegraph, March 21, 1932

"Rowly?"

He heard Wilfred's voice through a dense fog of pain. He struggled to sit up.

"Take it easy, old boy."

Rowland ignored him. Things would become clearer if he was upright. He groaned as he became aware of his body, and the damage done to it.

"Be careful." Wilfred moved pillows behind Rowly's back. "They cracked a few ribs…you're going to be tender for quite a while."

A doctor came in. He examined the dressing on the bullet wound to Rowland's right thigh, and prodded his rib cage in a way that left him gasping and weak. Then he consulted with Wilfred about his brother's injuries. Rowland didn't care—he just wanted the man to go. Eventually the physician did leave and Rowland was able to demand answers of Wilfred.

"Did the police…?"

"They've arrested Alcott—they want to speak to you as soon as you're up to it."

"I'm up to it."

"Just hold on a minute, Rowly, they'll get to you. This is such a flaming mess!"

"What time is it?" Rowland asked, still trying to put his head in order.

"Three in the afternoon."

Rowland was surprised so much time had passed. "You shouldn't have let me sleep so long."

"They had to take the bullet out, Rowly. I couldn't really go in and wake you for breakfast."

"Oh." Rowland looked down at his leg. It was heavy, on fire, and heavy. He moved it tentatively. He stopped pretty quickly.

"You're lucky...handguns make relatively small holes," Wilfred informed him.

Rowland told him where to go. Wilfred smiled.

"Where's Ed...? And Clyde...?"

"They wouldn't let anyone but family in until you woke up."

"I'm awake now." Rowland winced, almost wishing he wasn't. He noticed Wilfred looked older than he remembered him.

"Mr. Watson Jones—the real one—is just outside."

Wilfred opened the door and called for Clyde, who'd been pacing outside in the hospital corridor. "Rowly, thank God..."

Rowland smiled, or at least tried to. "Apparently, it's not a big hole. How's Milt? Did Ed tell you what happened?"

Clyde glanced at Wilfred. Wilfred shook his head.

"What?" Rowland noticed the exchange. "What the hell's happened?"

Clyde walked to his bedside. He didn't look at Wilfred. "They've arrested Ed. Milt's at the station seeing what he can do."

Rowland pulled himself up a little more, using Clyde's shoulder to steady himself. He spun his head round to Wilfred. "You let them arrest her!"

"For the love of God, Rowly...she shot you! I know you think you're in love with this girl, but she shot you!"

"It was an accident—she was trying to help me!"

"That's not what she said!"

"Rowly," Clyde interrupted. "Ed was hysterical, spattered with blood...she thought she'd killed you. She confessed to anyone who'd listen." Rowland fell back on the pillows.

"Ed's in gaol, and she thinks I'm dead?"

"Yes."

"And Milt went to help her with 'Red' branded across his forehead!"

"He wore a hat...Now that I know you're all right...well, not dead, anyway, I'll go down and see what I can do."

"No, wait." Rowland turned back to Wilfred. "Wil, you go down there, please? I don't care what you have to do. Engage every bloody barrister in Australia if you have to, but get her out!"

Wilfred looked at his brother as if he'd lost his mind. "No, Rowly—she shot you!"

"Alcott might have killed me if she hadn't," Rowland said coldly.

"Clyde…" He put his hand on Clyde's shoulder again and began to pull himself up, cursing under his breath as he moved his leg.

"What the devil are you doing?" Wilfred stepped toward him in alarm.

"I'm going to get Ed out of prison myself if you won't…Where are my blasted clothes?"

"Don't be an idiot, Rowly. Lie down."

"I'm not going to leave her there—it was a bloody accident!"

"Dammit, Rowly," Wilfred brought his fist down on the metal frame of the bed in frustration. "Very well, I'll go!"

"Bring her back here, so I know she's all right," Rowland said.

"You don't trust me?"

"I just want to see her. Go…please…now."

Wilfred called his brother a few choice names, but he went. Once he'd gone, Rowland allowed himself to fall painfully back onto the bed.

"Thank God for that," he breathed. "Wil can be the most stubborn bastard…"

Clyde poured him a glass of water and helped him drink. "Don't be so hard on him, Rowly," he said. "He's all right—any idiot can see you'd never make it out of that bed, and he went anyway."

"Wil was there…at Boongala?" Rowland frowned as he tried to piece muddled memories together. "You were, too?"

"I telephoned him just after you left," Clyde admitted. "He came straight over. We weren't sure who you were going to attack first, so we went to Alcott's house in Potts Point."

"I wasn't going to attack anyone." Even as he said it, Rowland wasn't sure it was the truth.

"That wasn't clear when you left," Clyde replied. "Anyway, Wilfred spoke to Alcott's father who told him Alcott had gone to see Campbell. Your brother made some calls, and all sorts of people, including the police, met us at Campbell's. Good thing the bridge was open, or we'd never have got there."

"So, you were both there."

"We didn't get there first. God, Rowly, it was like a war zone. The police said you'd been shot, Edna was screaming she'd killed you. There was a moment when we really did think you were dead. It was bleak. You should go easy on Wilfred."

Rowland raised his brows. "He hasn't signed you up to the Old Guard, has he?"

"Don't tempt me to thump you while you're in hospital. It wouldn't look good."

"Why did they arrest Ed? I wasn't dead—surely they could see that?"

"You were in a bad way when we arrived. Alcott and his friends weren't saying anything and Ed was the only one talking, or should I say, screaming, and all she was saying was 'I shot him…I shot him.' You can see why they don't send women to war."

Rowland sighed. "Well, I can tell them now. Given the belting I was getting, if she hadn't started shooting I may have ended up like Uncle Rowland…Ed just doesn't know how to hold a gun straight. It's a bleeding miracle she didn't manage to shoot herself as well." He smiled. "I wonder if Wil knows she shot me with his gun…you didn't think to take my paint box did you?"

"The police have it."

"Oh, good. I wouldn't want to have to ask Campbell for it now."

It was several hours before Wilfred returned, with both Edna and Milton. Apparently Milton had been so determined in his attempts to have Edna released, that they'd arrested him too. Wilfred was, however, better than his word and delivered them both.

Edna was in tears the second she entered the hospital room. She had convinced herself that Rowland was dead, that she had killed him, and nothing Wilfred had said in journey from the police station could reach her in her grief.

"Steady on, Ed," Rowland murmured as she threw herself at him, apologising through gulping sobs.

Milton reached past her and squeezed his shoulder. "Wasn't your best idea, Rowly." The bruises on Milton's face had darkened, as had the letters of the word on his forehead.

"I don't know...I did find Alcott."

Wilfred stood to leave. "I'd better get back," he said. "Kate will be frantic by now, and I still have some people to see. I'll bring her, and Ernie, to see you tomorrow."

"Thank you, Wil."

Wilfred clasped his brother's hand, and Rowland could sense by the weakened grip that he was tired. Rowland met his eye and said again, "Thank you, Wil."

Wilfred nodded. "Try to get some sleep, Rowly," he said looking meaningfully at his friends. "The police will want to speak to you tomorrow. I've posted some men at the hospital, just in case."

"So," Clyde sighed, as Wilfred shut the door behind him, "all this because you and your uncle have the same name."

"Had." Rowland's voice was dulled with sadness.

"I don't get it," Clyde shook his head. "You're

not even a Communist. What the hell did you do that was so offensive?"

"It's that class traitor thing," Milton, rubbed his forehead. "The right-wingers despise all Communists, but when it's one of their own, a man who should know better…well, they really see red."

Rowland groaned, in response to the pun rather than anything else. It was stupid, but it was a diversion.

Clyde nudged Rowland. "You really need to pick your friends more carefully, mate."

"You mustn't dwell on it, Rowly." Edna pushed the hair back from his forehead, as she had often known him to do himself. She could see through his flippancy to know he was struggling with the idea that his uncle had died because of him. "It wasn't your fault. It was that dreadful man, Alcott."

"It's a shame you managed to shoot everything but him." Rowland managed a smile. "Still, at least they've arrested him now. With any luck, Campbell's whole bloody house of cards, minus the queens, will fall down around him."

Milton looked nervously at Clyde.

Rowland saw. "What?"

Neither responded.

"For God's sake, I haven't got a bloody heart condition—what's happened?"

"Alcott and his mates are claiming they

thought you were a burglar, that they were just trying to restrain you, when Ed started shooting. Campbell's backing them up."

Rowland cursed, groaned, and cursed again. "Does Wil know about this?"

Milton nodded; he almost smiled. "You Sinclairs have bloody fearsome tempers—if Wilfred does half of what he's threatened, I think Alcott might think he'd be safer in gaol."

Clyde tried to give him some hope. "Look, Rowly, the police haven't talked to you yet. That may change things." He stood. "We should let you get some rest now, or Wilfred will have us. We'll be back first thing in the morning." As much as Clyde loathed leaving just after giving his friend the news that this might all have been for nothing, Rowland was clearly exhausted, and Edna and Milton weren't looking too flash either.

Milton took a small pewter flask from inside his jacket and slipped it under Rowland's pillow. "Chin up, comrade," he said. "We'll get the bastards eventually. We'll make the tyrants feel the sting of those that they would throttle; They needn't say the fault is ours if blood should stain the wattle."

Rowland stared at him blankly. "Good Lord, don't tell me you actually wrote something?"

Clyde groaned. "Bloody typical! You recognise

everything written by dead Brits, and you let the man steal from Lawson."

Edna smiled. "Shame on you, Rowly." She kissed his cheek. "We'll see you in the morning."

It was Wilfred who arrived first the next day. He studied Rowland over the top of his bifocals. "Good heavens, Rowly, you look a bit rough. I'll send a barber in later this morning."

Rowland pushed the hair out of his face and responded a little ungraciously.

Wilfred went on regardless. "We'd better organise some clothes as well...There's a few people lined up to talk to you, and I'd rather you didn't look like someone who might actually burgle a man's house."

Rowland pulled himself up gingerly. He had slept very badly. He was stiff and in more pain than he'd thought possible, yet Wilfred seemed to think that he needed a tie and jacket.

Wilfred pulled up a chair and sat down next to the bed. "We need to talk about how we're going to handle this."

"Handle what?"

"I've just left a meeting with Campbell. We've come to an arrangement."

Rowland bolted up, winced, but did not fall back. "Arrangement—what are you talking about?"

"This is such a bloody mess, Rowly. You didn't tell me you fabricated references to get this portrait commission with Campbell. What the devil were you thinking? Do you understand how serious forgery is these days? And then you left the bloody evidence with Campbell. He could have you charged at any time!"

"But if we explain…"

"Campbell is claiming your plan was to assassinate him, that you smuggled a gun into his house… my gun, for heaven's sake…for that precise reason. He's contending that this was an Old Guard plot, and that my neck is in it as much as yours."

"And what happened at his house…?" Rowland clutched his side and gasped as he moved too suddenly. "Ed was there too—she heard Henry admit they killed Uncle Rowland."

Wilfred's face softened slightly. "Rowly, as unsuitable as she is, I know you care about this girl—you do not want to involve her in this any more than she is already. Campbell's lawyers could make a Sunday school teacher sound like a harlot… and your Miss Higgins is no Sunday school teacher. However careless you are about your own reputation, you don't want to do that to her."

"No, I don't." Rowland swallowed. "So what does this mean?"

"It means, Rowly, that you could go to prison

for a significant period, the Sinclair name stands to be ruined and the Old Guard compromised." Even as he said this, Wilfred put his hand reassuringly on his brother's shoulder.

"And the police...Delaney?"

"They're sympathetic, but if Campbell pushes the issue, they'll have no choice but to arrest you... at least for forgery and deception, and possibly for attempted murder."

Rowland knew that somehow Wilfred had rescued him. What had he done?

"So this arrangement with Campbell...?" he asked.

"Fortunately, the New Guard is keen to avoid exposure of their less acceptable practices." Wilfred exhaled. "Campbell has agreed not to press charges against you, or Miss Higgins, or me."

"And in return?"

"The men who killed Uncle Rowland will plead guilty to simple assault, but no mention will be made of the Legion or the New Guard. They'll probably get a fine. The assault on you will be treated as a misunderstanding. I'll pay for the damage to Campbell's house and the new carpet to replace the one you bled all over."

Rowland said nothing, defeated, humiliated.

"Rowly, there's more."

Rowland clenched a fist in his hair, beyond

frustration, beyond anger. This was bad for Wilfred too. He knew it would have galled his brother to negotiate with Campbell.

"Whether or not you believe it, we've managed to the get the better end of this deal. I'm concerned that Campbell may change his mind and then there's Henry…"

Rowland bristled at the mention of Alcott.

Wilfred looked at him intently. "Exactly," he said sternly. "Your doctors tell me, that provided there is no infection, you should be able to walk on crutches in a week or so…I want you to go abroad."

Rowland laughed hoarsely. "Exile?"

"Don't be so dramatic. You could use some time away—to recuperate—and there are some business matters you could take care of for me. Take your, er, friends with you…it's not as if they have employers to miss them."

"How long?"

"I'm not punishing you, Rowly," Wilfred said gently. He paused. "A few months."

"And what will I come back to, Wil?"

Wilfred rose and closed the door to the hospital room. He sat down again. "If I have anything to say about it, Rowly, you'll come back to the Australia you left. There are thousands of men, right-thinking men who will protect what we have against both the Communists and people like

Campbell." He regarded his brother thoughtfully. "You're a young man, Rowly. You're impetuous. You hurtle headlong into things and go down in a blaze of glory. Older heads do things differently, quietly, more effectively."

"And you want me to just leave you to it?" Rowland's mouth was tight.

"You don't have a lot of choice." Wilfred sat back. "This mess has the potential to damage a lot of people. For all our sakes, you have to walk away."

Rowland twisted inside with what his brother asked, conflicted, resistant. Finally he nodded, resigned. Wilfred had kept him out of prison—he couldn't really refuse. He would do as he was told.

Chapter Thirty-seven

De Groot in Court

FREED FROM RECEPTION HOUSE
FURTHER ACTION BY POLICE
Remand on Three Charges

SYDNEY, Monday

Captain Francis Edward De Groot, an officer of the New Guard, who cut the ribbon during the opening of the Harbour Bridge on Saturday, and who was charged subsequently with being deemed to be insane and not being under proper care and control, appealed before a special Court at the Reception House this morning.

Mr. Macdougal S.M., after hearing the evidence, discharged De Groot without making any comment, after a doctor told the court that De Groot was sane.

Police officers under Detective

Superintendent MacKay, immediately took De Groot to the Darlinghurst police station, where he was charged with offensive behaviour, with having used threatening words to Inspector Stuart Robson, and with having damaged ribbon worth £2, the property of the New South Wales Government. De Groot was released on bail of £10 to appear at the Central Police Court tomorrow.

The leader of the New Guard (Colonel Eric Campbell) was with De Groot during the proceedings at the reception house and at the Darlinghurst Police Station. He supplied bail and drove away with De Groot and Mrs. De Groot.

A crowd of 1,000 men cheered Captain de Groot and Colonel Campbell whenever they appeared.

The Argus, March 29, 1932

"Good grief!" Milton lurched forward to support Rowland as his crutch slipped and clattered to the floor.

"Keep your voice down!" Rowland said urgently but quietly, as he resisted his own impulse to curse. "If that damned nurse hears you, she'll never shut up."

Milton grinned. Rowland had returned to

Woodlands House under the dedicated care of two senior nurses who worked round the clock in shifts. They were fearsome, humourless women who were impervious to any form of charm, and seemed to answer only to Wilfred. Stalwarts of the temperance movement, they treated pain with tea and readings from the Good Book. The physician, Maguire, a man of equally dour disposition, called twice a day.

Milton eased Rowland onto the couch.

"Do you want a drink, Rowly?" he asked as he saw the sweat beading on his friend's brow.

Rowland nodded.

Between Wilfred's determination that morphine was unnecessary, and his own refusal to lie quietly and heal, Rowland was having a hard time of it. Milton prescribed alcohol whenever the nurses were out of earshot.

"What do you want?"

"Anything, just hurry before she returns."

The door opened and, for a moment, they thought they were too late…but it was just Edna and Clyde. The sculptress was resplendent in a ball gown of ice blue taffeta.

Milton whistled.

"Why, thank you, sir." She dipped into a deep curtsey.

Milton waved her away. "The whistle was for Clyde. He's positively pretty."

"The tailor will be ready for you in a few minutes," Clyde growled as he fiddled with the cuff of his tailcoat. Rowland had instructed his gentleman's tailor to outfit his friends with dinner suits, tails, and whatever other attire they would need for their extended tour of the Continent.

He'd arranged for Edna to be fitted out by one of the more elite High Street boutiques. From what he'd seen so far, the "Sinclair party" was going to look smashing.

The sculptress sat unceremoniously on the arm of the couch and put her hand gently on Rowland's forehead. "Rowly, darling, you're a bit warm. Are you sure you didn't leave the hospital too soon?"

"This might help." Milton handed him a large glass of gin.

"Wilfred thought I'd recuperate better at home," Rowland said vaguely, not wanting to distress her unduly.

In truth, his brother had become concerned that the hospital was not safe. Wilfred was convinced that the New Guard now had Rowland Sinclair in their sights. He had taken Rowland home after just a few days and had surrounded the mansion with his own security. For the first time since Rowland had become master of Woodlands, the gates were locked and guarded.

Their passages aboard the *RMS Oceanic* had been purchased for a sailing in a week. Wilfred was determined to put his brother out of Eric Campbell's reach.

"You look outstanding, Ed." Rowland raised his glass to her and drank.

"Slow down," Edna said, alarmed by how he was throwing down his gin.

"I might not have much time before that nurse woman returns to ensure I'm miserable."

Edna smiled. "Nurse Conroy? She's busy. I think she might be a while."

"Really. What's she doing?"

"I heard her arguing with Mary Brown as I passed the kitchen…something about what kind of food you should be eating. Mary was quite indignant."

"Thank God for Mary," Rowland muttered. "That old crone's probably trying to poison me."

"Poor Rowly." Edna took his empty glass. "Would you like another?"

Rowland shook his head. "I don't need a hangover on top of everything else."

"You can top me up if you're offering." Milton handed her his own glass as he adjusted the black beret which sat over his brow. Selwin Higgins had presented Milton with his beloved beret so that the poet could hide the word which now marked his forehead. Milton hadn't taken it off since. To Rowland, that was just one more thing for which the New Guard should have to answer.

Clyde removed his tailcoat and sat down with the newspaper. "Looks like the Guard is going to show up in force for De Groot's trial," he said, scanning the page. "They're expecting some sort of stoush."

"And they're going to get it." Colin Delaney walked into the room. "MacKay's priming the boys to belt a few New Guard heads in." The detective walked over to shake hands with Rowland. "Blimey, Sinclair, I had a time getting past your security… You're better protected than the Premier."

"That's Wil," Rowland replied. "He's convinced that some overzealous Guardsman is going to finish me off."

Delaney's face was sober. "He's got a point. Things are tinder dry at the moment—any spark and people will lose their heads." He glanced at Rowland's leg. "How are you, anyway? You look like hell."

"Do you think Campbell will make his final putsch?" Rowland asked.

Delaney sat down. "He's getting cocky—issuing ultimatums left, right, and centre…They still have a load of public support—despite De Groot's antics at the bridge. Bloody Jock Garden's rallying the Communists and Union men."

Rowland watched the eye contact between Milton and Clyde. "Hell of a time to be leaving Sydney," he murmured darkly.

Delaney shook his head. "No, your brother's right." He pointed at Rowly sternly. "You're a marked man, Sinclair…and if this deal he's made with Campbell falls apart, the story that you tried to assassinate the New Guard's commander may just swing public opinion in their favour. You've no choice but to sit this fight out."

"Mr. Sinclair! What are you doing down here? If I had known you were going to ignore the doctor's orders for rest, I would never have allowed you to get dressed!" Nurse Conroy stormed into the room ignoring everyone but her errant patient.

"Rowly can rest here," Edna ventured courageously. Now she'd shot him, she'd become very protective.

Nurse Conroy puffed. Her considerable chest expanded imperiously. "Young woman, Mr. Sinclair is not a well man. I will not risk his convalescence for either his whim or your entertainment. Is that understood?"

Rowland groaned. The other men shrank into their seats.

Edna continued valiantly. "But we could make Rowly comfortable here, Nurse Conroy, and he wouldn't get so bored." She tried to appeal to the woman's compassion. "It hurts more when he has nothing else to think about."

"Young woman…" Nurse Conroy was not impressed or moved in any way. "Mr. Sinclair is not to have any form of excitement." She handed Rowland his crutches and stood back with her arms folded expectantly.

Edna patted his hand. "You go then, Rowly. I'll just change and pop in to sit with you. We can play cards." The sculptress looked pointedly at Clyde and Milton, who agreed cautiously but with nervous glances in the nurse's direction.

Nurse Conroy snorted.

Delaney stood. "Well, I'd better be getting on." He made a face at Rowland, out of the nurse's sight. "Cheer up, Sinclair. There's really nothing you can do now." The detective took his leave and headed back out to the increasingly tense streets of Sydney.

Rowland struggled to his feet. Clyde and Milton stood to help him. "Clyde," he said quietly, "could you find Poynton? He lives in Newtown. Get him to come meet me—he will need a little convincing."

"You want me to bring him here?"

"No, Campbell might have people watching...not to mention Wil's people."

"Well, how's he going to meet you?" Milton whispered. "There's no way you're going to get past Warden Conroy."

"Warden" Conroy cleared her throat impatiently as she waited by the door.

Rowland thought for a moment. "It'll have to be the day we leave...that tea house on the docks, the grimy little one. We're less likely to be seen there."

Clyde nodded. "I'll take care of it.

"Be careful...remember your name is mud with the New Guard."

Chapter Thirty-eight

NEW GUARD ACTIONS

Police May Intervene

SYDNEY, Tuesday

In the Legislative Assembly today, Mr. Heffron asked the Chief Secretary (Mr. Gosling) whether his attention had been drawn to the recent actions of the New Guard. Would he consider declaring the New Guard to be an illegal organisation?

Mr. Gosling said that some time ago he had regarded the actions of the New Guard as buffoonery, but now it was approaching criminality. The question of proceeding against members of the New Guard for breaking the law was one for the police.

The Sydney Morning Herald, April 4, 1932

The clientele of the tea house at the docks were, for the most part, those about to embark in the second- and third-class cabins of the passenger liners that left from the harbour. The establishment's windows were so caked with grime that it could offer its patrons a privacy forgone in the more fashionable, and well-maintained cafes. At a table by the murky window sat a heavily jowled man who smoked continuously and seemed to produce unreasonably large clouds of fumes whenever he exhaled. Seated with him was a young man with dark, slightly unruly hair. His eyes were so intense that they were recognisable as blue from across the room, despite the tobacco fog of the tea house. A pair of crutches leant against the back of his chair.

The two had been deep in conversation for over an hour. Earlier, there had been a strong tension between them—the older man had initially refused to sit, and at one point, had knocked the crutches to the floor. But something the younger man had said thawed the atmosphere and their heads had been bent close for a while. The younger man looked at his wristwatch, and reached round to grab the crutches. He struggled to his feet, gritting his teeth as he did so. His companion stubbed out his cigarette and stood also. The two shook hands.

"I'll see you when I get back," said the one on

crutches. "Remember, speak to Delaney when the time comes."

The other nodded. "You can rely on me. Good luck, Jonesy." Inevitably, he tapped the side of his nose.

Chapter Thirty-nine

Civil War

Mr. Lang's Bogey
ATTACKS ON COURTS RENEWED

GOULBURN

Speaking here to-night, Mr. Lang claimed that Mr. Stevens had stated that if the Labor Party was returned at the election, he and his colleagues in the Federal Parliament would declare civil war upon them.

"Was that an ultimatum Australians were going to sit down under?" Mr. Lang asked.

What Mr. Stevens said in effect, was that: "If you vote for Labor, the Federal Government will shoot you down. What sort of a cause must Mr. Stevens have, if he had to threaten the population with civil war unless he won the election?"

Mr. Lang said that Mr. Stevens' threat was idle. It was used simply to dragoon people of the State into voting for Stevens' policy—the policy that would bring misery and ruin to the people of New South Wales.
The Canberra Times, April 4, 1932

Kate Sinclair kissed her brother-in-law fondly. "You look after yourself, Rowly. Have a wonderful time."

Wilfred shook his hand. Rowland winced, trying to balance on a single crutch.

Wilfred frowned as he noticed. "You should have let me send Nurse Conroy with you."

"One day, Wil," Rowland said, "if I have cause to retain a nurse for you...I'll remember Nurse Conroy."

Wilfred smiled faintly. "I don't know what you mean, Rowly. She's a fine woman...came highly recommended."

"For what exactly?"

"I've had a word to the ship's doctor...he'll keep an eye on you." Wilfred glanced at Milton and Clyde who were skylarking with young Ernest a few yards away, and Edna who was bidding farewell to her father and the flock of eager young men who'd come to see her off. "You just make sure your friends don't disgrace us internationally."

Rowland's eyes darkened.

Kate nudged her husband. "Oh Wil, don't quarrel." She reached up to Rowland's ear and whispered. "He's actually quite glad they'll be there to look after you."

"You had best board now," Wilfred directed sternly. "It might take you a while to get up the gangplank."

Rowland looked up at the ship towering above them. Was he walking away when New South Wales needed the few men left who were still sane? MacKay's men had already faced off against the New Guard, on the day De Groot stood trial. The police had more than defeated the Guard; they had publicly humiliated Campbell. Guardsmen were trotted through Liverpool Street by their neckties, pounded and bloodied by a constabulary ordered to take back control. Had they succeeded, or would things simply escalate?

Wilfred put a hand on his shoulder. "Don't worry, Rowly. They won't get the better of us."

Rowland wondered briefly who his brother meant by "they," but he left it.

Ernest ran up to them, excited, and clambered into his father's arms. "You have to throw lots of streamers, Uncle Rowly. From up there," he pointed.

"Of course," Rowland replied. "I'll throw yellow ones. You watch out for them."

Ernest nodded solemnly. "Are you going to see the King?"

"Shall I give him your regards?"

Ernest smiled. "Don't be silly, Uncle Rowly, King George has his own guards...with big black furry hats."

"Oh, yes, I forgot."

Rowland finished his goodbyes, and turned to join his friends to board.

As Wilfred took his family to the best vantage point to wave the *Oceanic* off, a brass band struck up, signalling the passengers that final boarding had commenced. The Sinclair party moved slowly toward the stream of travellers making its way to the gangway.

"Oi, Sinclair!" Rowland just heard the hail above the music and the noise. "Sinclair!"

Harcourt Garden ran toward them, pushing through the crush. Clyde and Milton stiffened. Surely Garden wasn't going to challenge a man on crutches. The burly Unionist caught up.

Rowland regarded Garden warily; their last encounter, in Pyrmont, had been anything but cordial. "Harry," he said carefully. "What are you...?"

"I was here talking to some of the boys on the docks, when I caught sight of you." Garden stuck out his hand, grinning. "I hear the Boo Guard is looking for you."

Rowland took his hand. "So I'm told."

"I don't know who the hell you were working for, Sinclair, but you obviously got to that mongrel, Campbell. That makes you all right in my reckoning." He leant closer. "Did you really try to kill the Fascist bastard?"

Rowland met his eye. "No."

Garden winked. "Of course not—you're a gentleman, after all, eh, Sinclair? But still…it was a good try."

"Look, Harry…" Rowland thought now of the meeting of the Fascist Legion to which Poynton had taken him. Jock Garden's name had come up several times. "The men in hoods, the ones who beat up Paddy…"

"Paddy wasn't drunk, you're saying?"

"No, he wasn't…They're a dangerous mob; fanatical. Tell your father to watch out."

Garden nodded. "That Detective Delaney's already been round, but Dad thought the police were just trying to get him to back off. Thanks, Sinclair, I'll stick to old Jock like glue."

"We'd better go," Rowland glanced up the gangway.

"Goodbye then, Rowly," Garden slapped

his back warmly. "Don't worry, we'll be ready for them."

Again Rowland wondered who exactly fell under the category of "them."

Leaving Garden, they made their way onto the *Oceanic* and up to the first-class decks. Rowland gripped the rail of the promenade thankfully. Clyde and Milton had all but carried him up the stairs and the roll of the deck was not pleasant on crutches. Still, the atmosphere of excitement was contagious. He was beginning to feel less despondent about this exile...at least he would spend it in good company.

The ship's horn sounded its low, belching note. The crowds around them and below on the docks cheered and waved. The band played "Auld Lang Syne."

"Here you go, Rowly." Edna handed him several rolls of yellow streamers. "Ernie will be watching." Thousands of passengers all began hurling the colourful paper strips.

The tugs pulled the ocean liner away from the docks, its horn drowning out the crowds and the fanfare. Rowland watched as Sydney receded. There wasn't anything more he could do. He'd just have to hope to God that democracy would survive all these right-thinking men.

Epilogue

ARCHIBALD PRIZE
WON BY MR. E. BUCKMASTER

Portrait of Sir William Irvine

SYDNEY, Thursday

The Archibald Prize of £370 has again been awarded to a Victorian, Mr. Ernest Buckmaster of Melbourne, for his portrait of His Excellency the Lieutenant Governor of Victoria (Sir William Irvine).

Mr. Buckmaster was represented by five large portraits, all of which maintain a high standard of excellence in technique and delineation of character. His winning portrait of Sir William, shown seated against a sombre background, is imbued with quiet dignity and a sense of repose.

The Argus

Convicted of offensive behaviour, Francis De Groot was fined £4 plus costs. The Irishman's charge upon the Sydney Harbour Bridge opening ribbon aroused a public reaction that galvanised both the New Guard's supporters and its detractors. De Groot would later claim he took this action only to prevent Campbell from choosing a more extreme and dangerous plan.

Later that same month, as tensions heightened, Superintendent Bill MacKay commissioned a full police report into the activities of the Old Guard, rumoured to greatly outnumber Campbell's movement, and to be preparing for action.

In May, 1932, the Peace Officers Act was implemented by the Federal Government as across the State the loyal men of the Old Guard stood ready to be sworn. The Old Guard was poised for mobilisation.

On May 6, 1932, Jock Garden was assaulted by eight men in black hoods and robes. When Garden's sons came to his aid, the assailants fled but for one man who was cornered by the family's Airedale terrier. The resulting investigation saw the arrest of John Dynon, who gave the police the names of the other men, all members of the New Guard's Fascist Legion. On May 9, 1932, all eight were convicted of assault and sentenced to three months gaol. They unsuccessfully appealed the decision on the grounds that police provocateurs in their midst had incited the operation. While Eric Campbell denied any prior knowledge of the Fascist Legion, he maintained that many "red-blooded Guardsmen probably felt that Garden had been let off lightly with only a good hiding."

On May 12, 1932, Herbert Poynton confessed to Detective Constable Colin Delaney everything he knew about the New Guard, the Fascist Legion, and their activities. The information was a major blow to Eric Campbell and his movement. Poynton made no mention of Rowland Sinclair. It was never clear to police exactly what led Poynton to confess.

On May 13, 1932, Governor Sir Phillip Game, in what was seen as a retreat from Moscow's influence, dismissed the Lang Government. With Lang defeated, the secret, and less secret armies fell into decline, and the right-thinking men of New South Wales returned home to their wives.

Enjoy this excerpt from *A Decline in Prophets*, the next book in the Rowland Sinclair Series:

Prologue

Death wore a dinner suit.

His manners were perfect. Murder made sophisticated conversation while dancing the quickstep. He was light on his feet.

Annie Besant shuddered and closed her eyes. How clearly she saw the spreading crimson stain on the starched white dress shirt. That much was revealed… but no more. She surveyed the room. So many immaculately tailored men—all dashing, some charming, at least one was dangerous.

An old woman now, her celebrated clairvoyance was not what it once had been. The foresight was vague, useless for anything but tormenting her with a premonition of violence. The feeling was furtive, an occasional glimpse of a deep predatory darkness that lurked amongst the gaiety and cultured frivolity of the floating palace. A cold creeping certainty that one of the elegant gentlemen who gathered to dine, intended to kill.

Chapter One
RMS Aquitania

The *RMS Aquitania* is like an English country house. Its great rooms are perfect replicas of the fine salons and handsome apartments that one finds in the best of old English manor halls. The decorations are too restrained ever to be oppressive in their magnificence. There is no effort to create an atmosphere of feverish gaiety by means of ornate and colourful furnishings. The ship breathes an air of elegance that is very gratifying to the type of people that are her passengers.

The Cunard Steam Ship Company
Ltd.

It was undeniably a civilised way to travel… particularly for fugitives.

Overhead, crystal chandeliers moved almost

imperceptibly with the gentle sway of the ship. If the scene over which they hung had been silent, one may have noticed the faint tinkle of the hand-cut prisms as they made contact. As it was, however, the Louis XVI Restaurant was busy, ringing with polite repartee and refined laughter as the orchestra played an unobtrusive score from the upper balcony.

The tables in the dining room were round, laid with crisp white linen and a full array of cutlery in polished silver. Each sat twelve, the parties carefully chosen from amongst the first class passengers of the transatlantic liner. Waiters wove efficiently and subtly through the hall. Though neither as large nor as fast as the newer ships in the Cunard Line, the *RMS Aquitania* boasted a luxury and opulence that was unsurpassed. Her passengers cared less about arriving first than they did about doing so in the most elegant manner possible.

Rowland Sinclair, of Woollahra, Sydney, hooked his walking stick over the back of his chair before he sat down. He dragged a hand through his dark hair, irritated with the inordinately long time it seemed to be taking his leg to heal. It had been over seven months now since Edna had shot him. Early in the mornings the limp was negligible, but after a day contending with the constant roll of the deck, the damaged muscles in his thigh ached and he relied on the stick.

His travelling companions, who had come with him into temporary exile, were already seated.

Rowland glanced across at Edna. She sparkled, perfectly accustomed to the many admiring eyes that were upon her. Her face was rapt in attention to the man seated beside her, the fall of her copper tresses accentuating the tilt of her head. Rowland considered the angle with an artist's eye. The creaminess of her complexion was dramatic in contrast to the chocolate skin of the man upon whose conversation she focussed.

Jiddu Krishnamurti had dined with them before, and with him his eminent—perhaps notorious—entourage. Rowland found the man intriguing—it was not often that one broke bread with an erstwhile messiah.

On the other side of Edna, leaning absurdly in an attempt to enter the intimacy between her and Krishnamurti, sat the Englishman, Orville Urquhart. A consciously elegant man, he had been solicitous of their company since he first encountered Edna on board. Rowland regarded the Englishman with the distance he habitually reserved for those who vied for the attentions of the beautiful sculptress. Urquhart was broad-shouldered and athletic, but so well groomed that it seemed to counteract the masculinity of his build. His hands were manicured, his thin moustache combed and waxed, and even from across the table, his cologne was noticeable. Despite himself, Rowland shook his head.

He turned politely as the elderly woman in the next seat addressed him. "Tell me, Mr. Sinclair, will you be staying on in New York?"

"Not for long I'm afraid, Mrs. Besant. We shall embark for Sydney within a week of our arrival in New York."

"I take it the Americas do not interest you?"

Rowland smiled. "We have been abroad for a while," he said. "We're ready to go home."

Annie Besant, World President of the Theosophical movement, nodded. "I have travelled greatly through my long life," she said. "First, spreading the word of intellectual socialism, and then, when I found Theosophy, promoting brotherhood and the wisdom of the Ancients. It was always the greater calling... but I do understand the call home."

"To London?" Rowland asked, knowing that the city was where the renowned activist's work and legend had begun.

"No, my dear... I belong to India where mysticism has long been accepted."

"Indeed."

"I was in Sydney before the war, you know." She looked at Rowland critically. "You would have still been in knee pants I suppose, so you wouldn't remember. I'm afraid I was considered somewhat controversial." She smiled faintly, a little proudly.

"And why was that?" Rowland asked, expecting that she wanted him to do so.

"Free thought, and those who espouse it are always the enemy of those who rely on obedience and tradition for power," she replied.

Rowland raised a brow.

"I gave a lecture…'Why I Do Not Believe in God.'"

He nodded. "That would do it."

Annie Besant smiled. She liked the young Australian. Clearly, he was a man of means, old money—well, as old as money could be in the younger colonies, but his mind was open, despite a certain flippancy. His eyes were extraordinary, dark though they were blue. There was an easy boyishness to his smile and, she thought, a strength. He had often stayed talking with her when the other young people got up to dance. She put a hand on his knee—Annie Besant was eighty-five now—she could take certain liberties.

"Tell me, how did you hurt your leg, Mr. Sinclair?"

"Ed… Miss Higgins shot me." He glanced toward Edna, still talking deeply with Krishnamurti.

"A lovers' tiff?"

"Not quite. She wasn't aiming at me."

"So fate misdirected the bullet?"

He grinned. "Not fate—Ed. She's a terrible shot, I'm afraid."

"And her intended victim?"

"Oh, she missed them entirely."

"I see." Annie placed her hand over his and gazed into his eyes. "You have an interesting aura, Mr. Sinclair. I have been clairvoyant for some years, you know, but still, you would be difficult to read, I think." Rowland was a little relieved. He was less than enamoured with the idea of being read.

Annie Besant smiled again and whispered conspiratorially. "I would not be offended, Mr. Sinclair, if you were to take out that notebook of yours."

Rowland laughed. It was his tendency to draw whatever caught his interest…it was not always appropriate to do so and he regularly checked the impulse to extract the notebook from the inside pocket of his jacket. Whether or not she was clairvoyant, Annie Besant was perceptive.

"I should rather like to draw you, Mrs. Besant," he said as he opened the leather-bound artist's journal. "Actually I'd very much like to paint you, but I'm afraid my painting equipment is in the ship's hold."

"You must call me Annie. I think we are well enough acquainted now… Besant is just the name of the man who took my children." She sighed. "Of course that was well before you were born."

Rowland was already drawing. He was aware that Annie's activism had seen her lose custody and contact with her children. He was not really sure why he knew that—it was one of those snippets of information told in hushed tones that came one's way from time to time.

"Not that old line again, Rowly." Milton Isaacs leant in from his seat on the other side of Annie Besant. "Not every beautiful woman can be seduced with a portrait, mate."

Rowland ignored him but Annie chuckled. Milton and Annie Besant got on famously. Her past as a socialist agitator and reformist made her a hero to Milton, whose politics were definitely, and at times awkwardly, Left. She in turn was intrigued by the brash young man who called himself a poet, and made no effort to hide the letters of the word 'Red' which disfigured his forehead. Being too old to wait upon niceties, she had asked him about it on their first introduction.

"Are you particularly fond of the colour red, Mr. Isaacs?"

"It is a perfectly acceptable colour, Mrs. Besant," he had replied smoothly. "But it does not appear on my face with consent."

To receive a free catalog of Poisoned Pen Press titles, please provide your name, address, and email address in one of the following ways:

Phone: 1-800-421-3976
Facsimile: 1-480-949-1707
Email: info@poisonedpenpress.com
Website: www.poisonedpenpress.com

Poisoned Pen Press
6962 E. First Ave. Ste 103
Scottsdale, AZ 85251

CPSIA information can be obtained at www.ICGtesting.com
Printed in the USA
BVOW05s0922300516

449990BV00004B/123/P